THE LIE TREE

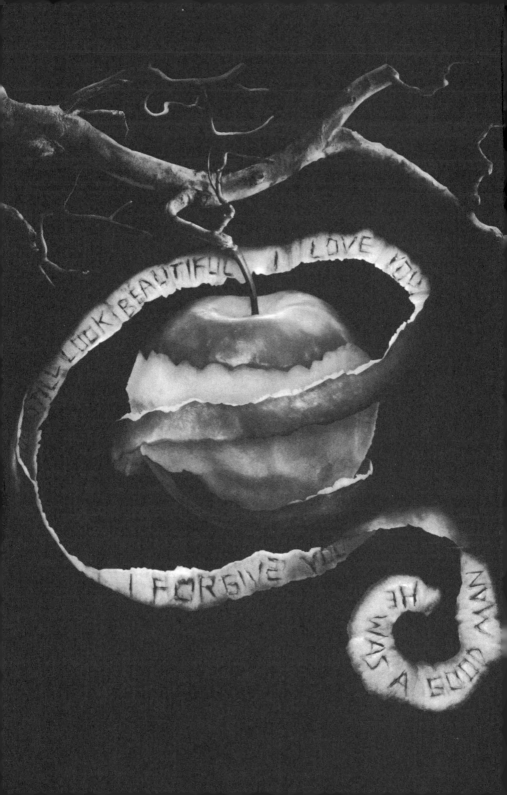

THE
LIE TREE

FRANCES HARDINGE

AMULET BOOKS
NEW YORK

Library of Congress Cataloging-in-Publication Data

Hardinge, Frances.
The Lie Tree / by Frances Hardinge.
pages cm
Originally published in Great Britain in 2015 by Macmillan UK.
Summary: On an island off the south coast of Victorian England, fourteen-year-old Faith investigates the mysterious death of her father, who was involved in a scandal, and discovers a tree that feeds upon lies and gives those who eat its fruit visions of truth.
ISBN 978-1-4197-1895-3 (hardcover) — ISBN 978-1-61312-899-2 (ebook)
[1. Gender role—Fiction. 2. Great Britain—History—Victoria, 1837–1901—Fiction. 3. Mystery and detective stories.] I. Title.
PZ7.H21834 Li 2016
[Fic]—dc23
2015028326

Printed and bound in U.S.A.
10 9 8 7 6 5 4 3 2 1

Amulet Books are available at special discounts when purchased in quantity for premiums and promotions as well as fundraising or educational use. Special editions can also be created to specification. For details, contact specialsales@abramsbooks.com or the address below.

THE ART OF BOOKS SINCE 1949
115 West 18th Street
New York, NY 10011
www.abramsbooks.com

To my father, for quiet wisdom and integrity,
and for respecting me as an adult
long before I was one.

Chapter 1

IN ONE PIECE

THE BOAT MOVED WITH A NAUSEOUS, RELENT-less rhythm, like someone chewing on a rotten tooth. The islands just visible through the mist also looked like teeth, Faith decided. Not fine, clean Dover teeth, but jaded, broken teeth, jutting crookedly amid the wash of the choppy gray sea. The mailboat chugged its dogged way through the waves, greasing the sky with smoke.

"Osprey," said Faith through chattering teeth, and pointed.

Her six-year-old brother, Howard, twisted around, too slow to see the great bird, as its pale body and dark-fringed wings vanished into the mist. Faith winced as he shifted his weight on her lap. At least he had stopped demanding his nursemaid.

"Is that where we are going?" Howard squinted at the ghostly islands ahead.

"Yes, How." Rain thudded against the thin wooden roof above their heads. The cold wind blew in from the deck, stinging Faith's face.

In spite of the noise around her, Faith was sure she could hear faint sounds coming from the crate on which she sat. Rasps of movement, breathy slithers of scale on scale. It pained Faith

1

to think of her father's Chinese snake inside, weak with the cold, coiling and uncoiling itself in panic with every tilt of the deck.

Behind her, raised voices competed with the keening of the gulls and the *phud-phud-phud* of the boat's great paddles. Now that the rain was setting in, everybody on board was squabbling over the small sheltered area toward the stern. There was room for the passengers, but not for all of the trunks. Faith's mother, Myrtle, was doing her best to claim a large share for her family's luggage, with considerable success.

Sneaking a quick glance over her shoulder, Faith saw Myrtle waving her arms like a conductor while two deckhands moved the Sunderly trunks and crates into place. Today Myrtle was waxen with tiredness and shrouded to the chin with shawls, but as usual she talked through and over everyone else, warm, bland, and unabashed, with a pretty woman's faith in others' helpless chivalry.

"Thank you, there, right there—well, I am heartily sorry to hear that, but it cannot be helped—on its side, if you do not mind—well, your case looks very durable to me—I am afraid my husband's papers and projects will not endure the weather so— the Reverend Erasmus Sunderly, the renowned naturalist—how very kind! I am so glad that you do not mind . . ."

Beyond her, round-faced Uncle Miles was napping in his seat, blithely and easily as a puppy on a rug. Faith's gaze slipped past him, to the tall, silent figure beyond. Faith's father in his black priestly coat, his broad-brimmed hat overshadowing his high brow and hooked nose.

He always filled Faith with awe. Even now he stared out toward the gray horizons with his unyielding basilisk stare, distancing himself from the chilly downpour, the reek of bilge and coal smoke, and the ignominious arguing and jostling. Most weeks she saw more of him in the pulpit than she did in the house, so it was peculiar to look across and see him sitting there. Today she felt a prickle of pained sympathy. He was out of his element, a lion in a rain-lashed sideshow.

On Myrtle's orders, Faith was sitting on the family's largest crate, to stop anybody from dragging it out again. Usually she managed to fade into the background, since nobody had attention to spare for a fourteen-year-old girl with wooden features and a mud-brown plait. Now she winced under resentful glares, seared by all the embarrassment that Myrtle never felt.

Myrtle's petite figure was positioned to impede anybody else from trying to insert their own luggage under cover. A tall, broad man with a knuckly nose seemed about to push past her with his trunk, but she cut him short by turning to smile.

Myrtle blinked twice, and her big blue eyes widened, taking on an earnest shine as if she had only just noticed the person before her with clarity. Despite her pink-nipped nose and weary pallor, her smile still managed to be sweet and confiding.

"Thank you for being so understanding," she said. There was the tiniest, tired break in her voice.

It was one of Myrtle's tricks for handling men, a little coquetry she summoned as easily and reflexively as opening her fan. Every time it worked, Faith's stomach twisted. It worked now. The gentleman flushed, gave a curt bow, and withdrew, but Faith could see he was still carrying his resentment with him. In fact, Faith suspected that her family had antagonized nearly everybody on the boat.

Howard shyly adored their mother, and when she was younger Faith had seen her in the same honeyed light. Myrtle's rare visits to the nursery had been almost unbearably exciting, and Faith had even loved the ritual of being groomed, dressed, and fussed over to make her presentable for each encounter. Myrtle had seemed like a being from another world, warm, merry, beautiful, and untouchable, a sun nymph with a keen sense of fashion.

However, over the last year Myrtle had decided to start "taking Faith in hand," which appeared to involve interrupting Faith's lessons without warning and dragging her away on impulse for visits or trips to town, before abandoning her to the nursery and schoolroom once more. Over this year, familiarity had done its usual work, picking off the gilded paint one scratch at a time. Faith had started to feel like a rag doll, snatched up and cast down according to the whims of an impatient child with an uncertain temper.

Right now the crowds were receding. Myrtle settled herself on a stack of three trunks next to Faith's crate, with an air of deep self-satisfaction.

"I do hope the place that Mr. Lambent has arranged for us has a decent drawing room," she remarked, "and that the servants will do. The cook simply cannot be *French*. I can scarcely run a household if my cook can choose to misunderstand me whenever she pleases . . ."

Myrtle's voice was not unpleasant, but it trickled on, and on, and on. For the last day her chatter had been the family's constant companion, as she shared it with the hackney-carriage driver who had taken them to the station, the guards who had stowed the family's luggage in the trains to London, and then Poole, the surly custodian of the chilly inn where they had spent the night, and the captain of this smoky mailboat.

"*Why* are we going there?" interrupted Howard. His eyes were glassy with tiredness. He was at the fork. Ahead lay either compulsive napping or helpless tantrums.

"You know why, darling." Myrtle leaned across to stroke wet hair out of Howard's eyes with a careful, gloved finger. "There are some very important caves on that island over there, where gentlemen have been discovering dozens of clever fossils. Nobody knows more about fossils than your father, so they asked him to come and look at them."

"But why did *we* come?" Howard persisted. "He did not take us to China. Or India. Or Africa. Or Mongia." The last was his best attempt at Mongolia.

It was a good question, and one that a lot of people were probably asking. Yesterday a flurry of cards carrying excuses and last-minute cancellations would have turned up in households all over the Sunderlys' home parish like apologetic, rectangular snowflakes. By today, word of the family's unscheduled departure would be spreading like wildfire.

In truth, Faith herself would have liked to know the answer to Howard's question.

"Oh, we could never have gone to those places!" Myrtle declared vaguely. "Snakes, and fevers, and people who eat dogs. This is different. It will be a little holiday."

"Did we have to go because of the Beetle Man?" asked Howard, screwing up his face in concentration.

The Reverend, who had shown no sign of listening to the conversation, suddenly drew in his breath through his nose and let it out in a disapproving hiss. He rose to his feet.

"The rain is easing, and this saloon is too crowded," he declared, and strode out on to the deck.

Myrtle winced and looked over at Uncle Miles, who was rubbing the sleep from his eyes.

"Perhaps I should, ah, take a little constitutional as well." Uncle Miles glanced at his sister with a small, wry lift of the eyebrows. He smoothed down his mustache at the corners of his smile and then followed his brother-in-law out of the saloon.

"Where did Father go?" asked Howard in piercing tones, craning his neck round to peer out toward the deck. "Can I go too? Can I have my gun?"

Myrtle closed her eyes briefly and let her lips flutter in what looked like a small, exasperated prayer for patience. She opened her eyes again and smiled at Faith.

"Oh, Faith, what a rock you are." It was the smile she always gave Faith, fond but with a hint of weary acceptance. "You may not be the liveliest company . . . but at least you never ask questions."

Faith managed a flat, chilled smile. She knew who Howard meant by "the Beetle Man" and suspected that his question had been dangerously close to the mark.

For the last month the family had been living in a frozen fog of the unsaid. Looks, whispers, subtle changes in manner and gently withdrawn contact. Faith had noticed the alteration but had been unable to guess the reason for it.

And then, one Sunday while the family was walking back from church, a man in a brown homburg hat had approached to introduce himself, with much bobbing and bowing and a smile that never reached his eyes. He had written a paper on beetles, and would the respected Reverend Erasmus Sunderly consider writing a foreword? The respected Reverend would not consider it and became ever more coldly irate at the visitor's persistence. The stranger was "scraping an acquaintance" in breach of all good manners, and at last the Reverend flatly told him so.

The beetle enthusiast's smile had drooped into something less pleasant. Faith still remembered the quiet venom of his reply.

"Forgive me for imagining that your civility would be the

equal of your intellect. The way rumor is spreading, Reverend, I would have thought that you would be *glad* to find a fellow man of science who is still willing to shake you by the hand."

As Faith remembered those words, her blood ran cold again. She had never dreamed that she would see her father insulted to his face. Worse still, the Reverend had turned away from the stranger in furious silence, without demanding an explanation. The chill haze of Faith's suspicions began to crystallize. There were rumors abroad, and her father knew what they were, even if she did not.

Myrtle was wrong. Faith was full of questions, coiling and writhing like the snake in the crate.

Oh, but I cannot. I must not give way to that.

In Faith's mind, it was always *that*. She never gave it another name, for fear of yielding it yet more power over her. *That* was an addiction, she knew that much. *That* was something she was always giving up, except that she never did. *That* was the very opposite of Faith as the world knew her. Faith the good girl, the rock. Reliable, dull, trustworthy Faith.

It was the unexpected opportunities that she found hardest to resist. An unattended envelope with the letter peeping out, clean and tantalizing. An unlocked door. A careless conversation, unheeding of eavesdroppers.

There was a hunger in her, and girls were not supposed to be hungry. They were supposed to nibble sparingly when at the table, and their minds were supposed to be satisfied with a slim diet too. A few stale lessons from tired governesses, dull walks, unthinking pastimes. But it was *not* enough. All knowledge— any knowledge—called to Faith, and there was a delicious, poisonous pleasure in stealing it unseen.

7

Right now, however, her curiosity had a focus and an urgent edge. At that very moment, her father and Uncle Miles might be talking about the Beetle Man and the reasons for the family's sudden exodus.

"Mother . . . may I walk on the deck a little while? My stomach . . ." Faith almost made herself believe her own words. Her insides were indeed churning, but from excitement, not the boat's jarring lurches.

"Very well—but do not answer anyone who talks to you. Take the umbrella, be careful not to fall overboard, and come back before you catch a chill."

As Faith paced slowly alongside the rail, the faltering drizzle drumming on her umbrella, she admitted to herself that she was giving in to *that* again. Excitement pumped dark wine through her veins and sharpened all her senses to painful edges. She wandered slowly out of sight of Myrtle and Howard and then dawdled, acutely aware of each glance directed her way. One by one these gazes wearied of her and slid off once more.

Her moment came. Nobody was looking. She sidled quickly across the deck and lost herself among the crates that clustered at the base of the boat's shuddering, discolored funnel. The air tasted of salt and guilt, and she felt alive.

She slipped from one hiding place to another, keeping her skirts gathered close so that they did not flare in the wind and betray her location. Her broad, square feet, so clumsy when anybody tried to fit them for fashionable shoes, settled silently on the boards with practiced deftness.

Between two crates she found a hiding place from which she could see her father and uncle a mere three yards away. Seeing her father without being seen felt like a special sacrilege.

"To flee my own home!" exclaimed the Reverend. "It smacks

of cowardice, Miles. I should never have let you persuade me to leave Kent. And what good will our departure do? Rumors are like dogs. Flee from them and they give chase."

"Rumors are dogs indeed, Erasmus." Uncle Miles squinted through his pince-nez. "And they hunt in packs, and on sight. You needed to leave society for a while. Now that you are gone, they will find something else to chase."

"By creeping away under cover of darkness, Miles, I have *fed* these dogs. My departure will be used as evidence against me."

"Perhaps it will, Erasmus," answered Uncle Miles with unusual seriousness, "but would you rather be judged here on a remote island by a couple of sheep farmers, or in England among persons of consequence? The Vane Island excavation was the best excuse I could find for your departure, and I remain glad that you chose to accept my arguments.

"Yesterday morning that article in the *Intelligencer* was read out at breakfast tables all over the country. If you had stayed, you would have forced your entire circle to decide whether they would support or snub you, and the way rumor has been spreading you might not have liked the decisions they would have made.

"Erasmus, one of the most widely read and respected newspapers in the nation has decried you as a fraud and a cheat. Unless you want to subject Myrtle and the children to all the barbs and trials of scandal, you cannot return to Kent. Until your name is clear, nothing good awaits any of you there."

Chapter 2

VANE

A FRAUD AND A CHEAT.

The words buzzed in Faith's head as she continued her damp promenade, staring distractedly at the passing islands. How could anybody suspect *her father* of fraud? His bleak and terrible honesty were the plague and pride of the family. You knew where you stood with him, even if where you stood was within the blizzard of his disapproval. And what did Uncle Miles mean by "fraud" anyway?

By the time she returned to the shelter of the saloon, Uncle Miles and her father were back in their seats. Faith sat down on the snake crate again, unable to meet anyone's eye.

Uncle Miles squinted at a rain-spotted almanac through his pince-nez, for all the world as if the family really were on holiday, then peered out across the seascape.

"There!" He pointed. "*That* is Vane."

The approaching island did not look large enough at first, but Faith soon realized that it was drawing up to them end on, like a boat with a tapering prow. Only as the ferry navigated around the island and began traveling down its longer flank could Faith see how much larger it was than the rest of the shoal. Great black waves shattered themselves against the deep brown cliffs, throwing up wild arcs of foam.

Nobody lives here, was her first thought. *Nobody could ever live here by choice. It must be where the outcasts live. Criminals, like the convicts in Australia. And people running away, like us.*

We are exiles. Perhaps we will have to live out here forever.

They passed pitted headlands and deep coves where solitary buildings skulked along the shoreline. Then the ferry slowed, turning laboriously with a churn of water to enter a deeper bay with a harbor ringed by a high wall, and beyond that ascending rows of blank-eyed houses, slate roofs slicked with rain. Dozens of little fishing boats tilted and shrugged, their cat's cradles of ropes ghostly in the mist. The gulls became deafening, all squabbling with the same broken note. There was motion on the ferry, a communal letting out of breath and readying of luggage.

The rain became fierce again just as the ferry came to rest beside the quay. Amid the shouting, rope-throwing, and maneuvering of gangplanks, Uncle Miles dropped coins into a couple of palms, and the Sunderly luggage was manhandled ashore.

"The Reverend Erasmus Sunderly and family?" A thin man in a black coat stood drenched on the quay, water spilling off the broad brim of his hat. He was clean-shaven, with a pleasant, worried sort of face, currently a little blue from the cold. "Mr. Anthony Lambent sends his compliments." He bowed formally and handed over a rather damp letter. As he did so, Faith noticed the tight-fitting white stock round his neck and realized that he was a clergyman like her father.

Faith's father read the letter, then gave a nod of approval and extended his hand.

"Mr. . . . . Tiberius Clay?"

"Indeed, sir." Clay shook him respectfully by the hand. "I

am the curate on Vane." Faith knew that a curate was a sort of under-priest, hired to help out a rector or vicar who had too many parishes or too much work. "Mr. Lambent asked me to apologize on his behalf. He wished to meet you himself, but the sudden rain . . ." Clay grimaced up at the leaden clouds. "The new holes are in danger of filling up with water, so he is making sure that everything is covered. Please, sir—will you permit me to have some men assist with your luggage? Mr. Lambent has sent his carriage to take you and your family and belongings to Bull Cove."

The Reverend did not smile, but his murmured acquiescence was not without warmth. The curate's formality of manner had clearly won his approval.

They were drawing looks, Faith was sure of it. Had the mysterious scandal reached Vane already? No, it was probably just the fact that they were strangers, loaded down with absurd amounts of luggage. Subdued murmurs around them caught her ear, but she could make no sense of them. They seemed to be a mere soup of sound with no consonants.

With difficulty, the Sunderly luggage was arranged into an ungainly and alarming tower on the roof of the large but weathered carriage and strapped into place. There was just enough room for the curate to squeeze inside with the Sunderly family. The carriage set off, jouncing over the cobbles and making Faith's teeth vibrate.

"Are you a natural scientist, Mr. Clay?" asked Myrtle, gamely ignoring the growl of the wheels.

"In present company, I can but claim to be a dabbler." Clay gave the Reverend a small, damp bow. "However, my tutors at Cambridge did succeed in hammering a little geology and natural history into my thick skull."

Faith heard this without surprise. Many of her father's friends were clergymen who had stumbled into natural science in the same way. Gentlemen's sons destined for the Church were sent to a good university, where they were given a respectable, gentlemanly education—the classics, Greek, Latin, and a little taste of the sciences. Sometimes that taste was enough to leave them hooked.

"My chief contribution to the excavation is as a photographer—it is a pursuit of mine." The curate's voice brightened at the mention of his hobby. "Alas, Mr. Lambent's draftsman had the misfortune to break his wrist on the first day, so my son and I have been recording the discoveries with my camera."

The carriage headed out of the little "town," which to Faith's eyes looked more like a village, and climbed a rugged, zigzag lane. Every time the carriage jolted, Myrtle clutched nervously at the window frame, making everyone tense.

"That edifice out on the headland is the telegraph tower," remarked Clay. Faith could just make out a broad, dingy brown cylinder. Shortly afterward a small church with a tapering spire passed on the left. "The parsonage is just behind the church. I do hope that you will do me the honor of calling in for tea while you are on Vane."

The carriage seemed to be struggling with the hill, creaking and rattling so badly Faith expected a wheel to fall off. At last it juddered to a stop and there was a sharp double rap on the roof.

"Excuse me." Clay opened the door and climbed out. An animated conversation ensued above, in a blend of English and French that Faith's untrained ear could not disentangle.

Clay appeared in the doorway, his face drawn with distress and concern.

"My most profuse apologies. It seems that we have a dilemma.

The house you have leased is in Bull Cove, which can only be reached by a low road that follows the shoreline, or by the high track that passes over the ridge and down the other side. I have just learned that the low road is flooded. There is a breakwater, but when the tide is high and the breakers fierce . . ." He crinkled his forehead and cast an apologetic glance toward the lowering sky.

"I assume that the high road is a longer and more wearisome journey?" Myrtle asked briskly, with one eye on the morose Howard.

Clay winced. "It is . . . a very steep road. Indeed, the driver informs me that the horse would not be equal to it with this carriage in its, ah, current state of burden."

"Are you suggesting that we will have to get out and *walk?*" Myrtle stiffened, and her small, pretty chin set.

"Mother," whispered Faith, sensing an impasse, "I have my umbrella, and I do not mind walking a little—"

"No!" snapped Myrtle, just loud enough to make Faith's face redden. "If I am to become mistress of a new household, I will not make my first appearance looking like a drowned rat. And neither will you!"

Faith felt a rising tide of frustration and anger twisting her innards. She wanted to shout, *What does it matter? The newspapers are tearing us to pieces right now—do you really think people will despise us more if we are wet?*

The curate looked harassed. "Then I fear the carriage will need to make two journeys. There is an old cabin nearby—a lookout point for spotting sardine shoals. Perhaps your boxes could be left there until the carriage can return for them? I would be happy to stay and watch over them."

Myrtle's face brightened gratefully, but her answer was cut off by her husband.

"Unacceptable," Faith's father declared. "Your pardon, but some of these boxes contain irreplaceable flora and fauna that I *must* see installed at the house as soon as possible, lest they perish."

"Well, I am quite happy to wait in this cabin and spare the horse *my* weight," declared Uncle Miles.

Clay and Uncle Miles dismounted, and the family's personal trunks and chests were unloaded one by one, leaving only the specimen crates and boxes on the roof. Even then the driver stared at the way the carriage hung down, grimacing and gesturing to indicate it was still too low.

Faith's father made no move to step out and join the other men.

"Erasmus—" began Uncle Miles.

"I must remain with my specimens," the Reverend interrupted him sharply.

"Perhaps we could leave just one of your crates behind?" inquired Clay. "There is a box labeled 'miscellaneous cuttings' that is much heavier than the rest—"

"*No*, Mr. Clay." The Reverend's answer was swift and snow-cold. "That box is of *particular* importance."

Faith's father glanced at his family, his eyes cool and distant. His gaze slid over Myrtle and Howard, then settled on Faith. She flushed, knowing that she was being assessed for weight and importance. There was a dipping sensation in her stomach, as if she had been placed in a great set of scales.

Faith felt sick. She could not wait for the mortification of hearing her father voice his decision.

She did not look at her parents as she stood up unsteadily. This time Myrtle said nothing to stop her. Like Faith, she had heard the Reverend's silent decision and had turned meekly to toe the invisible line.

"Miss Sunderly?" Clay was clearly surprised to see Faith climbing out of the carriage, her boots splashing down into a waiting puddle.

"I have an umbrella," she said quickly, "and I was hoping for some fresh air." The little lie left her with a scrap of dignity.

The driver examined the level of his vehicle again and this time nodded. As the carriage rattled away, Faith avoided her companions' eyes, her cheeks hot with humiliation despite the chill wind. She had always known that she was rated less than Howard, the treasured son. Now, however, she knew that she was ranked somewhere below "miscellaneous cuttings."

The cabin was set into the hillside facing out to sea, and was rough-hewn from the dark, glossy local rock, with a slanting slate roof and small, glassless windows. The floor inside was scattered with earth-colored puddles. Overhead, the rain's drumroll was slowing.

Uncle Miles and Clay dragged in the family's trunks and boxes one by one, while Faith shook out her dripping bonnet, feeling numb and useless. Only when her father's strongbox landed with a thump at her feet did Faith's heart skip. The key had been left in the lock.

The box contained all her father's private papers. His journals, his research notes, and his correspondence. Perhaps it held some clue to the mysterious scandal that had driven them here.

She cleared her throat.

"Uncle—Mr. Clay—my . . . my kerchief and clothing are very wet. Could I have a little while to . . ." She trailed off, gesturing toward her sodden collar.

"Ah—of course!" Clay looked a little alarmed, as gentlemen often did when something mysterious involving female clothing was in danger of happening.

"It looks as if the rain is letting up again," observed Uncle Miles. "Mr. Clay, shall we take a little turn on the cliff, so that you can tell me more about the excavation?" The two men stepped outside, and after a while their voices receded.

Faith dropped to her knees next to the strongbox. Its leather was slick under her fingers, and she considered peeling off her wet, skintight kid gloves, but she knew that would take too long. The buckles were stiff, but yielded to her hasty tugging. The key turned. The lid opened, and she saw creamy papers covered in various different hands. Faith was no longer cold. Her face burned and her hands tingled.

She began opening letters, teasing them out of their envelopes and holding them by their edges so as not to smudge or crumple them. Communications from scientific journals. Letters from the publisher of his pamphlets. Invitations from museums.

It was a slow, painstaking task, and she lost track of time. At last she came upon a letter whose wording seized her attention.

". . . challenging the authenticity of not one but all the fossils that you have brought to the eye of the scientific community and upon which your reputation is based. They claim that they are at best deliberately altered, and at worst out-and-out fakes. The New Falton find, they say, is two fossils artfully combined, and report traces of glue in the wing joints . . ."

A knock sounded at the door, and Faith jumped.

"Faith!" It was her uncle's voice. "The carriage has returned!"

"One moment!" she called back, hastily folding the letter.

As she did so, she noticed a large, blue stain on her wet, white gloves. With horror she realized that she had smudged the letter, leaving a thumb-shaped smear.

Chapter 3

BULL COVE

AS THE CARRIAGE RATTLED ALONG THE HIGH
route, Faith kept her hands tightly balled to hide the mark on her
glove. She was sick with self-hate. If her father looked through
his letters, he would spot the evidence of her crime instantly.
Who else had been alone with the strongbox? He would soon
deduce that she must be responsible.

She would be caught. She *deserved* to be caught. What was
wrong with her?

And yet all the while her mind gnawed at the wording of the
letter, simmering with outrage on her father's behalf. How could
anybody believe that any of his finds were fakes, let alone his
famous New Falton fossil?

Everybody had agreed that it was real. Everybody. So
many other gentlemen experts had examined it, prodded it,
exulted over it, written about it. One journal had named it "The
New Falton Nephilim," though her father never called it that,
and declared it "the find of the decade." How could they all be
wrong?

*He must have enemies. Somebody must be trying to destroy
Father.*

Dusk was settling as they crested the hill, then zigzagged down a rough and winding road. At last the carriage slowed, and Faith made out the yellow glow from an open doorway.

It was an old farmhouse, slate-roofed and built of jagged brown stone that looked like shattered caramel. On the other side of the cobbled courtyard stood a stables and barn. Behind them rose a domed greenhouse, its panes milky in the half-light. Beyond lay a lawn, then the edge of a dark, ragged copse, and a dim outline that might have been another building.

The carriage splashed its way through the puddles and came to a halt. Clay leapt out and handed Faith from the carriage while Uncle Miles settled with the driver.

"Good evening!" The curate gave Faith and Uncle Miles a hasty bow. "I shall not keep you in the rain!"

A manservant ran out and started unloading the luggage. Under the cover of the umbrella, Uncle Miles and Faith ran to the open door. A gaunt, middle-aged woman stood aside to let them enter.

"Mr. Miles Cattistock and Miss Sunderly? I am Jane Vellet—the housekeeper." She had a deep, mannish voice, and small, shrewd, unforgiving eyes. Her dress was striped in shades of dark green and buttoned high at the throat.

The hall was darker than expected, the only light coming from two lanterns perched on sills. There were black timber beams in the ceiling. Faith could taste paraffin on the air, and a host of other smells that told her the house was old, and had settled into its own way of being, and was not her home.

Soon Faith was sitting in front of a blazing hearth next to Uncle Miles and Myrtle, with a bowl of hot soup in her hands. If Myrtle felt any remorse at having left her daughter by the roadside, she hid it well. She was pink and purposeful, and had apparently reconnoitred the family's new abode and found it grievously wanting.

"They have *no gas at all*," she informed Faith, in a stage whisper. "They say that there is some to be had in the town, but out here we shall be surviving on lamps and dips. There is *no cook*, only a housekeeper, a housemaid, and a manservant. They all worked for the last tenants—two old invalid ladies—and were kept on. Apparently the housekeeper and maid 'managed' the cooking between them. But how shall they manage for a family of five? And there is no nurse for Howard—you must take care of him, Faith, until we can find someone."

"Where is Father?" asked Faith when her mother paused for breath.

"He went out to find a home for a botanic specimen as soon as he arrived," Myrtle answered wearily. "Apparently the greenhouse will not suffice. Instead he has been out in the Folly for an age, fussing over his plant."

"The Folly?"

"An old tower, apparently." Myrtle cleared her throat as the housekeeper passed through the room. "Mrs. Vellet, what *is* the Folly?"

"It was intended to be a spotting tower, madam," Mrs. Vellet answered promptly, "looking for Napoleon's ships. They never built forts here on Vane the way they did on Alderney. The gentleman who owned the house back then decided he should build his own defenses, like a good Englishman."

"Was it of any use?" asked Myrtle.

"He ran out of money before it was finished, madam, and then the war ended," answered Mrs. Vellet. "It was used as an apple store for a while . . . but it leaked."

"Peculiar place to put a plant," mused Myrtle. She sighed. "In any case, nobody is permitted to interrupt him or go anywhere near the Folly. Apparently the plant is frightfully delicate and exotic, and an untrained gaze will cause all its leaves to fall off, or something of the sort."

Faith wondered whether her father had retreated into the forsaken tower because it was the only place he could be alone. Her heart ached. She knew some great animals retreated from their pack when they were wounded.

Faith lost herself in the exhausted fog of her own thoughts and worries, while her mother rattled on. Before long, however, even Myrtle's ever-ready conversation was waning. The long journey had left them all depleted, like paintbrushes drawn across a broad stretch of canvas. Eventually it was noticed that Faith's head was drooping, and she was told to go to bed.

"You have the smallest room, darling," Myrtle told her, "but there was no help for it. You do not mind, do you?"

Mrs. Vellet took up a candle and offered to show her to her room. As they passed through the hall, Faith glanced through a door and saw that a small parlor had been conquered by her father's menagerie. The lizards stared through the glass. The elderly wombat snuffled and twitched in its sleep, which was virtually all it did these days. Faith frowned as she realized that she could not see the snake.

There was a stack of the family's trunks and boxes against one wall of the hall. With disbelief, she recognized the snake crate near the bottom of the stack. It had been abandoned in the cold hall as if it were just a hatbox.

Faith ran over and crouched beside it, pressing her ear against it. She could hear nothing from within.

"Mrs. Vellet—could you please have this box brought up to my room?"

Faith's room turned out to be tiny, less than half the size of her bedroom at home. The vigorous fire in the hearth cast light on a hand washstand with a chipped marble top, an elderly dresser, and a four-poster with curtains that had probably known another monarch. In the shadows beyond the dresser she could just make out another door, with great bolts on it.

"Would you like a posset brought up before you sleep?" asked the housekeeper.

"Do you have any dead mice?" As soon as the words were out of Faith's mouth, she became aware that this was perhaps not the best response. "My father has a Mandarin trinket snake!" she explained hastily, and watched Mrs. Vellet's eyebrows rise another fraction of an inch. "Meat . . . tiny scraps of fresh meat will do," she stammered, suspecting that she was not making the best first impression. "And some rags. And . . . a posset would be most agreeable, thank you."

Only when she was alone in the room did she open the crate and lift out the cage within. The trinket snake was a disconsolate figure eight in the bottom, sleek black except for the flares of gold and white. The patterning always made Faith think of a candlelight procession through an ink-black wood. Back at the rectory she had spent a lot of time with her father's little menagerie, and even taken on their care during his absences, but the snake had always been her favorite. He had brought it back from China eight years before.

When Faith reached in and stroked its back, she was relieved to see it flinch a little. It was alive at least. She placed the cage on the dresser, away from the chill draft of the window, but not too close to the fire either. It was a cool-weather snake, and too much heat would kill it as surely as too little.

Mrs. Vellet returned, and handed over a bundle of dry rags

and a bowl of beef scraps, before departing once more. Faith pushed the rags into the cage to serve as a nest, and filled the snake's water bowl from the jug by her bed. The snake ignored the meat, but it basked and bathed in the water.

Only when Faith was sure that the snake was not about to slither through death's door did she remember the ink stain on her glove. She tried to wash it out using the cold water in the ewer by her bed, but in vain. In the end she hid the gloves under the mattress.

Faith's clothes were tyrants. She could not step across a dusty road, brave the rain, sit in a wicker chair, or lean against a white-washed wall without something becoming damaged, gathering dirt, wearing smooth, or losing its stiffening. Her garments were always one misstep away from becoming a source of guilt. *Eliza had to spend hours brushing the mud out of your hem . . .*

Worse, they were traitors. If she slipped outside in secret, or hid in a cupboard, or leaned against a dusty door to listen, her clothes would tell tales on her. Even if her family did not notice, the servants would.

Faith retired, but found it hard to sleep. Strands of horsehair poked through the mattress cover and sheet. The bed curtains did not close properly and let in a clammy draft. The long day had printed itself on her brain, and when she closed her eyes she saw gray skies and dark, turbulent waves.

The wind rattled the shutters and bolted door, and sometimes behind its moan she heard a distant, roaring boom, like a sound from an animal throat. She knew that it must be a trick of the wind, but her imagination painted some great black beast out on the headlands, baying amid the storm.

She wondered whether her father was still self-exiled in the Folly. Faith sometimes felt that there was a connection between them, like a hidden root linking a mangrove tree to its little sprouting "children." For a moment she tried to imagine the link, and told herself that perhaps, somehow, he would be able to sense her feelings if she felt them hard enough.

I believe in you, she told him in her head. *Whatever anybody else says, I believe in you.*

Faith was jolted awake by the pounding of rapid footsteps against wood. She opened her eyes and as she took in the unfamiliar canopy above, her memories flooded back.

She pushed open her bed curtains, half expecting to see somebody running around her room. The footsteps had sounded so close, mere yards from her head. There was nobody there, of course, but as she listened she heard them again, and this time understood the rhythmic creak. It was the sound of somebody running up or down stairs.

The servants' stairs! Her room must be close to them, so close that she could hear them through the wall. Faith rose and stalked around the room, pressing her ear to the walls, and felt a frisson of triumph when she found the place where the sounds were clearest. She could even make out the distant murmur of conversation.

Most people would have been outraged at such a discovery. The whole point of the servants' stairs was that the servants could come and go without the family being forced to notice them. What good were they if they forced themselves on your attention, and woke you at dawn? For Faith, however, it was not an annoyance; it was a chance to listen in on the servants' invisible world.

Although, of course, she would not be using it for *that*.

The bolts on the mysterious door beyond the dresser were

rusty, but she eventually worked them loose. The door stuck and then opened with a judder, and Faith found herself blinking into sunlight.

It was a little roof garden, its pale stone slabs blotchy with dew. Around its perimeter ran a wrought-iron trellis, heavy with creeper, shielding it from the view of those below. White stone children, pocked by lichen and time, held out stone basins from which purple aubretia tumbled. At the far side she could see a little vine-trammeled gate, and beyond it a set of stone steps, presumably leading down to ground level.

Faith felt a smile creeping across her face. If she *had* been of a sneaking temperament, she would now have her own private means of leaving or entering the house unobserved.

She dressed, and continued her exploration. Walking down the main stairs she reflexively counted the steps, memorizing which ones creaked and which could be trusted to be discreet. Faith caught herself making mental notes of which bolts and latches would need to be secretly oiled.

No! Faith was giving up *that*.

She was soon to be confirmed, she reminded herself, and felt her usual lurch of fear at the thought. She would be an adult in the eyes of the Church and God. Her sins would be her own. Of course she had always felt immortal judgment swinging above her head, like a vast, deathly pendulum, but her youth had been a frail shield—an excuse. Now she was growing tall enough that the pendulum might strike her down with one mysterious swipe. All her evil habits needed to come to an end.

Nonetheless, murmured a scurrilous voice in Faith's head, the house at Bull Cove was showing some potential.

Entering the murky, wood-paneled dining room, Faith found her mother upbraiding the housemaid, a spiky, pretty, dark-haired girl of about fifteen, with an eternal smirk hovering in the corners of her mouth.

"No, Jeanne, it will not do at all!" Myrtle gestured to the board in the housemaid's hands on which lay two outlandishly long loaves of a sort Faith had never seen before. "When I ask for bread and butter, I expect slices cut from a *real* loaf of bread, *so* thick." Myrtle held up her forefinger and thumb, half an inch apart. "See to it, if you please."

The maid gave a brief, noncommittal pout, a shrug of the face, and departed with the board.

"What a house!" exclaimed Myrtle. "I could barely sleep a wink last night. I am sure that the rooms had not been aired. And what in the world was that frightful noise that boomed and bellowed all night?"

"Apparently that is the Great Black Bull," Uncle Miles told her with a twinkle. "When the storm is high the beast leaps from the bowels of the earth and bellows at the heavens. Or rather, it is a perfectly natural phenomenon caused by the wind blowing through sea caves."

"Well, I think it is too bad of the landlord to have leased us the place without mentioning the bellowing spectral cattle," Myrtle answered sharply.

"Ah, but according to local superstition, there is barely an inch of this island that does *not* have its own phantom," Uncle Miles rejoined, smiling. "Clay recounted some of the tales to me yesterday—wailing women, ghost ships, and so forth. Oh, and apparently Vane was a nest of smugglers during the war with the French. They say that one buried a good deal of treasure before he died, and for fifty years his ghost has been trying in vain to lead people to it."

"He cannot be very good at charades," Faith murmured under her breath as she sat down at the table.

"Well, on a more earthly note, it would seem that two cards were left for us this morning." Myrtle glanced at her husband. "One is from Dr. Jacklers, my dear—he says that he hopes to have the pleasure of calling on us at two this afternoon, and taking you to see the excavation.

"The other is from Mr. Lambent saying that the local geology society is meeting at his house at four o'clock, and that they would all be obliged if you would attend as guest of honor. Oh, and the rest of us are invited to afternoon tea. He offers to send his carriage for us."

The Reverend gave his wife a brief, cloudy look, inclined his head to show that he had heard, and then returned to the silent consumption of his breakfast.

"Perhaps we should *all* go to see the excavation with Dr. Jacklers," suggested Uncle Miles in hopeful tones. "We could make it a family outing."

"Could we?" Faith gave her parents a look of excited appeal. In her father's library at the rectory, she had spent long hours poring over books dedicated to the beasts of prehistory, marveling at the sketched bones of long-extinct creatures. She was thrilled by the thought of seeing a real, live excavation.

Myrtle looked to her husband, who gave the table a distracted look and cleared his throat.

"I do not see why not," he said.

Jeanne returned, set down a board gently with an air of studied innocence, and walked out again. The long loaves had been hacked into half-inch slices with aggressive thoroughness, and had not survived the experience. Tatters of bread lay in a heap of crust-shrapnel, glued into clots by dabs of butter.

"Jeanne!" Myrtle called after the departing and conveniently deaf housemaid. "Jeanne! Oh, this is too much! I shall have to take Mrs. Vellet to task—indeed I shall!"

From above came a muffled thunder, the sound of small, careless feet running, followed by a few experimental door slams. Myrtle winced, and glanced toward her husband, who was frowning at the ceiling with cool disapproval. Howard was not even supposed to be seen at such a time, and definitely not heard.

"Faith," Myrtle said in an undertone, "would you be a dear and take breakfast with your brother today, then help him with his lessons?" She did not even look at Faith for a response.

Faith cast a wistful farewell glance at the kedgeree, bacon, toast, and marmalade, and rose from her seat.

Myrtle had once explained to Faith that there was a right way to give an order to a servant. You phrased it as a question to be polite. *Will you fetch the tea? Could you please speak with Cook?* But instead of your voice pitch going up at the end, you let it droop downward, to show that it was not really a question, and they were not expected to say no.

It occurred to Faith that that was the way her mother talked to her.

Howard had two adjoining rooms assigned to him, a "night nursery" for sleep and a "day nursery" for his games, lessons, and meals.

"I hate them," he said, sipping his toast-and-water. "They

have rats in the dark. I can't sleep without Skordle." "Skordle" was Howard's rushed pronunciation of "Miss Caudle," his nurse-maid who usually slept in his room back in Kent. Faith secretly rather liked the name "Skordle" and thought it sounded like a mythical animal.

Faith did not like the nurseries much either, but for different reasons. For the last year she had felt like a seesaw, clumsily rocking between childhood and adulthood. It was always clear-est at mealtimes. Sometimes she would find that she had grown into an adult overnight with magical beanstalk speed and was allowed the honor of eating with her parents in the dining room. And then, without warning, she would find herself back in the nursery with Howard, eating porridge while an undersized chair creaked beneath her weight.

Nursery food was "plain" and "wholesome," which usually meant tasteless and boiled to the point of surrender. Day nurs-eries smelled of it, of potatoes and rice milk and twice-boiled mutton. The smell made Faith feel as though she was wearing an old version of herself that was too small for her. It itched.

"Other hand!" Faith reached out, gently taking Howard's por-ridge spoon from his left hand and putting it in his right. It was the usual battle.

The hard part came after breakfast when she had to wrestle him into his blue jacket. Howard loathed the jacket, which he had to wear for all his lessons. The left sleeve was stitched to his side, trapping his left hand so that he could not use it.

Howard's willful persistence in using his left hand was, Myrtle insisted, a "fad"—nothing to worry about, providing it was not encouraged. His pre-Skordle nursemaid, however, had been too indulgent, and Howard had developed some "bad habits."

"You know what Mother says! You have to learn to eat and

write properly before you go away to school!" The plan was to send Howard off to boarding school once he was eight.

Howard crinkled his face, the way he always did when school was mentioned. Faith swallowed down a little knot of bitterness and envy.

"You are very lucky, How. Some people would be grateful for the chance to go to a good school." Faith did not mention that she was one of them. "Listen! If you wear your jacket and finish your writing exercises, we can explore the garden afterward. You can bring your gun!"

Her bargain was deemed acceptable.

Outside, Howard ran around and "shot" the upper windows of the house, pointing his little wooden gun and uttering shrill cries of "Bang!" He shot the black crows that hopped stolidly away from his hurried approach and then spread lazy, unflustered wings to outpace him. He shot everything down the muddy, scrubby path toward the sea.

If his behavior were noticed, Faith would probably be scolded for letting him "wear himself out." There was always a fear that Howard, the one surviving son, would catch some fatal chill. Faith had already watched five younger brothers lose their grip on life and fold in on themselves like closing daisies. Some had been mere babes, others had eked out a few birthdays. The first two had been Howards, then her parents had tried their hand at a James and two Edwards, with similar poor success. It made the living Howard seem fragile, as if he were holding hands with his namesake brothers through the grim curtain.

However, Faith knew Howard far better than her parents did. She understood that he *needed* to wheel and race crazily until he tired, just as he needed his toy gun. He "shot" things that frightened him. Right now he was trying to make a whole strange new world feel safe.

Her gaze was drawn to the stubby tower, over by the edge of a copse. By daylight, she could see that the Folly was nothing but a one-storey stump, its chink-windows clogged with mortar and ivy, its stonework tea-stain brown.

It tugged at Faith's curiosity, but she had more pressing worries. Her incriminating gloves were balled up in her pocket. She needed to rid herself of them before they could be found by one of the servants.

The path forked as it approached the sea. The left-hand path climbed up to the cliff-top. Faith and Howard took the right-hand route, which weaved its way down to the pebble beach. There Howard ran amok, shooting nervous-stepping oyster-catchers, the mud-brown cliffs that rose on either side, and his own reflection in the wet sand.

There was a little boathouse on the beach with a rowing boat inside, and behind it a scramble of boulders. As Howard raced over the shingle, Faith slipped behind the boathouse and pushed the gloves into a narrow dark crack between two boulders. At once she felt lighter. Somehow the sting of guilt was always more acute when there was a risk that she might get caught.

Faith returned to the beach. She rather liked it, she decided, for all its dour colors and gray scud of clouds. In her head her father's books of natural history unfurled, and she found the words for what she saw: fleet, sharp-winged terns skimming the gray air. A snub black-and-white razorbill preening its plumage on a crag. Samphire, trembling its white flowers among the rocks.

Staring out at the distant headlands, Faith could see waves plume white as they chafed against the rocks. Here and there she could make out black cracks and triangular fissures at the base of the cliffs.

"Look, How!" she called against the wind, and pointed. "Sea caves!"

Howard ran over and squinted in the direction of her pointing finger, then sighted at the caves down his gun.

"Are there monsters inside?" he asked thoughtfully.

"Maybe."

"Can we go there in the boat and look?"

Faith glanced back at the little rowboat in the boathouse and then peered speculatively at the fraught sea. The dark openings tugged at her curiosity.

"Perhaps another day," she said, half to herself, "but we will have to ask Father and Mother."

When Howard had tired himself out, she led him back up the slope toward the house. Seeing the dun-colored Folly once again, she paused.

The night before, her father had spent hours in the Folly, tending to some mysterious plant. At the time she had thought he just wanted to be alone, but now she found herself remembering the crate of "miscellaneous cuttings" that had robbed her of a seat in the carriage. It was a strangely vague label, come to think of it. Her father was usually so precise.

"Howard, shall we look for lions around the Folly?"

Faith had to circle around the building to the side nearest the trees before she found its heavy wooden door. She could not be seen from the house, and the temptation was too great. She lifted the aged latch and opened the door.

Inside lay darkness. A strange smell reached her nose, with a coldness like mint that stung her eyes.

She looked upward and saw murky rafters, gray with spider-cities. The roof was intact, she realized with surprise, blocking out the daylight. Why would her father put a precious specimen somewhere that the sun could not reach?

Faith took a careful footstep into the Folly, her boot sliding slightly against the slimy dankness of the stone floor. She peered into the shadows of the little, round room.

There was something huddled against the far wall, a domed shape shrouded in an oilskin cloth, the rounded base of a plant pot just visible beneath the fabric. It was two feet high, small enough to have fitted in the crate.

Just as she was edging toward the strange shape, she realized that the cries of "Bang!" behind her were becoming louder and more excitable. In a guilty panic she fled back into the daylight, and quickly fastened the Folly door behind her. She looked around, fearing to see her father returning from some walk.

Instead she saw Howard aiming his gun into the thicket. A strange man was tramping through the bracken.

He was not one of the servants; Faith could see that at a glance. His clothes were worn, his hair uncombed, his beard shaggy. A wooden pail hung from one of his hands. A trespasser, then. His strangeness screamed threat in Faith's head. She felt every hair rise, as if she were an animal smelling another species.

Fourteen years of trained fears broke into full stampede. A strange man. She was a girl, nearly a woman, and of all things, she must never be near a strange man without protectors and witnesses. That way lay a chasm in which a thousand terrible things could happen.

"Bang!" shouted Howard. The man stopped and turned to look at them.

Faith scooped up Howard and broke into a struggling run

toward the house. She burst in through the front door and almost collided with her mother, who was just leaving the drawing room.

"Heavens!" Myrtle raised her eyebrows. "Faith—what is the matter?"

Faith put Howard down, and panted an explanation. Myrtle hurried to fuss over Howard, who realized that he must be hurt and promptly broke into a wail.

"Look after Howard, Faith—I will tell your father."

A few moments later, Faith's father strode into the parlor, where Faith was distracting Howard.

"Where was this man?" he demanded.

"Near the Folly," replied Faith.

"How close did he come?" demanded her father. Faith had never seen him so grimly agitated. She felt a little pang of warmth at his concern.

"About ten yards—he was walking past, downhill."

Mrs. Vellet came promptly at the Reverend's call. There was a slight, unhappy flush in the housekeeper's cheeks, and Faith wondered whether Myrtle had been "taking her to task" as promised.

"That sounds like Tom Parris," Mrs. Vellet answered immediately, when she heard Faith's description of the stranger.

"Perhaps you would tell me why this Parris was permitted to trespass on this estate?" The Reverend's voice was steely.

"My apologies, sir," the housekeeper responded swiftly, "but these grounds are the shortest way down to the beach. It is the best beach on the island for cockling, so . . ." She spread her hands, with an increasingly familiar air of self-absolution. *There it is, and there is nothing I can do about it.*

"No further trespass is to be permitted," the Reverend

announced starkly. "I have the safety of my wife and children to consider, and valuable specimens in the hothouse that I do *not* intend to leave at the mercy of the larcenous or idly curious. While I am leasing this property, I shall regard all those who trespass on the grounds as poachers. If you know these interlopers, inform them that I shall be investing in rabbit traps."

How close did he come? At first Faith had gratefully taken this as concern for her safety, and that of Howard. As she calmed herself, however, she started to wonder whether her father had meant something else.

How close did he come to the Folly?

Chapter 4

THE SEPULCHRAL CAVERN

AT TWO IN THE AFTERNOON, A CARRIAGE ARRIVED AT the house. A minute or so later a sturdy-looking middle-aged man with red cheeks, black whiskers, and strong white teeth was shown into the parlor. He introduced himself as Dr. Jacklers and shook the Reverend's hand with a series of tense little tugs, as if he were trying to pull it loose.

"Reverend! What an honor to meet you—I have read your articles in the *Royal Society Journal*!"

The doctor shook Uncle Miles's hand a little more uncertainly, despite Uncle Miles's insistence that he too dabbled in natural science, and that perhaps the good doctor had heard of his little pamphlet on fossilized shellfish. Myrtle cut her brother short with a cough.

When Faith was introduced, Dr. Jacklers seemed momentarily taken aback.

"Faith—ah, I do remember the story! I had thought . . ." He trailed off, holding his hand out, just high enough to pat the head of a small imaginary child. "Has it been so long? You look quite the young woman now!"

Faith thanked him, a little uncomfortably. She knew exactly

which event he meant, and it was a day she remembered with a jumble of happiness, wistfulness, and embarrassment.

She had been seven years old, and for once her father had suggested of his own accord that she take a walk with him down a beach. Faith had scampered along beside him, dizzily delighted that he wanted to spend time with her. For once his manner had been easy and kind. Now and then he had stooped to gather pebbles for his basket, and he had even paused to show one of them to her. It had been white, with little ruts and bulges that made a pattern.

"Do you think you could find stones like that?" he had asked her.

Delighted, Faith had run off and brought him every stone that she hoped might be special, though most simply glistened with seawater and dulled in his hand as they dried. At one point he had taken a sharp detour away from the water and beckoned her toward the base of the cliff.

"Try searching around here, Faith."

While he stood staring out to sea, she had scrambled among the boulders. At last she had seen it, a flat piece of stone with a spiral of indentations. She had brought it to him, held carefully in both hands, almost trembling with hope and doubt.

"Well done, Faith." Her father had dropped into a crouch. "That is a fossil—a very pretty one. Remember this moment. Remember finding your first fossil."

Much later, Faith had read newspaper articles about the find. Little Faith, harmlessly frolicking upon a beach, had brought her father a rock that she found pretty, and which he instantly recognized as a fossil of unparalleled interest. The journalists had loved the story, talking of "the artlessness of a child" and "an unwitting innocent opening the door to Nature's marvels." Whenever the Reverend introduced his daughter to fellow natural-science enthusiasts, those who remembered the story expected to see a small, wide-eyed image of innocence. Confronted with a clumsy specimen of not-quite-womanhood, they seldom knew how to react. She had tumbled off the safe, hallowed shore of childhood, and now she was in no-man's-water, neither one thing nor another, like a mermaid. Until she dragged herself up on the rock of marriage, she was difficult.

"So, young lady, did you ever find any other fossils?" asked Dr. Jacklers with a game attempt at gaiety.

Faith shook her head. That was the sting. Her first fossil had been her last. Her father had never taken her fossil hunting again.

It was as if he had opened a door to her that bright, salty day, but then closed it again. She tried to tell herself that it was not shut forever, that remoteness was just his nature. He let her read books from his library, copy out his notes in longhand, and take dictation, and these she took as signs that he still wanted her to share in his private world, and that the door might swing wide again.

Dr. Jacklers's eyes slid off Faith. She understood. As with the wet pebbles, her shine had worn off.

Howard's excitement about the family outing plummeted as soon as he learned that it did not involve daring the waves.

"But we found a little boat on the beach, and Faith said we could explore the sea caves!"

"Faith was joking, darling!" Myrtle gave Faith a look of pure exasperation. "The sea currents are *far* too strong. Howard, don't you want to see your father at work?"

Howard eyed his father nervously and clutched Faith's hand.

As the Sunderly family trooped down into the courtyard, Faith felt herself burn under the carefully bland gazes of the servants. Her boots felt clumsy and her collar too tight.

Faith could hear the tinkle of giggles as the front door closed. With the finely tuned instincts of the solitary, she guessed that the servants had already been laughing at her panicky return to the house earlier that day. So far her parents seemed to be engaged in a campaign to alienate everybody in the house, and now she had made herself a butt for resentful jokes.

The tide had gone down, so it was possible to take the low route around the headlands. On one side of the road rose a rugged cliff, and on the other ran the breakwater, a broad wall some five feet high. Faith wondered how fierce the breakers would need to be to threaten the road, and felt a tingle of excitement at the thought.

"So what has been found so far?" asked Faith's father.

"We are bringing up hand-flaked flints, Reverend, and bones—pygmy hippo, and a tooth that *I* think is mammoth." The doctor rubbed his hands. "I have been hoping for human remains—maybe even a skull. I am a skull man, Reverend.

"But . . . to tell the truth, I am very glad that you are here to set us to rights." The doctor cast a shrewd sideways glance at Faith's father. "I fear that those of us involved in the excavation have been getting in one another's hair. Lambent is a dabbler and has no patience. It is all we can do to stop him from blasting his way through the rock at every turn. But the cave is on his land, so we cannot do without him. Then there is our good curate . . ."

"Mr. Clay seems most pleasant," Myrtle remarked. It was a statement that was really a question.

"Oh, and he is! However, he has some odd, old-fashioned

views, for one of his years." The doctor smiled a lot, but there was something clenched about his smiles. "But he cannot be kept out of the matter either, for he *found* the cave. Or rather his dog found it. The poor brute fell down the hidden shaft and broke one of its legs—we had the deuce of a time fetching it up again.

"As for myself, I have read the latest works on cave hunting and the others have not, so they cannot do without *me* either." The doctor grinned mirthlessly.

Faith shifted uncomfortably. Her father had been called in as an expert, but it sounded as though the locals really wanted someone to settle their squabbles.

The route turned inland, rose gently, and then leveled. The carriage halted. Faith alighted with the rest of her family.

The land all around was craggy and turbulent. Here and there rose rock-crested ridges, with little gorges and dry stream beds twisting between them. On the seaward side, the descent seemed to be a clumsy mixture of level shelves and little cliffs, as if some giant had made a haphazard attempt at carving steps into the side of the island.

Dr. Jacklers led the Sunderly family along a sawdust-strewn path until they could peer down into the nearest gorge. Looking down, Faith saw a cluster of canvas tents. With mounting excitement, she realized that they flanked the mouth of a tunnel, cut into the slope of the hillside between two large boulders. The entrance had been reinforced by a timber lintel, and she could just make out some shadowy wooden struts within.

A tunnel into the past, she thought.

When the doctor called out a greeting, five men in earth-covered workman's clothes stopped what they were doing and stood by politely.

A sixth man, in gentlemanly dress, looked up at them and shielded his eyes, then bounded up the zigzag path to meet them.

"Mr. Anthony Lambent," was all the introduction the doctor managed before their host was upon them.

Lambent was more than six feet tall, and seemed even taller as he tore toward them like a blond hurricane. Faith guessed that he was probably in his thirties, but his stride still had a roaring youthfulness. His green coat showed daubs of mud, and his bright yellow cravat was askew.

"Reverend!" he shouted like a war cry, and pounced upon the Reverend's hand. Faith's father recoiled slightly, and briefly seemed to consider defending himself with his walking cane. Lambent barely allowed the doctor to complete his introductions before hurrying them all down the hill. "Come, let me show you around!" There was something unsettled and unsettling about him, like a horse that might kick.

Myrtle made a face as she edged carefully down the path, and Faith followed with the same caution. It was a difficult route for those who could not see their feet. Eventually Lambent noticed how far he had outpaced his guests and backtracked.

"Forgive me!" he said. "I am of a hopelessly restless constitution—I must be on the move all the time."

"Does that not make sleep uncommonly difficult?" asked Myrtle.

"Oh, indeed—for many years I scarcely slept more than two hours a night, in spite of all the doctors could do. I daresay I should have been forced to rely on laudanum. Thankfully now I have my dear wife, who has a wondrously calming influence on me. As soon as Agatha begins to talk, I find myself yawning."

Faith doubted his "dear wife" would thank him for the compliment.

When they reached the bottom of the hill, Lambent noticed Howard's wooden gun.

"Hullo!" He leaned over, bringing his face closer to that of Faith's brother. "Do we have a soldier here? Or is it a sportsman? Are you a hunter of big game, sir?"

Howard froze, staring up into Lambent's large, bewhiskered face, and gave an uncertain nod.

"Capital!" exclaimed Lambent. "What is it that you shoot, sir?"

Howard opened his mouth, and it stayed open. His eyes widened with panic and concentration. Small noises issued from his throat. Some of them were trying to be words.

"Li . . . li . . . li . . ."

Faith recognized the signs, and knew that shyness and fear had choked off Howard's voice in his throat. The more people stared at him, the worse it would become. She hurried over and placed a comforting hand on his shoulder.

"Lions," she said quickly. "Howard has been shooting lions."

Lambent threw back his head and gave an enormous laugh. "Stout fellow! I daresay you are ready to travel the world like your father, eh?"

Howard blinked nervously, staring at Lambent's blond mane.

"Crock!" called Lambent.

A tawny, broad-shouldered young man approached, and touched his forehead. He was almost as tall as Lambent, but kept his head a little ducked to make his height less intimidating. He moved with the leisurely care of a big man in a flimsy world.

"This is my foreman, Ben Crock. Crock, please look after the ladies while I show the gentlemen the section." He gave a smile and wink to show that the "stout fellow" Howard was included among "gentlemen."

And that was that. A lamp containing a composite candle was

fetched, and then Lambent led the way into the tunnel, followed by the Reverend, Uncle Miles, and even little Howard, clinging to his uncle's sleeve. The ladies were left behind to be looked after. Faith felt as if a door had slammed in her face.

Among the practical canvas tents, a wooden frame had been erected and draped with rich, red-tasseled cloths, so that it looked a little like a Bedouin tent with the sides open. Within was a divan, a small table, and several chairs, two of which were hastily brushed down so that Faith and Myrtle could sit. An inch of amber tea lurked at the bottom of a bone china cup on the table, a relic from another guest. Evidently this was where visiting ladies were stored.

Faith was not ready to sit down yet, however. At long last, she was at an excavation! A real *scientific* excavation. She looked around her, fascinated by everything, even the barrows piled with rubble.

At the far end of the gorge she could see Clay, fixing a camera to a tripod, while a boy of about Faith's age held it steady. She recalled that Clay had mentioned having a son.

In the nearest tent Faith could see a long table, covered in shallow, wooden boxes.

"Mr. Crock, may I look?" She pointed into the tent, too eager to be shy.

"Faith, you should not bother Mr. Crock!" Myrtle gave her a silencing look, but Faith could not be silenced, not at this moment.

"Please!"

"I see no harm in it." Crock gave them both a gentle smile, and held aside the tent flap for them to enter. As she drew near the table, Faith found that the boxes were painted with mysterious number sequences and contained tallow-brown lumps and shards of what looked like bone.

"Better not to touch them, miss," Crock advised quietly. "They would make a mess of your gloves. They are still wet from . . ."

"Seize," finished Faith reflexively, and she looked up at him. "Boiled horses' hoofs or something like that—to stop the ancient bones from crumbling when they dry." She had read of "seize" in her father's books, but this was the first time she had smelled it, and seen it treacle-sticky on bones older than the pyramids.

"Yes, miss." Ben Crock gave a slow blink. His patient blue eyes did not change expression, but Faith sensed him making a quiet mental adjustment.

Faith looked over the shards of bone and noticed one bone sliver that was set apart from the rest. She could not help giving a small gasp. At one end it tapered to a point. The wider end had a perfectly round hole bored through it.

"Mr. Crock! Is that a needle?"

"That's right, miss," answered Crock promptly. "Chiseled from reindeer antler using a stone tool, so the gentlemen think."

"Glacial era?"

"Dr. Jacklers says so."

Faith realized she was smiling. Being answered simply and without fuss was a relief that felt almost physical.

She thought of the needle being chiseled in the distant age of endless ice, when reindeer hoofs had pounded the snow even in Britain. She *did* wish she could touch it, she realized. She wanted to reach out across countless aeons and hold it, just as its maker had once held it. That would be like touching a star.

Only as they were walking out of the tent did Myrtle fall into step with her.

"Faith," she hissed, "*must* you make yourself so absurd?"

Before long, Lambent bounded out of the tunnel with the "gentlemen." Howard looked dusty and confused.

". . . so our tunnel has not broken its way into the cave yet," declared Lambent, "but that is nothing that a barrel of blasting powder cannot solve. Let me show you how we have been lowering ourselves into the cave from above!"

While Myrtle remained in the "Bedouin tent," Lambent led the rest of the Sunderly family up a much longer zigzag path. At the crest, Faith found herself staring at a dimpled, grassy plateau, tufted with low bushes.

"Tread carefully!" Lambent advised cheerfully. "This is where our curate's dog found an unexpected drop, and there may be more!"

Ahead, in the biggest dimple, was a large, freshly hewn timber platform. Faith realized that there was an oblong hole in the middle. Over the hole was a sturdy frame supporting a great spindle with a thick chain around it, a little like the mechanism for lowering a bucket into a well. Instead of a bucket, however, there hung a sort of roofless cage, with a square metal base and sides three feet high.

"I had this old mechanism moved from an abandoned mine on the other side of the island," Lambent explained. "The hauling is all done by *that* fellow." He pointed toward a sturdy-looking horse to whose halter the loose end of the chain had been attached. "We needed something of the sort—the drop is a good thirty feet."

Gripping Faith's hand, Howard stood on tiptoes to peer at the top of the shaft.

"Ah!" exclaimed Lambent. "Our young sportsman is sizing up the basket! Would you like a short ride in it, sir?" He glanced at the Reverend. "What do you think, Reverend? Would he like to be one of the very first people since the Stone Age to see those caves? We can lower him a dozen feet with one of the men and a lantern, just low enough that he can look down into the cavern."

A quiet light kindled in the Reverend's eyes. He looked at Howard, and she knew that the idea was taking hold. *His son*, seeing a prehistoric cavern while it still wore its mysteries. It would be a kind of baptism. He gave a barely perceptible nod of consent, and Faith felt an ache of loss and jealousy.

She was vaguely aware that an unhappy-looking Ben Crock was whispering into Lambent's ear. She caught the words "child" and "risk." But whatever his arguments were, they were waved away.

Lambent beckoned, but Howard clung to Faith's sleeve. His jaw was working again, his face reddening with frustration at his own trapped words.

"He will go down if *I* do," Faith whispered to her father, on impulse. She could not resist. Of course she would have preferred it if her father had turned to her and said, *Faith, I want you to see this, I want you to be part of this.* But if all she could do was ride her little brother's coattails, it was better than nothing.

And the Reverend did not quell her with a look. Perhaps he had noticed that Howard was looking a little less scared by the thought of Faith coming with him.

He gave a nod. Faith flushed with excitement as the men readied the basket, attaching an oil lamp to a hook on the frame. At Ben Crock's insistence they also hooked ropes onto the sides, as guy ropes to keep it from twisting.

One of the sides of the cage-basket was hinged like a door, and was held open so that Faith and Howard could enter.

"Sit down—that will be safer," called Crock, and they obeyed.

At the sight of his furrowed brow Faith's stomach gave a little fizz of fear, but the excitement was stronger.

Faith wrapped her arms around Howard as the chain was let out and their basket started to descend. They passed below the timber frame, and now they were flanked by red-brown rock, rippling and pocked. Howard's eyes were bright in the lantern-light.

"This is our adventure, Howard!" whispered Faith. "We are going back in time! Far, far back, to when this was a mountain tip, not an island. No sea, just land, covered in snow deeper than houses. Mammoths stamping around, making the ground shudder. Huge herds of reindeer, shaking their antlers. Shaggy rhinos big as shire horses. Saber-toothed cats."

The past was all around her. She could smell it. It did not feel dead. It felt alive, and as curious about her as she was about it.

The shaft was widening, as if they were descending through the neck of a bottle. The light from the lantern threw into relief the jagged walls of the shaft, and directly below there was darkness.

The metal chain told out with a tooth-tingling *clang-clang-clang* that echoed down the shaft. Then amid this monotonous music there was a faint *chink* and then a loud, dull *crack*.

The basket fell.

There was a second of utter weightlessness, and perfect light-headed despair. Then the basket was rattling against the rock walls, and Howard was screaming. Good honest terror hit Faith like a brick.

The basket came to a sudden halt, with a jolt that made it tip. As Howard pitched forward Faith flung an arm around him, grabbing the cage barrier with her free hand. Something heavy hit her hard in the back with a metallic rattle. It was a loose end of the chain fastened to the basket. The ropes were taut, Faith realized, and groaning as the basket swung and tipped over the dark abyss. These ropes alone had halted their plummet. There was shouting above, but the echoes muddied the words.

Clumsily, in jolts, the basket started to ascend again. Looking up she could just see a cleft of sky with heads silhouetted against it. As the basket swayed, Faith could see the slender ropes scraping against the rock and starting to fray.

"Hush Howard hush Howard hush Howard . . ." It was an incantation. Howard's sobs were the only real thing in the world.

The cleft grew closer. Arms were reaching down toward the basket. Faith grabbed Howard under his armpits and heaved him as high as she could. Her arms ached and weakened under his weight, and then the burden was lifted away. Howard's legs flailed as he rose, nearly kicking her in the head.

Then the basket started to ascend more quickly, and the arms were reaching down again, and this time they were clutching her hands, her arms. They had her. They heaved her up and out, and then she was sitting on the grass, scarcely believing she had survived.

Afterward there was a lot of shouting, most of it from Lambent, who was thunderstruck and incandescent. He was the local magistrate and would have the law on somebody, but it soon became clear that it would probably not be anybody present. The fellow who had sold him the old mining mechanism was the main target of his ire.

Howard was wailing. He needed to be examined for injuries, wiped with handkerchiefs, petted, comforted, and offered toffees. The Reverend was icily furious, but gradually relented in the face of apologies. After all, who could have expected such a thick chain to snap? And with the guy ropes in place there had been no real danger.

Unsteadily Faith walked over to Ben Crock, who was sitting on the grass, recovering his breath. There were raw, red rope burns on both his palms.

"Thank you," she said quietly, casting a pointed glance at his hands.

"No lady should have a scare like that while in my charge," was all he said. "I hope you can forgive me, miss."

Chapter 5

SKULLS AND CRINOLINES

THE SUNDERLY FAMILY WENT HOME TO CHANGE
their clothes, and to argue about what had just happened. For
a while it seemed that Myrtle would refuse to attend the Lambents' afternoon tea out of indignation. Only when she had been
assured a dozen times that her children had never been in any
real danger did she finally relent.

Faith said nothing. She still remembered her lurching horror
when Howard had seemed about to fall out of the basket. The
peril had certainly felt pretty mortal at the time.

Myrtle was not at all sure whether Faith was included in the
invitation to "ladies of the family." Had it been a dinner invitation, she would have been left behind with Howard as a matter
of course. Afternoon tea, however, was a slightly different matter. In the end Myrtle decided Faith could attend, though Faith
suspected that her mother simply wanted somebody to accom-
pany her as an unofficial lady's maid.

Because of the importance of the occasion, Myrtle agreed to
tighten Faith's "training corset" an inch more than usual. However, she quashed Faith's suggestion that she wear a longer skirt
in an adult style. Faith knew a few girls of her own age, and over

the last year she had watched their hems creep downward. Most of them had also just graduated to proper grown-up corsets, leaving Faith feeling self-conscious about her clumsy, loose, childish one. She sometimes wondered if Myrtle was keeping her a child for vanity's sake, rather than admit to being old enough to have a nearly adult daughter.

As they were about to leave, Myrtle noticed the crochet gloves on Faith's hands.

"Where are your kid gloves?" she demanded.

"I . . . do not know." Faith reddened. "I am sure I had them on the boat . . ." A tremulous hint that the unfortunate gloves had fallen overboard.

"Oh, *Faith*!" Myrtle's mouth tightened with impatience and annoyance.

Lambent's house stood on the top of a headland, less than a mile from the excavation. According to the battered wooden sign, the house was called "The Paints." It braced its four red-brick storeys against the weather, but the fences and little trees around it had surrendered to the wind, bowing and skulking close to the long grass. There was a large stable and coach house. Beagles barked in their kennels.

There were the usual delays, as Myrtle was maneuvered out of Lambent's carriage. Her crinoline, the bird's cage of whale-bone and linen that bulked out the back of her skirts, creaked and shivered, tipping to reveal her dainty, bow-covered shoes.

The Sunderly family had barely entered the hallway before they were intercepted by Lambent.

"Come through! Let me introduce you to everyone!"

He led them into what appeared to be a trophy room, its red-and-white check floor flecked with burrs and dog hairs. Antlers jutted from high plaques, throwing branched shadows across the walls. There were also African masks, Chinese jade carvings, a walrus tusk, a boomerang, and other souvenirs of strange and exotic lands.

A dozen guests stood around talking, most of them men. Faith recognized Dr. Jacklers and Clay, but the rest were strangers.

When the Sunderlys entered, Faith cast a nervous glance around the room, scanning every face for traces of coldness or scorn. Instead, when her father was introduced, she saw only enthusiasm, curiosity, and respect. If the venom of scandal had touched her father's name, nobody present appeared to be aware of it.

As usual, the adulation slid off the Reverend's stony reticence and was soaked up by the lace handkerchief of Myrtle's busy charm. She quickly made herself a favorite with the gentlemen, by being witty without being *too* clever. Meanwhile Uncle Miles produced the fossilized shellfish he kept in his tobacco tin and tried to show them to people, in spite of Myrtle's attempts to make him stop.

Faith found herself standing next to Dr. Jacklers, who clearly had no idea what to say to her.

"Do tell me about skulls!" Faith whispered. It was a bold suggestion, perhaps an unladylike one, and if Myrtle had been within earshot Faith would not have asked it. But Crock's willingness to answer her questions had given her a small surge of confidence. What if the rules were different in Vane? What if she could show interest in natural science without it seeming odd?

"Ah, you are just humoring an old man!" The doctor laughed, showing his strong, white teeth. But of course he let himself be humored. "I have a collection of skulls—not because I want to affright nice young ladies like yourself, but because I am writing a paper on the human brain and the roots of intelligence. I measure my patients' heads as well—even if they drop by with a sniffle I come up with some reason to wrap a tape measure around their skulls."

"So you are a craniometrist?" As soon as the words left Faith's mouth she saw the doctor's smile fade and knew that she had made a mistake. He had been enjoying his explanation, and now she had spoiled things by knowing too much. "Is . . . is that the right word?" She knew it was, but swallowed hard and made her voice hesitant. "I . . . think I heard it somewhere."

"Yes." The doctor's confidence slowly returned in the face of her timidity. "That is *exactly* the right word, my dear. Well done."

As he went on to describe his skull collection, Faith listened with an acid twist in her stomach. She was furious at herself for using too clever a term. Right now, somebody was *talking to her about science*, and if she sounded too knowledgeable he would stop. Yes, he was explaining things that she already knew as if she were half her age, but she should be grateful even for that.

Once upon a time, when she was nine years old and starting to make sense of her father's books, Faith had been so keen to show off her knowledge. Every time visitors came to the house she would bubble over with the latest facts she had discovered and the newest words to capture her imagination. She had wanted to impress—to prove to her father and everyone else that she was *clever*. Each time, her efforts had been met first by surprised laughter, then uncomfortable silences. Nobody was unkind exactly, but after a while they had politely ignored her as if she were a stain on the tablecloth. She had wept herself to sleep afterward, knowing that she had *not* been clever, she had been stupid, stupid, stupid. She had embarrassed everyone and spoiled everything.

Rejection had worn Faith down. She no longer fought to be praised or taken seriously. Now she was humbled, desperate to be permitted any part in interesting conversations. Even so, each time she pretended ignorance, she hated herself and her own desperation.

"The larger the skull, the larger the brain, and the greater the intelligence," the doctor continued, warming to his theme. "You need only look at the difference between the skull sizes of men and women. The male skull is larger, showing it to be the throne of intellect." The doctor seemed to become aware that he was not being entirely tactful. "The female mind is a different thing altogether," he added quickly, "and quite delightful in its own right! But too much intellect would spoil and flatten it, like a rock in a soufflé."

Faith flushed. She felt utterly crushed and betrayed. *Science* had betrayed her. She had always believed deep down that science would not judge her, even if people did. Her father's books had opened to her touch easily enough. His journals had not flinched from her all too female gaze. But it seemed that science had weighed her, labeled her, and found her wanting. Science had decreed that she could not be clever . . . and that if by some miracle she *was* clever, it meant that there was something terribly wrong with her.

"Ah, I recognize that refrain!" declared a woman's voice directly behind Faith. "Once again Dr. Jacklers is decrying us for our little skulls!"

It was a lady who had been introduced as "Miss Hunter, our postmistress and telegraph operator." She was short, neat, and black-haired, with a quickness of motion and gesture that reminded Faith of a moorhen. Her plump, gloved fingers were kept busy straightening and preening at her own clothes, but her gaze was steady and appraising.

"Forgive me, Doctor, do not let me cut you *short*." Miss Hunter smiled blandly. Faith was not sure whether she had imagined the slight emphasis on the last word.

There was no mistaking Dr. Jacklers's reaction though. His ruddy face became almost violet and he gave Miss Hunter a glance loaded with bitterness. He was by no means a tall man, and Faith wondered if Miss Hunter's remark was a veiled taunt about his height. Nonetheless Faith suspected that she was missing something.

"I am simply saying," the doctor persisted with an edge to his voice, "that the Almighty has designed each of us for our appointed place in the world . . ."

But these were fateful words. The conversation promptly exploded into a debate about evolution.

Natural scientists liked to argue and debate. Back at the rectory Faith had grown used to her father's guests smiling, bantering, and my-dear-fellow-ing over their tea, while racing their rival theories like prize ponies. The disagreements about evolution were always different, however. There was a crackle of fear behind them, a rawness like splintered wood.

The same rawness and tension filled the conversation now. To Faith's surprise, the mild, courteous Clay was one of the loudest and most fervent voices.

"Lamarck and Darwin are leading the world into a great error!" he declared. "If we say that species change, then we say that they were created imperfect! We criticize God himself!"

"But, Clay, what about the relics of extinct beasts?" protested Lambent. "The mastodon! The great cave bear! The aurochs! The dinosauria!"

"All slain in the Flood," answered Clay without hesitation, "or through similar catastrophes. Our Lord has seen fit to clean the slate many times, on each occasion creating new species to enjoy his world."

"But the fossils—most of them must be tens of thousands of years old at least, long before the Flood—"

"That is impossible." Clay's tone was adamant. "We *know* how old the world is, from scriptural records. It cannot possibly be more than six thousand years old."

The oldest gentlemen nodded approvingly at this speech. The other men looked pained and rather embarrassed. Clay seemed to notice the silence.

"Dr. Jacklers," he appealed, "you have said as much yourself! I remember you talking of such things with my father . . ."

"Perhaps I did, ten years ago." Dr. Jacklers looked uncomfortable. "Clay . . . everything has changed in the last ten years."

Faith was a naturalist's daughter and knew what the doctor meant. The world *had* changed. Its past had changed, and with it everything else. Once upon a time, everybody had *known* the story of the earth: It had been created in a week, and Man set in place to rule it. And the history of the world surely could not be more than a few thousand years . . .

But then gentlemen of science had worked out how long it took rock to fold itself like puff pastry. They had found fossils, and strange misshapen man-skulls with sloping brows. Then, when Faith was five years old, a book about evolution called *On the Origin of Species* had entered the world, and the world had shuddered, like a boat running aground.

And the unknown past had started to stretch. Tens of thousands, hundreds of thousands, even millions of years . . . and the longer the dark age stretched, the smaller glorious mankind shrank and shrank. He had not been there from the start, nor had the whole of creation been presented to him as a gift. No, he was a latecomer, whose ancestors had struggled up from the slime and crawled on the earth.

The Bible did not lie. Every good, God-fearing scientist knew that. But rocks and fossils and bones did not lie either, and it was starting to look as though they were not telling the same story.

"Truth has not changed!" exclaimed an elderly whippet of a man with white floppy hair. "Only the minds of those who doubt! May I point out that in our very midst we have the Reverend Erasmus Sunderly, whose greatest find bears dumb witness to the truth of the Gospel!"

All eyes were on Faith's father, who did not deign to raise his eyes.

"I was one of the first called in to examine his New Falton find," continued the old man. "When I looked upon it, and saw a fossilized human shoulder with faint traces of wings spreading from it, I felt . . . awe. At once I knew what it was. 'This,' I said, 'is one of the ancient Nephilim, and it is as authentic as I am. I would stake my reputation on it!'"

The Reverend's cheek twitched slightly at the word "reputation." Faith was filled with a terrible surge of sympathy. She wanted to feel happy that her father had such an ardent supporter, but the old man's declaration was a little too desperate. It made her nervous.

"My dear friends," said Lambent, "I do not think this is a conversation for mixed company."

The company unmixed itself. For a little while there had been a faint tension in the air, a feeling of politeness under strain. The ladies had been charming company, but now the gentlemen wanted them to depart and enjoy their afternoon tea, so that the men could have their scientific meeting and talk freely.

Faith's heart sank as she found herself trailing after the other ladies. *This is your future*, said a cruel voice in her head. *Walking away from scientific meetings you are not allowed to attend.*

As Faith got halfway down the corridor, her attention was caught by an open door. Beyond lay a tiny room that smelled of dust and formaldehyde. Daylight from high windows glinted on glass-fronted cabinets and the eyes of stuffed animals. A Cabinet of Curiosities, a naturalist's den.

Faith glanced after Myrtle and the other ladies, none of whom was paying her any attention. She felt a flare of rebellion, and a familiar singing in her ears. *If I cannot eat at the table, I can snatch at scraps.*

She slipped into the little room, closing the door behind her deftly and without a click.

Faith moved around the room, rapt, mesmerized, staring into case after case. Birds' eggs. Butterflies. Dry pinned-out hides of lizards and baby crocodiles. Papery remains of carnivorous plants, with thornlike teeth or tonguelike stamens. Every item had its own tiny, meticulously written label.

A stuffed mongoose was frozen forever in the black and yellow coils of a snake. The color and pattern of the scales reminded Faith of her father's snake, which made her feel a little uncomfortable.

As Faith peered at the exhibits in the biggest cabinet, she felt a queer, unpeeling sensation in her stomach. A stuffed albino badger lurked between a fly preserved in a glossy blob of amber and a tough-looking root shaped crudely like a person. In a great pickle jar, a pair of conjoined piglets floated in pallid eternal sleep.

"Freaks of Nature," read the central label.

And that is what I am, thought Faith, feeling sick. *A little female brain with too much crammed into it. Maybe that is what is wrong with me. Maybe that is why I cannot stop myself from creeping and spying.*

Faith had just crept out of the room into the corridor again when Myrtle reappeared, tight-lipped and impatient.

"What in the world delayed you?"

"Sorry, Mother—I was lost . . ." Faith trailed off, and with satisfaction saw her mother's annoyance ebb into weary resignation.

"This is no time for wandering or wool-gathering." Myrtle tugged Faith's straight collar a little straighter. "These ladies will be taking their measure of our family, and it is very important that we make the right impression. We cannot look too eager—if we let them talk down to us, then by tomorrow the whole island will be doing so."

Faith followed Myrtle to a green-papered drawing room where half a dozen ladies were seated and a silver tea service had been laid out. A fierce fire blazed in the hearth. Even compared to the pleasant warmth of the trophy room, this room was muggy and stifling.

In a wicker throne by the fire sat a woman that Faith had not seen before. She had a high, queenly forehead and a fine haze of pale blond hair gathered back into a bun. The blankets that swaddled her marked her out as an invalid.

"Please, do come in—so that my man can shut the door. The seats are warmest by the fire. I am Agatha Lambent." She had a deep, pleasant voice, but every sentence lilted mournfully downward, as though drooping under its own weight.

Back in the trophy room the gentlemen would be taking the leash off their conversation. Likewise, here in the drawing room, each lady quietly relaxed and became more real, expanding into the space left by the men. Without visibly changing, they unfolded, like flowers, or knives.

Faith could sense her mother making rapid judgments. Everyone had their place on an invisible ladder. It was easy to know that dukes were high above you, and chambermaids far below. But there were thousands of rungs, some at tiny differences in height, and Myrtle always wanted to determine everyone's level to a fraction of an inch.

Myrtle's blue gaze flitted quickly over the room and its occupants. Mrs. Lambent sounded as English as the Sunderlys, but the other ladies' murmurs of greeting had displayed the local accent. The local ladies' dresses were of good quality, but not quite up to date. Most of them were clearly wearing bell-shaped full crinolines, a style that had been fashionable a couple of years before. Myrtle, on the other hand, wore the very latest flat-fronted "half-crinoline."

With an inner wince Faith saw Myrtle sweeping forward confidently and dropping curtseys that were polite but a little condescending. She could see that her mother was claiming a position only a little lower than Mrs. Lambent, and slight superiority to the other ladies. Perhaps they were important ladies on this island, but they were all *provincial*.

"How very kind of you to invite us!" she told Mrs. Lambent. *And how kind of us to come*, her manner added in the sweetest tone.

Faith took a seat and tried not to squirm. The tightened corset made her feel much more adult, but it was hard to sit still, and the straps dug into her shoulders.

Myrtle was younger than most of the other women, but did not defer to their opinions. Instead, she countered with, "Ah, but I have always found in *London* . . ." or, "Well, I do recall a *London* gentleman once told me . . ." She had been brought up in London prior to her marriage, and that was her trump card.

Please stop, Faith begged her silently. *Must we make everybody hate us? What if we are stranded on this island for years?* Only black-haired Miss Hunter seemed unruffled by Myrtle's manner, watching her instead with the bright, anticipative air of one watching an amusing play.

I do not belong here, Faith told herself desperately. *I do not belong in this room of tea and bonnets and gossip* . . .

Faith tried not to listen to her mother, or to the thistly, resentful whispers elsewhere in the room. Instead she let her eyes drift around the room, and realized that it was covered in religious oddments—prayer books, samplers with lines from Psalms, and memento mori like china skulls and black wreaths. Perhaps Mrs. Lambent's illness kept her thoughts focused on the hereafter. Certainly she seemed determined not to go to hell for lack of ornaments.

"Faith!" hissed Myrtle.

Faith started, and found that Mrs. Lambent's large eyes were regarding her solemnly. She reddened, realizing that she had probably just been asked a question.

"Do forgive Faith—she is still recovering from the voyage yesterday." Myrtle gave Faith a far from forgiving look.

"It must have been very trying," Miss Hunter agreed. "Particularly since I understand you brought none of your own servants with you?" Her smile was a little too sweet.

"The house we have leased is fully staffed," Myrtle responded quickly.

"Oh, I do not blame you at all!" Miss Hunter spread her plump, well-shaped hands. "There is always so much trouble when you mix two lots of servants—we all know how they gossip!"

Faith's cup clicked against her saucer. Miss Hunter's words were too close an echo of her own suspicions. The Sunderly family had not brought their servants because they did not want to bring gossip with them.

"I do hope you will find you have everything you need on Vane," Miss Hunter continued amiably. "We are not without society, and most of the London fashions reach us sooner or later. We even . . . receive the London papers. Usually a day late, but news is not milk—it keeps well enough." Her tone was dry, but now with an unmistakable barb. "I am *particularly* fond of the *Intelligencer.* Do you ever read it, Mrs. Sunderly?"

"I prefer the *Times*," declared Myrtle, with unnecessary hauteur, her spoon tracing hasty circles in her cup.

Faith kept her head bowed, hoping that her face did not show her feelings. She had started to hope that no dark rumors about her father had reached Vane. There was no mistaking Miss Hunter's veiled meaning, however.

Faith glanced at her mother, and saw that Myrtle's cheeks had turned pale.

Mother knows. The accusations against Father—Mother must have known about them all this time.

We didn't outrun the Intelligencer *after all. It followed us all the way to the island. Miss Hunter must know about the scandal already . . . and soon everyone else will too.*

Chapter 6

YELLOW EYES

AS LAMBENT'S CARRIAGE TOOK THE SUNDERLY family back to Bull Cove, Faith tried to work up her courage. She needed to speak with her father. She needed to warn him about Miss Hunter's words, and to let him know that whatever happened, she was on his side. It was torture seeing him bear so much alone.

When at last they reached home, and Jeanne had taken their coats and hats, Uncle Miles lit a taper and fumbled for his pipe, preparing for his customary stroll and smoke.

The Reverend halted him at the door. "Miles—if you're stepping outside, stay near the house. Earlier today I had the gardener set rabbit traps."

Uncle Miles coughed out an incredulous lungful of smoke.

"Erasmus—is that wise? In the dark . . . if people are unaware of the danger . . ."

"I hardly see that allowing nocturnal intruders to prowl the grounds can be described as either 'wise' or without danger," retorted the Reverend. "Now, if you will excuse me, I must visit the Folly." He strode out into the garden.

A little while later the Reverend returned with a small,

wooden box in one hand. As he came in, stamping the soil from his shoes, Faith rallied her courage.

"Father, can—"

"My dear, I wonder if I might speak with you?" Myrtle spoke at the same time, drowning out Faith's more hesitant voice. She wore the expression of careful alertness she always used when addressing delicate subjects with her husband. "There is something I need to mention to you."

"It will have to wait," the Reverend responded curtly. He stared down at the box in his hand. "Everything will have to wait. There is a matter that requires my immediate attention— *all* of my attention. I shall be in the library, and under no circumstances must I be disturbed." The Reverend had claimed the library as his study from the first day, and it was now sacred ground.

Faith's father had mastered the art of making his words sound gravestone-final, his decisions irrevocable. The library door closed behind him. The moment was lost.

Faith joined Howard for supper, then helped him say his prayers and put him to bed, wondering how she had become governess and nursemaid in one. Howard was sleepy but tenacious, wrapping his arms around her every time she tried to leave.

As she stroked her brother's head and lulled him to sleep, a faint sound jerked Faith from her thoughts. It was a short, sharp cry, not unlike a vixen but very like a child, and it came from the darkness outside. Doors below opened and closed. There were hushed conversations, exclamations of alarm, and hurried steps.

Faith slipped from her brother's room and hastened downstairs, finding her mother, her uncle, and Mrs. Vellet in the drawing room, in tense, hushed debate.

"Madam, we must send for a doctor . . ." Mrs. Vellet was insisting.

"I cannot consent to that without my husband's permission . . ." Myrtle cast a nervous glance in the direction of the library.

"Has he forbidden it?" asked Uncle Miles. "Does Erasmus even know that there is a maimed child on his doorstep?"

"He gave instructions—strict instructions—that he was not to be disturbed," Myrtle's tone was meaningful, and her expression seemed to take the wind from her brother's sails. Even warmed by port, Uncle Miles was not one to risk the Reverend's temper. "Miles—is there a chance that *you*—"

"Myrtle, if I had money for the doctor I would send for him straight away, but right now I simply do not have the funds."

"Mrs. Vellet—" Myrtle turned to the housekeeper "—if the boy is brought into the kitchen, can he not be bandaged there?"

"Yes, madam." Mrs. Vellet seemed to be having some difficulty maintaining her usual composure. "But the trap has hurt him badly, and there is only so much we can do."

All three were too caught up in their conversation to notice Faith slipping away to the library.

Father would want to know. Of course he would want to know.

She knocked. There was a silence, and then a faint sound that might have been a cleared throat, but which sounded just enough like a muffled word.

Faith turned the handle and opened the door.

The gas lamps were turned down to a mere glow, but the brass reading lamp on the desk bathed the scene in a quivering halo of light. Behind the desk sat her father, reclining back in his chair. As Faith entered he turned his head very slightly in her direction, and frowned.

Faith opened her mouth to apologize, but the words died in her mouth. Her father's posture, always ramrod-straight, was now oddly slumped. She had never seen his face so pale, so slack. Her skin tingled.

There was a clammy smell in the room, she realized, the cold scent she had noticed in the Folly. Now it ran little ice-fingers down her throat, through the nerves of her teeth, and across the backs of her eyes. The air was alive with it.

"Father?"

Her own voice sounded odd, as if a faint down of sighs clung to it. As she gingerly advanced, her footsteps were muffled in the same strange, feathery way. On every side the air seemed to be stirring itself in little mouthless breaths.

A pen trembled between her father's loose fingers, ink pooling on the paper beneath the nib. A few sentences had been scrawled in clumsy, lopsided letters, unlike the Reverend's usual handwriting.

His pupils were tiny and impenetrably black. In the lamplight it seemed that the gray of his eyes had jaded to a murky, troubled yellow. As she watched, the flecks and blotches of his irises seemed to shift and stir like waterweed . . .

"Father!"

The discolored eyes fixed on her, their gaze sharpening. Then his jaw set and his brow slowly creased.

"Get out." It was a whisper, but with more venom than Faith had ever heard in her father's voice. "Get out!"

Faith turned and ran from the room, heart pounding.

"Faith!" Myrtle appeared in the hallway, just in time to see

Faith closing the door behind her. "Oh—has your father finished his work for the evening? Thank goodness—I must speak with him."

"No!" Faith reflexively put her back to the door.

She could not make sense of what she had just seen, but she knew he wanted to keep it a secret. Faith remembered tales of strange opiates smoked in secret, with fumes that entranced gentlemen's wills and enslaved their minds. What if her father's troubles had driven him to become an opium eater? She could not expose him. He was facing enough scorn and scandal already.

"I . . . I went in to tell him about the boy in the rabbit trap," Faith said quickly.

"What did he say?"

Faith hesitated. The only safe answer was to say that she had been ordered out of the room and given no answer. It was true besides.

"We should send for a doctor," she heard herself say.

Myrtle hurried away to give orders to Mrs. Vellet, relief visible on her pretty, rounded features.

Faith was flabbergasted by her own nerve. Her lie would inevitably be exposed. Her mind mouse-scampered with the agility of practice, trying to find a way out, but she could think of no excuse or explanation. She could not imagine facing her father and telling him that she had given false orders in his name.

Father has to understand, she told herself. *If I had not, he might have been discovered, or blamed for letting the boy bleed. I am protecting him.*

At the same time, the thought that she had claimed a tiny part in one of her father's mysterious secrets filled her with a small, quiet glow.

A few minutes later, Faith looked out through the window and saw Uncle Miles, the household manservant, and Mrs. Vellet helping a shorter figure toward the house. When they drew close enough for the window's light to fall on them, she could make out the face of the boy, who looked about fourteen years old. He was alarmingly pale, cheeks shiny with tears, face crumpled with pain. The cloth clumsily tied around his ankle was blotched with dark. The sight of it filled her stomach with an animal, sympathetic tingle.

Faith was not allowed into the kitchen. Sitting in the nearby dining room, however, she could easily hear the boy's high sobs of pain, and the panicky conversations within.

". . . No, hold the pad steady!"

"Mrs. Vellet—it's soaked! It's leaking through my fingers!"

The manservant Prythe arrived with more makeshift bandages. As he opened the kitchen door, Faith caught a fleeting glimpse of the wounded boy lying on the hearthrug, Jeanne clamping a red-soaked cloth to his ankle. The boy was cursing through clenched teeth, his eyes tightly shut.

"I won't have language like that in my kitchen," Mrs. Vellet could be heard to declare, as the door shut. "What would you do if you bled to death right now, and got dragged down to hell for having a wicked tongue?"

Dr. Jacklers's carriage arrived within the hour. He bowed to Mrs. Sunderly and Faith, but had a businesslike frown rather than his sociable smile.

"How is the boy?" he asked immediately. "Serious, you say? Well, I would hope so—I have just left a good mug of spiced cider cooling on my dresser, and I would hate it to be wasted for nothing." He asked for a tot of laudanum to numb the patient's pain, and a hot cup of tea to help himself recover from the cold of his journey. "I never like to work with numb fingers, and a man is best warmed from the inside out."

The house became a little calmer after the doctor's arrival. After an hour he emerged, his hands washed and his bag packed once more.

"How is the poor child?" Myrtle asked meekly.

"Well, the teeth of the trap missed the bone, thank goodness, but they spiked two holes into the meat of his calf. I have washed the rust and dirt out of them as best I can, and swabbed the wounds with carbolic acid." The doctor seemed to become aware that Myrtle was blanching at his words, and changed the subject. "He is bandaged and made watertight now, so I might as well take him home—I know the Parris family."

After a moment Faith realized why the name Parris was familiar. The man she had met in the woods and had run from was called Tom Parris, according to Mrs. Vellet. The wounded boy was the right age to be his son. Perhaps the whole family liked cockling.

As the doctor's outdoor clothes were brought, he looked around and frowned, seeming slightly offended. Faith wondered whether he had been expecting her father to emerge and greet him.

"Thank you *so* much for coming out at such an hour!" Myrtle gave him a charming, vulnerable smile and extended a hand for him to take. Dr. Jacklers's disgruntlement evaporated like dew in the morning sun.

Much later, after the household had retired for the night, Faith quietly rose from her bed and donned her dressing gown. She slipped downstairs and peered through the keyhole of the library door. It showed her little except a bookcase and a patch of floor, but they were both still lamplit. Pressing her ear to the keyhole she could make out the furtive scratch of nib on paper, occasional mutters, and tiny noises that might be made by the shifting of a chair.

Relief washed over Faith. She had imagined her father sprawled and unmoving, or struggling for breath. Now these images melted away, and instead her mind's eye saw him still seated at his desk—alive, conscious, and busily writing.

She curled her hand around the knob, but hesitated, the metal chilling her palm. She could not forget her father's eerily shifting eyes, the whispering sickness of the room, and the venom with which he had ordered her out. Instead she crept back upstairs and slipped back into her cooling bed.

When at last she slept, her mind remained unsettled. She dreamed of scrambling through a cold garden full of frost-furred trees. At its heart she came across her father's enormous stone head, jutting above the ground as if he had been buried to the neck. His eyes were yellow-stained glass, and behind them dark shapes shifted, blotting and muting their light. His face was stifled with moss, but when she tried to claw it off, the stonework came away too.

Chapter 7

A CREEPING FROST

FAITH'S MIND WAS WATCHFUL, EVEN WHILE sleeping. The first early morning movements in the house nudged her from her dreams into a half-wakened state. She could hear a distant door banging, the slosh of water, the tumble of logs from a woodpile.

Her outdoor coat wrapped around her nightshirt, Faith slipped downstairs, just in time to see Jeanne walking up to the library with a tea tray.

"It is quite all right, Jeanne," said Faith, trying to imitate her mother's air of confidence. "I will take in the tray."

Jeanne looked at Faith in surprise, then glanced at the door. Faith could see the older girl's curiosity unsheathing itself like a cat's claw.

"Yes, miss."

After Jeanne had departed, Faith took up the tray and slipped into the library, which was almost pitch dark. The same cold smell hung in the room, but now with an added sour staleness, like rotten oranges. Faith set down the tray and hurried over to open the window and shutters, so as to let in the light and clear the air. If the smell was the scent of an opiate, she did not want anybody else to notice it.

As daylight seeped into the room, Faith could see that the Reverend was still sitting in his chair, wearing the same clothes as the night before. His body lolled forward on to his desk, and Faith felt a frisson of panic, until she realized that she could hear him breathing.

The desk was heaped with open books and scrawled papers. The Reverend's writing box and travel chest were open, their carefully guarded contents scattered over chairs and even the floor. On the edge of the bookcase a candle had been left to burn down, so that there was a blackened scar in the shelf above and waxen stalactites trailing below.

It felt blasphemous seeing him asleep. Even in rest his face had the sedate severity of churchyard marbles or ancient statuary. He was unyielding stone, and judgments carved deep. He was a place where you needed to tread quietly and whisper.

"Father?"

The Reverend stirred, then slowly lifted his head and sat up.

His eyes were their usual gray, but with a filmy distance. The mists lifted with uncanny speed, however, and his gaze became skewer-sharp.

"What are you doing in this room?"

Faith froze. A moment before, she had felt that she was protecting him. Now that very thought seemed childish and presumptuous.

"Jeanne brought your morning tea. I thought . . . I thought you would not want her to come in. You seemed . . . last night you seemed ill . . ."

"I gave instructions that *nobody* was to come in here!" Her father blinked hard and stared through Faith, frowning as through she were a very poor telescope. "I . . . am not ill. You were mistaken. Did you tell anybody that I was ill?"

"No." Faith shook her head emphatically.

"Has anyone else been in here?"

"I do not think so . . ." Faith trailed off. Her father's eye had caught on something, and as she followed his gaze she saw a new bundle of kindling by the fireplace and a freshly filled coal scuttle. Faith had forgotten that most of the fires were set at five in the morning. Clearly one of the servants had come in to set the fire, found the sleeping Reverend, and departed again, leaving the fire-making supplies ready to be used when needed.

The Reverend glanced around at his strewn papers, now with an air of alarm and urgency.

"Were these papers scattered thus when you first came in?"

Faith nodded, and the Reverend began scooping them up and heaping them back into his writing box. A few pages showed rough ink sketches, and he paused to stare at them.

"What do these mean?" he murmured under his breath. "I deserve an answer—I have given everything for an answer! How can I make sense of this nonsense?"

Faith hurried over to help. The sketches were strange and hard to distinguish. A rat-shaped creature rested its forepaws on a broken oval. A dragon-like beast reared a scribbled head. A half-human face with a heavily sloping brow glowered with hostile stupefaction. She saw little more before the drawings were snatched out of her hands.

"Do not touch those!" the Reverend told her abruptly.

"I was only trying to help." Faith's desperation won out over her prudence. "I just want to help! Father, *please* tell me what is wrong! I promise not to tell anybody!"

Her father looked at her in surprise for a few seconds, and then his gaze dulled with impatience.

"There is nothing wrong, Faith. Bring me my tea, then leave me to my work."

The rejection stung, as it always stung. Somehow there was never a callus to protect her.

Faith ate a nursery breakfast of weak, cold tea and eggs boiled soft to the point of liquescence. She was preoccupied and groggy from broken sleep, and noticed only at the end of the meal that Howard was furtively using his fork and knife in the wrong hands again.

When Faith came downstairs, she ventured to the dining room and peered through the door. There was her father, drinking tea with her mother and uncle over the remains of their breakfast. He showed every semblance of his usual composure. His hands were steady as he turned the pages of his newspaper.

"There you are, Faith!" Myrtle caught sight of her and beckoned. "You must come into town with me today. We must buy you some new kid gloves, since you have lost yours—though I do not know how you could be so careless!"

Faith flushed and mumbled an apology.

"Be ready to go out as soon as you can." Myrtle gave her husband a slightly warier glance. "My dear . . . if you see Dr. Jacklers at the excavation today, will you settle matters with him?"

"Dr. Jacklers?" The Reverend surveyed his wife as if she were an incomprehensible squiggle under his microscope. "What matters?"

Faith's heart sank and she suddenly wished with miserable intensity that she had admitted everything to her father that morning. It was too late though, and the crisis had arrived. Her terrible impudence in speaking for her father was about to be discovered.

"The fee for treating that young boy caught in the rabbit trap last night . . ." Myrtle faltered.

"*What?*" The Reverend rose to his feet, casting a thunderous look out toward the garden.

"You . . . said that we should send for the doctor." Myrtle's brow wrinkled uncertainly, and her eyes slid toward her daughter.

Faith swallowed hard and met her father's gaze. His expression was cloudy, changeable and hard to read. There was ill weather there, and the makings of a storm. She saw his thoughts surge silently toward a conclusion, but could not tell what it was.

Then he slowly sat down again and smoothed his disheveled paper.

"When I sent for the doctor," he continued coldly, "I assumed the boy's family would bear the brunt of the cost. I scarcely see why trespassers should be allowed to pick our pocket like this, but . . . since I shall be seeing Dr. Jacklers, I will settle his fee. I shall of course speak to the magistrate as well, and see that the law is brought to bear in this matter."

Faith listened in shocked relief. Somehow, miraculously, the storm seemed to have passed harmlessly. Her father had backed up her story. Now Faith felt that they shared more than a secret—they were joined in a conspiracy. She could not quite understand why this had happened, or how.

"Which trap *was* it?" the Reverend asked, apparently as an afterthought.

"It was among the trees, just past the Folly," said Uncle Miles. "Erasmus, I do hope you will move that trap—it is right on the edge of a steep slope that rolls down to the bottom of the dell. Somebody who tripped that trap might fall badly and break their neck. And . . . it is not quite legal, you know."

The Reverend nodded solemnly to himself, but Faith was not sure how much of Uncle Miles's advice had penetrated. Indeed, she wondered if he had heard anything after the word "Folly."

One of the gentlemen at the Lambents' gathering had gallantly offered to put his driver and carriage at Myrtle's disposal for the morning, so that she could "see something of the town." When the vehicle arrived and proved to be a dog-cart, Myrtle's face showed a flicker of surprise and disdain before her smile reasserted itself. Myrtle rode beside the driver, and Faith was left perched in the breezy, backward-facing seat at the rear, watching the road unscroll below her feet.

As the dog-cart carried Faith and her mother along the low coast road to town, Faith was still trying to understand her father's behavior and her own reprieve. The wind was fierce, dragging a patchwork sky of blues and grays, and forcing Faith to cling to her bonnet. Tiny spits and spots of spray tickled Faith's cheeks and gleamed on her eyelashes.

The little harbor town was a more pleasant sight by damp sunlight than it had been on the day of the Sunderlys' arrival. The houses were painted in whites, ochre yellows, and vivid blues. The sunlight gleamed on the inn signs and the hanging bell in the tiny, lopsided town square. Everything smelled of the sea.

Myrtle asked the driver to wait in the square and then daintily dismounted, followed by Faith. Today Myrtle's cape, dress, and bonnet were all blue, bringing out the color of her eyes.

One of the smarter buildings had pictures of elegant bonnets and gloves on the sign above the window. Inside, it was tiny but immaculate. Five or so bonnets in fashionable styles perched on wicker heads. Along a marble counter was proudly arranged an assortment of gloves, some long with buttoning at the wrist, some short and practical for daywear.

The shopkeeper was a rather small woman with a rather large nose and a restrained air of self-importance. She listened as Myrtle picked out a style of kid gloves, then disappeared into the back of the shop to find some for Faith to try on. When she returned, however, there was an extra stiffness in her manner.

"My apologies, madam, but it would seem we have nothing in your daughter's size at present."

"Nothing?" Myrtle's eyebrows rose. "Why, that is absurd! My daughter has not even tried on a glove yet!"

"Madam, I am sorry," the shopkeeper answered smoothly, "but I am unable to help you."

As Faith and Myrtle emerged on to the street, Faith thought she heard enthusiastic whispering coming from the back of the shop.

"How peculiar," commented Myrtle, with dogged matter-of-factness. "I wonder how—oh, look, Faith, it is two of the ladies we met last night!"

Sure enough, the black-haired Miss Hunter was walking crisply along the other side of the street, next to an older woman with dusty-brown hair. Myrtle directed a charming smile toward the two women and dropped a small curtsey.

Miss Hunter's eyes settled upon them, and then slid off, like a water drop from wax. She turned to offer her companion some murmured deadpan comment, and the two of them continued their walk, without offering Myrtle and Faith the slightest acknowledgment.

"They did not see us," said Myrtle, a slight wobble in her voice. Her eyes had a childlike, haunted expression.

Faith felt something settling in her stomach like a stone. It was no longer anxiety; it was a heavy dread of the inevitable. They had been snubbed. Snubs were reserved for people below your notice. Yesterday they had been an accepted part of "society" in Vane. Something must have changed, for now Miss Hunter knew she could snub them with impunity.

"Mother . . . can we go home?" Faith scanned the crowd, seeing a few surreptitious glances but no friendly faces.

"No!" Myrtle pulled her cape around her. "After braving that dreadful coast road, I intend to see the best of this meager little town."

The milliner's shop was suddenly shut as they approached. The woman at the patisserie was just French enough not to be able to understand Myrtle, but seemed to have no trouble with anybody else. The little apothecary was so very busy that somehow he never noticed them waiting to be served.

"*Please* can we go home?" begged Faith under her breath. She could feel dozens of covert, derisive gazes like dull hail.

"Faith, must you always whine so?" hissed Myrtle, who was now pink-faced.

In that moment, Faith almost hated her mother. It was not just Myrtle's stubborn refusal to retreat in the face of humiliation; it was the utter unfairness of her retort. Faith had spent her life choking back protests and complaints, and was bitterly aware of all the feelings she swallowed down every day. To be accused of *whining* was so wildly unjust that it left her feeling slightly weightless, as though she had stepped off the edge of the world.

As they walked, Myrtle's eyes brightened.

"We shall go to the church," she declared. "I told Mr. Clay that we might visit to choose a box pew."

The dog-cart took them up the hill, and they alighted outside the little church. It proved to be empty, so Myrtle led the way to the little parsonage, a small, hunched building that was apparently being slowly crushed by the weight of a marauding honeysuckle bush.

In the largest window a collection of little photographs had been arranged facing outward, some of them touched with color. It made the building look suspiciously like a shop. Faith wondered whether Clay was using his "hobby" to make a little extra money.

As they approached, Clay himself opened the door, and seemed flabbergasted to see them.

"I . . . Mrs. Sunderly—Miss Sunderly . . ." He looked over his shoulder for a moment as if in search of reinforcements. "Would you . . . ah . . . like to come in?" Faith could not help noticing that Clay looked extremely uncomfortable. "Ah . . . this is my son, Paul."

A boy of about fourteen stepped forward and politely took their capes and bonnets. Sure enough, it was the boy Faith had noticed with Clay at the dig. He was dark and slight of build like his father, with a rather rubbery-looking mouth that Faith thought could become angry or sullen in the wrong circumstances.

"Do sit down," said Clay. "Er . . . how can I help you, ladies?"

"Well, I called to ask about renting a box pew for the family," declared Myrtle, "but . . . to be candid, Mr. Clay, I am here as much in hope of seeing a friendly face as anything else." There was a little break in her voice, and a poignant light in her big, blue eyes. "We have been ill-used all over town this morning and I . . . perhaps it is very stupid of me, but I do not know why. Please be honest with me, Mr. Clay—have I done something perfectly dreadful to offend everyone?"

Faith dug her nails into her palms. Outside, Myrtle had been an obstinate martinet, and now, in the company of a gentleman, she had suddenly become a trembling little fawn.

"Oh, Mrs. Sunderly—please do not imagine such a thing!" Clay had melted. They always melted.

"Is it because of that dreadful business last night with the poor boy who was hurt on our grounds?" asked Myrtle.

"That . . . did not help, Mrs. Sunderly. However, my son Paul here tells me that the young fellow is doing better than expected."

"He may keep the foot," said Paul in an offhand tone. His wide-apart brown eyes had no smile in them. He was about the same age as the injured boy, and Faith wondered whether they were friends.

"However, the biggest problem . . ." Clay faltered to a halt, and gave Faith an uncertain glance.

Myrtle read his hesitation and turned promptly to Faith. "Faith—perhaps you would like to look at some of Mr. Clay's photographs?"

"Indeed!" Clay leapt at the suggestion. "Paul will show you around."

Faith let herself be led to the far end of the room by a woodenly polite Paul. On the shelves and mantelpiece clustered framed, stiffly posed pictures, most no bigger than a hand's palm.

"This one is a trick photograph." Paul pointed out an image where two men faced each other, one seated playing a cello, and the other standing dressed as a conductor, baton raised. At a second glance, Faith saw that the men were identical, like twins. "The same man was photographed twice. You cannot even see the seam where the images were joined."

Another caught Faith's eye. In the foreground sat a little boy about two years old, but looming behind him was a human shape shrouded in a dark cloth, so that it was almost invisible against the dark background.

"Sometimes the little children squirm or cry if we sit them down alone, and that blurs the picture." Paul pointed to the dark shape. "So we seat the mother behind them to comfort them, but hide her under a cloth."

Glancing toward the other side of the room, Faith saw Clay hand Myrtle a newspaper, and point out a particular headline. Myrtle read and read. The paper trembled in her hands.

The *Intelligencer*. In truth, Faith had already guessed what must have changed everything. The scandal surrounding her father had arrived in Vane, formally and in print.

"Perhaps you would like to look in here." Paul's voice interrupted her thoughts. He was gesturing toward a small wooden box with binocular-like eyepieces. Faith recognized it immediately as a stereoscope, a clever device that showed each eye a slightly different photograph, so that the view seemed to be in three dimensions. Reflexively, she raised it to her eyes and peered in.

As the picture swam into focus, she felt sheer shock, like a jolt in her chest. It was a murder scene, the culprit brandishing a blade over the prone red-daubed body of a woman in an alley. There was a long wound visible from her solar plexus down her belly.

Faith lowered the stereoscope slowly, feeling a little shaky.

Until now, the stereoscope images she had seen had been exotic landscapes, or whimsical images such as fairies pouring sweet dreams into the heads of sleeping children. This gruesome image was not one that ought to be shown to "ladies."

Paul met her eye a little too steadily and coldly. He *was* angry, Faith was sure of that now, angry with her whole family on his injured friend's behalf. So he had decided to vent his feelings by scaring the easiest mark—the dull, prim, shy Sunderly daughter. It was a reckless, stupid piece of malice, and he knew he would get into trouble. His eyes *dared* her to get him into trouble.

Suddenly Faith was angry too—wildly angry with Vane, with the stupidity of the rabbit trap, with her mother, with snubs and snickers and whispers and secrets and lies. What made her most angry was knowing that if she gasped, or stormed off, or made a fuss to get Paul into trouble, then in some way he would have won. She would have proven that he was right—that she really was just the dull, prim, shy Sunderly daughter, and nothing more.

And so she did none of these things. Instead she smiled.

"I once helped my father with the taxidermy of an iguana," she said quietly. "We had to make a cut just like that before we pulled out the innards." The passing seconds became dangerous and spacious. The rules tinkled silently as they broke.

It was hard to tell whether Paul was taken aback by her response. Certainly he did not speak for a few moments.

"I am accustomed to handling something a mite bigger than a lizard," he said at last. He moved to another shelf, and Faith followed.

The first card on the shelf caught her attention. It displayed two photos, both showing the same pretty young girl, her hair carefully combed. One showed her with her eyes closed, under a label "Fast Asleep." The other was marked "Wide Awake," and showed her gazing out of the photograph.

"My father paints in the eyes," said Paul, "if the family wants them to look natural." It took Faith a second or two to process his words and realize what she was looking at.

The little girl in the picture was dead and had been photographed as a memento. She had been carefully positioned by her loving relatives to look as if she were just resting.

The other pictures on that shelf were of the same breed, Faith realized, now that she knew what to look for. Many of them were family groupings, where one member lolled a little more than the rest, or had to be propped up with cushions, chair backs, or supporting arms.

No such photographs had been taken of Faith's little departed brothers. They were remembered through other mementos, their baby bottles carefully preserved, or their hair sewn into samplers. However, she had seen a memorial picture of this type once, of a woman apparently sleeping peacefully in a chair, a book on her knee.

"I help position them," said Paul. "You have to pick the right time—when they are not too stiff." Again his expression was blandly courteous. *Your turn*, said his eyes.

"How did you position that one?" Faith pointed to a little picture of a small boy sitting alone and unsupported in a playroom, a toy soldier in one hand.

"That picture is different." Paul hesitated. "My father photographed that little boy . . . then cut out the head, really careful, and glued it on to an old photograph of me. He has always taken lots of pictures of me, so that he can turn them into portraits of dead customers when he needs them."

"Do you have your own copies of the original photographs?" asked Faith.

"Of course not." Paul gave a short shrug. "Why waste albumen paper if it isn't for a customer?"

"How does it feel," whispered Faith, "to come back to your memories and find yourself missing and a dead person in your place? I would feel as if I were *disappearing*. I would wonder if my father wanted to remember me at all. Do you ever have nightmares where you wake up and find that there is nothing of you left, just a dead person sitting up and wearing somebody else's face?"

She saw Paul flinch. She had touched a nerve, and that knowledge made her fiercely happy.

Chapter 8

A STAINED CHARACTER

IN SILENCE, MYRTLE AND FAITH RODE BACK TO
Bull Cove. As they alighted from the dog-cart, both noticed a
solitary figure standing by the corner of the house, sheltered
from the wind. It was Uncle Miles, his brow creased and his
pipe protectively cupped in one hand. He gestured to gain their
attention, then beckoned with furtive eagerness.

"Miles!" exclaimed Myrtle, as she approached him. "I thought
that you would be at the excavation by now! Did my husband
leave without you?"

"Oh no, we have been to the site already, more's the pity."
Uncle Miles spoke in hushed tones. "I thought I should try to
catch you before you trotted into the house. There has been the
deuce of a row, and now we are all treading on eggshells." He
raised his eyebrows in a meaningful way. "Certain people came
back from the dig in a foul temper, and heaven help the rest of
us if we *think* too loudly."

Faith felt her neck and shoulders tense. When her father was
in his darker moods, his path needed to be smoothed with the
greatest care. He was not a violent man, but if he made a decision in a cold rage, he would keep to it ever after.

Myrtle stepped forward and took her brother's arm.

"Let us take a little turn in the grounds, Miles," she murmured.

Faith followed her uncle and mother on to the lawns, remaining just close enough to overhear and just far enough that they might assume that she could not. The trio promenaded away from the house.

"Myrtle, old girl," Uncle Miles said at last. "I think most people would say that I am a patient man. But today has truly tried my patience. Our dear Reverend has tried me to the fraying point."

"What happened at the excavation? Why are you both back so early?" Myrtle's tone was a little flat, as if she had already guessed at the answer.

"No carriage came for us this morning. In the end we had to pay some fellow to give us a ride in his cart. And when we arrived, nobody would allow us on the site! After all their letters declaring that they *must* have the great Reverend Erasmus Sunderly, they turned us away from their precious excavation! Worse, our path was blocked by a line of hired hands and the foreman, Crock. Lambent did not even come down to talk to us."

"Could it have been a misunderstanding?" asked Myrtle, without much air of hope.

"Well, that is what I tried to suggest, but the Reverend was having none of it. At the excavation site he was given a letter, and after he read it there was no reasoning with him. He insisted on marching up to the Paints, knocking a dent into their door, and then leaving a message so curt it would not surprise me if Lambent set a lawyer on him for defamation. Myrtle, you know that I always do my best, but every time I find some oil for troubled waters, your husband snatches it from me and uses it to burn a bridge."

Following silently behind, Faith burned with rage at the way her father had been treated. One day a guest of honor, lionized and courted. The next day, barred from the grounds like a disreputable tinker.

"There are copies of the *Intelligencer* on the island," Myrtle murmured.

"That explains it." Uncle Miles sighed. "Still, to pass judgment on a fellow without hearing his side of the story . . ." He shook his head. "You had better tell Erasmus about the *Intelligencer*—at the moment he has it in his head that the story got out through the servants snooping and gossiping. How many people have heard about it?"

"Everyone." Myrtle's voice trembled slightly. "This morning we were snubbed all over town."

"It would have been a hundred times worse in Kent," Uncle Miles insisted, a little defensively. "Your husband does not see it that way, of course. I have done my best to help your family escape your woes, Myrtle, but to hear Erasmus talk, you would think that I had lured you to this island with malicious intent."

"He does not mean it," Myrtle said quickly.

"Erasmus never says anything he does not mean," Uncle Miles retorted. He sounded genuinely annoyed. Unlike his sister, he was not prone to flashes and fizzes of ill humor. Most of the time his easygoing nature acted as a sort of padding and offense simply bounced off. When a barb did penetrate, however, it remained there forever.

"We need to leave Vane, Miles." Myrtle adjusted her white scarf to protect her throat. "Go farther afield—the Continent, if necessary. I need you to help me persuade him."

"Sorry, Myrtle, but right now I feel a need for some sort of apology from that husband of yours," her brother answered stiffly, "and I would bet ten guineas that he has no intention of giving it. Until he does . . ." He sighed and lifted his shoulders in a shrug, and then lowered them again, letting responsibility slide off.

Even without Uncle Miles's warning, Faith would have known that a storm was breaking as soon as she entered the house. Quiet people often have a weather sense that loud people lack. They feel the wind-changes of conversations, and shiver in the chill of unspoken resentments.

It was Mrs. Vellet, not Jeanne, who came to claim their bonnets and capes.

"Mrs. Sunderly, I wonder if I might have the privilege of a word?" The housekeeper's voice was carefully hushed but huskily emphatic. "Forgive me, ma'am, but this is an important matter."

"Oh." Myrtle let out a breath and smoothed her hair. "Very well, but first have tea brought to us in the parlor. There is only so much importance I can tolerate right now without refreshment."

Although it evidently took an effort of will, Mrs. Vellet held her tongue until Faith and Myrtle were installed in the parlor with a tea set between them. Then, at last, she received a nod from Myrtle.

"Madam, Jeanne Bissette is a good girl—a decent, hard worker. She may be a little pert and silly at times like all girls her age, but she has been serving in this household since she was thirteen, and there has *never* been a word spoken about her honesty. Madam, she freely admits that the newspaper was in her possession, but surely that is not a *crime*—"

"Mrs. Vellet!" interrupted Myrtle, eyes widening. "What in the world are you talking about? Has Jeanne been complaining of her treatment here?"

Mrs. Vellet took a breath, folded her hands, and composed herself with visible effort.

"Madam . . . your husband believes that somebody has been searching through his papers. One of his letters is a little smudged . . ." She gave a small impatient shake of the head. "To me it looks as though a drop of water has fallen on it, but the Reverend is very certain that it has been smeared by a wet finger."

A wave of heat rushed through Faith. She had let herself hope that the smudge would go undetected. But, no, her father had noticed it. She was sure that she must be glowing a guilty scarlet.

"He insisted that all the servants should be made to show their hands. Jeanne was found scrubbing hers under the pump behind the house, so she fell under suspicion."

The first rush of panic ebbed. Faith's heart slowed enough for her to think clearly and understand the housekeeper's words. She herself was not suspected. Her father had found the evidence of her crime, but had not traced it to her.

"And . . . was there ink on her hands?" asked Myrtle.

"Yes, miss—but not pen ink. Printer's ink from a newspaper." Mrs. Vellet dropped her gaze and stirred a little uncomfortably. "When she was asked about it, she turned out her pocket and handed over the newspaper straight away. She says she found it in town—she knows she should have left it where it lay, but she was curious and hoped to read it after she had finished her work."

There was a short expressive silence, in which Mrs. Vellet did not mention why Jeanne had been curious, and Myrtle did not ask. Faith had no difficulty reading between the lines, or guessing which newspaper it had been.

"Who has the paper now?" asked Myrtle.

"Your husband confiscated it," answered the housekeeper.

"I will bear your character references in mind," declared Myrtle a little wearily, "but I think I must speak to Jeanne myself, so that I can decide what is to be done. Send her to me, as soon as she can be spared from her work."

"Her work? Madam, your husband has dismissed her! She is packing her belongings, and has been told that she must leave this house first thing in the morning."

Only Faith, who knew her mother very well, saw Myrtle stiffen slightly and try not to react. Running the household and managing the staff were Myrtle's domain. The Reverend expected his wife to carry out his wishes, but never before had he bypassed her completely.

Faith's hands were shaking. The blame that should have landed on her head had missed her, and struck somebody else to the ground. She set her cup on its saucer lopsidedly and it tipped, spilling hot tea over her wrist and down her dress.

"Oh . . . *Faith*." Myrtle sounded utterly exasperated. "You stupid, clumsy girl. Go and change your clothes, and then . . . oh, read your catechism."

Faith came downstairs for dinner in her freshly laundered blue dress. Its cleanness made her feel worse, like a poison-pen letter in a crisp new envelope.

The thought of telling her father the truth filled her with utter panic. If her father shut her out, the sun would go dark and her dreams would fall to dust. She needed that tiny hope of winning his regard, respect, and love. She could not bear the thought of losing it forever.

And Jeanne can always find another place, murmured a desperate voice in her head. *I cannot find another father.*

It soon became clear that dinner would be a subdued affair. Uncle Miles had consented to come back indoors, but had asked that his food be brought to his room on a tray.

Faith's father was late to dinner, stalking in steel-eyed and taciturn. He was not, however, nearly as late as the dinner. The family had been sitting for half an hour before the first dish arrived.

It was carried in by a frightened-looking young girl Faith had never seen before. The new girl seemed half dazzled by her task. She spilled soup onto the tablecloth every time she tried to use the ladle. When her skirts brushed Myrtle's spoon off the table so that it hit the floor with a clang, she started so badly that she knocked over the cream jug. The Reverend was forced to pull back his chair to escape the advancing tide.

"This is insupportable!" His voice was not loud, but icy enough to slice through all other sounds. "Is this child a local imbecile, or has someone dragged a donkey on to its hind legs and wrapped an apron around it?"

The girl's eyes were brimming as she attempted to mop up the worst of the cream with her apron.

"Enough—you are making it worse." Myrtle's voice was a little impatient, but less sharp. "Go and change your apron, and have Mrs. Vellet fetch a fresh tablecloth." The girl seized the chance to flee the room.

"She is quite hopeless," Myrtle declared, with a fragile lightness of tone, "but she was all that could be found at short notice. I wonder . . ." She paused, and Faith saw her neat lace collar bob slightly as if she had swallowed. "I wonder if perhaps it might be worth keeping Jeanne on a *little* longer, just to spare ourselves such trials."

"She leaves in the morning," the Reverend stated flatly.

"Nonetheless I wish . . . I do wish, my dear, that you had given me the chance to talk to the girl, and perhaps handle this my own way—"

Faith's father abruptly slammed both knife and fork down beside his plate, and fixed his wife with a glare. "I might have done so, had I seen any evidence of your competence to deal with the matter! I had thought that you were equal to the task of managing this household, but it seems I gave you *far* too much credit.

"A man's home should be his refuge, the one place where he can be master without being embattled. Is that too much to ask? Instead, I am served chill offal at the dinner table by ill-washed servants who slouch, spill, slam doors, and show not the slightest respect. The maids make free with my private papers, and half the household turns a blind eye to poachers and vagrants stamping across the grounds. I am plagued and thwarted in the very place where my wishes should be law."

Myrtle's blue eyes widened, then she dropped her gaze. Her face slowly flushed, and the knife in her hand trembled a little.

"I . . . I am very sorry, dear," she murmured, almost inaudibly.

"I know to my cost that there are limits to the female understanding," the Reverend continued bitterly. "Nonetheless, I hear that other wives manage to keep their servants in some sort of order, and prevent their household from descending into a disgusting shambles." He stood abruptly, casting his napkin down on the table, and walked out of the room.

Faith felt a terrible tearing sensation inside her, as she always did when her father spoke to her mother that way. She wanted to be on her father's side, and it hurt when her sympathy was dragged to her mother's. She could almost sense the waiting ears outside the door, reveling in Myrtle's humiliation. Her mother doubtless knew they were there too.

Myrtle retired to her room, complaining of a headache. The carnage on the dining room table was cleared, and the dishes borne away to the scullery.

Leaving the dining room, Faith heard faint sounds of sobbing. It seemed to be coming from the direction of the servants' stairs, next to the kitchen. Peering around a corner, she glimpsed Jeanne huddled at the foot of the stairs, crying uncontrollably.

The housemaid's expression was shocked, drawn and bewildered. Her eyes were swollen, and even her mouth was puffy from crying.

Faith drew back around the corner. It was no good though. In her mind's eye, Jeanne Bissette was no longer pretty, confident, and contemptuous. Now she could only picture the older girl looking like a slapped child. Perhaps Jeanne did not expect to get another post. Perhaps Jeanne had nowhere else to go.

Chapter 9

CONFESSION

I CANNOT. IT IS NOT POSSIBLE.

And yet here Faith was, outside the library, one hand poised ready to knock.

She felt sick, her mind still squirming and looking for reasons to flee. Faith tried to imagine God watching her, willing her to take the noble course. But in her head, God had her father's face. Even now a foolish part of her brain felt that if her father did not know what she had done, God would not know either, and then it would not really be a sin.

Faith knocked. And now it was too late. She could not turn back.

The door was snatched open to reveal her father. When he saw Faith, his look of irritation faded a little. Evidently he had been expecting somebody less welcome.

"Faith. Is something wrong?"

"Father—I need to talk to you." Faith said it quickly so that she could not lose courage again.

Her father spent a second in silent scrutiny and then gave a nod of assent.

"Very well," he said, and held open the door. Faith entered, and her father closed it behind her. "Sit down, Faith."

She did so, unsure whether her father's gentle tone should make her feel reassured or nervous.

"I think I know what you wish to talk about." Her father settled himself behind his desk. A lot of his angry energy seemed to have ebbed out of him. Now he just seemed somber and tired. "You are still worried about my health, are you not? And you fear that I am angry with you for coming into my study uninvited." The glance he gave her was not unkind.

Faith swallowed and said nothing. These *were* things that worried her, but they were not at the front of her mind.

"First of all, you need not worry about my health," her father went on. "As I said before, you were mistaken. I was not ill yesterday evening, simply weary and too caught up in my work to give you much attention. As for your invasion of my study, that evening and the following morning . . ." He clasped his hands and gazed earnestly at Faith. "It was ill-done, and I shall be extremely disappointed if you ever do so again. However, I am willing to believe on this occasion that you meant no harm or disrespect. I will overlook the incident, Faith. We shall say no more about it."

He gave a small nod and evidently expected Faith to leave the room. She remained where she was, feeling foolish.

"You have something further to say?" He had already picked up one of his pens and opened his notebook, a clear cue for her to leave.

"Father . . ." Faith's vision was jumping slightly with each beat of her heart. "I . . . I . . . I was the one who smeared your letter."

The pen was set down. The book was closed.

"What did you say?" The kindness in his gaze had wilted away.

"It was not Jeanne. I . . . I did it." Faith could not even tell whether her voice was audible.

Her father stared at her for several long seconds.

"That letter has been in my strongbox since we left Kent." Faith's father rose from his seat. "Are you saying that you deliberately *opened my strongbox?*"

"I am so sorry—" began Faith again.

"You had the ungodly temerity to pry through my papers? Did you look at the letter? What other papers did you read?"

"Just the letter!" protested Faith. "I . . . looked at some others, but only a glance. I am sorry, I should not have done it, but I did not know what else to do!" Her frustration gave force to her voice. "I knew there was some dreadful reason for us leaving Kent, and nobody would tell me what it was! I just wanted to know!"

"What? Are you attempting to *justify* your behavior?" Her father was now shaking with anger. "No! Not another word. Be silent, and listen.

"It seems I must judge you anew. I had thought you a dutiful daughter, with an honest heart and a keen sense of what she owes to her elders and betters. I had not thought you capable of this skulking, deceitful behavior. Evidently your character has been allowed to drift dangerously astray. Honesty is commendable in a man, but in a woman or girl it is essential if she is to have any worth at all.

"Listen, Faith. A girl cannot be brave, or clever, or skilled as a boy can. If she is not good, she is nothing. Do you understand?"

Faith felt as if she had been physically struck. Deep in her heart there had been a tender, tiny hope of understanding and forgiveness. Even now as she looked at its crushed remains, she knew she had to plead for absolution. And yet somehow she did not.

"But I *am* clever." She did not say it loudly, but she said it. She heard her mouth shape the words.

"What did you say?"

Seven years of swallowed thoughts could be silent no longer.

"I *am* clever! I have *always* been clever! You know that it is so! I taught myself *Greek*! Everybody talks about Howard, and how brilliant any son of yours will be—but at his age I had read *The Pilgrim's Progress* and *A Child's History of England*, and I was learning the Latin names of the plants in the garden! Howard can barely sit still long enough to be read *Little Goody Two-Shoes*!"

"How dare you!" interrupted her father, advancing to stand over her. "How dare you raise your voice to me! How dare you speak of yourself in this vaunting, arrogant way! Where did you learn this repellent vanity? Is this my reward for encouraging you and allowing you access to my library and collections?

"Have you lost your wits, or merely your sense of gratitude? Do you believe that you are *owed* the clothes you wear, the roof over your head, or the food laid before you? No. You are not. Every child begins their life in debt to the parents who house, clothe, and feed them. A son may some day pay back that debt by cutting a figure in the world and raising the family's fortunes. As a daughter, you *never* will. You will *never* serve with honor in the army, or distinguish yourself in the sciences, or make a name for yourself in the Church or Parliament, or make a decent living in the professions.

"You will *never* be anything but a burden, and a drain on my purse. Even when you marry, your dowry will gouge a hole in the family coffers. You speak so scornfully of Howard—but if you do *not* marry, some day you will need to court his charity, or find yourself without bed and board."

Faith could not form words. She felt breathless and winded. Hot tears tumbled down her cheeks. In her mind she saw the sunlit beach where she had found her fossil, her first fossil. A sun disappeared behind a black wall of cloud, and a father was gone, and a little girl was stumbling around alone, a broken piece of rock in her hand.

"All that a daughter can do," the Reverend said more quietly, "in recompense for the debt she cannot pay, is to hold steadfastly to the path of duty, gratitude, and humility. That is the very *least* a father can expect, is it not?"

Smothering her sobs with one hand, Faith nodded. She hated herself for nodding. But the light on the beach was dying.

Her self-respect had suffered a head-on collision with love, a clash that generally only ends one way. Love does not fight fair. In that moment her pride, the gut knowledge that she was right, even her sense of who she was, meant nothing, faced as she was with the prospect of being unloved.

Faith's father moved back to his desk and turned his back to her, restlessly pushing his papers around. She took advantage of the respite, shakily pulling out her handkerchief and wiping her face. Her insides seemed to have been scraped out. All those feelings and thoughts she had bottled up for years had burst free . . . and been crushed with apocalyptic thoroughness. She no longer knew what she felt about anything.

She was vaguely aware that her father had paused in his stirring of his papers. He picked up one sheet and studied it.

Several seconds passed, and then he pulled out the chair from behind his desk and drew it over toward Faith. He sat down in it, so that there was barely a foot between them. He was still blurry with her tears.

"Faith." His voice had lost some of its cold energy. "You truly are sorry to have acted and spoken the way you did, are you not?"

Faith nodded again.

"And this foolishness of yours—it really was because you were worried about me, and wanted to help me?"

"Yes!" managed Faith.

"And you still wish to be of help to your father?"

"Of course!" There was something in Faith's innards again now. A little solidity. A little hope.

"Good." The Reverend passed Faith the paper he held. It was a map of Vane, she realized. "Howard said that the pair of you saw sea caves from the beach. I need you to point them out on this map."

Baffled, Faith peered at the crinkled ink outline and then pointed out the places where she thought she remembered seeing the dark mouths of the caves.

"He mentioned a little boat on the beach as well. Think hard—did it seem seaworthy?"

"Yes, I think so." Faith racked her memory. "It looked newly painted—no holes."

The Reverend frowned and then seemed to come to a decision.

"Faith—fetch your cape, but be sure that nobody sees you. I need you to assist me with something, and nobody—*nobody*—must know of it."

Chapter 10

THE SEA CAVE

WHEN FAITH SLIPPED OUT THROUGH THE BACK door in her cape, her father was already waiting outside, wearing his stout coat, thick scarf, and deerstalker.

"Take this," he whispered, passing her a lantern shrouded in thick fabric. "Keep the cloth open a sliver, but make sure the light does not shine toward the house." The lantern was heavy and smelled of whale oil. He turned and led the way toward the Folly.

The night was cold and starless, with just a few streaks of purplish pallor in the west. A single bat skimmed past and vanished, rapid as a heart-flutter.

Faith advanced across the grounds gingerly, fearful of stepping on a man-trap in the long grass, her ankles tingling apprehensively. Her father gave her an impatient glance over his shoulder and beckoned to her to hasten.

"I must be back at the house by midnight," he whispered curtly as she drew level with him. "Pray do not dally."

In the darkness the Folly seemed larger, and grimly prison-like. Her father opened the door and disappeared into the darkness.

When he reemerged, his arms were filled with a familiar

cloth-shrouded pot, and he was clearly struggling with the weight. With a muffled clink of terra-cotta on wood, he lowered it carefully into the wheelbarrow that stood by the entrance. Once again Faith's nose filled with a strange, cold scent.

The Reverend took up the handles of the barrow. "Light the way ahead for me, so that I can avoid the stones," he whispered, pointing down the path that led seaward.

As the ground descended toward the beach, the path became rugged and tussocky, and the way more difficult. Whenever the wheel jolted, a little rustle of dropped leaves sounded from beneath the cloth, and each time her father drew in breath through his teeth. Whatever plant lay concealed beneath the cloth, it did not seem to be in good health.

On the beach the winds were colder and fiercer. The sea was black but for the seething shore and brief scars of white foam. The cliffs seemed higher than they had by daylight, like giant bites taken out of the sky.

There was a sudden surge of wind, and some unseen crack or cliff hollow gave off a throbbing whine not unlike a voice. Faith's father tensed, turning his head toward the source of the sound. He lowered the barrow, one hand sliding into his pocket as he listened. Eventually he relaxed.

As they continued on their way, Faith cast an occasional glance at his pocket, which bulged slightly and seemed to swing more heavily than usual. It was the one in which he always carried his little pocket pistol when he was out collecting fauna samples. The gun was single shot with a stubby little barrel, but had been powerful enough to take down a Scottish wildcat at twenty feet.

Carrying a cloaked lantern meant secrecy. Bringing a pistol

meant danger. Who did her father fear? Faith looked around her, and her imagination peopled the cliff-top with peering heads and flitting figures each time the treeline shivered. Pebbles bouncing in the surf became the clatter of footfalls.

With difficulty, her father manhandled the barrow across the beach to the little boathouse. There he stooped by the rowboat, examining it by the rays from the lantern, and knocking on the wood. After a while he nodded to himself.

Taking up the boat's mooring rope, he began dragging it across the shingle toward the waterline. It moved grudgingly and slowly.

"Get behind the boat, and push," he ordered, raising his voice to compete with the wind.

Faith's heart plummeted, her worst suspicions confirmed. Her father really *did* mean to take the boat out in the middle of the night.

With deep misgivings, Faith clambered into the boathouse. She stripped off her gloves and tucked them into her pocket, then braced her hands against the clammy woodwork and pushed the boat as hard as she could. She struggled forward, hearing the deep crunch of the prow splitting the shingle. By the time her father called to her to halt, her arms were aching and cold water was rushing around her boots, drenching her feet. Faith felt the boat shift and drift under her grasp as the water lifted it.

With visible effort, her father lifted the precious plant pot. Faith held the boat as steady as she could while the pot was settled near the stern.

"Father," ventured Faith, "how will we see the rocks?" Avoiding rabbit traps in long grass was one thing, but negotiating submerged rocks on a dark night was quite another. She remembered her mother's warnings about currents, and the gossip about shipwrecks along the coasts.

"You will sit in the prow with the lantern. Keep watch while I row, and warn me if you see rocks."

Faith stared out across the black shifting mass of the ocean. Every time a foam crest flared, she imagined it breaking on hidden rocks. Nonetheless, she hitched her skirts as best she could and clambered into the boat, while her father held the little vessel steady. Her father needed her, and whatever dangers were ahead they would be facing them together.

Her weight settled the boat on the shingle again, but her father gave it a last great heave that set it afloat, and then waded out and climbed in behind her.

"Take this." He passed Faith the map of Vane. "You must guide me to the caves." He settled himself with his back to Faith and the prow, and took up the oars.

She twisted in her seat so that she was sitting sideways, able to look ahead past the prow, or back toward her father and the beach. The map fluttered in her hands, threatening to break free. She flattened it against her lap, pinning it in place with the lantern's weight, as her father began to row.

At first, each breaker made a solicitous attempt to cast them back on to the beach. Faith's father worked the oars with an angry energy while the surf hissed around them. When the boat struggled into deeper water, the character of the waves changed. Now they tipped and jostled the little vessel, like great black wolves in a playful mood.

The distant headlands were jet silhouettes. There was no hope of making out the deeper dark of the caves. Faith tried to remember how it had all looked in daylight, the cliffs and inlets, the staggered headlands, the powdery clouds of far-off seabirds.

The waves grew bigger and less playful, rolling under the boat with menacing unconcern. Whenever the boat tipped, every fiber in Faith's body was braced for the capsize, the freezing shock of the water. She had never been taught how to swim, but her common sense told her that that scarcely mattered. If she fell overboard, her layers of skirts might keep her afloat for a few seconds, but then they would soak up the seawater and become a terrible deadweight, tangling her legs and dragging her down to the seabed.

As the boat bucked and the oar blades splashed onward, Faith had an uneasy feeling that to her left the lightless cliff range was looming taller than it should, and that the beach behind was sliding to the right. Whenever her father let his oars hang slack for a moment, the blades drew little white wakes in the water's surface.

"There is a current!" Faith stared up at the various black and featureless cliff-lines, trying to work out where she was. "It is pulling us to the left—I mean, to port!"

Toward the cliffs, she tried not to say. *Toward the rocks.*

Her father said nothing but began hauling on the oars with greater vigor. With each heave the boat's nose twitched toward starboard, but then started to drift back to port.

Faith was so hypnotized by it that she almost missed a flare of foam thirty feet ahead. It flung itself up in an outward spray, like a convolvulus bloom. Only once the scattered froth fell did she see it settle upon a jutting form, outlining it for a second in white . . .

"Rock!" she shouted, holding up the lantern to see better. "A rock straight ahead!"

"How far away?"

Faith opened her mouth to answer, but then her lantern's light caught a much closer trail of white. In the slick valley between two waves, a black jagged shape tore the surface for a telling second.

"Ten feet!" Faith steadied herself on the edge of the boat and then drew in her breath as yet another rocky point bared itself like a tooth-tip, closer still. The waves around her crested and swirled. "They are all around us!"

There was a grating sound from beneath the boat, like a great, blunt claw being drawn along the boards. Reading the eddies of the water, Faith leaned over the side, plunging her hand into the icy water and grazing herself on the rough barnacles of a submerged rock. She pushed off it as hard as she could, nearly losing her balance and then fell back into the boat with a sopping sleeve and stinging fingers. The lantern in her other hand swung and clattered, the flame shrinking to a blue sprite, before growing tall and yellow once again.

Behind her, Faith could hear splashing, a cacophony of wood and metal, and her father's gasps for breath as he wrestled the oars. There were no more grating sounds from below, however, nor could she make out the trickle or gush of a leak.

Salt-matted strands of Faith's hair whipped her face and stung her eyes. All the while, the cliff stealthily loomed larger and larger, cutting out ever more of the sky. At its base waves raged, champed, tore each other, and bled white.

Faith became aware that she could hear a loud and rhythmic rush and hiss, rush and hiss. A little farther oceanward, she saw a wave strike the cliff. Nearly all of it detonated in spray, but part of it seemed to disappear into the rock. She could hear it roaring hollowly, and after a few moments the water surged back out, turbulent and gleaming. It took Faith a moment to understand what she was seeing.

"Father, I can see a cave!"

As the boat drew nearer, the roar grew louder and more ominous. Soon Faith could make out the cave's mouth, a deeper blackness gaping like a cat's yawn.

The waves had them now, the oars helpless against the churning of the white water. The spray stung Faith's eyes. At last a breaker seized them and bore them helplessly forward, into the mouth of the cave itself. The sky went out like a lamp, leaving only the radiance of the lantern. The roar of water and rock was deafening, echoing.

The belly of the boat ground against a glistening slope of shingle, complained, and beached. The roar went out with a fierce sibilance of water and stuttering of pebbles. Ahead, Faith could see that the cave floor sloped upward. Beyond toothed openings, other chambers quivered in the dull, discolored lantern-light.

Behind Faith, the Reverend got to his feet, letting go of the oars.

"Stay where you are!" he said sharply, as Faith adjusted her position. "Your weight will keep the boat grounded." He took the lantern from her, clambered out of the boat and waded through the ankle-deep retreating water to the prow. He seized the mooring rope and climbed up on to a stone shelf, where he made it fast to a top-heavy pillar of rock.

The next wave came in at a terrifying speed, and the boat rose, then descended to ground itself once more. The Reverend returned, the lantern's handle looped over one arm, and carefully lifted the great pot out of the boat.

"Wait here." Her father disappeared into the throat of the

caves, carrying the pot as tenderly as if it were a wounded child. The light receded with him, leaving Faith in darkness.

The cave smelled of the sea, but it was not a cheerful seaside smell. It reeked, as if the sea were something old and evil. This sea licked the flesh off shipwrecks, leaving the bare wooden bones in the lightless deep. Its mermaids were green-skinned and squid-eyed with long, hooked fingers and breath that smelled of old fish.

At last Faith's father returned, carrying nothing but the lantern. He loosed the rope and jumped back into the boat without a word. When the next wave came to lift them, he used the oars to push away from the rising floor with all his might, so that they were still floating free when the wave retreated. It hurried them back out of the cave, the sky returned to them, lividly bright after the cave's darkness.

The waves tried to sweep them back toward the cliffs, but the Reverend rowed and rowed tirelessly, and at last Faith saw the cliff start to recede, the rocks become fewer and the waves less turbulent.

The haul back to the shore was a long one. Faith could no longer see the beach they had set off from, but thankfully she remembered a jutting poplar at the top of the cliff. Now she kept her eye upon that solitary spike on the skyline and aimed for it, calling out instructions to her father when they veered off course. The foam-fringed shore came into view, and at last the keel ground into the shore. Father and daughter climbed out and manhandled the boat back up the beach. Faith found that her legs were weak, her hands too numb to grip properly. The two of them leaned against the boat for a short while to recover, breathing plumes of mist into the cold air.

"Good girl, Faith," the Reverend said at last. "Good girl." And suddenly Faith was no longer cold.

They walked back toward the house, Faith pushing the wheelbarrow. She felt unsteady, but somehow, impossibly, there was dry ground beneath her boots. They had faced danger together, and had survived. She had been tested, and had passed.

They left the wheelbarrow by the greenhouse. As they drew closer to the house, however, her father stopped and studied his pocket watch once more by the lantern-light.

"It is nearly midnight," he murmured. "I am out of time. Faith—go in, and go to bed."

"You are not coming in?" Faith's concerns leapt to attention once again, like guard dogs. "Is something wrong? Shall I come with you?"

"No!" he replied abruptly. "No, that will not be necessary." There was a long pause. "Faith," he began in a quieter tone, "nobody must ever know that I left the house this night. Listen to me. If you are *ever* asked, you must tell them that we stayed up talking in my study until well after one in the morning. Do you understand?"

Faith nodded, though the nod was a half-lie. She did not really understand.

"I am not going far, and will be back very soon." Her father hesitated. "Faith, are your boots wet?"

"Yes," confessed Faith, touched by his concern. The walk from the beach had been squelchy and unpleasant.

"See to it that they are dry by morning, or the servants will notice and gossip about it. Nobody must suspect what we have done, nor where we have been. You must make sure there is no clue, no evidence."

He took a step away from the door, and hesitated. He glanced over his shoulder at Faith, but the lantern was shrouded again and his expression lost in darkness.

"Show me how clever you can be, Faith."

Clever. That one small word warmed Faith as she crept up the outside steps to her private roof garden and eased open the door to her room. She slipped inside and hastily removed her cape, dress, and petticoats.

Show me how clever you can be. Surely that meant that she was *permitted* to be clever—that he was acknowledging that she *could* be clever?

She would prove herself. She would not be caught out, or betray his secret.

Faith removed the cover from the hearth, teased life out of the dormant embers with kindling and paper, then used a taper to light the candle on the mantelpiece. By its light, she examined the damage to her clothes. Her cape was covered in burrs and stained with bilge grime. The hems of her dress and petticoats were drenched with seawater and her stockings were sopping wet. Even the inch-high heels on her boots had not saved them from a soaking, and there was every danger that the sodden leather would shrink and crack as it dried out.

However, this was not the first time Faith had hidden evidence of a secret outing. She slipped on her night clothes and then crept out of her room and downstairs, her damaged clothing bundled in her arms.

As she hoped, the scullery was dark and empty. She stealthily filled a sink with water and then stirred in soap shavings, starch for stiffness, and a handful of salt to stop the dye running. Then, very carefully, she rinsed her stockings and then the wet hems of her petticoats and her dress. Her nerves were as brittle as glass and she jumped at each rattle of the shutters.

When her clothes no longer smelled of the sea, she wrung them out, stole a jugful of bran from the pantry, and crept upstairs again. Her newly washed clothing she draped over the fireguard to dry. Using her buttonhook, she unfastened the tiny, fiddly buttons on her boots. Then she filled them with the bran, which she knew would soak up the moisture from them, buttoned them up tight so that they would keep their shape, and left them by the fire.

The room was still cold, so Faith slipped into bed. She wished she could call for a warming pan, and hoped she would not catch a chill. With a blanket wrapped around her, she sat up brushing the grime from her cape and plucking off burrs. The smell of the fire-cooked bran was at least a dry and comforting one. Her thoughts were warmer and more comforting still.

Faith's father had called on her in his time of need. She felt as if a door long shut had opened between them, if only a crack.

He cannot shut me out again, whispered part of her mind. *Not this time. I know too much.*

Even as this thought passed through her mind, though, the brush faltered in her hand. Ever since they had set off on their nocturnal adventure, she had felt a nagging, miserable sensation in her gut. It was a thought she had been trying not to think, an idea she had been edging around as if it were a rabbit trap in the grass.

Her father, her beloved, revered father, had been shocked to hear about her secretive, deceitful behavior. And yet he had ordered her to creep through the night with him by the light of a covered lantern, and to tell nobody about it. He had torn her apart for concealing the evidence of her secret deeds . . . and now she was doing the same thing again, on his own instructions.

Father. The grim patron saint of honesty. The harsh light of judgment. He had asked her to lie to save his secrets.

And now he had gone out into the darkness once more with a pistol in his pocket, and had asked her to give him an alibi.

Chapter 11

THE HORSESHOE

A BANG ON THE DOOR SHOCKED FAITH FROM SLEEP.

She lay there for a few seconds amid the jagged shards of her dream. She had been on trial, standing in a dock that was filling with seawater. The court had been angry that she would not give the name of her accomplice. The judge had worn her father's face.

"Fa-a-aith!" It was unmistakably the voice of Howard, petulant and disgruntled. "I cannot do my collar!"

If Howard was awake, then it was nearly breakfast time. Faith had overslept.

She leapt out of bed, trying to comb her thoughts straight. She pulled her dress and petticoats off the fireguard. They were dry now—not immaculate, but far less incriminating than they had been. Faith put the fire cover back in place and quickly swept up every stray crumb of mud.

Opening her windows and shutters, she found the world had been swallowed by mist. She shook the bran out of her boots onto the stone flags of the roof garden. With satisfaction she saw sparrows and pigeons flit down to dispose of the evidence.

"Fa-a-a-aith!"

Faith opened the door, and Howard blundered in, his paper collar on backward.

"It hurts!" He tugged at it. "I want Skordle!"

Faith calmed Howard down, straightened his jacket and collar, and then sang to him while she plaited her hair and dressed. By the time their breakfast was brought up to them by Mrs. Vellet, both of them were sitting in the nursery, only slightly unkempt.

Howard did not want Faith to leave him after breakfast. He was bored to the breaking point and desperate for her to stay, read with him, play with him. It was an hour before she could finally slip away.

Downstairs, all was quiet. There was no sign of either of her parents, only Uncle Miles reading in the drawing room.

"Good morning." Uncle Miles blinked at her over his book.

"Where is everybody, Uncle Miles?" asked Faith.

"Your mother insists that she has a headache, and has taken breakfast in her room. Your father has not risen yet, and nobody is in a hurry to bang on his door."

"He is probably tired." Faith did not meet her uncle's eye as she sat down. "It is my fault. I kept him talking late last night—we did not go to bed until one o'clock."

"So late? Is something wrong?"

"No," Faith insisted hurriedly, her face turning hot. "I . . . have just been worrying about my confirmation."

"Good Lord, was that it?" Uncle Miles sounded a little taken aback. "Well, I commend your piety. I am not sure I could have worried about my confirmation for ten minutes straight, let alone until one in the morning."

It was done. The words were spoken. For better or worse, Faith had given her father an alibi. She knew that it had sounded convincing. She knew she ought to feel happy and proud that her voice had sounded shyly natural. But instead she felt only a confused sense of guilt.

What had she just done? She had obediently opened a door and stepped through into blackness, without even knowing if there was a floor on the other side.

You are doing your duty to Father, she told herself. *There cannot be any wrong in that. You need to trust him. It is just like Abraham. God told him to kill his son, so he went to fetch a knife. He did the right thing, even though it looked evil. He trusted God to understand right and wrong better than he did.*

But, whispered another voice in her head, *maybe he should not have done. And anyway, Father is not God.*

Faith gritted her teeth and tried to find resolve. Instead a sly thought slipped into her head, both terrifying and thrilling.

I can make Father tell me the truth.

He must. I know too much. He has to take me into his confidence about everything now—the plant, the scandal, and wherever he went after we came back last night. He can't shut me out anymore.

"Are you sure?" said Uncle Miles.

Faith started, before realizing that her uncle was not talking to her. Mrs. Vellet was discreetly stooped next to his chair, murmuring in his ear.

"Yes, sir." The housekeeper's voice was tactfully low, but Faith could make out her words. "All the other boots were outside the doors this morning, but not his. So I looked at the hooks, and his overcoat and hat are missing too."

Faith's blood ran cold.

"That is peculiar." Uncle Miles frowned and stood up. "Perhaps we should try knocking on his door again."

Faith rose, but did not follow her uncle as he headed upstairs, brow furrowed. She alone knew that her father had gone out in the dead of night. Now it looked as though he had not come back.

Her mind was full of pictures more terrible than the scene in Paul Clay's stereoscope. She imagined her father bleeding in his own rabbit trap, or wounded by some enemy, and too weak to call for help.

She could not wait while others searched the house in vain. Faith quietly made her way to the front door and slipped out of the house.

The mist flattened everything and sucked out all color. Trees became intricate smoke-hued doilies. Buildings were featureless outlines, eiderdown gray.

Faith tiptoed to the sites of the rabbit traps, and found nobody sprawled in their toothed maw. There was no one in the greenhouse or the Folly. She even edged her way into the dell and called out among the ghost-trees. Nobody answered. There was no sign of her father on the road that faded as it climbed the hill into the mist.

Sounds were startlingly real in this world of ghosts. Faith could hear her own breath, and the click of stones under her feet as she hobbled down the path to the beach. At the fork in the path she passed the wheelbarrow, lying on its side, one handle raised as if hailing her as a coconspirator.

The rough path gave way to pebble beach, and each step became a high-pitched *chhh* of little stones rasping. The night before, the cliffs had been inky and massive. This morning they were gray paper. She could have thrown a stone and torn them.

She stared down the beach, hoping to find her father's outline. The far end of the beach melted into mist, and with a jolt she realized that she could not see the little rowing boat.

She broke into an uneven run, skirts hitched. No. *No!* The boat had to be there! He could not have taken it out a second time! It would have been mad to do so, without Faith to hold a lantern! The idea enslaved her imagination. It was too horrible to be anything but true.

Faith hobbled, almost turning her ankle . . . and then slowed. With calm innocence, the mist thinned just enough for her to make out a gauzy white shape, with a familiar curve of a prow. The boat *was* there after all. The mist had deceived her.

Faith covered her mouth with both hands, not sure whether to sob or be sick with relief. She turned to walk back to the house.

And it was then, of course, that she saw it.

Halfway up the nearest cliff, slung over a jutting tree, was a black shape. It looked like a horseshoe, ends pointing down so that the luck would drain out.

It was a silhouette and nothing more, but Faith knew what it was. Humans are always looking for one another, and human eyes have a gift for spotting the human shape. With cruel clarity, she knew she was looking at two legs hanging loosely, two dangling arms, the curve of a back.

It was a man who was draped over the tree. The cold air was a knife in Faith's throat as she ran back to the house.

Ten minutes later, Faith and Myrtle sat on the parlor's chaise lounge, tea cooling in their cups. Uncle Miles and the manservant, Prythe, had hastened out to the beach with stout rope.

Myrtle was bundled in several of her nightgowns, over which was draped a floor-length shawl of yellow Oriental silk. Faith sat gripping her saucer, bargaining with the silent seconds.

Let it be somebody else, or let him be alive, she begged Fate. *Let him be safe, and you can take my left foot.* The clock callously told out second after second after second after second, and no news came. *Let him be safe*, she raised her offer, *and you can take my whole left leg.* Tick, tick, tick, and nothing. *Let him be safe, and you can take both my legs.* The clock was relentless.

Somewhere a door opened and there were hushed voices out in the hall. Then there was a gentle knock, and Uncle Miles put his head around the parlor door.

Faith's heart was beating so hard she could feel it. Uncle Miles met her desperate gaze and then quickly dropped his own.

"Myrtle," he said very quietly. "May I speak with you for a moment?"

And in that second, Faith knew.

She was very aware of herself, of her own lungs filling and emptying. She could feel where the china saucer dented her fingers, and the shapes of her teeth against her dry tongue. Something warm was spilling from her eyes down her cheeks. Suddenly she was hotly, unbearably alive.

The room was still there. Myrtle was standing up and the clock was ticking and the bald white sky was staring in through the window. But an invisible wave had gone out, and now everything looked beached and stranded. Faith watched her own hands put down the cup and saucer.

Myrtle joined Uncle Miles at the door, and he murmured and murmured in her ear. One of his hands hovered protectively by her side, not quite cupping her elbow, but ready to support.

"Where?" Myrtle's voice was bruised and unguarded. "Where is he?"

"We've put him in the library."

Myrtle pushed past her brother and out of the room. Uncle

Miles followed, and barely seemed to notice Faith taking up the rear.

In the library, Prythe stood by the wall, cap in one hand, looking miserably uncomfortable. The two chairs in which Faith and her father had sat still faced each other in mute conference, but now they had been moved to one side to make room.

There was a blanket spread on the floor. There was somebody on the blanket. Faith looked and looked and could not look away, but her brain decided not to see. Only when she blinked was there an image imprinted on her mind's eye, a half-mask of dark blood, open eyes, and pale, slack hands. A thousand hopes blew out like candles.

Faith stood in the doorway, leaning on the door frame. Her arm shook.

I should have bargained better, said a stupid, pointless voice in her mind. *I should have offered all my arms and legs, right from the start.*

Chapter 12

TIME STOPS

MYRTLE STARED DOWN AT HER HUSBAND'S shape on the blanket, her eyes bright but empty. The color and expression slowly drained out of her face.

"We will send for the doctor," Uncle Miles said quietly, "but . . . we have held a mirror over his mouth and there is no sign of breath. We have pricked him with a pin, and there is no reaction." He glanced across and looked appalled as he noticed Faith in the room. He said nothing though; it was too late to spare her.

Myrtle did not seem to hear him. She drifted away from her brother and Prythe, both of whom seemed to be tensed to catch her if she fell, and came to a halt near Faith, facing the mirror on the wall.

One of her blond ringlets hung down beside her cheek, and shivered in a draft. It had a childlike poignancy, and Faith felt a pang of tortured tenderness. She reached out to her mother impulsively, but her fingers halted against the cool silk of the yellow shawl. She could not throw her arms around her mother after all. If she did, something inside her would break.

Myrtle gave Faith's hand a brief squeeze, but she continued staring into the glass, her eyes starry and distant. Slowly her ungloved hands rose and started making small adjustments to her hair, tucking away stray tresses and teasing crushed locks back into shape. She rubbed hard at her lower lip, and watched as the blood rushed back to give it a rosier hue. Her gaze dropped to her Oriental shawl, and her brow creased slightly.

"I am too pale for yellow," Myrtle muttered under her breath. The words were very quiet, but Faith was close and she caught them.

"Myrtle," prompted Uncle Miles.

"You found him in the dell," said Myrtle, without turning around.

"No, old girl—I told you, he was at the beach, halfway down the cliff. He must have fallen from the top . . ."

"How many people know that?" Myrtle asked sharply.

Uncle Miles looked taken aback. "Only the four of us in this room," he replied, after a moment's thought.

"Then you found him in the dell." Myrtle turned to meet her brother's eye. "Miles—you said yourself, there is a steep slope where anybody might fall and break their neck."

"But—"

"Miles, please!" Myrtle exclaimed. "It *must* be done this way. Think of how it will *look* if he fell from the cliff-top. Think of what that would mean for *us*."

Faith felt the words like a blow. What did it matter how *anything* looked, ever again? But Myrtle was already turning to the manservant.

"Prythe . . . my family is indebted to you for the service you have done my husband this morning. You must allow us to show our gratitude. If we can count upon your discretion in this matter, then we shall be even more grateful."

With that she walked forward with a rigid calm and dropped

to sit on her heels beside the prone figure on the blanket. Faith watched her mother's pink, carefully groomed hands pull open the jacket and slide into the inside pockets, pulling out her father's pocketbook and purse. Myrtle stood, and turned to Prythe, placing a coin in his hand.

"Thank you, Prythe. May we count on you?"

Prythe stared down at the sovereign in his palm, and the color drained from his face. "Ma'am." He looked shocked, almost stricken, but his eyes were bright as he looked at the coin. "I can hold my tongue in the general way, but . . . if the constable should ask, I would not wish to mislead him. And if I am asked to swear on the Bible I cannot lie." Hesitantly, and with obvious reluctance, he offered the coin back.

"I would not ask such a thing of an honest man," said Myrtle, making no move to take the money. "There should be no need for constables or Bibles. All I ask is your silence."

"Yes, ma'am," whispered Prythe.

A faint sound caught Faith's ear, a slither of sole on tiles.

"Someone is outside," she said reflexively.

Uncle Miles tweaked open the door and peered into the hall.

"Did anyone overhear us?" demanded Myrtle.

"I am not sure," answered her brother. "I did see somebody, passing toward the servants' stairs. Jeanne, I think."

"Jeanne." Myrtle was carefully, absently searching through banknotes in the pocket-book. "Someone must tell the girl that we have decided to keep her on after all."

Uncle Miles departed to talk to Jeanne and the other servants, and Prythe left to fetch Dr. Jacklers.

Myrtle looked around the room and then hurried to her husband's desk, where she began hastily leafing through the papers.

Faith's stomach turned over at the sight of her mother's neat fingers carelessly handling the sketches and notes over which he had been so fiercely protective.

"What is it?" Faith asked, fighting the urge to snatch the papers out of her mother's hands. "What are you trying to find?"

"There may be a letter," Myrtle said without looking up. "A . . . private letter that we would not wish others to see."

"Let me look," Faith said through her teeth. She swallowed, and forced calm into her voice. "Leave it to me."

Myrtle hesitated. "That would give me a chance to change my clothes," she muttered under her breath. "Very well. But be quick! We do not have much time."

Faith nodded.

"Good girl," Myrtle said hurriedly. As she hastened from the room, she patted Faith's cheek. Faith flinched from the touch. The words burned.

As soon as the door closed behind Myrtle, Faith hurried to the desk and made a pile of the loose papers, then hastily searched the desk drawers, the writing box, and the strongbox in the corner. There were a couple of envelopes stuck within the pages of books, so she snatched those too.

Everything else was lost, but she could still protect her father's secrets. Faith's hands shook as she glimpsed her father's handwriting between her fingers. Her face was hot. But she was helping him in the only way she could. She could hide his papers where nobody else would find them.

With the bundle of papers wrapped in an antimacassar from one of the chairs, Faith sneaked out of the library.

As she crept along the hall and up the stairs her sharp ears caught the sound of conversation in the kitchen, where it seemed all the servants were holed up. The voices were hushed and a little hysterical, but with a hard, excited, curious edge. To judge by the smell, everybody was being "fortified" with hot cider.

Outside her father's room, she hesitated, then turned the handle and entered. His room would be searched soon enough, so it was best if she did so first. The darkness smelled of book must, varnish, and his tobacco. His dinner coat glowered darkly from its hook on the back of the door.

She snatched up a couple of letters and a ledger from his bedside table and filched two notebooks from jacket pockets. Then, on impulse, she ran a hand under the bed. Her fingers brushed a rough corner, and she drew out a thin, leather-bound book.

Adding this to her finds, she slipped into her own room, which was lit only by the pale daylight from the window.

When Faith pulled the cloth off the snake's cage, it flinched into a coil, then raised its head curiously, mouth slightly open to let its dull pink tongue flicker. She hushed it, opened the cage door, then reached in a slow, unthreatening hand, and let the snake slide up her arm.

Faith pulled out all the rags that the snake had been using as a nest. She divided the bundle of papers into two piles and placed them on the floor of the cage, then covered them with rags so that they did not show.

"Guard them for me," she whispered to the snake, and eased it back into its cage.

When Faith returned to the library, Myrtle had returned.

"Where have you been?" Myrtle demanded without preamble, but did not wait for an answer. "Stay with me—the doctor will be here soon."

Myrtle was wearing her blue dress with the demure high collar and pearl buttons, but a few of them were undone, showing her white throat. Her hair was brushed to a golden gleam, and carefully arranged, but one girlish curl was loose at her temple. She was still pale, but powder had made the paleness even and comely. She looked disheveled, distressed, vulnerable, and very pretty.

There was a strong smell in the room, something dark brown and spirited. Looking across at her father's desk, Faith saw the glass sherry decanter that usually stood in the dining room. A little sherry lurked at the bottom of a large glass. Had those been there before? Faith had not noticed them, but perhaps she had been in too much of a hurry.

Myrtle stiffened, holding up a hand to bid Faith be still.

"That is Dr. Jacklers! I hear his carriage."

Myrtle pulled her cut-glass bottle of smelling salts out of her reticule. She uncorked it, and raised it to her nose, flinching away a moment later with a wince and gasp. After she had done this a second time, her eyes were swimming. She put away the bottle and blinked rapidly. By the time Dr. Jacklers was shown into the room, a tear was tracing a gleaming path down Myrtle's cheek.

For a long time, Dr. Jacklers looked at the figure on the floor. Myrtle hovered nearby, twisting her hands and answering his questions, while silver tears slid hypnotically down her face.

Faith sat nearby, her thoughts churning. Her father on the beach, her father in the dell. Why was her mother so determined to lie?

"I am so very sorry, Mrs. Sunderly," the doctor said at last. "I cannot advise you to hope. His neck is broken . . ."

Myrtle gave a small, vulnerable noise, somewhere between a gasp and a sob. She turned away and bowed her face over her handkerchief.

"I wish we had never come here!" she said, her voice a little muffled. "Those trespassers . . . he was convinced they would steal his rare botanic specimens. So he set rabbit traps, and kept rushing to that dreadful dell every time he heard a noise out there. I suppose he must have fallen in the dark and struck his head against something . . ."

"Your husband was found in the dell?" The doctor's eyebrows rose. "Madam, I must confess that surprises me, given the nature of his injuries. I am loath to grieve you with such details—"

"Please." Myrtle turned back to face him, her mouth tremulously resolute. "Do not spare me. I must know."

"Well . . . I fancy two ribs are cracked, suggesting a longer fall than you could suffer in that dell. The wound on his forehead is deep, but there is another great bump to the back of his head, under the hair. To me that looks like a longer tumble, with some rolling. Mrs. Sunderly—there is no delicate way to ask this—is it possible that he was found somewhere else, and that your friends have misled you in order to spare your feelings?"

"My husband is dead," Myrtle said softly. "What feelings do I have left to spare?"

Faith felt the color rise to her face. She could brush away her mother's lie like a cobweb. But how many of her own strands of untruth would she destroy with the same gesture? Besides, her last experiment with truthfulness had burned her to the core.

"Well," the doctor said under his breath, "perhaps the drop was high enough . . . if he managed to pitch forward with some force." He sighed. "Pardon the question, but did your husband appear preoccupied yesterday? Out of spirits?"

Myrtle stiffened, her face pale and pained.

"Dr. Jacklers," she said with fragile hauteur, "what in the world are you trying to say?"

Faith knew exactly what the doctor was trying to say. In a flash, she realized how this must look to him. The disgraced man creeping out of his house by night to plummet to his death, rather than face a terrible scandal . . .

"Forgive my clumsiness." The doctor looked mortified and out of countenance. "I am simply trying to understand . . ."

"Perhaps," Myrtle said with dignity, "this is a matter we should discuss in private." She turned to her daughter. "Faith, will you please go to Mrs. Vellet . . . and have her stop the clocks."

Faith took her cue and left the room, feigning a few receding steps. Then she stooped and put her ear to the keyhole.

". . . a whole decanter before bed?" Dr. Jacklers was asking. "Was this usual?"

"Of late it had become so." A sigh. "It is not the first time he has suffered a fall. It is just the first we were not able to conceal."

Faith smothered a gasp of pained indignation. How *dare* her mother say that? How *dare* she paint the Reverend as a blundering drunkard, tripping over his own feet? Then Faith remembered her father sitting torpid and yellow-eyed, his room filled with the exotic, clammy scent. What if her father really did have yet more secrets?

"Dr. Jacklers, I do not know what to do." Myrtle's voice was low and tearful. "I am so used to hiding my husband's . . . habits . . . and I would wish to hide them still, to protect his memory. But now you have made me frightened. Did you really think my husband had 'pitched himself forward with force'? Will everyone else think that too?"

"Mrs. Sunderly . . ." The doctor stopped abruptly, with a slight gasp. There was a short silence.

Faith took her ear from the keyhole and peered through instead.

Her mother was standing very close to the doctor. Her ungloved hands were wrapped beseechingly around his, a strange, shocking intimacy. The doctor's face was brick red.

"I have *children*," Myrtle said. "I am desperate. Please, tell me what to do."

"I . . ." The doctor coughed and dropped his gaze. "You have my word that I will do everything in my power to . . . to spare you and your family trouble. My solemn promise. The injuries . . . there are ways that, ah, things can be phrased. Please, please do not distress yourself, Mrs. Sunderly."

He did not, Faith noticed, make any attempt to pull his hands away.

Faith drew back from the keyhole, her face burning. She could not bear to see or hear anything more. A warm, slow anger was filling her bones like lava, and it had nowhere to go.

Instead, she tiptoed down the hall to the corner, where the grandfather clock swung its pendulum for each monotonous *click*. It mocked her, pretended that time still mattered, that there was still a day to be told out, that the world was still turning.

The glass front was cold against her skin as she opened it. The pendulum slowed to her touch. The clock's hands twitched under her fingers, so she gripped them until the ticking stopped. Her mind calmed as she imagined the earth giving up its giddy spin and drifting untethered through the void.

Faith stood there for a long time with her fingers on the motionless hands. She felt like the murderess of time.

Chapter 13

FALSE PICTURE

IT WAS A HOUSE OF THE DEAD NOW. ALL THE curtains were drawn. Dark cloth was draped over every mirror, like a dull lid drooped over every eye.

The air was heavy, so heavy that Faith thought the whole house might sink into the ground. Voices were hushed, fragile and mothlike. Footsteps were trespassers.

And yet, all afternoon people came to visit, on foot and on horseback, even to the despised Sunderly household. For there was death in the house, and death was a business.

One cart rolled in heaped with bundles of cut flowers. A jobmaster dropped by to show off a little black coach and two dark horses. Mrs. Vellet was sent out to town, and returned with a dressmaker and trunks bulging with black cloth.

The funeral would be the next day, Myrtle had decided.

"Very soon, isn't it?" Uncle Miles had protested. "Old girl, there is another boat to the mainland in a few days. If he were kept in the ice house, we could take him back with us to Kent and see him settled in the family plot."

"No." Myrtle had been immovable. "We bury him here in Vane—and as soon as possible." She refused to be drawn further.

The rush felt indecent, but it was just another indecency. Faith found she could not bear the living. She could not bear the servants' hard-eyed curiosity, or Uncle Miles's platitudes and shrugs. Howard's questions tore her in two. Most of all, she could not bear her mother.

Somebody needed to take on the duty of the "wake," and sit by the side of her father. Faith was all too willing to volunteer.

The Reverend had been washed, dressed in his best clothes, and laid out on his bed upstairs. One might even imagine that he had passed away there, flanked by loved ones and with the good book in his hand. It was a lie, but a comforting one. There were scented candles all over the room now, and vases of flowers. They made the room seem sacred, even though Faith knew that they were there to mask any smell.

It was not the first time Faith had been alone with the dead of course. She had watched five younger brothers wane, felt the trusting pressure of their small hands in hers. And later, each time, she had done her part in keeping watch over the body for the wake. There always needed to be somebody watching over the newly dead, just in case they turned out not to be dead after all. It was best to know these things before anyone was actually buried.

There would be no movement, however. She knew it in her blood. She knew it from the crashing stillness that filled the room. Dead people bled silence.

On the bedside table lay the great black family Bible. Many times Faith had looked through the family's births, deaths, and marriages scrawled onto the blank pages at the back. Her brothers were there, with the dates of their deaths. And now Erasmus

Sunderly would be added to the names, another little human life crushed flylike between its great pages.

At least in the flickering candlelight he no longer looked helpless, the way he had on the blanket down in the library. His features might have been carved from marble, unchanging and incorruptible. Here he was his own altar.

Faith never wanted to leave this stillness. She never wanted to leave him. She did not know what she felt. Her emotions were so large and strange that they seemed to be something outside her, vast cloud patterns roiling and colliding above while she watched.

Suicide. The great mortal sin.

"I do not believe it," she told him. "I *know* you would never do that."

But could she be sure of anything anymore? How many secrets *did* her father have? What if he had taken his mysterious opiate again and flung himself to his doom in a fit of drugged melancholia?

Faith was too tired to think, and too tired not to think. All the while her mind kept picking at what she knew and did not know, numbly dropping the pieces before she could fit them together properly.

She understood now why her mother had lied about where the body was found. A broken neck in the dell looked like an accident, a misstep in the dark. After all, why would anybody hurl themselves down a small, wooded incline when there was a cliff nearby?

But he did not even need a cliff. He had a pistol.

Faith pressed her fists against her temples.

He had a pistol.

She remembered his nervous, reflexive reach for the gun, while they were down on the beach. He had been expecting some sort of danger. And now he was dead.

Why had he insisted that he needed to be back from the boat trip by midnight? And why had he been so desperate to conceal the mysterious plant?

As she recalled their stealthy journey with the plant in the wheelbarrow, a troublesome sense of wrongness tickled her mind. Again she saw the misty image of the wheelbarrow as she had seen it that morning, lying on its side at the fork in the path . . .

But . . . it should not have been there. Father and I left it by the greenhouse.

The smoky uncertainties in her head began to coalesce, and solidified into a suspicion.

The mist was starting to lift as Faith walked through the grounds once more, retracing her steps along the path. And there indeed was the wheelbarrow at the fork.

It might mean nothing. Maybe Prythe rose early and moved it.

But she continued to walk, this time along the path that led to the cliff-top. It was a rugged climb, and rocky in places. It looked as though the footpath doubled as a temporary stream in wetter weather.

She reached the grassy top, and the breeze filled her cape. Looking down, she could see the shallow waves drag their foam crescents like fingernails down the beach. Directly below her, halfway down the cliff, the black-barked tree that had caught her father quivered as if beckoning to her.

Here the path was a muddy track trampled through the

grass. Faith stooped to peer. Not far from the brink, she could make out a deep groove pushed into the mud. It was just wide enough that it might have been left by the wheel of a wheelbarrow.

When Faith entered the drawing room, Uncle Miles looked up from his book and his furrowed brow smoothed a little.

"How are you faring, Faith?"

There was nothing good or cheerful that Faith could say.

"Uncle Miles . . . can I ask you something? You said that when my . . . when my father was turned away from the excavation, somebody gave him a letter."

"Oh." Uncle Miles raised his eyebrows ruefully and closed his book. "Yes, and it upset him immeasurably. I suppose we shall never know who wrote it."

"It was unsigned?" Faith's interest sharpened to a point.

"It must have been. Your father kept demanding to know who had written it. Suddenly everybody was his enemy and he would not hear otherwise. Ben Crock found it among his day's papers and handed it over, but said he knew nothing more about it."

"What did it say?"

"Your father would let nobody see it." Uncle Miles shook his head. "On the journey home he kept insisting that somebody had spied on him, or betrayed him, or read his papers. And when we reached home . . . he tossed the letter on the fire."

"There you are, Faith!" Myrtle was in the drawing room with the dressmaker. "There is a black cambric dress that might do for you, if it is taken apart and made up in your size."

Faith stared at the black dress draped over a chair. There was wear at the collar and shine at the elbows. It was a dress that had already mourned.

"Mother—can I talk to you?"

"Of course," Myrtle said absently, without looking up from a book of plates showing elegant women in full crêpe dresses. She tapped a picture and passed the book to the dressmaker. "This one, with the fashionable cut. I cannot simply throw away my half-crinoline. And you are sure that we cannot work in a little glossy silk? Must it all be lightless and dull?" There was indeed something deathly about the crêpe. It was a mass of fine threads, rough and scratchy to the touch. It seemed to suck light.

The dressmaker assured her that there was no help for it, and Myrtle accepted this with poor grace.

"And everything is so *expensive*," Myrtle muttered under her breath. "But we must do things decently. Mrs. Vellet, surely there must be someone on Vane with old crêpe for sale?"

"I can make inquiries, madam . . . but folks do not like to keep it in the house once mourning is over. Bad luck, they say. Besides, madam, crêpe does not last well. It snags easily, and gets a shabby look, and falls apart if you wash it or get caught in the rain."

"Mother, *please* can I speak with you privately?" Faith could not suppress her impatience.

"Yes, Faith, yes. As soon as you have been measured."

Faith had to stand there with gritted teeth as she was draped with bombazine, paramatta, and black ribbons and flicked with a tape measure. She was forced to listen as her mother chose, quibbled, and haggled, veering between obstinate extravagance and startling meanness. Yes, she unquestionably needed the black chiffon parasol. But no, black glass jewelry would certainly do instead of jet. Yes, she would certainly need the bonnet with the extra ribbons. But no, the family would not need a wealth of other black clothes, some of theirs could be dyed black to suit.

At last the dressmaker left the room.

"What is it, Faith?" Myrtle took a moment to study her. "You are quite white! I shall ask Mrs. Vellet to bring you a little broth."

"I want to talk to you about Father—about the cliff . . ."

Myrtle's expression of distracted concern slipped away in an instant. She moved quickly to the door, opened it, then closed it again.

"Not another word," she said quietly and firmly.

"But—"

"Do not talk about the cliff—not to me, nor to anybody else."

"I found a mark at the top," Faith persisted. "I think something terrible happened—"

"It does not matter!" erupted Myrtle. She closed her eyes and let out a long breath, then continued in a quiet but barely controlled tone. "I know it is hard for you to understand, but *all* that matters is how things appear. We have our story. *That* is what happened."

Faith felt stifled with frustration and disgust. Why had she even tried to talk to her mother? Why had she expected her to care?

What more could Faith say anyway? The pistol, her father's hurry to be back at the house by midnight, his desperation to hide the mysterious plant . . . she could not reveal any of these without breaking her father's confidence. He was beyond her protection now but his secrets were not.

As Faith was leaving the room, she glanced over her shoulder and saw Myrtle trying on a black ribbon choker. In that moment, Faith hated her mother.

. . . . .

135

In the late afternoon, Clay arrived with his camera, tripod, and case of chemical bottles. His son struggled in behind him with a collection of stands.

It was to be a memorial photograph, a family photograph. A beloved father at the heart of his family. A picture to show friends and relatives at home, a card to send to close acquaintances.

Faith remembered Paul Clay showing her the after-death photographs in the shop and watching for her reaction. Now he showed no inclination to meet her gaze, and she did not seek his.

The Reverend Erasmus Sunderly had been brought down to the drawing room for the photograph, his clothes straightened and his hair artfully brushed to cover the wound at his temple. For so long he had been the center around which the house revolved. It made Faith sick to see him moved around and positioned, like a doll at a tea party. Now the Reverend sat in state in his great armchair, his hand resting upon the page of an open Bible.

Myrtle was meekly placed beside him in a straight-back upholstered chair. The full widow's gown was still being adjusted to her size, but she had dressed as darkly as she could, in deep blues and a black shawl. She appeared very pretty and mournful, and Faith hated her composure. Howard was hunched at their feet, his wooden lion in his hands to distract him. All Faith could see of him was his bowed head, and the vulnerable curve of his tensed back. The lion's jaws *clack-clack-clacked*, over and over.

Faith stood immediately behind her father's chair. She let one hand creep up so that it rested on his sleeve, and felt a little throb of comfort and solidarity at the touch.

"Could you please take a step backward, miss?" Paul Clay was behind her, holding a slender stand with a sturdy base and a pincer-like attachment at the top.

Unwillingly Faith stepped back, losing her contact with her father. She felt Paul move her plait to one side, then gently fasten the stand's clamp on either side of her neck.

Her eyes stung, and she hated Paul Clay, hated his flat, coldly polite voice. She reached behind her head, found his hand, and pinched the flesh of it as hard as she could. She willed him, dared him, to cry out and disgrace her, but he did not. When she released him and let her arm return to her side, he returned to his father, face unreadable.

"The stand will help you hold position," explained Clay.

Stand exactly here and do not move, or you will spoil the picture. Say this, and only this, or you will spoil the story.

The Sunderly family held still, staring into the black eye of the camera. Faith thought of chemicals fizzing, and her image burning its way into the glass negative, indelible, immortal. She wondered whether it would have haunted eyes, thoughts whirling trapped behind them like bats in a turret.

"There," said Clay, as tenderly as if he were bringing a baby into the world. "We have it."

After he had fixed the negative, Myrtle called him over to whisper with her by the fireplace. Faith tried not to overhear, but could not help it.

". . . I am so friendless on this island, I do not know what I will do if I cannot count on your help." Myrtle's eyes were wide and childlike. "If you are clever enough to paint the photograph so that his eyes appear open, surely you can change the picture in other ways? The wound on his temple still shows a little. Can you hide it with paint?"

And so the photograph, with its lie of a happy family, would have more lies laid over it, and yet more . . .

Faith could not bear it. She left the drawing room quietly and quickly. The hall was kinder, colder, and darker. At least she was alone.

But then the door creaked open behind her, and she turned to find that Paul Clay had followed her. There he stood, saying nothing, watching her in the same cool, masklike way as before.

"Did it hurt when I pinched you?" she demanded. There was something wrong with her lungs. Every breath filled them with pins and needles. "Tell me that it hurt!"

He took a breath, then held it for a second or two before speaking.

"It should be a good picture," he said at last. "Dignified. Not all of our customers . . . That is to say, he makes a good . . ."

"A good what?" Faith's blood felt like magma. "A good corpse?"

"Why are you spitting fire at me?" Paul snapped back, raising his voice for the first time. "I didn't make him so!"

"No? Well, *somebody did*."

The words were out, and Faith's breathing became faster, easier.

She no longer believed that her father had tumbled off the cliff in a drugged frenzy. Instead she imagined a nocturnal figure struggling up the path with a laden wheelbarrow, halting at the very top to tip its burden over the edge. A falling body, bouncing cruelly off the rocky face and lodging in a tree. And then the other figure creeping away, abandoning the wheelbarrow where the path forked.

"You all hated him—everybody on this filthy, stupid, miserable island. *And one of you killed him*." She turned and ran upstairs, because death would be better than letting Paul Clay see her cry.

Not an accident. Not suicide. Murder.

Chapter 14

THE FUNERAL

THE DAY OF THE FUNERAL WAS A NUMB, exhausted gray. The black-clad bearers muttered as they maneuvered the coffin down the stairs. Their boots left mud on the carpet. The front door was opened, and the coffin carried out "feet first." Faith had heard that this was to stop the dead looking back into the house and calling one of the living to join them.

I wish he would, she thought.

One cold coach ride later, the Sunderlys dismounted and paraded toward the church porch, Howard and Uncle Miles walking behind the coffin as "men of the family." The hired mourners walked beside them with long poles swathed in crêpe, like sinister butterfly nets.

When the family entered the church, it took a moment for Faith's eyes to adjust.

She had thought that she might find the church empty except for the priest, all of Myrtle's set-dressing prepared for a performance with no audience. She had been mistaken.

Nearly every pew was crammed with figures, all turning to watch the Sunderly family's entry. Most were complete strangers.

The box pews, on the other hand, were all but empty. Dr. Jacklers sat at the far end of one, looking extremely uncomfortable. The respectable families, the great and the good of Vane, were nowhere to be seen.

As they walked to their box pew, Faith could feel gazes like a trickle of cold water down the back of her neck. Myrtle raised her chin and glided in like a dark queen, the candles glittering on her black glass jewelry, the gold of her hair just visible beneath her heavy veil. The whispering hushed as her black skirts brushed over the floor's marble memorial slabs. Faith felt a moment's unwilling admiration for her mother's defiant poise. It was somewhat daring for females to attend a funeral service at all, but Myrtle had been adamant that she would not "hide away."

The Sunderly family settled themselves in their pew, Faith wishing that its walls were seven feet high. Some of the comments had caught her ear as they walked to the front.

"What does 'the trap rc-baited' mean?" she could not help asking quietly.

"It means," Myrtle murmured from beneath her veil, "that there are some envious old hags in this church. And that I have chosen the right dress."

"I told you it was a mistake to hold this on a Sunday," muttered Uncle Miles. "Everybody's day off—leisure aplenty to come and goggle."

Clay looked so frail in his surplice, dwarfed by his oversized pulpit. His voice was earnest but faint, as though tired of fighting the shadows that hung from the vaulted ceiling.

"We brought nothing into this world, and it is certain we can take nothing out. The Lord gave, and the Lord hath taken away; blessed be the name of the Lord . . ."

A rustle of hymnbooks. A familiar psalm, sung to an unfamiliar tune. And then Clay was talking and talking again, of falling and rising and sleep and redemption. His words were lifeless pebbles on an endless beach, and Faith wanted it all to be over, over, over. She wanted her father to be safe under the clod, away from this chill, hostile darkness and the bushfire crackle of whispers.

At last the curate's voice came to a soft stop and there was a thunder of shoe-shuffles and shifting pews. Myrtle nudged Faith, and she realized with passionate relief that the service was done. She stood, and with the rest of her family paraded out toward the gray daylight, so that they could follow the coffin to the grave.

There was a rush of motion ahead of them. Instead of waiting to follow them out, the congregation was pouring from the pews and surging out through the porch door.

The Sunderly family emerged into the daylight, and Faith saw that the crowds had not in fact rushed off with rude haste. The churchyard was full of people, standing, squatting, sitting on monuments, all watching the approach of the casket.

For a moment, Faith could not see the waiting grave. Then she noticed a man with a spade drooping in his hands, his brow furrowed with conflict and uncertainty. At his feet was the long, dark crease of a hole, but there were four or five people defiantly standing in it, their heads just visible, their elbows resting on the turf edge. Others stood massed in front of the grave, arms folded, a human barrier three rows deep.

"What in the world is all this?" exclaimed Clay.

"They can't bury him here," said one of the men at the heart of the group. He was tall and strongly built, with dark hair and a pugnacious face. Faith recognized him at once. It was Tom

Parris, who had startled her by chance in the woods at Bull Cove. Tom Parris, whose son had been caught in the Reverend's trap.

"What do you mean, Tom?" The curate looked flabbergasted. "Why ever not?"

"This is holy ground," Tom answered curtly. "No suicides. That Sunderly threw himself off a cliff, and we don't care who says different. We know where he was found."

Only Faith caught a flicker of Tom's eyes toward a member of the crowd. She followed his glance, and her gaze lodged upon a familiar figure. Jeanne Bissette, the housemaid, meek in her Sunday best and black armband, but with a fierce satisfaction in her eyes.

She told them where Father was found. She told everybody.

"If they want to bury him," Tom continued relentlessly, "there's a crossroads two miles down the road. We'll even give them a sharpened stick to keep the ghost down. But not here. Not next to our families' stones."

"But this is cruel—cruel!" Myrtle was shaking with feeling, her poise broken for the moment. Faith hardly recognized her mother's voice.

There was an uproar of other voices. Uncle Miles and the priest both pushed forward through the crowd, and Faith saw them in earnest debate with Tom, the crowd's spokesman. After a while she saw Uncle Miles turn and give his all too familiar resigned shrug. *I tried*, it said. Howard mewled faintly, and Faith realized that she was gripping his hand too tightly.

Clay returned to Myrtle and Faith.

"I have never seen our people so adamant!" he said. "But I can promise you, nobody will be staking your husband and burying him at the crossroads!"

"Oh, thank you, thank you!" exclaimed Myrtle.

"No, that old law was thrown out in my grandfather's day," the curate continued, furrowing his brow. "But they are correct that a suicide cannot be buried on holy ground. I am so sorry, Mrs. Sunderly, but since the manner of the Reverend's death has been called into question, I shall have to refer the whole matter to Mr. Lambent as magistrate."

"We cannot bury him?" A fat, cold raindrop struck Faith on the cheek.

"Do not worry," Clay answered hurriedly. "I am sure there is some confusion and everything will be settled easily."

"And if it is not?" demanded Myrtle.

"Well . . . then . . . there is a meadow not far away where they bury the little babes born out of wedlock. Unconsecrated, but within sight of the church spire—"

"No!" exploded Faith. Her father eternally cast out, shamed in death and cut off from the Church . . .

"No, not that!" declared Myrtle, the fervent glitter of her eyes just visible through the heavy veil. "It *must* be holy ground." She lowered her voice. "These people—they cannot stay here all day. Can we not wait, and bury my husband when they are gone?"

"Mrs. Sunderly," the curate answered sadly, "I have promised them an inquest. If I go back on my word . . . well, we may put him in the ground, but I do not think he would stay there."

Uncle Miles remained at the church with the priest and the hearse, to talk to the protesters and see "what difference good sense and money will make." He did not hold out much hope, however. The coffin was moved down into the church crypt "for the moment."

"We must have it settled today!" Myrtle kept saying, as the coach weaved north along the low coast road. "The funeral breakfast—the coach and hearse—the hired mourners—all is arranged for today! We cannot afford . . ." Her voice trailed off.

"Why can we not go back home to Kent and bury Father there?" demanded Faith.

"Do you think people would not ask the same questions there?" snapped Myrtle. "A sudden death right after a breaking scandal? Other doctors would be called in to examine him, and they might not be as . . . reasonable as Dr. Jacklers. No, by the time we return to the mainland, your father must be decently buried, with a doctor's testimony that he died of an accident, so that nobody can argue. The burial must be here, and it must be today!"

When the coach drew up outside the Sunderlys' house, Myrtle seemed to come to a decision. She called Mrs. Vellet over and passed Howard into her care. Then she rapped on the ceiling of the coach.

"Driver—take us to the magistrate's house!"

The driver objected—he was not a hansom cab, and had been hired for a funeral, not "gadding about." Myrtle coldly carried her argument through use of coin.

Faith felt a creeping discomfort. Widows in full mourning were not supposed to make house calls, she knew that. In fact, it was shocking for them to visit anybody or be seen out in public. But what else could Myrtle do?

"They must understand," she announced, apparently answering Faith's unspoken thought. "They must see that this is an emergency."

Yes, thought Faith. *They must.*

With some apprehension, she watched the road wind

its way up to the Paints, looking ever more affronted and wind-beleaguered. The little black coach drew up, serenaded by the usual dog barks.

Faith and Myrtle dismounted, and there was another argument with the driver, who was less than keen on waiting. Another coin persuaded him to stop for a while, but he made it clear that he did not mean to "lose his Sunday."

He looked frightened. Faith guessed that he was worried about the throng in the churchyard. Perhaps he did not want to be seen nailing his colors to the mast of a sinking ship.

Mother and daughter climbed the steps and rapped with the great knocker. The wheezing servant they had met before opened the door, and looked surprised as he recognized them.

"We need to speak to Mr. Lambent, on a matter of urgency," explained Myrtle. "As both a friend and a magistrate."

The servant was most apologetic. Mr. Lambent was out of the house and would not be back for several hours. Mrs. Lambent was at home, however. Would Mrs. and Miss Sunderly care to wait in the parlor, while he found out whether Mrs. Lambent was accepting visitors?

The parlor was small and smelled of disuse. Myrtle paced, with a sweep and swish of her long black skirts, and Faith clasped her hands so tight they hurt, trying to tame the unruly rookery of her thoughts.

"It is better than nothing," Myrtle muttered under her breath. "If we can talk her round, then she may win her husband to the cause."

Here the clocks were not stopped, and the rose-painted carriage clock showed them all too clearly the creep of time. A quarter of an hour. Half an hour. Three quarters.

When they had been waiting for nearly an hour, the servant

brought them a freshly sealed letter on a silver plate, and left them with it. Faith read it over Myrtle's shoulder.

> *Mrs. Sunderly,*
>
> *You must pardon me for taking so long to respond, but when I first heard that you were waiting in my parlor, I was not disposed to believe it. Although I appreciate that things are done differently in London, I did not think that the Capital had lost all sense of propriety, decency, and good taste.*
>
> *I will confess that I was already surprised at your decision to hold your husband's funeral on a Sunday. That is all very well for farmhands and factory girls, but there is little excuse for a respectable family to desecrate the Sabbath in that way.*
>
> *This visit is another matter. When I buried my first husband, I retreated into mourning like an anchoress into her cell. For that first year, nothing would have persuaded me to sully my husband's memory by gallivanting around in public. I would sooner have joined him in his grave.*
>
> *Thus, with great regret, I cannot in all conscience agree to receive you.*
>
> *Your obt servant,*
> *Agatha Lambent*

Myrtle stood staring at the letter for a while. Her shoulders rose and fell as though she was having trouble breathing, and then wordlessly she walked out of the parlor. The old servant hurried to open doors for them, until Faith and Myrtle were out in the courtyard once more.

Faith felt sick with anger, mortification, and misery. They had been kept waiting on purpose and then dismissed as cruelly as possible.

"That poisonous, hateful hypocrite!" Myrtle was bristling. "How dare she preach at us! An 'invalid,' is she? I caught a scent of her 'medicine,' and I know gin when I smell it!"

There was no sign of the coach in the courtyard, nor in the stable block or on the road. The driver had held true to his threats and had left.

"Oh, I cannot *bear* to beg that woman for use of their carriage!" exclaimed Myrtle. But there was no help for it, so she returned to knock on the door once more.

Nobody answered.

They knocked and knocked, but there was no response. Once Faith glanced up at a first-floor window and glimpsed a face, peering between the curtains. She thought it looked a little like Miss Hunter.

"How far is the house?" asked Myrtle at last.

"Four miles," said Faith, remembering the map.

"Then we shall have to walk quickly," said Myrtle in a tight, small voice, "if we are to outpace the rain."

They failed. The rain caught up with them halfway. First it menaced them with freak patters that left individual dark splashes on their clothes. Then the patter became a rattle, then a rush, that filled their ears and whitened the air. The road turned to mud under their feet, jumping and frothing as if it were boiling.

Myrtle's little chiffon parasol could not contend with the weather. Soon it was slick and slack, water forcing its way through and running in rivulets down its handle. Their bonnets became sodden, sagging under the weight of the moisture.

With unwilling pity, Faith saw Myrtle's beautiful mourning outfit ravaged by the weather. Her black skirts and stockings were soon thick with mud. Worse, the crêpe of her dress began to come apart, the glue that bound the silk fibers melting away.

As they stumbled, Myrtle began to cry. Not with pretty, artificial, smelling-salt tears, but like a little child, with great, racking sobs. Mother and daughter stopped under a tree for shelter, but it provided little defense. Myrtle cried and cried, each sob cutting a ragged line through Faith's heart.

"We are nearly home," Faith heard herself saying, in the tone she might have used with Howard. "We are nearly there. It is not so bad."

She ran out into the rain, looking for a cottage or hut, anywhere they could take cover. In the middle of a leafy crop field she thought she saw a figure and called out, only to realize that the distant shape was a scarecrow.

Myrtle barely looked up when Faith returned with the scarecrow's coat. Faith put it around her mother's shoulders, covering the worst holes in the disintegrating dress.

It was a long walk back, and by the time they reached the house both were shivering violently. Mrs. Vellet looked appalled, and sent for hot water to be boiled for baths. Somewhere around the corner, however, Faith heard a small, stifled shriek of laughter. It sounded like Jeanne.

Even when she was alone, all Faith could think of, all she could hear, was that laugh, that squeal of incredulous, delighted mirth. It stuck in her like a knife.

Faith stood alone in her room, drenched to the skin, and wondered where her tears had gone. There had been some earlier; she remembered them, hot and helpless. Now she felt as if all the weeping had been scoured out of her.

She thought of the laugh. Jeanne laughing. Then she remembered the stereoscope image of the murdered woman, and imagined her with Jeanne's face.

She imagined the church burning with all the people inside. She saw herself standing outside with a flaming brand, watching the door jump and rattle as they tried to get out.

There was a long mirror in Faith's room, decently cloaked in crêpe.

When there's death in the house, mirrors are hungry, her nursemaid had told her long ago. *If we don't cover them, they suck in the poor dead soul and trap it. And if a living person looks in one, sometimes they see the dead person staring back, and get pulled into death too.*

In a house of death, anything might be waiting there in the mirror. Waiting to steal your soul.

She reached out and took hold of the crêpe, feeling its rasping roughness. With one tug she pulled it down.

In the dull light of the room, the mirror might have been a gilt-edged doorway. On the other side of the portal Faith saw a young witch with eyes like fierce stars. Her hair snaked in loose, slick tendrils over her shoulders. Rainwater glistened on her cheeks. Her simple, high-collared dress was a hungry, mineshaft black. She sucked the light from the room.

Was this Faith, the good girl?

The girl in the mirror was capable of anything. And she was anything but good, that much could be seen at a glance.

I am not good. Something in Faith's head broke free, beating black wings into the sky. *Nobody good could feel what I feel. I am wicked and deceitful and full of rage. I cannot be saved.*

She did not feel hot or helpless anymore. She felt the way snakes looked when they moved.

Chapter 15

LIES AND THE TREE

"SHHHHH . . ."

The trinket snake flinched when she opened its cage. It tugged itself into a tighter coil, then calmed as it tasted Faith's scent on the air. They were kin. It slid up her arm with the lazy beauty of ink flourishes in water. Its scales were dry silk and leather, evening cool. The flicker of its tongue tickled her cheek.

Faith's fingers crept under the cloth and bedding and closed upon her father's papers. Instead of a guilty sense of sacrilege, she felt only excitement.

I am all that you have left, Father. I am your only chance of justice and revenge. And I need answers from you.

She stiffened as she heard rapid steps outside and the faint echoing slop of water in a metal vessel. But it was only a servant fetching water for her mother's bath. They would not bother her.

Faith had dropped out of the household's thoughts like a coin into the lining of a coat. Quiet people often do. And nobody would be surprised that she had retired to her room. After the trials of the day, everybody would expect her to need to lie down. Exhaustion was the natural, the *ladylike*, response.

For now, they could think what they liked if it bought her some privacy.

She pushed her travel trunk against the door so that she could not be surprised. Her sodden outer clothes she removed and hung up. Then she fed and stoked the fire and settled down in a chair with the papers, so close that the heat seared the skin of her cheeks and hands. She could see her skirts start to steam. It made her feel like a salamander, or some misty female monster of myth. Her hair was drying into stiff tentacles.

By the ruddy light of the hearth, she began to examine her father's papers.

There were a great number of them. Many were letters from other scientists, filled with wordy compliments, clever jokes in Greek, reminiscences, and introductions. There were invitations to give lectures, debates about the age of certain teeth, or the best recipe for "seize" to preserve bones. Some papers appeared to be bills of sale, accounts, or receipts. There were even some tattered and stained sheets with royal crests and swirling calligraphy in a mix of English and French. Faith realized these last must be passports and visas from the Reverend's travels.

As hours passed, and her clothes dried on the guard, Faith leafed through delicate sketches of poisonous plants and tropical birds, maps of excavations and meticulous observations. There followed the scrawled sketches she had glimpsed before, after her father's strange, yellow-eyed episode. Again she was struck by how different they were from the other drawings, how feverish and crude.

Finally her fingers rested on the leather book she had found under his bed. She had left it until last because it looked so much like a journal or private diary. But she could no longer allow him secrecy.

She opened it, and began to read the words carefully inscribed in her father's precise, elegant hand.

A Study of the Alleged Virtues of the "Mendacity" Tree

I first heard of the so-called Mendacity Tree when on a visit to southern China in 1860. My visit proved ill-timed, and as I was traveling through the Yunnan region I heard rumors of the fresh conflict between British and Chinese forces. Uncertain where I might meet hostility, I sought accommodation in a riverside village and waited for further news.

There by chance I made the acquaintance of one Mr. Hector Winterbourne, a fellow natural scientist. He was a veteran of many excavations and a fanatical collector, with a passion for monstrosity and oddity of all sorts. Pleased at the chance of an educated conversation with one of my countrymen, I spoke with him for the greater part of the night.

He waxed fervent about his latest obsession, a plant he had encountered in an obscure legend three years before. This tree was said to resemble a creeper, but to bear citrus-like fruit possessed of extraordinary properties. The plant thrived in darkness or muted light, and would only flower or bear fruit if it was fed lies.

This I dismissed as plainly fantastical, and was surprised when my companion did not share my skepticism. When I asked him how a plant could be "fed" a lie, he said that the falsehood needed to be whispered to the Tree, and then circulated widely. The more important the lie, and the larger the number of people prevailed upon to believe it, the larger the fruit.

Should anybody consume that fruit, he claimed, they would be granted knowledge of a most secret sort, and on a matter close to their heart.

Faith stared. What was this fairy tale? Why had her famously rational father written of such a thing? At the same time, her thoughts slid to the shrouded plant pot her father had been so desperate to conceal.

When I pointed out the absurdity of such a notion, Winterbourne showed me a piece of dried peel, not unlike that of a lime, and assured me that two years before he had purchased a Mendacity fruit at considerable price and consumed it. He would not divulge the "secret" he had learned, but grimly assured me that it was of no small import.

He said that he had bought this fruit from a Dutchman named Kikkert, who had set himself up in the Indies as an information broker. Winterbourne believed that Kikkert had been "feeding" the Tree by passing false information to some buyers, so that he could sell the fruit to others, or learn secrets worth a high price. It was a dangerous game, and Kikkert fled town before Winterbourne could learn more.

Winterbourne believed that he had traced the Dutchman's movements to Persia, but there had lost track of him. It was by the merest chance that he had recovered the trail. Winterbourne had come to China to assist with an excavation, but on the verge of departing had heard reports of the sudden and suspicious death of an old Dutchman matching the description of Kikkert. Now Winterbourne was traveling upriver to investigate, and to see whether he could find any trace of the legendary plant.

That night I retired, filled with the conviction that Kikkert had been a charlatan and that my new friend was little short of a madman. Nonetheless, as I attempted to sleep I found that the notion of this plant had taken possession of my imagination. His very earnestness, after the fact, impressed itself upon me. All those who thirst for knowledge must be tempted by the thought of learning untold secrets with one bite.

I rose next morning, interested in speaking with Winterbourne again, only to discover that he had chartered a boat at dawn and departed upriver with his entourage. By the time I heard of the British victory, I had decided to abandon my erstwhile plans. Instead I resolved to follow Winterbourne and learn more of his mysterious plant.

When at last I arrived at the town that had been mentioned to me, I made inquiry and discovered that—

Faith startled as a loud bang sounded at her door, causing her travel chest to jump half an inch.

"Faith!" It was Howard's voice, sounding petulantly hoarse. "Fa-a-aith!"

"Howard . . . I am asleep!" Faith looked around her at the papers scattering her lap. "I am ill! I am lying down!"

"I stepped on a grave," came the plaintive cry. "My foot is muddy. Can I come in?"

Howard's voice tugged at Faith. He did not want to be alone, she knew it. His world had ended just as hers had, and he did not understand how or why and the phantasms of his own mind were bellowing at him from the dark places. But when Faith thought of opening the door she felt terror. There was a pit outside, filled with *his* fears, *his* confusion, and *his* misery, and if she fell into it she would tumble down, down, down, until there would be no Faith left for solving mysteries, or righting wrongs. She would lose this strange wild fire, and right now she needed it.

"Never mind your foot!" she called back as evenly as she could manage. "Just . . . be a good boy, and . . . copy out some Scripture." It was all she could think of to say, to pretend that it was just another Sunday. "If you are very good and quiet, and write out your lines, everything will be better in the morning. Oh—write with your right hand, How!"

Faint, scuffing steps moved away across the landing. A moment later Faith heard the nursery door shut quietly and with painful care. She felt a numb ache at the sound. There seemed to be no guilt left in her, just a bruise where it should have been.

All was quiet again. Faith prised open the journal again, and found her place once more.

. . . and discovered that the Winterbournes had taken rooms in a shabby inn. When I visited it, however, I found the establishment in disarray. Hector Winterbourne had been discovered raiding the house of a man thought to have been murdered, and was under arrest on suspicion of involvement in that murder.

I prevailed upon the local authorities to let me visit Winterbourne, and found him in a pitiable state. Like many confined to those noxious cells, he had contracted malaria, which was rife in those parts. I promised to do all I could to secure his freedom, and he confided in me his latest suspicions about the location of the Mendacity Tree, begging me to find it if he could not.

I was unable to save him. His fever killed him in his cell before I could arrange his release.

Following his instructions, however, I found a little stone hut in the bamboo forest a few miles from Kikkert's house. Within its dark, dank recesses I discovered a dry-looking, vine-like plant that appeared to have dropped most of its leaves.

My extrication of the specimen from this murky enclosure was nearly catastrophic, both for the plant and for myself. While I had noted Winterbourne's comments regarding the Tree's preference for darkness, I had not anticipated the violence of its reaction to daylight. Only by hastily covering the plant with my coat did I avoid disaster. Never again would I be so incautious.

It took a long while for the specimen to recover from this incident. Through careful experimentation I discovered that it thrived on dank or moist air and was best nourished by slightly brackish water. Rather than relying on the sun's rays, it suffered ill effects from all brilliant light and most particularly the beams of natural daylight. By nurturing it in the right conditions, I eventually succeeded in coaxing it back to health.

There followed several meticulous sketches of a plant at various stages of recovery. First a small tangle of blackened, dead-looking vines, stripped of foliage. Then sketches of tiny scroll-like buds, which gradually unfurled into slender, forked leaves.

I must ask myself why I devoted so much time to this project, and neglected so many others. It is possible that from the earliest moment I felt a yearning to discover something of wonder.

I have lived long enough to see the death of wonders. Like many others, I have dedicated my life to investigating the marvels and mysteries of Creation, the better to understand the designs of our Maker. Instead, our discoveries have brought us doubt and darkness. Within our lifetime, we have seen Heaven's lamp smashed and our sacred place in the world snatched from us. We have been dethroned and flung down among the beasts.

We thought ourselves kings of the ages. Now we find that all our civilization has been nothing but a brief, brightly lit nursery, where we have played with paper crowns and wooden scepters. Beyond the door are the dark wastes where leviathans wrestled for millennia. We are a blink of an eye, a joke amidst a tragedy.

All these thoughts were unspeakable torment to me.

Faith had never, never heard such despairing words uttered by her father, or anyone else for that matter. She sometimes sensed the great cracks of doubt that the revelations of science had opened up under people's feet. But nobody mentioned them, not directly. They stepped over them or edged past them and said nothing.

Thus I began my experiments with the Tree, which of course necessitated the use of falsehoods. It was not my habit to indulge in deception, but in the event this acted in my favor. Since deceit was known to be contrary to my nature, none was expected from me. I began with a small lie, which I whispered to the plant, conscious of the absurdity of the proceeding. I adopted a counterfeit illness, and feigned a limp for the better part of a month.

For the very first time since its germination, the plant flowered, producing a small white bloom resembling that of a lemon tree. The petals fell away, and it bore a tiny fruit, slightly smaller than a common cherry, which quickly ripened to olive green streaked with gold.

I resolved to pluck and eat the fruit, taking all reasonable precautions. The flesh was surpassingly bitter. As to the effect upon my faculties, I have never eaten opium and thus cannot compare the experience, but I suspect it was not dissimilar.

In this state of bedazzlement I found myself a traveler in the country of my own body, my veins red-gold and fierce as lava streams, my spine a mountain ridge, my lungs catacombs. I traveled all the way down to the promontory of my left big toe, and there discovered simmering, noxious green lakes that turned my stomach.

Not two months after this vision I suffered pain and swelling in that toe for the first time. My doctor confirmed that it was the onset of gout, a condition that I have suffered ever since. My vision, therefore, had conveyed to me a truth that at that time was known to nobody, least of all myself. However, it was not a particularly edifying, useful, or impressive truth.

Considering the matter, however, I had a moment of insight. The lie I had told pertained to my own personal health, as did the secret I had been granted. Was it possible that lie and secret were linked, and that the plant fed a certain lie would release a secret on a connected matter?

My first experiment had been an attempt to learn whether the Tree truly possessed the bizarre qualities that Winterbourne had claimed. Now that it began to seem possible, I dared to ask myself another question. What secret unfathomed by man did I actually wish to uncover?

It was easily answered. There was one thing I wanted, nay, needed to know.

For a long time I had been losing my grip on the rock of my faith, as wave after wave of new knowledge struck me cruelly. My former certainties were now broken timbers on the tide. I needed to know, once and for all, wherefore came Man. Was he crafted in God's image and given the world, or was he the self-deluding grandson of some grimacing ape? If I knew, then my turbulence of mind would be over. I could recover my peace of mind, or resign myself to despair.

Faith halted, staring at the page. She felt shocked, as if she had seen her father break down in front of her. The Reverend's faith had always seemed vast and invulnerable as a cliff-face. She had never guessed at the doubts secretly quarrying their way into the heart of the rock. It was like learning that God had ceased to believe in Himself.

I resolved that I would wrench this knowledge from the Tree. It would be done to calm not only my mind, but all those similarly tormented and bewildered.

If I wished for a secret relating to the origins of Man, then my lies must relate to it also. To earn a secret so profound, I would need to tell momentous lies, and make as many people as possible believe them. My great project unfurled before me, and I could see what needed to be done. I was respected as a natural scientist, consulted, trusted. If I made claims, they would be believed. If I presented fossils or finds, they would not be questioned. I could fabricate at will, and I would not be doubted.

In the interests of Truth, I would lie. I would deceive the world, then bring back knowledge that would benefit all of Mankind and perhaps save its soul. I would muddy the waters for a time, so that in the end they might run truly clear. I would borrow from the Bank of Truth, but in the end would pay back in full and with interest.

"No," whispered Faith. "No. No. No."

But the next page and the next were filled with meticulous details of his falsehoods. There were careful sketches of fossils, before and after his painstaking alterations.

The largest picture showed his most famous find, the New Falton Nephilim, as it had been before he assembled it. Not a winged human shoulder, but a faint tracery of fossilized feathers glued to the stony shoulder of another creature, with a precision and artistry that were almost beautiful.

"Choose a lie that others wish to believe" was written beneath it. *"They will cling to it, even if it is proven false before their face. If anyone tries to show them the Truth, they will turn on them and fight them tooth and nail."*

And he *had* chosen such a lie. A beautiful proof of the truth of the Bible story of the Nephilim. Faith remembered the old man at the Lambents' house, so feverish in his belief in the fossil, so *devout*. The "Nephilim" had been a floating timber in the cruel new seas of doubt. Of course people had clung to it.

The scandal, the outcry, the accusations of fraud . . . it was all true. Her father *had* faked fossils. He *had* lied about his findings. He *had* deceived his friends, his colleagues, his family, and the world.

Nothing less than this would have convinced Faith. Nothing less than this confession in her father's distinctive, precise hand. She could no longer feel shock or surprise, only a sense of ever-spreading darkness. A frail, lost part of her wheeled helplessly in that dark, like a dove in a shadowed vault, crying, *Who was this man, then? Whom have I loved all these years? Did I know him so little?*

But she *had* loved him. She had loved him too hard and too long to loose her hold even now. She had nailed her very heart and soul to his mast.

Faith wrapped her arms around the little journal and held it tight to her chest, eyes squeezed shut. She imagined him soldiering on toward truth through a poisoned jungle of concealment, danger, and enmity, courageous but solitary. How lonely his secrecy must have been!

"You did it to help mankind," Faith whispered. "They did not understand you, but *I* do." She could forgive him, even if nobody else could. That made him more human, and brought him closer to her.

She flicked hastily past the drawings of his false fossils, unwilling to look at them. They were followed by records of his visions. These were generally vague and difficult to comprehend, and this appeared to infuriate him.

The first showed him a shadowy jungle where a cruel-beaked shadow glided slowly downward, light flecks catching on its reptilian eyes and its blue-and-scarlet feathered wings. The second showed islands boiling into being like swelling bubbles in a porridge pot, their volcanoes spewing white smoke. Another revealed a skirmish, a band of small, unshaven men in rough hides battling larger, manlike creatures with thick necks, their sloping faces and limbs so thickly muscled that they looked unreal.

The last vision was the most detailed.

I was at my club, and somebody placed On the Origin of Species *in my hands. I tried to read it, but the words skimmed and danced before my gaze. When I raised a hand to rub at my eyes, my fingers tickled my face. They were covered in fur.*

In the silver back of my snuffbox I saw my own face reflected. Above my cravat yawned a tawny, wolfish jaw with long incisors and canines. Hurriedly I raised the book before my face to hide my disfigurement and peered over it to see whether anybody had noticed my transformation.

The club was in disarray. The footmen swung from the chandeliers, monkey-faced and cackling. One member bared rodent teeth in a snarl, fighting a toad-featured rival for a plate of oys-

ters. Another flailed his arms, upsetting crockery, and gobbled everything within reach of his pelican bill and slack, sack-like throat. A dropped cigar set a curtain on fire, but nobody moved to put it out. Instead the smoke only caused more howls, roars, hisses, and screeches.

I tried to keep my head, and made my way out of the room. I was looking for the old man whom I knew ran the club and lived on the topmost floor. He would explain everything and put things to right.

With every set of stairs I climbed, however, things became worse. On the first floor the members had torn off their waistcoats, crawling and capering in their shirtsleeves. Their faces were distorted to the likenesses of beasts I had never seen before, some with scale-crested brows or monstrous tusks. On the second floor the members were all but naked, sliding and slithering through puddles of spilled port, slender tongues darting from their lizard mouths.

On the third floor I found myself before a door with gilded paneling, and knew that beyond it I would find the old man.

As I reached for the door, my name was spoken. My daughter Faith was standing beside me.

I felt terror and outrage at the sight of her. She should not have been in the club at all, and I did not wish her to see my fangs and fur. The greatest horror was seeing her succumb to the curse of that place. As I watched, the youthful skin of her face started to split, showing the scales beneath.

This apparition owed itself to the fact that my daughter had intruded into my library and interrupted my vision. I believe that she nearly roused me from it, but as my mind started to surface I was coherent enough to banish her hence.

Faith swallowed. Now at least she understood the strange,

quiet savagery of her father's response when she had roused him from his stupor. But what damage had she done in interrupting him? Had she robbed mankind of an eternal truth?

When my daughter was gone, I opened at last the gilded door.

There was no chamber beyond. Instead a terrible foaming cataract struck and engulfed me. The room filled with water in an instant. I was spun around and over and then drifted down, down, down. I was no longer in a building but in an interminable murky sea. My lungs breathed the water, and I knew with despair that I would sink into an ever deeper darkness for millennia multiplied by millennia, and never drown. I was alone, but for tiny motes of gold that swam, circled, and hunted each other.

And that was the whole of my vision. That was the entire reward for my efforts, sufferings, and trials.

I had entertained high hopes of this vision. It was the fruit resulting from my fabrication of the so-called New Falton Nephilim, and I had left it to swell and ripen far longer than any of the others. I felt entitled to expect that it would justify all the sacrifices I had made. The fickle world was turning on me, but at least I would achieve my goal.

Instead, this latest magic-lantern show has filled me with further turmoil and dread. I am not blind to the interpretation that can be placed upon its images: the relentless turning back of the clock, the regression of Man into Beast, the return to a primordial slime. That is the easy explanation, but to accept it is to resign myself to despair. I must seek further. My quest cannot end thus.

After everything I have done, I find myself empty-handed and at a dead end. I must coax another fruit from the Tree, but I cannot see the way. However ingenious a falsehood I contrive, nobody will now believe me. If I cannot rescue my reputation, all has been for naught.

There followed some two dozen pages of sketches, jottings, and tables of figures, but Faith's mind was too full to take them in. She closed the book slowly.

No wonder he had been so protective of his plant, and so reluctant to talk about it or let it out of his sight. No wonder he had snatched his papers from Faith's hand, and lost his temper when she admitted to having opened his strongbox.

Faith had hoped that there might be information in the journal that could somehow be used to clear his name. That hope was dead. No, nobody else could ever be allowed to read it! If the contents became public, he would be proven a fraud, and probably remembered as a madman to boot.

So, was this madness? Had this obsession and all these visions been a symptom of a diseased mind?

Perhaps. Or perhaps right now Faith was the only living person who knew the location of the Mendacity Tree, a wonder of the earth, which might draw forth untold secrets and unravel countless mysteries.

Faith had to know, one way or another. If the Tree could deliver secrets, then perhaps it would unravel for her the mystery of her father's death.

Chapter 16

ANGRY SPIRIT

AT ABOUT EIGHT O'CLOCK, THE HOUSEKEEPER
brought a supper tray to Faith's room. Faith thanked her,
declared that she would be turning in early, and declined the
warming pan. The housekeeper departed, and Faith was left to
herself for the night.

She gobbled her food down quickly, then quietly put on
the rest of her damaged funeral clothes once again. Everyone
had already seen them wet and muddy, so probably would not
notice if they became wetter and muddier overnight. She lit a
lantern to take with her, but turned the flame low and covered
it with a cloth, just as her father had done.

She slipped out through her private door into the roof garden, which still dripped and glistened after the recent rain. The
sky overhead was still grimly gray. As she slipped through the
gate and down the steps, she could hear the busy clatter of pans
and voices in the scullery. She took an oblique route across the
garden, creeping behind the outbuildings so that she was less
likely to be spotted.

Faith hurried along the seaward path, hoping that she had
remembered the tide table correctly. When she reached the

beach, she was relieved to see that the tide was low and the sea calm, just as she had hoped. If she was right, it would ebb for another hour, then start coming back in. The waters would be calmer, and the currents would be her friend.

Feeling exposed, Faith scanned the cliff-tops, but could see no sign of anybody watching her. The half-dry tendrils of her hair whipped her face.

It was difficult dragging the boat by herself, but she finally wrestled it into the water. She clambered in and used one of the oars to push away from the shore.

Faith had never rowed before, and soon discovered it was much harder than her father had made it look. At first she tried to row facing forward so that she could see where she was going, pushing the blades through the water instead of pulling, but the oars floundered weakly and kept rattling out of their sockets. She made much better headway when she rowed facing backward, as her father had done. Very soon she was out of breath, and the muscles in her arms and shoulders ached. She was all too glad that she had loosened her training corset before coming out.

Whenever she twisted around in her seat to look ahead, she seemed to be heading straight out to sea or about to founder on a submerged crag. Thankfully the rocks were easier to see by twilight than they had been at night.

And there in the gray light was the sea cave, like a dark Gothic arch. Its open mouth swallowed each wave, then vomited foam.

Heaving furiously at the oars, she brought the boat close to the cave. Once again a wave swept her into its mouth, but less violently than before, and the boat ran aground far closer to the cave entrance.

Faith clambered out onto slithering rock, half deafened by the echo of the water, and tethered the boat to the same column as before. She took up the lantern, hitched her skirts, and scrambled up onto the rocky platform beyond the boat, then through the rough, triangular hole into a larger cave beyond. Here the light was dim, only a little leaking in from the cave mouth behind her. Remembering her father's warning about the plant's "violent reaction" to light, she kept her lantern almost entirely covered, allowing only a sliver of radiance to play across her surroundings.

The cave was roughly domed, cracks and streaks running down the ceiling like vaulting. Here and there she could see shadowy fissures and openings leading to other caves.

On the far side of the cave, on a jutting oblong shelf of rock, stood a shrouded shape, the terra-cotta pot just visible beneath the cloth.

There was something strange in the echoes of the vaulted cave. The roar of the nearby sea had been softened and twisted, so that the air seemed full of sighs. Faith could not help glancing over her shoulder, thinking that somebody had just let out a long breath immediately behind her. That cold smell was bitter here, making her eyes sting.

Slowly Faith slithered her way up the sloping stone floor. When she stood by the rocky shelf, she reached up and slowly pulled at the cloth. She felt resistance, the tug of thorns, and then the oilskin came away, revealing a black, indistinct tangle that spilled over the edges of the pot, a scribble of shadow on shadow.

The not-noises in the cave became louder, as if the breathers had drawn closer. Gingerly she raised her lantern, letting a little bar of quivering light fall upon the plant.

The light glistened on slender, blue-black leaves, long thorns, dull golden pearls of sap glowing on black knobbed stems . . . and then before her eyes Faith saw the illuminated foliage flinch, wrinkle, and subside, hissing with the angry sibilance of a beast disturbed.

Hastily she turned the lantern's beam away again, so that the plant became an inky, indistinct mound once more. Even when the hissing desisted, she did not dare illuminate the plant again. Instead, she reached out and gently stroked her fingers through its foliage, seeing it by touch.

To her relief, the light did not appear to have done too much damage. The leaves were cold and slightly clammy, and left her fingers covered in a moist stickiness like honey. She could find no fruit.

Imaginary ants led a parade up her spine. There was no mistaking the shape of the leaves, which forked then tapered to two narrow points. She had seen their likeness painstakingly sketched in her father's journal. This was the Mendacity Tree, his greatest secret, his treasure and his undoing. The Tree of Lies. Now it was hers, and the journey he had not finished stretched out before her.

She lowered her face until her mouth nearly touched the leaves. The smell was a snow-bite behind her eyes, and ached in her temples.

"Father cannot come to you anymore," she whispered. "He is dead and in the church crypt. I want to find out who murdered him. Will you help me?"

There was no reply. Of course there was no reply.

"Do you want a lie?" asked Faith, feeling as though she were offering some dangerous animal a treat. She almost expected it to bristle again, like a hungry wolf.

Choose a lie that others wish to believe, her father had written.

Faith remembered the conversation at the graveside, and Tom's suggestion that her father be staked "to keep the ghost down." She thought of Howard's superstitious terror, the stopped clocks, and the cloaked mirrors.

"I have a lie for you." She closed her eyes and whispered, "My father's ghost walks, seeking revenge on those who wronged him."

Something very gently stroked her face, and Faith pulled back, opening her eyes. There was no sign of motion among the plant's glossy leaves. She would leave it here, where it was unlikely to be discovered. Her father had chosen its hiding place well.

As she slowly retreated from the central cavern it seemed to her baffled ears that the echoes had a new timbre. She almost thought she could hear faint traces of her own words in the air, swaying and unfurling.

A stake through the heart at the crossroads, so the dead cannot find their way home . . .

Slipping back into the darkened house in her ravaged black dress, Faith herself felt a little like a lost soul returning. She paused to listen, but all was still quiet. Everybody had gone to sleep. The house was hers.

So what should she do? Where should she start?

Faith narrowed her eyes, then smiled in the darkness as inspiration dawned. She crept into the kitchen, where she was sure she had seen . . . yes.

The careful light of her lantern showed her a bell board on the wall, just above head height. There were seven bells, each dangling at the bottom of a spiral curl of metal, which in turn was attached to one of the seven wires running horizontally across the wall. Each bell had a different label—Master Bedroom, Second Bedroom, Third Bedroom, Drawing Room, Library, Nursery, Dining Room. The bell pull in each of these rooms tugged a hidden wire, which zigzagged unseen through floors and walls and rang the corresponding bell in the kitchen.

Squinting in the imperfect light, Faith set about unfastening the wires for the Master Bedroom and Third Bedroom and swapping them over.

She crept to the library, and found her father's tobacco box on the desk. She took a pinch and fed it to a candle flame, watching it fizzle and blacken, leaking a scented, bluish plume of smoke. Then, with a letter opener, she slashed a hole in the crêpe covering the mirror, so that a silvery gash was visible through the cloth like a half-open eye.

One last stop. She tiptoed upstairs, listened again for any sign of motion in the bedrooms, then crept into her father's room, closing the door carefully before uncovering her lantern.

The room was still filled with vases of wilting flowers. There was a long crease in the bed where his remains had rested, but his effects had been tidied away into trunks and boxes. The family Bible lay closed on the bedside table.

Faith's mind filled with a thousand angry ideas, but she restrained herself. Too much at once would betray her. She opened the Bible, and hastily leafed through until she found Deuteronomy 32.35.

To me belongeth vengeance, and recompence; their foot shall slide in due time: for the day of their calamity is at hand, and the things that shall come upon them make haste . . .

She left it open on that page, with a single flower petal under the vengeful quotation.

The bell pull by her father's bed was a red corded rope with a tassel. Faith climbed on a chair and used her father's razor to saw through the cord at a high point, so that it was close to snapping. Only then did she leave the room.

If they want a ghost, they will have one.

Chapter 17

A GHOST-KILLING GUN

FAITH WAKENED FROM A DREAM OF BEING BUR-
ied under rubble to find herself still weak and aching. For a
while she lay there, trying to work out why her back, shoulders,
and arms were so sore.

Then everything returned to her in a cold, dark rush. Loss,
the funeral, the journal, the touch of the Lie Tree's leaves
against her face. Her mind spent a few moments in cold, helpless free fall, before her anger spread its wings and buoyed
her up again.

She struggled out of bed. Her arms felt heavy as lead, and
maneuvering them into the sleeves of her spare mourning
clothes was a painful process. These muscles had never before
been used in earnest and were shrieking in protest.

Her hair was a mess of tangles, woven by wind and salt. She
attacked it with her brush until it recovered some of its smooth-
ness and sheen.

Faith tweaked aside the curtain and peered outside. It was
another gray, restless day. The wind fluted in the flues and flattened glossy spirals in the grass, and the trees flung up their
boughs like drowning sailors.

She had a murderer to find, and an island to frighten. Frightened people sometimes made mistakes, and it was a good day to be a ghost.

Faith grasped the blue corded bell pull that hung by her bed and gave it three long, deliberate pulls.

She imagined the servants below staring agog at the bell board as the bell for the empty master bedroom impossibly twitched and chimed. Minutes passed, and nothing happened. Then she heard uncertain steps ascend the servants' stairs and walk along the landing. Faith knelt by her bedroom door and pressed her eye to the keyhole.

Jeanne was hovering outside the Reverend's room, eyes wide, twisting her hands nervously together. As Faith watched, she grasped the door handle and entered the room. Faith was fairly sure she heard a muffled gasp.

Creak. Creak. Faint, cautious footsteps from inside the room. Then there was a short squeal of surprise. Jeanne burst onto the landing in disarray, the red corded bell pull in one hand, and sprinted from view.

Faith smiled to herself as the other girl's steps thundered down the servants' stairs. She had guessed that somebody would give the haunted bell pull an experimental tug. If she had left it unsawn it would have caused the bell for *her* room to ring, and perhaps somebody could have deduced the truth.

Pressing her ear to the wall, she could hear muted conversation taking place somewhere on the servants' stairway.

"You *broke* it?" Prythe was asking, incredulously.

"I only pulled gently!" Jeanne could be heard exclaiming, her voice defiant but shaken. "It came away in my hand! There's all manner of things amiss in that room . . ."

Faith stroked her hand down the bell pull, feeling its roughness under her fingers, tempted to pull it again. No, that would be too much, too fast. Her victims needed time to wonder, to whisper, to tell each other frightened stories.

An hour later, when Jeanne brought the breakfast tray to the day nursery for Faith and Howard, she seemed to have lost her usual self-possession. The cups rattled as she set down the tray, and she barely spared Faith a glance, bobbing the briefest distracted curtsey as she left. Whatever she thought of the mysterious bell, she evidently did not suspect the prim, shy daughter of the house.

Faith could hardly concentrate on her breakfast as she sat at the little wooden table with Howard.

What did she know about the murderer? Almost anybody on Vane *could* have been in Bull Cove that night. However, her father had talked as though he had an appointment at midnight. This had to be somebody that he was willing to meet, though not without a pistol. If he expected danger from this enemy, though, why meet them at all, let alone secretly and unaccompanied in the dead of night?

Then there was the mystery of the pistol. He had gone out armed, but for some reason this had not saved him. And when his body had been laid out, the pistol had been missing from his pocket.

"Other hand, How," she said reflexively, noticing her brother had quietly swapped his cutlery again.

"No!" Howard shouted, in a sudden fit of rebellion. He was shiny-faced and breathless, his face locked in an expression of slightly frantic discontent. Faith could see that he had slept badly, and once again felt a soul-bruise that was not quite guilt.

"Howard . . ."

"No, no, no, no!" Howard shrieked more loudly, pushing

away his plate so that it nearly knocked Faith's breakfast into her lap.

She tried to stay calm, but felt her temper fraying. He was clawing for attention, and it actually felt as though his small, clumsy fingernails were scraping at her mind.

"Behave yourself!" she snapped, losing control. "Or I will put you in the blue jacket!"

It was an ill-judged threat. Howard's mouth fell open and he started to bawl.

"I ha-a-ate you!" he wailed, his words broken and thick with sobs.

The jacket, with its trapped left sleeve, was only meant to be worn when Howard was writing. It was not supposed to be used as a general punishment. Howard liked to understand how things worked, and needed to know that the world was fair. Unfortunately the world was *not* fair, and every time he collided with this fact he lost control completely. If Faith did nothing, he would scream himself sick.

No, the world was not fair. Faith jumped from her seat and stalked across the room, looking for something to kick.

When she glanced back at Howard, he looked very small in his miniature wooden chair. None of this was his fault. He had every reason to be miserable.

Relenting, Faith sat down with a rustle of black skirts. She reached into the trunk of Howard's toys and pulled out his model theatre.

The theatre was box-shaped, its card and paper intricately painted in reds, golds, and greens, with crests, swirls, and angels. The front frame had painted curtains, and you could look through it onto the stage itself, which tapered and receded to a tiny backdrop of blue sky, hills, and a castle.

Faith pulled out the landscape backdrop. There were three others to choose from, one showing the same hillside scene by moonlight, one depicting an indoor scene with pictures and a chandelier, and one with a green-tinted woodland scene. With a deliberate air of absorption, Faith slotted the nocturnal scene into place.

Very quickly Howard stopped screaming. He wandered over and dropped himself heavily beside her to sit cross-legged. Howard was always captivated by her "shows."

"I want Juggler," he said. "And . . . Wizard. And the Devil."

The actors were tiny paper figures, glued to slender sticks so that they could be moved around the stage. Most of them had been created by Faith, carefully drawn, colored, and cut out.

There were slots in the side of the stage, so that Faith could slide the figures in and move them from side to side. They could not move forward or backward though. This frustrated Howard, and several puppet sticks had been broken as a result of this frustration.

Today, as usual, Howard wanted fighting.

"Juggler fights the Devil!" he demanded, thumping his knees.

The tiny green-and-yellow jester fought the red-horned devil to and fro. Today Faith let the Devil win, with much roaring, and flipped the Juggler on to his back to show he was "dead." As always, this made Howard laugh, with a wildness that Faith thought owed something to terror.

"Wizard fights the Devil!"

The Devil fought the Wizard, the Knight, and the Sailor, one by one, and killed them all.

Howard laughed, too high and too loudly. His eyes were round and alarmed, fixed on the grimacing Devil.

"They get up again—all get up—they kill the Devil!"

"But, Howard, they are dead . . ." Faith stopped herself. She flipped the little paper corpses neatly back on to their feet. They mobbed the Devil, who subsided howling on to his back. There was a silence.

"I want the Wise Man," said Howard quietly, as he always did after a fight.

The Wise Man was a Chinaman, with a limpet-shaped hat and a long mustache. His eyes were lopsided, because Faith had drawn him when she was a lot younger and less skilled with a pen, but he was Howard's favorite.

She shuffled him on to the stage.

"Why, it is young Master Howard!" she trilled, in a high, querulous, little-old-man voice.

Howard laughed and hugged his knees. It was the same frightened, exhilarated laugh as when the characters "died." By long tradition, the Wise Man was the only puppet clever enough to see past the stage and notice Howard watching.

"Do you have a question for me today?" Faith asked in her Wise Man voice.

Howard hesitated, his tongue resting against his lower lip, scratching at the sole of his shoe with one fingernail.

"Yes," he said very quietly. "Is the Devil dead?"

"Oh yes, quite dead," the Wise Man assured him.

For most of his six years, Howard had looked to Faith to be his oracle, his almanac, his source of all truth. He had believed everything she told him. This tide was changing though. *Girls don't know about sailing*, he would say suddenly. *Girls don't know about the moon.* There was never any malice or spite in it; he was simply repeating some nugget he had panned from the confident river of adult conversation. There were things that girls did not know, and Faith was a girl. Each time he said such a thing it was a shock, and Faith felt her domain of expertise breaking apart like an ice floe.

Howard still consulted the Wise Man, however, without shame. The Wise Man was not a girl, and the Wise Man knew everything.

"Will the Devil come back again in the night?" Howard's mouth was trembling now. "I heard it in the dark. It went into Father's room. I heard its teeth."

Faith held her breath for a moment, her skin tingling. She had thought herself unnoticed as she crept around the house in the dead of night. But Howard had heard her footsteps. He had heard her sawing through the bell rope with a sound like gnawing teeth.

Howard talked to everybody. He had no guile. He would tell everybody about the steps he had heard, and the sound of teeth. How could she keep him quiet?

Then again, perhaps she did not *need* to keep him quiet.

"How did you know it was the Devil?" asked Faith–Wise Man. "Did it have strange, echoing footsteps?"

Howard picked at his shoe sole and frowned. Then his brow cleared and he nodded.

"Did everything get colder as it passed?" persisted Faith–Wise Man.

Again Howard hesitated, then gave a small shiver and nodded his head. He was not exactly playacting, Faith knew. He now believed he had heard the spectral echo and noticed the uncanny cold.

"Oh, then it was probably just a ghost!" the Wise Man remarked cheerfully.

Howard did not look reassured. "Is it . . . because . . . I trod on a grave?"

"No, no—it won't have been looking for you, Master Howard. Ghosts won't come after a good little boy who says his prayers and copies out his Scripture right-handed. They only hunt *bad* people." Faith had no desire to terrify him.

Howard chewed on his knuckle, making his finger shiny with spit. He seemed a little comforted.

"But . . . if I was . . . bad, and the ghost came back," persisted Howard, "could I *shoot* it?"

Faith's mind leapt back to the image of her father on the beach, jumping at shadows and reaching for his hidden gun. The pistol had been missing from his pocket when his body was brought back. Perhaps it had simply fallen out when he was hurled off the cliff . . . but if she found it somewhere else, perhaps that could tell her where her father had been struck down.

Another thought slipped into Faith's head. She imagined her father's pistol snugly in her hand, its ivory warmed by her grasp. She could not picture her father's murderer—in her mind the enemy was a person-shaped abyss, a roiling storm cloud crackling with malice. Faith thought of leveling the pistol to point at the dark shape's head, and squeezing the trigger . . .

"Yes, Master Howard," she creaked, in her Wise Man voice. "But you need a special ghost gun for that, just as you need an elephant gun for elephants." The little paper figure tottered and shuffled conspiratorially. "Why don't you ask that lazy sister of yours to take you for a walk and see if you can find one?"

Ten minutes later, when Faith led Howard downstairs in his new black outdoor clothes, she found the house quiet. Uncle Miles had departed early to visit Lambent, and Myrtle was still indisposed in her room.

"Good-bye, Mrs. Vellet," Howard called out politely as Faith led him past the drawing room. "I am going out to find a gun to shoot the ghost!"

Mrs. Vellet, who had been watering the flowers, flinched and spilled water over the tablecloth. Jeanne, kneeling in the hearth, dropped her dustpan with a clatter, scattering ash.

"Howard!" protested Faith, casting the housekeeper an embarrassed, apologetic look. "I am so sorry, Mrs. Vellet," she added. "I do not know where Howard gets these ideas."

"But there *is* a ghost!" declared Howard, with bell-like clarity. "I heard it walking around last night—"

"Why don't we go out for a nice walk?" Faith interrupted quickly, taking Howard's hand and guiding him out through the front door. She managed not to smirk as feverish whispers broke out behind them.

She knew that if you wanted somebody to believe something, there was no point forcing it down their throat. Far better to give them a hint, a glimpse, a taste, then snatch it away from them. The faster you ran, the more they would give chase, and the more likely to believe the hard-won information when they caught it.

"Let us go down and search on the beach, shall we?"

As they walked along the path, Faith kept an eye out for any glint of metal or ivory among the long grass, just in case the pistol had fallen out of her father's pocket while he was being carried back to the house. She saw nothing but the wavering grass and the purple-headed nodding of thistles.

On the beach, Howard scrambled over shingle and boulders, rivalling the gulls with his whoops. He was not exactly an image of mourning, but Faith thought that she understood. He was tumbling through feelings that he did not understand, and only knew that he wanted to run and scream.

Faith searched among the boulders, at first directly beneath the crooked tree where her father had lain, then in wider circles, prying into crevices, combing the pebbles with her fingers. The pistol could only have bounced so far.

"I cannot find it!" called Howard.

"No," said Faith thoughtfully. "I do not think it is here."

If her father had not lost his pistol in his fall, then where? Perhaps when he was attacked? The true scene of the crime had to be close by. Even with a wheelbarrow, transporting a body could only be difficult and tiring.

They walked back toward the house, and Faith took a detour into the wooded dell. Now and then unseen birds broke the uneasy peace with a stutter of wings, or called their cut-glass questions to the gray sky. Ferns stroked gently at Faith's skirts.

After ten minutes of searching, she gave up. A dozen pistols might be nestling among the undergrowth and she would never find them.

Just as they were leaving, they chanced upon a clearing where emerald green moss was thick as fur. Howard was fascinated, and began jabbing his heel into it, laughing as it broke away in chunks and revealed the black earth.

"Faith, look!" he shouted, as his heel mashed and tore the green. "Stamp!"

Something caught Faith's eye, a narrow strip of darkness against the green. She walked over and stooped to peer.

"Faith!" called Howard from a little distance. "Faith, look! Look at this!" The little impacts of his heels thudded and squeaked, growing closer and closer. "You're not looking, Faith! Faith!"

The dark strip was not a shadow. It was an indentation. Faith reached out, and her gloved finger traced a narrow groove.

"Stamp!" Howard's small heel stamped on to the mark, obliterating it and nearly catching her fingers.

"Howard!" Faith jumped to her feet. Howard beamed up at her, and for a moment she wanted to slap his proud little face.

When he saw her expression, Howard's smile wavered, then wilted into a downturned pout.

"I was talking to you!" he retorted. "You didn't look when I told you to!"

Faith turned away, biting her lip hard and fighting to compose herself. The damage had been done, and done innocently enough.

"Never mind," she forced herself to say. "It does not matter." They walked out of the dell, Howard lashing at ferns with a stick and Faith fighting back her frustration.

It had been there; she had seen it! A narrow rut, just wide enough to have been made by a barrow wheel. And now it was gone.

Faith's mother had been right after all. The Reverend Erasmus Sunderly really had met his fate in the dell.

When they returned to the house, Jeanne was ready to claim Faith's bonnet and cape.

"Faith, I want to search for the ghost!" declared Howard.

"Oh, Master Howard, you will wear out Miss Faith!" exclaimed Jeanne. "Miss—you do look tired, and you are not yet recovered. Why not let me look after Master Howard for a while?" In spite of the polite words, her tone was briskly insistent and she had already taken Howard's hand. Jeanne was overstepping her place, and clearly knew it, but she had the hard-eyed confidence of a strong personality confronting a weaker one.

And Faith played her part. She looked confused and distressed, but too shy to object as Jeanne led Howard away.

"Now, tell me about your ghost!" she heard the housemaid whisper as they turned the corner.

Faith tried to control her expression. She had filled Howard with her lies like a tiny Trojan Horse, and now he was being wheeled into the enemy camp.

At one in the afternoon, a tinker stopped his cart at the back of the house. He seemed well-known to Prythe and Jeanne, who came out to chat with him.

Crouched in her rooftop-garden aerie, Faith watched them unseen through the creeper-draped railings.

"Don't worry about old Vellet," Jeanne was saying. "She won't be back from her afternoon walk for a bit. Same thing each day. She says she's inspecting the grounds to see that all is well. *I* think she goes somewhere quiet and smokes a pipe." There was a ripple of laughter.

"So . . . the cord just broke?"

"Mrs. Vellet says it's rats in the joists, nibbling the wires," said Prythe. "Well, that was a good, strong pull for a rat. If it gets much bigger, we can fasten a cart to it."

"That's not all." Jeanne was warming to her theme. "You can *smell* him in the house, like he's just brushed past you. The house is cold as a tomb. And sometimes things are moved about, aren't they?"

"There's a pot missing from the greenhouse," agreed Prythe.

Faith was learning something interesting about ghosts. They were like snowballs—once you set them rolling their legend grew without your help.

"No surprise, I say." Jeanne gave the upper windows of the

house a wary glance. "He *murdered* himself, poor damned thing. No wonder he can't rest, with a mortal sin on his soul."

The tinker said something else, of which Faith only caught the words "in her scarecrow coat." He nudged Jeanne, who laughed so loudly she had to cover her mouth.

Faith withdrew into the house once more, seething with vengeful thoughts. For the moment, none of the servants was in the house. She might never have another opportunity like this.

In the library, she plundered the crates of her father's stuffed exhibits. The black vulture, glistening raven, and screaming parrot she lined up on the desk, so that anybody entering would be confronted by three gaping, black-tongued beaks and six cold glass eyes.

Most of the clocks had been set in motion again. She halted each one as she passed. The dead man had left the house but had not gone to his rest. Nobody had the right to feel safe, or to let life restart.

On the dining room mantel she left a stuffed lizard, tucked behind a candlestick and nestled amid the billows of crêpe.

When she reached the door to the servants' stairs, she hesitated. Each time she trespassed, there was a moment where the seal broke, the threshold crossed. This felt like something more, however. She was stepping into a forbidden world, one that she usually had to pretend did not exist.

Faith opened the door. The stairs beyond were far plainer, narrower, and steeper than the main ones, and were lit only by little windows. There were no banisters. She climbed as quickly as she dared, knowing that at any moment the servants might return inside.

At the top, the stair opened into a long, dim room with a high wall on the right-hand side and a sloping ceiling that came down to a few feet above the floor on the left. Evidently the attic had been divided into two rooms. Through a door on the right, Faith could look into the other room, which contained a small four-poster, a green rug, and a pretty but battered little dresser. Faith guessed that it must be the housekeeper's room.

Near the entrance to the nearest room was a simple bed. There were two heavy boots beneath it, and Faith guessed that it must belong to Prythe. Beyond it a thick curtain cut off her view of the rest of the room, acting as a decorous makeshift wall. Faith advanced into the room and pulled back the curtain. Behind it lay another simple bed, which could only belong to Jeanne.

There was something in the plainness that shocked Faith. She stepped toward Jeanne's bed, seeing the little treasures tucked in the box beneath it and scattered on the nearby shelf. A wooden comb, a darning egg, a couple of coils of ribbon, and a muslin bag with "JB" embroidered on to it. She touched the bag, and it made her feel like a thief in a way that handling velvet or satin never had.

Faith was prepared to be cruel. However, she had not expected to feel mean.

Then she remembered Jeanne smirking as Faith's father was denied a grave, and laughing at Myrtle's humiliation and misery. Out of her pocket Faith drew an object that she had taken from one of her father's trunks. It was parchment-yellow, smooth, and cool. It clicked like knitting needles as she turned it over.

Faith carefully slid the cat skull into Jeanne's bed, then patted the blanket back into place. As she crept back down the stairs she kept thinking of it, staring empty-eyed into darkness in its little cloth cave.

Chapter 18

A SIBLING QUARREL

BY THE TIME UNCLE MILES RETURNED FROM HIS visit to the magistrate's house it was three o'clock, and Myrtle agreed to receive him in her bedroom. Wrapped up and propped on cushions, she was still looking unusually waxen-cheeked, and red around the eyes and nose. She was, however, well enough to maintain a shell of her usual manner and insist on Faith's presence.

When Uncle Miles entered, Myrtle sat up.

"Well?" she demanded. "Did you speak to the magistrate? What did he say?"

Uncle Miles glanced over his shoulder, then very carefully closed the door behind him. He sat down in an armchair and let out a long breath.

"He was very pleasant." Uncle Miles frowned at his gloves as he pulled them off. "He was very polite. And I fear he was quite adamant that there *must* be an inquest. If members of the public are asking for one—"

"Pish-tosh!" exclaimed Myrtle. "He is the magistrate! It is his choice!"

"What does an inquest mean?" asked Faith, bubbles of apprehension rising within her. "What will happen?"

"I am very sorry," Uncle Miles explained, "but it means that your father cannot be buried yet. I fear we cannot even take him elsewhere to be buried until this has been settled. There has to be an investigation, and then . . . a hearing. A little trial to decide the cause of death."

Faith was torn. On the one hand, she *wanted* her father's death to be investigated, so that his murderer could be caught. On the other, everyone on Vane seemed convinced that he had killed himself. Once it was clear that the Reverend really had been found dangling from the cliff tree, they would probably take that as proof of his suicide.

"When?" Faith asked. "When is this trial?" Her only hope was to find enough evidence of his murder before the "hearing."

"They have not set the date yet, but it could happen any day." Uncle Miles looked extremely uncomfortable. "My dears, it is all very legal and complicated, and there is no point distressing yourselves over the details—"

"Please, Uncle Miles!" Faith interrupted. "I *do* want to know the details!"

Uncle Miles looked surprised at her outburst, but gave a small shrug of surrender. "Sometimes when there is a sudden death . . . and things do not look quite natural . . . the magistrate gives the parish constable permission to summon a coroner, who investigates. At the inquest the coroner decides upon the cause of death, with the help of a jury of twenty-three local men. In this case, the coroner will be Dr. Jacklers."

"So Dr. Jacklers will be investigating, and will be the final judge," said Myrtle, her eyes narrowed. "Do you know, Miles, I believe I am really *quite* ill. I shall need to send for the doctor tomorrow—when I am looking a little better."

"Doctor's fees? On top of everything else?" Uncle Miles

frowned and exhaled. "No, Myrtle, old girl. I must put my foot down. At this rate you will burn through all our money."

"*Put your foot down?*" Myrtle interrupted sharply. "*Our* money? The money is not yours, Miles. As usual, *none* of the money spent has been yours."

Uncle Miles colored and frowned. "That brings me to something else I wanted to discuss," he said.

There was a thunder-heavy pause. Uncle Miles gave Faith a fleeting glance, and after a moment Myrtle did the same.

"Faith," said Myrtle, "could you . . ." She trailed off, and waved one hand wearily.

"I shall go and read my catechism," Faith said swiftly, and meekly left the room.

Listening at a door on a twisting landing always has its perils. Anybody might open their door and emerge. Somebody might arrive from either of the two staircases and discover one kneeling there. It was hard to focus on the sounds beyond the door, and stay alert for approaching steps at the same time.

Now and then it was worth it, however. Faith bit her lip and gently pressed her ear to the keyhole.

"Myrtle," Uncle Miles was saying, "you need to consider your position. I know what you have been trying to do all this time—how careful you have been with appearances—and it was a valiant effort, but *it has not worked.* The cat is out of the bag. What do you intend to tell the inquest if you are called to testify?"

"I shall tell them exactly what I said before," answered Myrtle firmly. "My dear husband had a very tragic accident."

"You understand the danger if the truth comes out?" Uncle Miles cleared his throat. "If things . . . come to the worst, I shall do everything I can for you . . . but right now you must follow my advice."

"What *are* you advising, Miles?" asked Myrtle suspiciously.

"You must give me all the money you still have, and as many of Erasmus's possessions as possible. We will pretend that they were mine all along—or that he gave them to me."

"I see!" Myrtle's voice was icy. "So that is where this conversation is twisting!"

Faith was angry but bewildered. What was the "danger" her uncle was talking about? Why was he demanding all of her father's possessions?

"It is the only sensible course!" Uncle Miles sounded tired but kind. "You must see that! However much Dr. Jacklers admires you, he cannot ignore evidence. Prythe will not lie under oath; he told us as much."

"No," Myrtle said slowly, "but *you* could."

"I beg your pardon?"

"*You* could testify. *You* could tell them that you found Erasmus in the dell."

"You are asking me to perjure myself?"

"You know what is at stake."

There was a long pause.

"No, Myrtle," said Uncle Miles at last. "Unless you are willing to do what I have asked . . . I am afraid I cannot bring myself to do what *you* ask." He gave a sigh of infinite abused patience. "Well . . . at least let me look after your husband's live specimens to stop them from dying of neglect. I should probably have a glance through his papers as well. I meant to examine them for you yesterday, but could not find them anywhere."

Faith tensed, feeling her jaw clench. No! She could not let her uncle take charge of the Lie Tree or her precious snake! And the journal and vision sketches must never be seen by anyone but herself. In fact, it hurt to think of handing over any of her father's papers. They were a genie bottle, holding her father's thoughts, voice, and secrets, and they were hers. *She* was their guardian.

"Miles." Myrtle's voice was knife-sharp. "Why are you suddenly so interested in Erasmus's papers and specimens? You cannot abide responsibility—it brings you out in a rash. When did you become so eager to trudge through paperwork and adopt an incontinent wombat?"

"Well . . . the flora and fauna need the right treatment, and there might be important matters among the papers requiring immediate action! Debts. Assets. Deeds. Obligations. Appointments, or . . . or even a will."

"Have you become a zookeeper and a lawyer since breakfast?" asked Myrtle.

"Myrtle, this is childish!" Uncle Miles's voice was uncharacteristically agitated. "You and I both know that you have no chance whatsoever of making sense of Erasmus's papers! You *must* let me look at them!"

"Where were you all day?" Myrtle's voice now had a hard edge of suspicion. "You cannot have spent six hours being turned down by the magistrate. Who else did you speak with? What have you heard? Miles, I *know* you."

There was a pause.

"You are . . . not thinking straight, Myrtle." Uncle Miles sounded calmer, but as if his calmness was costing him effort. "It is . . . my fault. I should not have raised these subjects when your nerves were overwrought—"

"Oh, do not speak to me that way!" spat Myrtle. "I am *not* nervous, Miles! I am *not* overwrought! And I am *not* surrendering, not yet! I shall stay on Vane and fight until Erasmus is respectably buried—"

"How?" asked Uncle Miles, his tone hardening. "How will you

stay here? How much money do you have left in Vane? How soon will you have to pay rent on the house, and the servants' wages? How long before we cannot order food for the household?"

There was a long pause.

"I thought as much." Uncle Miles's chair creaked as he stood. "Think about passing Erasmus's effects over to me, Myrtle. I know you will do the sensible thing in the end. But do not leave it too long."

Faith heard her uncle's chair scrape, and left her place by the door, scampering back to her room.

For a moment she wished that she could un-hear the conversation. She did not fully understand it, but the whole thing sounded ominous, like a squabble between conspirators. She had dug down and broken into yet another vein of secrets.

Faith had barely returned to her own room when she received a summons to her mother's chamber.

"Faith, close the door behind you and sit down. Tell me—are your father's papers somewhere safe?"

It was the phrasing that undid Faith. Not *"Did you hide the papers?"* but *"Did you hide them well?"*

Rapidly she weighed her options. She could deny all knowledge of the papers' whereabouts, but Myrtle knew that they had vanished while Faith was alone with them. If Faith's room was searched in good earnest, the papers might be found in the snake cage.

"Yes," she said. "It seemed the best—"

"Yes, indeed." Myrtle cut her short. "Good girl. Will you fetch them for me, please?"

No. Never.

"I . . ." Faith fought to keep her face placid as her mind raced. "I can bring them to you . . . but a lot of them are in Greek, or written in the codes Father used for his notes. *I* can translate them, but it is not easy—"

"Oh, save us! Greek?" Myrtle gave a little groan and a despairing shudder. "That is no use then. *You* will have to read them for me. Let me know what you discover. And let nobody know that you have them. Your uncle will probably ask after them—tell him nothing without my permission."

"What does he want with them?" inquired Faith, glad of the chance to ask the question.

"I do not know," answered Myrtle, "but I know my brother. He has excellent qualities, but in his dear, gentle way he is *always* looking to gain as much as he can, for as little effort as possible."

Faith took a moment, trying to align this description with her cheerful, mild-tempered uncle. After her latest bout of eavesdropping, this was easier than it had been.

"Did you see any papers that might be worth money?" Myrtle asked abruptly. "A letter of credit, a will, an IOU, or anything of that sort?"

"No." Faith watched her mother, marveling at her matter-of-factness.

"If your uncle is interested, there *must* be something valuable." Myrtle bit her lip acquisitively. When Faith left the room, Myrtle was twisting the rings on her fingers and staring pensively into space. Faith wondered what would have happened if Myrtle had claimed the paperwork, and whether she would already have sold off the Lie Tree to buy more dresses.

A poisonous realization crept unbidden into Faith's mind. A wife always had to go begging to her husband for housekeeping money, but a widow could spend her inheritance however she pleased. The Reverend's death had possibly left Myrtle in control of real money for the very first time.

As she lay awake that night, Faith tried to fit all the pieces together. She had so little time! There could be an inquest any day, and when the family's purse was empty the Sunderlys would have to leave Vane in search of more funds, maybe even returning to Kent, or to London where Faith knew her father had savings in the bank. Faith had hoped to investigate subtly and let the fruit of the Lie Tree ripen and swell over weeks. Now there could be no long plans, no slow and safe stratagems.

A short, sharp shriek from above her head jolted her from her thoughts. It took her a moment or two to remember the cat skull in Jeanne's bed. Floorboards creaked above, and she could hear somebody going into high-pitched hysterics, and then other indistinct voices, lower-pitched and soothing.

Faith felt neither triumph nor guilt. The darkness was lonely, and time was running out. She thought of the Lie Tree in its roaring cave, and oddly this made her feel a little less alone.

As sleep cradled her, she imagined her lie spreading silently like dark green smoke, filling the air around the house like a haze, spilling from the mouths of those who whispered and wondered and feared. She imagined it soaking like mist into waiting leaves, seeping like sap down gnarled, slender stems, and forcing itself out into a small, white spearhead of a bud.

Chapter 19

GENTLEMEN CALLERS

DR. JACKLERS WAS INVITED TO CALL AT TWELVE. He arrived at ten, throwing the house into confusion.

When Mrs. Vellet came in to report his arrival, Myrtle was in the drawing room, and the dressmaker had just pinned her into a new dress to check the fit. She was not, in short, ready to play the poignant invalid.

"Of all the people I cannot afford to offend!" Myrtle was flustered beyond measure. "Tell the doctor that I am dressing and that I will be with him shortly. Put him in the library. It has skulls—he will like that. Offer him some tea."

"I beg your pardon, ma'am," Mrs. Vellet answered carefully, "but he says he has arrived early on official business. He begs your permission to make a view of the grounds, ma'am."

Myrtle turned pale and spent a moment chewing her lip.

"We cannot very well deny him," she said reluctantly. "Put Prythe at the doctor's disposal."

"And what shall I do with the young Master Clay?" asked Mrs. Vellet blandly.

"Master Clay?" Myrtle's eyes widened. "Is he here too?"

"Yes, ma'am. He arrived at the same time as the doctor's carriage. He has come to deliver several large bunches of flowers, ma'am."

"Flowers," breathed Myrtle. Her pink, pretty countenance flitted butterfly-like between satisfaction, anxiety, and cool calculation. "We cannot afford to offend the Clays *either*," she murmured. "Make Master Clay comfortable in the conservatory—with some crumpets or cake."

Faith was barely listening. Dr. Jacklers was at the house investigating the Reverend's death. This might be her only chance to talk to him and persuade him that her father had been murdered.

Talking to Dr. Jacklers would be a betrayal, of course. She would be destroying the family's story. Myrtle would be furious. Perhaps she would be more than furious.

You understand the danger if the truth comes out, Uncle Miles had said.

Faith did not understand the danger, but remembering his words she felt a sudden qualm. Perhaps telling the truth really would bring trouble on the family. But how could she let such an opportunity slip through her fingers? She owed it to her father to try.

Faith found the doctor on the grounds, walking in the direction of the cliff-path.

"Ah, I am sorry that you should come upon me like this, Miss Sunderly . . . I am about my duties, I fear." He drew a folded paper from his inner pocket, opened it, and held it out to show its big red wax seal.

. . . as magistrate of the county of Vane do require and permit that Doctor Noah Jacklers shall be called upon as coroner in the inquest of the Reverend Erasmus Sunderly . . .

It had been signed at the bottom by Lambent. His handwriting and signature were large, swooping, and chaotic, a lot like the man himself.

"Do you understand the meaning of the word 'coroner'?" asked Dr. Jacklers, and smiled when Faith nodded. "Good, good. Now, usually a coroner would call in a medical expert, but, ah, since *I* am the only medical expert on the island, I must call in myself." He chuckled briefly.

Faith thought that it must be very relaxing being Dr. Jacklers, deaf to the crunch of other people's feelings beneath his well-intentioned boots.

"And so, you see, I must take a look around the grounds."

"Please let me come with you!" Faith said quickly. "I want to speak with you. There is something you need to know."

The doctor gave a puzzled frown, but followed it with a small bow of consent.

They walked away from the house, Faith fearing all the while that Myrtle might notice her from the window and call her back to the house.

She could not help observing that the doctor was dressed rather well. He wore a blue velvet waistcoat criss-crossed with gold thread, his mustache had been carefully trimmed and waxed, and a gold pin glittered in his cravat. There was a self-conscious eagerness in his manner that grated on her.

She remembered her mother standing close to the doctor and grasping his bare hand, and something twisted sharply in her gut, like the neck of a chicken being wrung. She could have felt sorry for him, if her father was not still lying in the church crypt. Wooing a widow before she was out of mourning was bad form. Beginning a courtship before her husband was even in the ground was sickening.

"What was it you wanted to say?" asked the doctor.

"I was walking in the dell yesterday." Faith took the plunge. "Doctor, there is a place where the moss is scuffed—"

"Ah, I see." The doctor gave her a look filled with patience and sad mirth. "I am sure there is. What a dear, loyal young woman you are!"

It took Faith a moment to realize what he meant, and then the blood rushed to her face.

"No, there really is such a place, and not of my making! Please! Let me show you!"

However, the doctor only gave her a sad, kind look, and continued walking in the direction of the cliff-path. When she caught up with him, he was standing at the very edge, staring down like a stocky hawk contemplating a stoop.

"That tree halfway down—split, and showing white wood," he murmured. "That is a fresh break."

"Sir—did you see this wheel mark?" Faith pointed to what was left of the wheelbarrow rut, now sadly softened with rain.

Dr. Jacklers gave it only the briefest glance. "Oh, that is a mark left by the edge of somebody's boot. There are doubtless a hundred such, now that everybody has been tramping to and fro."

It was a blow, but Faith did not choose to be discouraged.

"Tell me, Dr. Jacklers, could somebody survive that fall if that tree below caught them?"

"I suppose so . . . yes. Though they would be lucky to escape without broken bones."

"Then . . . if Father jumped, why do so above that tree?" Faith moved toward the brink, two yards to the doctor's left. "I would have leapt *here*."

"Miss Sunderly, you are too close to the edge!"

"There is a clear drop here, down to the rocks," said Faith.

"Nothing would catch me if I fell."

There was a sudden gust of wind, and the doctor lunged for Faith, catching at her arm. She recoiled, and for a moment was off balance, the hungry gray void gaping and roaring as she tipped toward it. Then her slithering boots found their footing again. She drew back a step from the precipice. She could not say for certain whether the doctor's clutch had steadied or unbalanced her.

Faith felt no fear, but the doctor's eyes were full of it. They were the color of good coffee, and puckered at the corners from reading. He flinched, as if somebody had shone a bright light directly into his gaze. And for a moment, just for a moment, it was as if he could see her properly.

Then he blinked, and let go of her wrist. She could see his workaday thoughts swing back into place like a curtain.

"You see, that is why you should be careful and pay attention," he said briskly, but not quite chidingly. "A slight young thing like you could be carried away by the wind, and then where would we be?"

I am flesh and blood, not a fairy. I would break and bleed just like you.

"I can see," continued the doctor, with what was probably meant as gentleness, "that you do not wish to believe that your father ended his own life."

"I find it hard to believe that he would do so," Faith answered, "and impossible to believe that he would do so *clumsily*."

"Then what is your explanation?"

"You said that you found bumps on the back of my father's head as well as the front. Could he have been struck from behind, and fallen forward?"

"Ah. So that is the measure of it." The doctor sighed, and gave her a sad little smile. "Miss Sunderly, do you know the coroner's worst enemy? Novels. You are a keen novel-reader, yes? I know that shy, dreaming look."

For a tiny instant Faith wondered whether it would benefit the doctor's investigation if he experienced a cliff fall firsthand.

"I quite understand the appeal," the doctor went on indulgently. "Why suffer dull reality when you might have kidnaps, murders, family secrets, and hidden passages aplenty, eh? And so you young ladies come to the coroners with your heads full of fantasies and phantasms, overheated notions, and wild suspicions—"

"I am surprised they all fit into our little female skulls," Faith responded a little tartly. She saw the doctor blanch, but pushed on earnestly. "Father was hated on Vane from the start. The day he died, a letter—"

"Listen, my dear. There is not a man, woman, or child on this island that I have not known for years. Oh, we have our share of the 'criminal classes' . . . but no murderers. Trust me. I would know them by the slope of their foreheads." The doctor turned away from the cliff with an air of finality. "There now, you can set aside your monstrous imaginings. Have I put your mind at rest?"

"I see how it is," was all Faith could say.

"I will not mention these notions of yours to anybody," Dr. Jacklers remarked graciously. "And I urge you not to do so either."

I see how it is. I will have no help from the law. If I want the killer found, I will have to do it myself.

Back at the house, the doctor was welcomed and shown into Myrtle's presence. Faith slipped upstairs, simmering with frustration. By the door she found a discreet corked pot, which proved to contain a dead mouse. Evidently Mrs. Vellet was willing to supply deceased rodents on demand, but preferred to avoid discussing it.

Faith carried it into her room. She felt some of the tense coils in her stomach loosen as she watched the snake pour like oil out of its cage. Its jaws gracefully gaped and enclosed the furred dollop, head first. The mouse disappeared inside the snake's lacquered body, and Faith let the reptile slide up her arm and around her neck.

At that very moment, she heard a sound out on the landing. Somebody was stealthily and carefully turning a door handle. Having recently turned that very handle herself, she recognized the pattern of tiny creaks. It was the door to her father's room.

Faith burst from her room and came to a halt on the landing. The snake tensed into angles, disturbed by the sudden motion.

Paul Clay was standing in the doorway of the Reverend's room.

"What are you doing here?" Faith demanded.

Paul stared at her aghast, his gaze dropping to the snake around her neck.

"It was a dare . . ." he began, stepping back out onto the landing.

"You *thief*!" hissed Faith. "What did you steal?"

"Nothing!" He glanced down at the scissors in his hand. "I just wanted . . . some hair. They dared me to bring back some hair. But I didn't want to prise open the coffin, and then Dr. Jacklers took it away for coroner business. I thought there might be some in his room . . ."

"How *dare* you!" Faith felt so angry that it would not have surprised her if big, black wings had burst from her shoulders. A lock of hair was the most personal gift or memento. Nobody but a close loved one should have such a treasure, and certainly not every trespassing gawper with scissors. "He is dead, and graveless. Is that not enough? Do you people have to cut him apart as well?"

Paul flinched, and glanced toward the stairway with a look of panic. As he did so, Faith realized that she could hear steps ascending. The moment the other person came into view, Paul would be discovered, a trespasser among the family's rooms. One little scream would seal his fate, and assert Faith's own innocence.

But Faith did not scream. Instead she found herself seizing Paul's sleeve and towing him at speed down the landing and into her own room. He gave a gasp when he realized that they were in her chamber, but she did not give him time to speak, dragging him out through the second door onto the roof garden.

She quickly lowered herself to sit on the little wooden stool.

"Sit down," she hissed, "or they can see you from below!"

Paul obeyed, settling himself on the opposite side of the roof garden, looking at her with a slow, wary incredulity.

What had she done? Faith was alone with a strange man. Not a doctor, relation, or close friend of the family. She had been told, over and over, that a woman *was* her reputation. She was a bubble that could be burst with closeness. On the landing she had been a black pillar of power and rage. Out here, she suddenly felt appallingly fragile.

She realized that her back was pressed against the trellis, as though her reputation could yet be saved if she maintained the maximum distance possible. In Paul's eyes she saw the same creeping panic. He had flattened himself against the opposite wall.

"Why did you do that?" he whispered.

"Why did you let me?" she retaliated.

There was a long silence. Neither of them had answers.

She was intensely aware of Paul's otherness, as if they were warriors from rival tribes meeting in the hinterlands.

And yet here she was.

"Who dared you?" Faith asked at last, a belligerent edge in her voice.

"Some friends." Paul's tone was noncommittal, but Faith was learning to see through that. "People are saying your father's spirit is walking—"

"Who?" demanded Faith. "Who says that?"

"Everybody, all over the island."

All over the island. Faith's falsehood had spread more quickly than she could have dreamed.

"They knew I helped move his body for the photograph," Paul went on, "but they wagered I wouldn't come back and touch him again, with his ghost hanging over, watching. The hair was supposed to be proof."

"What were the flowers supposed to prove?" asked Faith, recalling that he'd arrived with some.

Paul took a moment to study his knuckles, and Faith had the feeling he was embarrassed.

"My father sent them," he said. "He thought that you might need some . . . to freshen the house."

The gesture was almost reasonable, Faith had to admit. However, Clay was still sending flowers to a new widow. She wondered whether Clay's wife was a jealous sort.

"I did not see your mother at the funeral," she said, following the thought.

"She stopped coming to them after her own," Paul answered simply.

Faith could not say anything kind or bland to him. It would have sounded false and wrong. The pair of them were beyond such things. She said nothing instead.

"What was the doctor doing here?" asked Paul in his turn.

"He is the coroner. He came to investigate my father's death."

Paul allowed himself to look actually interested.

"Did you tell him what you tried to tell me? Did you tell him that you think somebody murdered—"

"Do you mean my fantasies and phantasms?" Faith retorted. "My overheated imaginings brought on by too many novels?"

"You *did* tell him!" Paul's eyes widened, and Faith could not be sure whether he was impressed or incredulous. "You *believe* it."

"And you do not," Faith said bitterly.

"Nobody liked him, but it was not a killing business." Paul narrowed his eyes. "He nearly lamed my friend, and acted curmudgeonly to everyone, and then turned out to be a cheat and a hypocrite to boot. But you do not *kill* a man for that."

Faith gritted her teeth against this description of her father, but she was still seething with the explanation the doctor had refused to hear. She could not hold it in. There was a dangerous joy in *talking*, even with this enemy. It made Faith realize how she had been trapped in her own head. Trapped in the house. Trapped in the Sunderly family.

"Well, somebody murdered him for *some* reason," she snapped. "The morning before he died, someone handed him an unsigned letter. It upset him. He would not talk about it. He burned it. Then in the middle of the night he went out into the darkness. I think he went to meet somebody. I think the letter forced him to do it.

"His pistol is missing. He did not shoot himself, so if he took it with him when he went out, it must have been for protection."

203

"If somebody attacked him, why didn't he shoot them?" asked Paul. He was staring at her again, the cold, ruthless, speculative gaze she had first seen on his face.

"I do not know," Faith admitted reluctantly. "But he had wounds to the back of his head as well as the front. I think he was struck from behind."

"Did anybody hear a carriage or a horse come by that night?" asked Paul thoughtfully.

"No." Faith thought back. "The wind was loud though."

"And they might have stopped at a distance, then walked. Or maybe they came by boat or on foot." He narrowed his eyes. "This house is miles from anywhere. Anyone who came out here would have been missing from their home for an hour or two, in the middle of the night. Unless they were in your house already, of course."

Faith nodded slowly, taking his words on board. The biggest shock, however, was hearing somebody answer her as if her thoughts were not absurd. Just for a moment, she wished that she did not hate Paul Clay.

Her next words surprised her.

"I want you to help me," she said.

"Help *you*?" Paul gave a huff of a laugh. "Why would I?"

"We cannot leave the island until my father is buried properly," Faith declared coldly. "Your father is sending my mother flowers. The longer we stay, the closer they become. Do you want me for a sister?"

Paul glared daggers at her, and for a moment Faith thought he would leap to his feet and leave.

"I would rather be skinned alive," he said.

"Then help me find my father's killer," said Faith, "and you need never see me again. You know the island. You can talk to people. You can find out whether anybody was out that night for no good reason. You can go where you please—"

"I have studies!" protested Paul. "I have work, helping my father—"

"Nobody shuts you in a room with your catechism, or expects to know where you are every moment of the day," persisted Faith. "You can go for a walk by yourself, or talk to people in the street. It is not the same."

Paul's stare was maddeningly hard to read. He was like his father's camera, she decided. He barely blinked, and took in every detail without mercy.

"What do I gain from it?" he asked after a long pause.

Faith hesitated, then slowly took out her locket. A lock of her father's distinctive dark auburn hair was curled inside, cut during the wake. It pained her deeply to think of disturbing it, but she needed an ally.

"What will your 'friends' do if you come back without some of my father's hair?" she asked. "Will they tease you? Call you a coward?"

Paul reddened, and Faith knew that her barb had struck home. She carefully pulled the little tress free, then prised it in two. One half she tucked back into the locket. The other she held out between finger and thumb.

"Come and take it," she said.

Paul looked at the hair, then at Faith, clearly conflicted. The sacred, inviolable distance still stretched between them. Then he rose to his feet, nervously stooped so that he could not be seen from the grounds. The movement disturbed the snake, which drew itself into a muscular zigzag with a faint hiss. Paul flinched and drew back a step, and the sight filled Faith with the same wild malice she had felt during their first conversation.

"If you like dares so much, Paul Clay," she said, "then come. *I dare you.*"

Paul seemed hypnotized by the slow ooze of the snake's ebony and gold body.

"Don't look so scared," Faith whispered. "This breed of snake does not bite." She saw one of Paul's hands twitch, as if he was considering reaching out. "It strangles," she added helpfully, and saw him recoil with satisfaction. "You don't dare, do you?"

He edged his way forward, and then lunged and snatched the hair from between her fingers. As he did so, she grabbed his sleeve, holding it fast.

"If you tell *anybody* the secrets I have told you today," she whispered fiercely, "then I will tell everyone that you were too frightened to cut the hair yourself. I have the other half of the lock, and I know which part of his head it was cut from, and you do not."

The snake slithered down past her wrist, its head gliding against the back of Paul's hand. He yanked himself free and withdrew a few steps, rubbing his hand with his other palm, clearly mortified and angry.

"Do *you* take dares?" he retaliated. "There is a ratting at the lookout hut on the coast road every Monday night. Come and find me there—we can talk about your precious murder."

Faith had heard of ratting, a "sport" for tavern cellars. Terriers were dropped into a pit of rats and commanded to kill them as quickly as possible. Paul knew she could not be seen at something of that sort. He was raising the stakes.

"Will I see you there then?" he asked, with a very slight smile. "No, I thought not."

A gust of wind stirred the leaves, making them both jump.

"I ought to go," Paul said, in a quieter, less combative tone.

He nodded toward the grounds. "Is the coast clear?"

Faith turned to peer out through the mesh of leaves and trellis. There was nobody in sight. She looked back at him and nodded.

Paul trotted across to the creeper-covered gate and vaulted neatly over it, disappearing from her view. She heard a faint patter as he descended the steps.

Faith sat and listened. There was no outcry. He had not been discovered. *They* had not been discovered.

She could not believe that she had held a clandestine conversation alone with a young man. Paul was about her own age, but that was old enough for scandal purposes. Faith felt scalded, sick and unclean. Her clothes felt itchy. If she looked in the mirror, she feared she might see something broken and used.

Why had she brought this about? What was it about Paul Clay that made her do and say mad, savage things?

At the same time she felt painfully awake, and as if a weight had been taken from her. She had thrown her dice wildly, but perhaps she had an ally now. Not a friend, but it was better than nothing.

Faith kept remembering Paul floating neatly over the gate. It had looked so easy. It had looked like flying. She wondered how it felt.

Only later did it cross her mind that Paul had been very quick to trust her word that the coast was clear. After all, she could have sent him right into the arms of capture, then fled into her room and feigned ignorance of his trespass. Strangely it had not occurred to her to do so, not for one moment.

Chapter 20

A SMILER IN THE WOOD

PAUL CLAY WAS NOT A FRIEND. HE HAD, HOW-
ever, given Faith a precious glimpse of the rest of the island, and
one important fact: her lie was taking hold.

Even now, everybody on Vane was talking of the Reverend's
ghost. Was this enough? Could a fruit be swelling on the Lie
Tree? Faith needed to visit the sea cave again. She needed to see
the Tree, to know whether she was wasting her time.

This time, however, she would prepare properly.

Secluding herself in her room on pretense of faintness, Faith
returned to her father's notes to study them in more detail. When
she recalled her first encounter with the plant, Faith felt a little
embarrassed. She had approached it like an altar and whispered
to it like a confidante. Her actions had all been shockingly bereft
of scientific method.

She was a *scientist*, she reminded herself. Scientists did not
give in to awe and superstition. Scientists asked questions, and
answered them through observation and logic.

The plant had no ears. How could it know when it had been
told a lie? It had no brain. How could it know the secrets of the
world? It hailed from exotic climes, so how could it understand

the Queen's English? How could secrets be contained within a fruit, and how could knowledge be eaten?

If her father was wrong about the Lie Tree, she needed to know. If he was right, then these questions needed answers. "Magic" was not an answer; it was an excuse to avoid looking for one.

Faith leafed through the crammed journal pages, deciphering her father's notes and comments.

A great puzzle—the plant's ability to live, grow, and purify the air without the benign radiance of the sun. Energy must be acquired from another source in order to enact its necessary chemical processes.

Warmth absorbed from the air? Improbable, since the plant appears to thrive in cold, damp environments. Insectivorous like the sundews? If plant is cave-dwelling, powerful wintry scent may convince lost creatures that an opening to the outside is nearby. No such predation observed, though prey may be imperceptibly small and borne in by air currents. Could glutinous sap entrap them?

Faith recalled the sticky moistness that had covered her fingers when she touched the plant and felt a sudden desire to wash her hands.

A new theory: the plant may be a symbiote. It remains dormant until it establishes a psychical connection with an intelligent member of another species, after which it is able to sustain itself through the flow of invisible energies not unlike those described in the now derided theories of Animal Magnetism. Could lies transmit nourishment through ripples in the Magnetic Fluid?

Could consumption of the fruit strengthen the connection, trig-
gering a Crisis and an incidence of Unobstructed Vision?

Faith vaguely remembered reading about "animal magnetism" in her father's library back at the rectory. It was an old theory that everything and everyone existed in a sort of invisible spirit soup, with currents running to, from, and through every animal and person. Blockages in the flow made you ill. If you learned to channel and direct it, you could affect other beings, some-times heal them. If all your blockages were destroyed, you went into a trance called "the crisis," where it was said that sometimes you could see right through solid objects. Faith had never heard of plants generating "animal magnetism," but the Tree was no ordinary plant.

It may be that I reach in vain for rational explanations. I have wondered whether the Tree may date from the Earliest Days, its lightless leaves, useless flowers, and seedless fruit souvenirs of a more Fortunate Age, now lost.

Those last words made Faith uncomfortable. They hinted at the inexplicable and brought back the memory of the whisper-ing cave. She felt a lurking fear that her bridge of science might fail her and come to an uncanny halt, leaving only a drop to dark and secret waters . . .

She would not succumb to superstition. She would be gov-erned by her mind, not her fears.

Faith tiptoed to her father's room, fairly confident that she was now unlikely to be interrupted in the "haunted" chamber. There she found a case holding her father's field kit. It contained his little brass field microscope, corked jars for trapping insects, a tin box or 'vasculum' for botanic samples, bottles of different acids for testing rocks, a little compass clinometer, a goniometer, and calipers. Another box held a niche where his pistol should have been, some lead shot, a bag of copper percussion caps, a dismounting key, and a small powder flask. She also scavenged a small metal ruler, a battered old pocket watch, and a folding knife.

Low tide was an hour later than it had been two days before. She made her compromise with the light and tide, heading out a little later than before, but not the full hour, for she did not dare face the journey in the full dark.

It was in the darker twilight that she crept out of the house in her ruined funeral clothes, flitted between the outbuildings, and hastened down the path to the beach.

The current was stronger than it had been on Faith's last little voyage, but for now it was with her. Her aggrieved muscles were grateful for this as they strained at the oars.

The strange boom of the breakers echoing within the cliff was welcoming to her, like the deep-throated bark of a guard dog that knew her. This time the lurching wave that drove her boat into the cave mouth filled her with a fizz of excitement instead of fear.

She tethered the boat and clambered back to the Lie Tree's cavern, taking care not to jolt her lantern or the field case. The split seams around her shoulders let her move her arms more freely, making it easier to climb.

Before entering the cavern with the Tree, she stopped to drape her shawl over the lantern. Too much radiance would injure the plant, but her father had succeeded in sketching it, so it must be able to endure *some* light. The lantern now gave off a much duller glow, but just enough to light her way.

As Faith entered the cavern, she thought she heard a welcoming rush of sighs, a susurration of recognition. She could just make out the outline of the Tree, a blot of blackness that seemed larger than before.

"I have returned," Faith whispered to it, then stopped herself. She was talking to botanic specimens again.

As she drew closer, her eyes adjusting to the dark, she could no longer delude herself. It was not a trick of the shadows. The plant *had* grown.

Reaching out, she could feel that its bristling creeper-like tendrils were now spilling over the side of the pot. She followed them by touch as they splayed out across the stone shelf like octopus tentacles, some drooping down over the edge toward the cavern floor. Beneath the leaves the undulating vine was thick and woody, as if it had been growing for some time.

"That is *impossible*," breathed Faith. She had never seen a plant grow so fast, let alone without sunlight. "That . . . is *not obeying the laws.*"

Her voice sounded absurd even to her. Was she expecting the plant to apologize and become obediently natural?

She swallowed and took out her father's folding knife. "I am sorry about this," she whispered, "but I am here to study you."

While the soft cacophony of wave-roars and rock-sighs billowed about her ears, Faith began examining the plant. There was too little light for her to take measurements with her ruler and calipers, but she managed to take rubbings of the leaf veins using pencil and paper. She cut samples of forked leaves, spines, and pieces of bark, then scraped away a blob of oozing sap, putting each specimen into a separate jar. It was an unnerving task, and Faith felt as though she were trimming the toenails of a dragon. She even waved the compass around the Tree, squinting at the dial to see whether she could detect magnetic fields.

All the while, as she stroked her fingers through the leaves, she was searching for a flower, a bud, anything. In her father's sketches the flowers had been white, so she hoped they might show up even in the darkness. She squinted at the plant from all sides, at first slowly and methodically, then with increasing desperation.

There was nothing. Perhaps there never could be anything. Perhaps the Lie Tree was itself a lie.

She felt utterly crushed and foolish. Only now did she realize how certain she had been that the plant would not betray her, and that she would find *something*.

Then, as she gave the foliage one more despairing pat, something small and round fell from one of the tendrils. It bounced off the rim of the pot, landed on her skirt and rolled down the slope of the fabric.

Faith gave a squawk of panic. She snatched at it, and was just fast enough to catch it between two of her knuckles. She let out a long breath. If it had bounced away into the darkness, she would probably never have found it again.

The Tree had not let her down after all. The tiny fruit was half an inch across, and wore some cream-colored, papery tatters that looked like the dried-out remains of a flower. It was perfectly round and textured like lemon peel. She could just make out pale streaks against its dark hide.

Faith could only hope that it was ripe. She could scarcely glue it back on to the Tree.

She hesitated. It was tempting to take the fruit back to her own room, so that she could eat it in relative safety. At Bull

Cove, however, she would run the risk of being discovered semi-conscious and yellow-eyed. Here at least she had privacy.

Her mind was made up. She would eat the fruit here and now, in the cave.

Everything needed to be observed properly and methodically, including her own reactions.

Faith found a "seat" in the entrance cave where the boat was tied. Here she could sit with her back against a stone pillar where a stalagmite and stalactite had melded into one. She removed the lantern's coverings to give herself more light. Her little hand mirror she propped on a ledge, so that she could see her own face reflected. Using the battered pocket watch she timed her own pulse. It was rapid, and she realized that she was frightened.

She sat down, and lashed herself to the stone pillar using a damp rope from the boat. She did not know sailors' knots, but she hoped it would be enough to stop her wandering into the sea in a drugged daze.

Faith made a note of the time on the clock. She laid her notebook and pens on a stone shelf within reach. Then she took her knife and very carefully cut the Lie fruit in half.

Instantly the cold smell became so intense that she winced. Blinking as her eyes stung, she held up the fruit to examine it more closely. The flesh seemed to be made up of dozens of tiny juice-filled cells, like that of a lemon, but a deep, rich red.

A dribble of juice ran down Faith's hand on to her wrist, and reflexively she raised her hand to her mouth and licked it off. The taste was searingly bitter, worm-juice and rotten walnuts. Her tongue went numb. Pins and needles spread through the skin of her mouth.

Faith did not give her resolve a chance to falter. With her thumbnail she eased the red flesh of the fruit free from the peel. It came away trailing downy white strands like a spider's web. Bracing herself, she pushed the red pulp into her mouth.

She tasted bitter ice, and her throat tightened. Only by covering her mouth with both hands did she stop herself from gagging and spitting the fruit out again. She struggled to swallow, and briefly the pulp was a clinging sour mass at the base of her tongue. Then she forced it down, shuddering and grimacing.

It was done. She had eaten the fruit. It was too late to turn back. Almost immediately her fears set upon her.

She could feel the cooling slither of the fruit flesh down her throat, then a numb tingling started to spread through her chest. Faith drew in breath after hasty breath, and each was a little harder than the last. It felt like somebody was stealthily drawing in the laces of her corset, a little at a time, cutting off her air.

There was a sound in her ears that she hardly recognized as her own heartbeat, a *whump, whump, whump* like a carpet being beaten. Her tongue and throat were paper dry. Before her eyes, colors deepened, darkened, and crawled with motion. It came to her that the world was a tapestry, and she was watching it being eaten by black beetles.

She was in a tunnel, racing ever faster into darkness, while great black wheels spun and hummed on either side of her, and the world shook with a heartbeat quake . . .

She was fighting it, fighting the darkness and drum of it, the helpless swoop and fall of it, and the fight was terror. She fought to keep the light, her wits, her control, and screamed inside as she felt all of these things pulled away from her like petals . . .

. . . and then they were gone, and there was no more panic.

Only a deep and silent soul-fear rolling on like unheard thunder, too strange and strong for her to really feel it.

Faith walked through a midnight forest. The trees were pure white and rose high above her head, disappearing into a blue-black darkness. There was no wind, and yet the snow-white leaves shivered and whispered.

She raised one hand to push aside low-hanging foliage, and felt her fingertips brush paper. The trees were flat and pale. The ragged-torn ferns stroked the skin of her hands, paper-cutting her, slyly cruel.

She was not alone.

Beside her walked a figure, warmly familiar. She could hear the crunch of foliage under heavy boots. Then there was a snuffled exhalation that she recognized.

"Uncle Miles," she said aloud. "Uncle Miles, why are we here?"

"It is all for the best," came the answer. "The very best." His voice sounded strange. It was droning and slack, like that of a sleepwalker.

"I know this place!" Faith felt a gnawing sense of familiarity, but it brought unease, not reassurance. "We do not belong here! Why did you bring us here?" Out of the corner of her eye she could just make out the plum-colored cloth of her uncle's coat. The moonlight fell unevenly, and he was only visible in fits and starts.

"They promised me . . ." murmured Uncle Miles.

"Who? What did they promise you?" Faith turned to face her uncle, and found that she could hardly see him. He was flat, perfectly flat, and from the side she could see only a paper-thin edge.

"The fellows at the Royal Academy laugh at me," moaned the

flattened shape. "I hear them. At the clubs. Old Miles—he never gets his name on a paper, never gives a lecture, never names a species. Follows his brother-in-law around like a dog. I *needed* to bring him here. *They* asked me . . ."

"What do you mean?" Gripped by apprehension, Faith seized her uncle's arm and pulled him around to face her.

His eyes were crude splotches of Indian ink, his mouth a smiling smear. The broken moonlight glimmered on his clumsy, sausage-like hands and the rough spirals that patterned his waist-coat. From top to toe he was a childish drawing, but one that narrowed its blot-eyes and leaned forward to peer into her face.

"They wanted Erasmus," said the ink mouth, flexing and undulating. "They only ever want Erasmus . . ."

"Who? What do you mean?" Faith gripped her uncle's arm more tightly, and to her horror felt it crumple under her grip. She released it and stepped back, but her uncle was emitting a thin hiss. His long, papery arms reached for her, one now deformed and creased.

"Tell me!" Faith struck out in a rage born of terror. Her slap caught his arm, and ripped it from his shoulder. The great paper head lurched toward her, and she lashed out, ripping a great tear in it, through one eye and down his cheek.

"Always Erasmus," he hissed. "So I brought him to them."

And he was so horrible, so misshapen, swaying there before her, that Faith struck out again and again, tearing and ripping and rending. Fragments of Uncle Miles drifted on the air like snowflakes and streamers. At last all that was left was a paper mouth, fluttering like a butterfly, still shaping doleful, slack words. She caught it between her fingers, pinching it cruelly and stretching it almost to the tearing point.

"What have you done?" she demanded.

"They promised that I could take part in the excavation," whined the mouth. "My name would appear on their paper. Recognition, at last! But only if I could persuade Erasmus to come too. He had already turned them down. It was hard to convince him . . . but then there was the scandal. I saw my chance. *Vane is my chance.*"

"You *used* us!" exclaimed Faith. "You brought us here to help yourself! You just wanted to join the excavation! Why did they ask for Father? Why?"

But she tugged too hard on his grimacing mouth, and it tore.

Looking desperately around, Faith saw another familiar figure in the distance. The sight of it filled her with a hot, welling sorrow, and she could not for that moment remember why.

"Father!" she called, and ran through the paper forest after the receding shape.

The figure moved away from her faster than she could run. It seemed to glide, and she had the uncanny feeling that its legs were not moving.

"Father, wait for me! There is something wrong! We are not supposed to be here!"

She thought he might slow. She thought he might turn. Neither of these things happened. Instead there was a disturbance in the foliage above, a scattering of paper leaves, and then a great shadow hand reached down into the woodland.

Faith screamed out a warning. The sound of the scream went on and on, even when she had no more breath to give it. Her father's head was crushed between a great finger and thumb. For a moment she saw him, staggering, half of his head a mangled mess. Then the hand closed into a fist around him, and dragged him upward out of view.

"No!" Faith sprinted forward. "Bring him back!" And then, as she heard sounds of rending from above, "I will kill you! I will *kill* you!"

There was a pause. Craning upward, Faith could just make out a huge dark shape amid the tree cover, silhouetted against the star-freckled sky. Above her, foliage rustled, boughs creaked and thwacked. Dry white leaves fell onto her upturned face. The hand was coming down again.

Then, and only then, did black terror consume Faith. She looked down, and for the first time saw her own body properly, a ragged girl-dress outline criss-crossed with wild black scribbles. She was paper. She could be ripped apart with ease. She had made a terrible mistake.

She dropped to the dark ground and wriggled under the white ferns, wincing as she felt herself crumple and slightly tear. She lay there stiller than still, while the great hand felt its way blindly through the forest. Looking for the source of the screamed threat. Looking for her.

Seconds drew themselves out to a breaking point. Faith's heartbeat seemed to be slowing too but getting louder, sending vibrations through the ground. The pallor of the trees was trembling and fading, the shadows encroaching. Then somewhere above, the moon guttered and went out, and all was darkness.

Chapter 21

SPONTANEOUS COMBUSTION

ROAR AND HISS. ROAR AND HISS. FAITH DID NOT know where she was, except that she was somewhere cold and painful. There was a clammy ache in her limbs and neck.

She opened her eyes a slit, and blinked at a blurred vista of shadowy stone. After a few blinks the pale blobs became stalagmites, and the dark smudges became openings to other caverns. Faith was still slumped against the pillar, the rope digging into her waist.

She was shivering. Everything ached. Her mouth was dry and tasted of lime and bile. Even her eyes felt dry, and her lids rubbed awkwardly when she blinked. However, she had survived.

Her dream was still a shadow in her mind. She blinked as her muddled thoughts tried to disentangle reality from the strands of phantasm.

Faith remembered tearing Uncle Miles to pieces . . . but that had not happened, she realized with unutterable relief. She was not in a paper wood, and a giant hand was not looking for her. She had not seen her father die. Then she remembered that he really *was* dead, however, and felt a tumbling sense of loss.

She pressed her fists against her temples, trying to squeeze thoughts from her numb brain. A great hand reaching down into a bone-white forest . . . there was something familiar about that image. It had been eerie because it should have been comforting, harmless, comical . . .

"Howard's theatre," she whispered, as realization struck. "I was in the forest of Howard's toy theatre."

Faith's lantern had burned itself out, and yet she could still make out her surroundings. Pale light was seeping in through the cave's seaward entrance. She fumbled for her pocket watch. To her horror, it was five in the morning.

She needed to leave! If she was not back soon, she would be missed and asked a thousand questions to which there were no good answers. Then she remembered the Tree. She could not leave until she had fed it another lie.

With numb, trembling hands she managed to unpick the knots in the rope and struggled free. When she hauled herself to her feet, the cavern danced ring-a-roses for a moment. Steadying herself with one hand against the wall, Faith tottered to the entrance of the larger cavern and gazed into the darkness. She could just make out the inky outline of the Tree.

What could she say? Her vision had not identified her father's murderer. What *had* she learned?

Until now, she had assumed that the killer must be somebody her father had angered since arriving in Vane—a frustrated cockler, a friend or relation of the boy maimed in the rabbit trap, or somebody angered by the treatment of Jeanne. If her vision had shown her the truth, however, somebody had planned to kill her father long before the Sunderly family arrived on the island. Whoever they were, they had persuaded Uncle Miles to bring his brother-in-law to Vane, and into a trap. They had played on Uncle Miles's ambition, and he had snapped up the bait.

If this was true, then one thing was certain. The murderer had to be somebody involved with the excavation. Who else could have bribed Uncle Miles with the offer of an invitation? Perhaps the incident with the malfunctioning basket had not been an accident at all. Who could have guessed that Faith and Howard would be ones to ride in it, rather than their esteemed father?

There were three keen natural scientists involved in the excavation—Lambent, Clay, and Dr. Jacklers.

Faith weighed each of them in her mind. When she remembered Mr. Lambent bounding around the site with impulsive enthusiasm, or his forthright anger after the basket incident, it was hard to imagine him plotting a cold-blooded assassination. Then she remembered the neat precision of his curiosity cabinet, the immaculate labels, the pristine evidence of an ordered mind. There was more to him than met the eye then. His bluster might be sheath to a dangerous knife.

Dr. Jacklers seemed honest to the point of tactlessness, but he was a cauldron of bitterness. He was the sort to collect grudges, she suspected, and rear them tenderly. And if he was the murderer, what better role to take than coroner and medical expert investigating for suspicious circumstances?

Clay had always seemed gentle, mild, and baffled. No, not always. Faith remembered the flare of passion when he had spoken so adamantly of the Bible, and calamities, and a young earth. How would he have reacted if he learned of the Reverend's great deceptions? Zeal was like gas, most dangerous when you could not see it. The wrong spark could light it at any time.

None of them had an obvious reason for murdering her father. But the Reverend's frauds and dealings with the Tree could have made him many enemies. One of his lies might have done somebody a real injury. Natural scientists who had vouched for his fossils would look like fools now, their reputations in shreds. Perhaps one of his visions had shown him someone else's dangerous secret, driving them to find a way of silencing him.

She needed to know more about all three men. The Lie Tree might tell her something, if she could think of the right lie. A lie about the excavation leaders. A lie that the islanders would wish to believe. She thought of the old tales of the smugglers' gold.

Faith leaned forward toward the waiting shadows. "The excavation is not really a dig for dusty old bones," she whispered. "The leaders are lying to everybody. They are looking for smugglers' treasure, and they want to keep it all for themselves."

The cavern echoed the surge of the water with a husky roar, as though the Tree had drawn in Faith's words with one breath.

The tide had come in while she had been unconscious, and when she found the boat it was afloat, tugging impatiently at its rope. As she rowed unsteadily out of the cave, the early morning light sliced into Faith's brain, making her wince and blink.

When she opened her eyes again, she noticed that she was on fire.

A small fleck of something on her sleeve gave a hungry fizzle as the sunlight touched it, then withered. The cloth beneath it ignited, a tiny flame starting to eat a moth-hole into the fabric. The threads glowed red as they caught.

Faith stared stupidly at it, until a pain in her arm convinced her sluggish brain that the flame was real. She let go of the oars, scooping up water in her hand and splashing it on the flames. At the same time she became aware that four other small spots on her clothing were smoking and glowing ember-red, one on her bodice and three on her skirts.

For a moment Faith could only think that she was spontaneously combusting. She had heard tales of such things. Men and women going about their own business suddenly caught fire from within and burned to ashes within seconds, sometimes leaving their clothes intact.

In panic, she splashed water on her face, skirts, sleeves, and bodice. She continued to throw water over herself even after the burning patches were reduced to charred holes. Only when she could be sure that she was no longer igniting, did her heart stop galloping. She could not understand what had happened, but at least it was no longer happening.

It was a hard row back to shore and Faith had to lean over the side of the boat several times to be sick. By the time she was sneaking through the grounds, dawn had well and truly broken. The sunlit green of the lawn burned her eyes as she tottered heavily toward the house, doing her best to stay behind cover. Singed, half blind, stupefied, and sea-splashed, she struggled up the steps, through the roof-garden door, and into the blessed, kindly darkness of her room.

She dropped into a chair and drank water straight from the jug, shuddering with each gulp. Then she opened the shutters and curtain a crack to let in a sliver of sunlight, just enough to let her undo her buttons and laces. She had just stripped off her renegade funeral garb and slipped back into her nightgown when a polite knock at the door made her jump.

"Wait a moment, please!" The room was littered with incriminating evidence of her night outing. As Faith hastily scooped up her discarded clothes, she accidentally kicked her father's field kit, which was lying open on the floor. One of the little sample jars tumbled out, and rolled into the slender shaft of sunlight.

Inside were a few leaves cut from the Tree. As the morning light touched them, they charred and shriveled, then erupted into searing white flame. There was a *whoomph*. The glass of the jar blackened, then cracked with a sharp retort.

"Miss Sunderly?" Mrs. Vellet's somber velvet tones were touched with concern. "Is anything amiss?"

"No!" called Faith, as she hurriedly tried and failed to pick up the hot jar, which promptly fell into two pieces. She kicked them under the dresser and pushed the window open, frantically trying to waft out the eye-watering lime-scented smoke. "I—I will be there in a moment!"

Once all the evidence was hidden, Faith opened the door, dreading to think how much crashing, creaking, and blundering must have been overheard.

"I am very sorry to have troubled you, Miss Sunderly." Mrs. Vellet was stiff as ever, but wore a tiny, discomfited frown. Faith wondered why the housekeeper had risen so early, and why she had come to Faith's door in person. The pause stretched. "I thought I would ask whether you wished for breakfast at the usual time, or whether you were planning to rise a little later. If you had not . . . slept well, miss."

Faith stared at the housekeeper, trying to decipher the lines of her face. The housekeeper knew something. She had heard something. Perhaps she had seen something. Until Faith was certain how much Mrs. Vellet knew, she could not frame a covering lie. She knew that she herself must look disheveled and shadow-eyed.

"Thank you," Faith said carefully. "I *would* like a later breakfast, if you please." She could not resist the prospect of some more sleep.

"Very good, miss." Seconds passed, and the housekeeper still stood there. "Miss Sunderly," she began again, and to Faith's surprise dropped her voice to an earnest monotone, "if you will forgive me for saying so . . . your father would not expect you to put yourself through this."

Faith felt her face tighten and her stomach clench like a fist.

"If you must go down there at night," Mrs. Vellet continued, "there is a cloak in the hall that will give you a measure of warmth. But it is a long, cold walk to the church, and a wake ends when the dead leave the house. Your father loved you—if you died of influenza, that would be poor thanks for his care in raising you."

It took a moment for Faith to disentangle Mrs. Vellet's words and understand her meaning. The housekeeper did not know where Faith had been, but she had heard or seen enough to know that Faith had been somewhere. She had jumped to a conclusion—that Faith had been continuing her own private wake, walking to the church to sit by her father's coffin like a dog on its master's grave.

Brimming with relief, Faith looked down so that her gaze could not be read and gave a little nod of acknowledgment. From under her lashes she saw the housekeeper give a small, formal bob, then withdraw. Faith closed the door, and then her eyes.

She had come so very close to being discovered. Even now, Mrs. Vellet could report her for sneaking out by night, but Faith did not think she would. No, if that had been her plan, Mrs. Vellet would have gone straight to Myrtle, rather than approaching Faith for a sotto voce conversation.

It could be kindness. Faith felt hollow at the thought. She had needed kindness before, and had received none. Now it was too late and she did not know what to do with it.

When Faith woke again, she was aghast to discover that she had slept through to the afternoon. As she emerged groggily from her room, however, her anxiety gave way to a rather mortifying realization. Nobody had missed her at all.

Myrtle was busy trying on a new veil and shawl. Both were newly arrived "gestures of sympathy," the former from Dr. Jacklers, the latter from Clay. Evidently their rivalry was proceeding apace. Faith winced internally, looking at the good-quality paramatta shawl. She suspected that it would have been a painful expense for the ill-paid curate. Faith caught herself wondering what Paul had thought of it, and her mind flinched from the memory of their strange confrontation and his impossible dare.

As it turned out, Clay had also delivered the first print of the family photograph. Faith's hand shook as she held the little square card. There was the Reverend Erasmus Sunderly, reposed and dignified in his chair, Faith a pace behind him. He looked eerily unblemished, his painted eyes coolly interrogative.

"Can I keep this print?" Faith reflexively pulled the card closer to her chest. "Please!"

Myrtle sighed. "Oh, very well."

Faith needed to find a way to infiltrate the excavation site, if she wanted to spread her new lie and continue her investigations. Right now she was trapped in Bull Cove, and the excavation leaders were frustratingly out of her reach.

Uncle Miles, however, was not.

After dinner Faith hunted him down and discovered him in the library, reading a copy of *Prehistoric Times*. It gave her a jolt when she walked in and found him sitting in the chair that had recently been used by her father.

There he was, round-faced and amiable, sitting by the fire with his pipe. Uncle Miles, who had always been there in the background, a warm and unthreatening presence, like a cat curled up on a windowsill.

Uncle Miles who had brought the whole family to Vane for selfish reasons, playing into the murderer's hands. Faith could not forget her vision, or the way his daubed, grotesque face had torn under her fingers.

"Good evening," she said, and managed to make her voice sound natural.

"There you are, Faith." Uncle Miles folded his paper, then regarded her with a serious smile. "How nice to see one sober, sensible face!"

"Has everybody else been drunk and silly?" Faith perched herself on the edge of a seat.

"After a fashion." Uncle Miles gave a sigh of exasperated mirth. "Everyone seems to be drunk on ghosts! They are terribly convenient ghosts as well. Whenever anything is broken or spilled, it is the ghosts. Whenever anything is missing, the ghosts are to blame."

Faith, the puppeteer of the local ghost, quietly folded her hands.

"Have many things gone missing?" asked Faith, wondering how many of her own "borrowings" had been noticed.

"I am afraid so." Uncle Miles proceeded to give quite a long list of missing items. Some of them were indeed items Faith had borrowed, such as her father's field instruments and his spare watch. However, the household was also missing a few plants, a couple of silk cravats, a tobacco jar, and other odds and ends. Clearly Faith was not the only person taking advantage of the confusion to acquire things they wanted. "The truth is, we need a proper inventory of your father's effects."

Faith said nothing but bristled quietly. Compiling a "proper inventory" would probably involve a search of the house.

Uncle Miles drummed his fingers on his paper. "Faith, you are . . . well, a big girl now. May I talk to you as a full-grown young lady?"

Faith nodded. Oddly his words made her feel that she was being treated less like an adult, not more.

"Well, it seems that I need your help. Your mother . . . is not well, not herself . . ."

"Overwrought?" suggested Faith, keeping her face deadpan.

"Exactly. And so there are important things that have gone astray. Faith, I'm sure you want to help your mother. Do you have *any* idea where she might have put your father's private papers?"

"No," Faith faltered, keeping her expression innocent. "But I suppose I *could* look out for them." She watched her uncle with fascination. How calculating he was! Why had she never noticed this side of him before? But she was calculating too, and right now her calculations told her that this was the moment to ask him questions, because he wanted her as an ally.

"Do you think perhaps Father took his papers with him when he went to give that talk to the local society?" she asked. "Per- haps we should try to ask somebody at the dig? They might know."

"No, I, er . . . well, as a matter of fact I *have* been talking to them." Uncle Miles coughed, and looked a little embarrassed. "I have been back to the excavation a few times. I thought . . . build a few bridges with my scientist brethren, put some minds at rest . . . They are not really such terrible fellows, you know."

"They brought Father all the way across the sea, and then they turned on him." Every word she spoke was carefully judged, but Faith could not stop real feeling from creeping into her voice.

Uncle Miles looked alarmed by her display of emotion. Faith dropped her own gaze quickly.

"I know," she said, letting her tone deflate. "I understand why they did it. I know about the rumors, and the *Intelligencer*."

"I am sorry that you had to hear about that." Uncle Miles sighed. "Try to see it from the gentlemen's point of view! If they had continued to associate with your father, with such a scandal breaking, all their findings would be thrown into doubt! Nobody would take their discoveries seriously!"

"Yes," said Faith, "I see. That would be terrible." Somehow she managed not to sound sarcastic. "Anyway, it's not *your* fault, Uncle Miles. You just wanted to help us." From under her lashes she saw her uncle's posture relax slightly. "Whose idea was it to invite Father anyway? I suppose it must have been Mr. Lambent."

"Nobody seems to remember." Uncle Miles spoke gently but rather carefully. "It seems that it was suggested one evening at a dinner, and everybody took to the idea. Now, of course, nobody wants to admit to having come up with it."

Who was at the dinner? Faith could not ask the question. It would sound odd, and Uncle Miles was unlikely to have an answer.

"I suppose you are right, Uncle Miles." Faith let her shoulders droop. "We do need to build bridges. Can I help? When you next go to the excavation, can you take me with you?"

"To the excavation?" Uncle Miles seemed taken aback. "Well, I have no objection, but . . . we would need to ask permission from the gentlemen running the dig. The Sunderly surname may be a problem, you see . . . and I am not sure your mother would approve . . ."

It was difficult to look at Uncle Miles, now that Faith understood him better. She could almost see thoughts squirming behind his placid face, like worms in a bun. He was sizing her up, wondering if her presence would jeopardize his hard-won admittance to the dig.

The murderer had made use of Uncle Miles's ambition, but perhaps Faith could use it too. Better still, Faith had been slowly learning that the excavation leaders were not united. Under the jovial surface lurked rivalries, distrust, and resentment—cracks just waiting for her to drive in her chisel.

"Uncle Miles," she said, "if you will be seeing Dr. Jacklers, could you give him a letter from me? I . . . wanted to thank him for trying to help Father."

"A letter? Of course—I see no harm in that."

Faith managed not to flinch when her uncle patted her hand. She remembered his paper grimace, and her fingers itched.

Chapter 22

THE CHISEL
IN THE CRACK

Dear Dr. Jacklers,

I am very sorry for being so foolish, and bothering you with my fancies. Thank you for putting my mind at rest. If you visit our house again I would very much like to apologize in person.

Faith narrowed her eyes at her letter, then added a postscript.

PS. Perhaps you would like to measure my head at the same time. I would very much like to help you serve the Cause of Science.

The letter was delivered the next morning, and Dr. Jacklers called by later that same day. He spent an hour talking to Myrtle, and then happily joined Faith for tea in the drawing room.

"Miss Sunderly, what an excellent thought!" The doctor's delighted gaze kept creeping to the top of Faith's head, presumably assessing her cranium. "It is always a joy to measure a head *properly*! So few people will brave my instruments! And your case, Miss Sunderly, is a special one. Genius, they say, is passed down through families, and your father possessed a remarkable mind."

Faith noticed that he had brought with him several boxes and cases with heavy straps. She had been expecting a tape measure, and the mention of "instruments" was a little worrying.

"Now, do not be alarmed," said the doctor in a sprightly tone, as he reached within one case and started pulling out bizarre contraptions. "These are merely measuring devices, and will not hurt at all. My word—I have so few chances to use these!"

The first was a gleaming pair of calipers, its pincers large enough to grip a melon. The second was a four-sided wooden frame, with adjustable screws, that was clearly designed to fit over the head.

As the doctor took these out of the box, Faith caught sight of a small painting within. It showed the head and shoulders of a neat-featured, black-haired woman in a pale yellow dress. Curiously, somebody seemed to have scrawled over the painting in ink, marking out the "comparative" of the skull, the angle of her face, and so forth.

"That looks like Miss Hunter," Faith said reflexively.

"It is nobody," the doctor responded, immediately and rather sourly. "It is an old picture of an Unknown Lady. Though . . . like Miss Hunter, she does have a short skull. There are many ill traits that can be found in a short skull. Ingratitude. Shallowness. Inability to understand her own best interests."

This seemed quite a lot of venom to direct against the poor stranger in the painting. For the first time, Faith started to suspect that Miss Hunter might have ungratefully, shallowly, and misguidedly refused to become Mrs. Jacklers.

"Where would you like me to sit?" asked Faith, eager to change the subject.

"Mmm? Oh, it does not matter as long as the back is not too high,"

Faith settled herself in a wooden chair, and a moment later she felt the calipers grip her, one metal pincer resting on the back of her head, the other pressing into the base of her forehead, just above her nose.

"Dolichocephalic skull, like your father," the doctor muttered, his temper recovering a little.

His words did not surprise Faith, nor was their meaning lost on her. It had already crossed her mind that, when engaged in his duties as coroner, the doctor had probably seized the opportunity to measure her father's head. She gritted her teeth and kept her expression bland as chalk.

The calipers were withdrawn and the wooden frame lowered on to Faith's head, so that its crosspiece was settled on the top of her skull. It had four drooping vertical arms, and Dr. Jacklers twiddled the screws until the arms pressed against the front, back, and sides of her head.

"My mother was very pleased with the veil," she said meekly. "And the lovely shawl!"

"Shawl?" The doctor paused. "There was no shawl."

"Oh!" Faith blinked. "I beg your pardon! Now I remember— the shawl was from Mr. Clay."

"Mr. Clay gave your mother a shawl?" asked the doctor in outraged, suspicious tones.

Faith knew that she might be providing Clay with an enemy, but she could not afford to be sentimental. Besides, any man of the cloth chasing a brand-new widow deserved everything he got.

"Yes," she faltered. "It arrived yesterday."

There was a long pause.

"That measurement seems too large," the doctor muttered at last. "Are you tensing your face muscles? Please try not to exert your forehead." The screws were tightened until she was unsure whether he was measuring her head or trying to crush it down to the right size.

"That feels rather tight, Dr. Jacklers!" Faith exclaimed, as the pressure became bruising. She wondered whether she had been rash, putting her skull at his mercy. He was, after all, one of her suspects.

"I am trying to acquire a credible reading," growled the doctor with rather ill grace. "Of course, the best way to be sure of your cranial capacity would be to fill your skull with seeds, just as I do with empty skulls, but you would hardly thank me for that!"

Just as she was wondering whether she would end up with a rectangular head, the screws were loosened and the frame lifted away. While Faith gingerly felt her forehead and temples, Dr. Jacklers wrote down a set of figures in a notebook. Glancing across, Faith could see that the columns had headings like "facial angle," "cranial index," "breadth," "circumference," and "length."

"How did I do?" she asked.

"Your head is longer than I expected," the doctor admitted. "No doubt a gift from your late father." He frowned again at his figures, and Faith saw him round a couple down.

"Dr. Jacklers," said Faith timidly, "can I ask your advice?" She reached for her sketchbook and spread it for the doctor's view, turning page after page. "I wanted to thank you—to be of help to you and the other gentlemen—and I know Mr. Lambent's draftsman has broken his wrist. Do you think I would do instead?"

The doctor watched as Faith leafed past sketches of birds and still lifes of deer antlers, then put out his hand to halt her. The page showed a cross section of a hillside, neatly sliced by lines into layers, with labels such as "broken medieval pottery," "fragment of Roman wall," "clay soil," and "pygmy hippo and aurochs bones."

"Is that a drawing of an excavation section?"

"Yes—Father taught me how to draw them." It was a lie. Faith had seen such diagrams before, and understood them a little, but she had carefully copied this picture from one of her father's books that very morning. "Would that help?"

The doctor was tempted, she could see it. But then he glanced over at her, and she saw herself reflected in his gaze, a young girl out of place amid rubble and bones. He started to shake his head.

"I would not want to be any trouble though," Faith declared swiftly. She shut the book. "I know that you have Mr. Clay to take photographs, and that he probably needs the money. I would hate to steal his commissions and make difficulties for him."

A little candle of malice lit in Dr. Jacklers's eyes. Faith could guess what he was thinking. If Faith was making sketches, the excavation would not need so many of Clay's photographs. He would lose his importance at the dig and have less money to buy presents for pretty widows.

"Miss Sunderly, do not concern yourself. That is an excellent idea! Are you sure that your mother can spare you?"

"I believe so," answered Faith, a little uncertain. "To tell the truth, I think I have been under everybody's feet lately. Do you think Mr. Lambent and Mr. Clay will mind though?" It was her role to be doubtful, hesitant, and ultimately persuaded.

"Leave it to me," said the doctor grimly.

Waiting for the verdict from the excavation leaders, Faith busied herself in her room with scientific investigation.

Remembering the way that her clothes had caught fire, and

the strange occurrence with the sample jar, Faith decided to perform some careful experiments, this time with a jug of water at hand.

First she tied a tiny piece of Lie Tree leaf on the tip of her knife and moved it into a narrow shaft of sunlight. It ignited instantly, a leap of white flame consuming it in a second with a hiss. A frail mote of gray ash floated down to the floor. The same thing happened when she repeated the experiment with thorns, blobs of sap, or fragments of bark.

It was true then. Fragments of the Lie Tree burst into flame at the touch of sunlight. There had probably been tiny fragments of foliage on her dress that morning, and they had ignited as she left the cave.

After singeing herself a few times and slightly charring the windowsill, she knew a little more. Bright light from candles and lanterns only caused a leaf to fizz and wilt. Daylight immediately reflected in a mirror's surface triggered instant combustion, as did direct daylight. Indirect daylight seemed to have no effect, providing it was dim and diffuse enough. Lantern-light muted by enough layers of gauze also seemed to be harmless to the specimens.

"Father must be right," Faith murmured to herself. "The Tree *must* be cave-dwelling—somewhere the sun never reaches. But *why* does it burn? Chemicals, I suppose—oils, volatile. Maybe that's why it smells so strongly. But why does it *let* itself burn?"

How could bursting into flames be an advantage? How would a tree like that *evolve*?

"Maybe it is a defense," she said aloud. She imagined plant-eating animals venturing into caves, chomping the Tree's slick leaves. As they emerged, muzzles sticky with sap, they would suddenly find their faces singed and searing. They would learn to avoid that ice-cold reek.

"But that answers nothing," she muttered, as she jotted down her thoughts. "Volatile oils are stored energy. Where does the Tree find its energy?"

Her father had theorized about the Tree feeding off a "psychical connection" with an "intelligent member of another species." Her pen halted on the paper. If the Lie Tree was "connected" to anybody at that moment, it could only be herself. And it was growing. But she did not *feel* as though something were draining out of her. As she looked at her notes, she felt energized, alive.

If Faith could understand the plant, perhaps she could understand something about daylight, the vegetable kingdom, truth, or even the human soul. Her awe of the plant was giving way to a hungry curiosity.

A little before dinner, a letter arrived for Myrtle from Dr. Jacklers, asking whether she might spare young Faith over the next few days for some sketching tasks.

Myrtle was only slightly happier than she might have been if Faith had suggested leaping down the excavation shaft. Sending a young girl to a dig full of laboring men was scarcely proper. Dragging her from the bosom of her family straight after bereavement was irregular. Expecting her to assist the excavation, after her father had been so terribly snubbed, was downright peculiar.

It was Dr. Jacklers who had asked though, so Myrtle spent the whole of dinner talking herself round.

"Uncle Miles will be with you, so it is not *completely* improper," she conceded. "And perhaps the invitation is some sort of apology for the way our family has been treated. Faith—the Lambents have slighted us dreadfully, but please be as civil to them as you can bear. If they can only be persuaded to be reasonable, then everybody can forget about this ridiculous inquest."

Jeanne served the food like a sleepwalker. There were dark shadows under her eyes, and she kept forgetting what she was doing mid-ladle. She picked up each napkin gingerly, as if expecting to find horrors lurking beneath. At one point a servants' bell rang in the kitchen, and she nearly jumped out of her skin.

The excavation is not really a dig for dusty old bones. The leaders are lying to everybody. They are looking for smugglers' treasure, and they want to keep it all for themselves.

That was the lie that Faith needed to sow into the minds of the islanders. Back in her room, she set about creating the first seed.

She had borrowed a sheet of her father's writing paper and one of his pens. Carefully she began to write, glancing at her father's journal now and then so that she could copy his handwriting as closely as possible.

17th May 1865
Proceeds of 2nd Cavn to be Divided as Below:
Mr. A. Lambent   763
(plus additional 100 for ownership of land)
Rev. T. Clay   763
Rev. E. Sunderly   763
All further finds to be divided equally

She examined it with real pride. It looked smudged and hurried, just as she had planned. Better still, it was unclear. There was nothing to show what the numbers meant. They could be pounds, guineas, doubloons, or mammoth teeth. All that anybody could tell from reading it was that *something* had been found in large quantities and divided between three men . . . and that Dr. Jacklers had not been included.

Faith was learning that you only had to provide part of a lie. You could rely on other people's imaginations to fill the gaps.

She chewed her lip, deciding where to leave the note. It should be found, but it should not look as though it had been left to be found. Discovering it should feel like a tantalizing accident.

Her eyes fell upon the glass spill vase on her mantelpiece. Of course! There was a similar vase on every mantelpiece, filled with stick-like rolled paper spills, so that people could light them from the fire and use them to light pipes or candles. Carefully she rolled her paper until it looked like a spill. Then she unrolled the last few inches again, so that a curl of paper was loose and the first line of writing just visible.

She crept down to the library and placed it among the other spills in the brass vase on the mantelpiece. Anyone who found it might fancy that it had been sitting there for days and only just begun to unravel. Faith looked at it, nestling among the other spills, and felt like an artist.

When she checked the library again a couple of hours later, the new spill was gone.

Chapter 23

INFILTRATION

THE NEXT MORNING, FAITH FOUND HERSELF stepping out of Dr. Jacklers's carriage at the excavation site, accompanied by Uncle Miles. For once the sky was clear and the sun bright, but Faith felt only a turbulence of nerves, gripping her sketchbook so hard that the edge dug into her fingers. She had no idea whether the doctor had persuaded everyone to accept her presence, or whether she would find herself a bone of contention, chewed by rival dogs.

"Perhaps we had better ask the driver to wait a few minutes, just in case," said Uncle Miles. Evidently he was thinking along similar lines.

Faith was relieved that the first person to approach was Ben Crock, and even more relieved to find that he had been expecting her. As before, his manner was careful and polite. He showed no signs of ordering her off the site.

"I am sure the gentlemen will want to greet you properly, Miss Sunderly, but they are busy setting up a commemorative photograph right now."

As she followed the foreman and her uncle down the zigzagging path into the little gorge, Faith felt a little glad that she had not robbed Clay of all his photographic commissions.

Down by the tunnel, a gleaming, dome-headed figure immediately caught her eye. Lambent was dressed in a most peculiar array of garments. A shining white pith helmet was perched on his head. He wore the top half of a brilliant white linen suit, but with Turkish-style purple pantaloons, gathered at the knee into high boots. He also seemed to be carrying a tropical fly-whisk, and flicking its plume of horsehair at imaginary flies.

Faith was not sure whether he had deliberately dressed this way, or whether items of his collection had simply fallen on him.

Clay's camera tripod stood facing the entrance of the tunnel. The cloth-draped "Bedouin tent" structure had been moved, with all its genteel furniture, so that it stood slightly to one side of the tunnel entrance. On the divan reclined a solitary figure in a dark green dress.

Dr. Jacklers was kneeling in front of the tunnel entrance and shuffling this way and that on his knees in response to Clay's instructions. When he saw Faith and Uncle Miles, however, he leapt to his feet and came over to greet them.

"We should find you somewhere in the shade . . ." He looked over his shoulder at the draped structure. "Lambent—what about having Miss Sunderly sit next to your wife? If one lady lends gentility to the picture, why not double the effect?"

Lambent stopped dead and appeared to observe Faith for the first time. His smile faded and he looked away, appearing deeply uncomfortable. Faith wondered whether he had intended to avoid noticing her.

"Yes," he said, after a pause that was slightly too long. "Why not?" His pained tone told Faith everything she needed to know. She was permitted on the site, but she was not welcome. Had the doctor made his suggestion in her absence, she suspected that Lambent would probably have given a very different answer. Instead, the magistrate had been put in a situation where he could not refuse without being incredibly rude.

With deep misgivings, Faith walked forward to the tent. As she drew closer she could see that it was indeed Agatha Lambent seated in the shadow, dressed in a green dress and bonnet, and swaddled in scarves and lace shawls almost to suffocation. On the table beside her gleamed a silver tea set, and an unhappy glass vase of lilies that threatened to pitch over with every gust.

"Good afternoon, Mrs. Lambent," murmured Faith as she sat down, keeping her tone civil with some effort. She remembered the day of the funeral all too clearly.

The older woman did not look at her, but continued nursing a small glass of clear liquid in her shaky, lace-gloved hands. A caprice of the breeze left Faith downwind of Mrs. Lambent for a moment, and a strong smell seared her nostrils. Myrtle had been right, Faith realized. Mrs. Lambent's "medicine" was indeed strong liquor.

"We should be shown discovering something!" declared Lambent, recovering his composure. "Where is the aurochs horn?" The four gentlemen hastened away to the other tents, debating the matter.

Agatha Lambent stirred herself and moved forward on the divan, so that she partially emerged from the shade. Faith realized that the older woman must be doing so to make herself clearly visible to the camera. She moved to do likewise, but was brought up short by a sharp cough from Mrs. Lambent.

"Miss Sunderly." Mrs. Lambent spoke quietly, hardly moving her mouth. "If you have any sense of consideration and decency, you will stay with your face in shadow. This photograph is to be a *carte de visite*, for circulation among our acquaintance, perhaps even for publication. Your name will *not* be among those written beneath it. We cannot have the name of Sunderly linked to this endeavor."

Faith felt warmth stealing up from the little cauldron of anger she kept at her core.

"I know that you did not ask to appear in this photograph," Agatha Lambent conceded. "Dr. Jacklers and my husband have put us both in an impossible position. For my husband's part in that, I apologize."

Faith found that she was trembling from head to foot. Suddenly meek silence was impossible.

"If you want to apologize, Mrs. Lambent," she said under her breath, "you can apologize for shutting us out of your house on the day of my father's funeral, and forcing my mother to walk miles in the pouring rain."

Agatha Lambent narrowed her eyes and sniffed.

"I see that you have your mother's manners," she murmured coldly.

"*You* cannot talk to *me* about manners," answered Faith, just as icily. "Do not worry—I shall stay in the shadows. I have no more wish to be seen with you than you have to be seen with me."

Before she could say anything else, the gentlemen returned. Clay positioned himself behind his camera, and Dr. Jacklers and Lambent knelt before the tunnel entrance. Lambent held a curling horn, discolored and honey-sticky with seize and varnish. Both men stared at it with pantomimish solemnity.

"Where shall *I* stand?" called out Uncle Miles. There was an uncomfortable silence.

"Erm . . ." Dr. Jacklers cleared his throat. "Actually, Cattistock, you would be of great service if you were to stand just *behind* the ladies' tent, and hold the cloth down to stop it billowing and spoiling the photograph."

With a rather stony look on his round, pleasant face, Uncle Miles walked past, presumably to station himself behind the tent.

Clay fiddled with his camera, adjusting the accordion-like bellows so that the front of it slid forward.

"Hold position!" he said, and removed the lid from the lens.

The seconds crawled by. Faith gritted her teeth. She was glad of the shadows, she told herself. She was pleased that she did not have to sit with the sun in her eyes for over a minute.

After what felt like five minutes, Clay covered the lens with the lid once more. "Thank you—it is quite safe to move now!"

"Back to work, everyone!" called out Lambent, flicking at imaginary mosquitoes with his whisk. The laborers stopped watching, and Dr. Jacklers, Uncle Miles, and Lambent strolled back to the tents. Clay's head and shoulders disappeared beneath the "hood," the black cloth attached to the back of the camera. From within the camera could be heard the faint clink of bottles.

"Thank you, Miss Sunderly," murmured Agatha Lambent without looking at her.

Faith tightened her grip on her fan, hearing its sandalwood slats creak under the strain. She did not want to be thanked by this woman, particularly not in such a low, sincere tone.

"Whether you believe it or not," continued the magistrate's wife, "I am usually kind. However, I am a good wife first and foremost. My husband is standing for Parliament, and his reputation must be protected at all costs."

"Then perhaps you should have stopped him from wearing those pantaloons," Faith murmured, as she rose from her seat.

"A wife cannot always rein in her husband's impulses,"

answered Mrs. Lambent gravely, "but she must always strive to protect him from the consequences."

Faith walked away without looking back. She had been insulted, but at least she had not been turned off the site.

She slipped one hand into her pocket and closed it around a small, cold coin. It was a reminder that revenge was possible, even in the enemy's camp.

The arrival of the Sunderly daughter had not gone unnoticed, and Faith could feel the weight of hard, wondering gazes. She was relieved when Crock approached her once again.

"Miss, I was thinking you might want to wait until the men stop for lunch before you make any sketches in the tunnel. Until then, if you would care to make some drawings of the best finds, I could move a chair into that tent for you." He nodded toward the tent where Faith had seen the ancient bone needle.

"Yes, thank you, Mr. Crock!" Even though Faith felt like an imposter, it was so refreshing to be treated like a useful member of a team, rather than some kind of strawberry ice that needed to be kept in the shade.

She followed him as he carried a folding chair into the tent, set it up, and dusted it down for her.

"I am sorry for your loss," Crock added in a quiet tone.

Faith stared at him, feeling as though somebody had pulled away the ground beneath her feet. It was, she realized, a perfectly natural thing to say in the situation. However, nobody else had said it.

"Thank you," she said.

"How is your family?" he asked.

Faith thought of drenched sobbing on the highway, ransacked drawers, desperate hunts for ghost-killing guns. All the polite answers died on her tongue. She shook her head silently.

"So . . . you needed to be out of the house for a while." Crock nodded slowly. "And coming here, you feel closer to your father." His gaze was very earnest and very blue. He had outdoor eyes, Faith decided, reflecting the light of countless skies.

His compassion cut Faith to the quick, as she thought of her many ulterior motives. At the same time, she realized that he was partly right. This strange scent of dust, cloven earth, and boiled horse hoofs really did make her feel that she was breathing the air of her father's world.

"Mr. Crock, did anybody ever find out why the mining-basket chain broke?"

"We haven't found the broken link yet," answered the foreman with a frown. "It must have dropped down the shaft after it snapped and fallen down a crack. When we find it, we'll know. Meanwhile, we're keeping the guy ropes short, and only lowering folks one at a time."

"Could a thief have crept in by night and damaged it?" asked Faith.

"Yes, if he had cat's feet." Crock nodded toward the laborers. "We have three navvies on the site, and they sleep here in the tents. I pity any thief who broke *their* rest."

Faith's curiosity was sparked by the missing link. Perhaps Crock was right and it had really fallen down a crack. She wondered, however, whether a stealthy hand had hidden it. Perhaps it had not broken through rust or fatigue. Perhaps it had been filed through.

When the laboring men stopped for lunch, Faith was shown to the tunnel and provided a chair, an easel, and a small folding table. A lantern's yellow light showed her the tunnel's timber supports and its rugged earth and rock walls.

Faith's mouth was dry. To maintain her cover, somehow she

would need to create something that could pass for a skilled drawing of rock strata. Somebody had cut grooves into the walls with a trowel to make the strata clear for her, but she could hardly make out the difference between the layers. She could only hope that everybody else around her knew even less about section drawings than she did.

In case anybody was watching, she made a great show of holding her pencil at arm's length and calculating the slope of the strata, then making confident-looking dots and tiny crosses on the paper.

At one point she was unnerved to realize that Crock was looking over her shoulder at her sketchbook, eyes bright in the lantern-light. Kind as he might be, the foreman was most likely to see through her squiggles and dots. She risked a few faint lines, copying the slope of the trowel grooves.

There was a rustle. A few papers had been placed on the table next to her.

"Mr. Lambent's draftsman made a few rough sketches, before he broke his wrist," said Crock. "I thought you might have a use for them." He left again before Faith could thank him.

The sketches were unfinished, but the draftsman had managed to capture the shape of the hill. Better yet, the drawings had scribbled labels for the strata, such as "black cave earth," "flint," "shale," and so forth.

Gratefully Faith corrected her lines and labeled the layers as he had indicated. For some time she had dearly wished that the whole of Vane would sink beneath the gray and turbulent sea. Now she admitted to herself that, should such a calamity occur, she would not be sorry if Ben Crock came upon a boat in time.

. . . . .

Faith's gratitude to the foreman was not enough, however, to make her reconsider her plans. She was there, after all, to cause confusion and conflict.

She had been discreetly observing the laborers. They were divided into two groups, she realized. Three strongly built men with Irish accents took care of the actual digging inside the cave and emerged with barrows of rubble. Two locals were on hand for the rest of the fetching, carrying, sweeping away underfoot gravel, and pushing barrows of rubble to a nearby heap. The two groups barely seemed to speak a word to each other.

Only the local men interested her. If she wanted to infect Vane with an idea, she needed to put it into their heads first.

She found her chance in the mid-afternoon, not long before Uncle Miles was due to take her home. The two men had stepped aside to take a short rest and enjoy their allowance of beer. Their barrow full of rubble was unattended. Out of her pocket she took the coin and dropped it in among the broken rocks, so that it was just peeping out. It was an old Spanish silver piece-of-eight that Faith's father had brought back from his travels. The blackened tarnish around the edge made it look mysterious.

A little later, Faith saw the laborers return to the barrow. One of them stooped to stare at it intensely, then dug his elbow into his friend's ribs. Both whispered and glanced about furtively, then one man plucked something out of the barrow and pushed it hastily into his pocket.

By the end of the second day, Faith drew fewer stares at the excavation site. She was not precisely accepted, but she was no longer quite so interesting. Her sketches were improving too, thanks to some late-night consultation of her father's books, and everyone seemed happy to leave her to it.

She soon found that, under cover of sketching, she could set up her folding chair and easel wherever she pleased and eavesdrop to her heart's content, watching the scene from beneath her lashes.

Very soon, with her deft pencil, she might have drawn a map of the little camaraderies and frictions that ruled the excavation.

Dr. Jacklers was happier than she had ever seen him. He was forever consulting his precious copy of the *Reliquae Aquitanicae*, the latest and most exciting book about cave artifacts. Possessed of this source of cave-hunting lore, the doctor ruled supreme in the tunnel itself. He drove pegs into the cave floor and ran taut "datum line" strings between them, dividing the area into grids so that it could be dug up a square at a time. Ben Crock nodded courteously, agreed to anything suggested, and then altered the doctor's orders slightly when passing them on to his men.

Lambent strode around the site and involved himself in everything. He examined newly excavated hyena bones and axes from the Glacial Age, became excited about them, ran into his house with them, ran out with books from his library, and put the artifacts back in the wrong box. Crock quietly followed his rampages, setting everything straight in his wake.

Despite her famous ill health, Agatha Lambent came by again. She spent her visit sitting like an invalid queen in her billowing shelter, spectating with regal distance. Ben Crock could frequently be seen stopping before her divan throne to make solicitous inquiries, his cap in his hand. Perhaps he was afraid that, without regular attention, she would fall over in the wind and break.

To Faith's surprise, Miss Hunter also visited. She showed no interest in the actual dig, but was content to drink tea with Mrs. Lambent. Her arrival had a remarkable effect upon both Dr. Jacklers and Lambent. The former stormed off to the farthest corner of the site and stared moodily at mammoth teeth. The latter appeared to lose all interest in the dig and joined the tea-drinking in the "Bedouin tent."

Crock was the glue that held everything together. He kept the site under control, without raising his voice or drawing attention to himself. He appeared to have eyes and ears everywhere, and an uncanny ability to detect problems in the bud and nip them. In short, Faith quickly deduced that if she wanted to spy, steal, connive, or do anything else underhanded, then Crock was likely to be her biggest problem.

The two local men, on the other hand, had changed their manner since the incident with the coin. They looked more alert and hungry, and were given to secretive, animated conversations in corners. Several times Faith noticed them surreptitiously searching through the rubble in their barrow, and wandering into parts of the site where they did not usually work.

"Maybe something in it after all," she heard one of them say, failing to notice her inside the nearby tent. "Maybe old Sunderly wasn't happy with his share."

"Or perhaps the others wanted a *larger* share, and he knew too much," suggested the other. "They left out the doctor, didn't they?"

Faith's jaw ached with trying not to smile. Whoever had found her half-rolled paper spill had clearly read it, and shared its contents with others. If word had reached these men, it was probably gossip all over the island. Her plan was working.

In spite of everything, there was real pleasure in the thought of her lie sending tremors through Vane, knocking her enemies off balance. She was filled with pride and a sense of power. She was *good* at this . . . and getting better.

Chapter 24

TREMORS

ON SUNDAY, OF COURSE, THERE WAS NO WORK at the excavation, nor any possibility of Faith visiting the site. On Myrtle's insistence, the whole Sunderly family, dressed in their night-hued best, braced themselves, and went to church.

As they entered all conversation died among the waiting congregation. Faith felt sick. It was too much like the funeral day a week before. As the family trooped up the aisle, however, the whispers sounded nervous, not venomous. When they arrived at the box pew in which they had rented space, those already seated in it moved out without a word, taking pains to avoid passing too close to them.

Clay, who had seemed so lost and ineffectual during the funeral, now stamped up into his pulpit with a purpose. His sermon was about the dead, respect for the dead, kindness to those they left behind. What sort of people were they if they mocked the deceased? Were they inviting vengeance from the unseen powers?

Halfway through this sermon there was a muffled squawk from somewhere in the main body of the church, followed by concerned cries.

". . . fainted!" somebody called out.

Trapped in her box pew, Faith could not look around. From the noises behind her she could tell that somebody was being carried out. After a pause, the sermon continued.

After the service, as the Sunderly family was leaving the churchyard, Clay hurried after them, his brow creased with concern.

"Mrs. Sunderly, Mr. Cattistock—I am very sorry to tell you this, but I am afraid your maid Jeanne Bissette was taken ill during the service. She is recovering now . . . but she refuses to leave the church."

"Why ever not?" demanded Myrtle.

"I am afraid a rather grotesque fancy has taken possession of her imagination. I shall try to dissuade her from it, but she believes herself cursed. Haunted. She absolutely refuses to leave holy ground."

Myrtle's face was invisible under her veil, but she was silent a moment and seemed to be taking his words on board.

"I have heard some of the rumors," she said softly. "How widely believed are these stories? Will all our servants use them as an excuse to abandon us?"

Clay opened his mouth, then closed it again, looking pained.

"I am sorry, Mrs. Sunderly. I fear the tales are commonly regarded as fact. Every day people visit the parsonage, demanding to know why I have not 'done something about the ghost.'"

"Then . . . if you told them that burying my husband would lay the ghost . . ." suggested Myrtle.

"Alas, decisions regarding his place of burial are no longer in their hands or mine. The law must decide." Clay looked uncomfortable. "And . . . I could not in conscience encourage their superstitions, which are too far entrenched already. Some claim to have *seen* the ghost, walking the cliff-paths near your house. Just yesterday, a sizeable donation was left on the church altar, with an unsigned note asking me to say prayers for the, er, unquiet spirit.

"As for Jeanne Bissette, her fear appears quite genuine. Indeed, she seems to be in a dangerously nervous state."

It was only later that evening that one of Clay's chance remarks struck Faith with new force. Somebody had anonymously paid a "sizeable" amount for prayers to lay the ghost. They had also left an unsigned note, like the one that had lured Faith's father to his death.

Somebody out there was desperately afraid of the Reverend's spectre, and just as desperate to hide their identity. Perhaps Faith's "ghost" had done more than feed the Lie Tree. Perhaps she had frightened the murderer.

Chapter 25

RIDING THE BEAST

A LIE WAS LIKE A FIRE, FAITH WAS DISCOVERING. At first it needed to be nursed and fed, but carefully and gently. A slight breath would fan the newborn flames, but too vigorous a huff would blow it out. Some lies took hold and spread, crackling with excitement, and no longer needed to be fed. But then these were no longer *your* lies. They had a life and shape of their own, and there was no controlling them.

Some ideas caught more easily than others, of course, and there is no spark quite like the promise of treasure.

As she rode with her uncle in the doctor's carriage on the third morning, Faith could not help noticing that along the lonely road to the dig there were now a few idlers, leaning against the breakwater with their hands in pockets, or chatting in the shadow of the cliff. There was something lazily purposeful about them, like gulls with an instinct for scraps gathering over a boat's wake.

As they neared the site, the carriage passed the pile of broken rubble from the excavation. Three of the local children were picking over the broken stones with hungry zeal.

At the site itself there was an air of tension. Spotting Lambent in earnest conversation with Dr. Jacklers and Ben Crock, Faith set up her easel within discreet eavesdropping distance.

"Some bee has flown into their bonnet," the doctor was saying, "and unless we know the species of bee and where it sits in the bonnet, we cannot shake it out."

"I have asked them what they mean by it," said Crock. As usual he was slightly bowed, so that he did not rival Lambent for height. "They made sour faces at me, and slouched away without giving proper answer. One of them called me a 'dog in the manger,' and said he supposed I was 'getting my portion.'"

"Your *portion*?" The doctor's face darkened. "What, are those fellows turning scientist? What interest can these oafs possibly have in fossils and bones? Unless . . . Can it be that somebody has been offering them money for specimens?"

"There is worse, sir," interjected Crock. "The navvies tell me they chased two intruders from the site last night."

"Vagrants?" suggested Dr. Jacklers.

"Vagrants would head to the tunnel for shelter," said Crock, "or the tents for easy pickings. These men were at the top of the shaft, cranking up the mining basket."

"Museums!" Lambent struck his palm with his fist. "I knew this would happen! Some museum must have got wind of our discoveries. You know how they are, always ready to steal glory and specimens from the gentleman scientist! They must have agents on Vane! Fossil-thieves! Mammoth-snatchers!"

"The navvies recognized one of the men," Crock continued. "They say it was Stoke." Peter Stoke was one of the two local men who worked on the site.

"Stoke!" Lambent glanced toward the man in question. "Are they sure? Do you believe them?"

"They seem certain, sir, and I cannot imagine why they would lie."

"Will you excuse me, gentlemen?" said Lambent, who had been swelling with annoyance throughout Crock's explanation. "It seems I must have a discreet word with Stoke."

Lambent strode over to the two Vane men, who were loading rubble into their barrow, in order to have his "discreet word." As it turned out his "word" was neither discreet nor singular. There were many words, some of which echoed back down the gorge.

". . . criminals . . . see you in jail if you do not leave my sight right now!"

Both the local men departed, casting alarmed and resentful looks over their shoulders as they did so.

Lambent strode back to join his friends. "Crock, I believe we shall need to hire two more of your navvy friends," was all he said.

This was not the end of the matter. Trouble waited its moment and struck in the early afternoon. Faith was examining one of her sketches when she happened to look up out of the little gorge toward the top of the nearby ridge.

"Who is that?" she asked reflexively.

It was just a human head and shoulders, silhouetted against the sun, peering down into the gorge.

Crock, who was standing within earshot, looked up and was just in time to see the silhouette before it ducked out of sight again. He said nothing but broke into a sprint and started scrambling up the side of the gorge, ignoring the zigzag path.

There was a *cra-thock* noise. It seemed to Faith that a rock some ten yards away suddenly jumped in the air, then landed and rolled around. Then she looked at it, and saw that it had cracked in half. It had not "jumped"; it had been thrown down from a height.

Faith jumped to her feet and sprinted for the tunnel. Canvas tents might slow a thrown rock, but she would be safer in the tunnel.

On the ridge above she could hear a lot of confused shouting. One of the voices belonged to Crock. There followed sounds of a very brief scuffle, more shouting, then quiet.

After a little while, Uncle Miles appeared at the entrance to the tunnel.

"Faith, I am afraid we must cut our day short. There has been some trouble, and there may be more. A handful of local men have been causing a ruckus, talking about navvies taking local men's jobs—some confused talk about gold too. Lambent has advised us to leave in case they come back."

"Was anybody hurt?" asked Faith.

"Nobody on our side," answered her uncle. "On that subject, remind me never to pick a fight with Ben Crock. I would sooner go fisticuffs with a locomotive."

It was enough. It had to be enough. There were people in Vane who believed in the smuggler's gold sufficiently to sneak into the site, search the rubble, and throw vengeful rocks. It was time for Faith to visit the Lie Tree again and discover whether her efforts had borne fruit.

When dusk came, Faith slipped out through the roof garden in her funeral clothes once again. This time she wore the cloak Mrs. Vellet had recommended. The housekeeper had been right; it did make her much warmer.

The rowing seemed easier this time. Her back muscles were growing accustomed to the strain, and her mind was too busy to panic about the rearing of the waves. The sea cave sucked her in, and she beached in the cavern full of bellow and roar.

Faith braced herself, cloaked her lantern, then clambered into the Lie Tree's cavern.

At a glance she could see that the dark mass of the Tree had grown larger once again. The pot was no longer visible, lost in the mound of black foliage. The tendrils that spilled onto the stone shelf now almost hid it, trailing down the pale stone sides. As she drew closer, her foot hooked in something. Looking down, she realized that there were now dark, weaving vines splaying outward, as if a giant, many-legged spider had been swatted against the floor.

Faith continued to approach, stepping carefully in the spaces between the vines, anxious to avoid crushing a fruit by accident. Again she heard the cacophony of little breaths in the air around her, molten words, untethered sounds.

"Why do you grow this way for *my* lies?" she asked aloud. "My father's were more important, and believed by many more people."

Maybe it's because it likes me. It was an idiot thought, and yet Faith could not quite push it away. *Or maybe it's because I like it.*

She found the fruit with its frill of dead petal nestled in the great central cluster of leaves. It was larger than the last, almost an inch in breadth. This time she had brought a rug to lay under her, a cushion to support her head and neck while she was unconscious, and a water flask.

I know that this will be unpleasant, she told herself as she cut open the fruit, *but I know that it will probably not kill me.*

She quickly crammed the fruit pulp into her mouth, choked, grimaced, and washed it down with water. The darkness came for her and beat her like a drum until all the light was gone.

. . . . .

Faith knew, even as she stood there on the grass, that she was slipping on an old memory like a shoe.

She was nine years old, and the whole family was visiting London, and as a special treat they had gone to see the Crystal Palace. She had been dazzled by the palace's glassy vastness and had been a little frightened in the Great Maze.

And then, of course, they had gone to see the dinosaurs.

The great beasts had been given their own landscape. It made them look at home, alive, as though one had discovered them in a chance moment of stillness. They had been caught basking on the little islands, strolling between the trees, and luxuriating in their private lake.

Some crouched froglike, reptilian mouths so broad they seemed to grin. Slender plesiosaur necks snaked up from the water. Ichthyosaurs lay half beached, raising their heads into the air to gape their tapering toothed snouts, their eyes eerily segmented like oranges. The huge, humpbacked megalosaurus seemed about to turn its vast, reptilian bulk around and sway off between the trees.

Faith held Nurse's hand and How slept in his green perambulator. Mama was beautiful in the blue-tinted shade of her parasol. Papa, who knew everything, was talking about how the models were made, and about the scientists who had thrown a dinner party inside one of the iguanodons. The sun was bright, and there were white, fluffy goose-feather clouds. The strolling crowds were loud and laughing and all the ladies were pretty.

And then the megalosaurus slowly blinked its dull, sorrowful eyes, shifted its low-slung weight and started to move.

Suddenly Faith was holding nobody's hand. She was no longer nine years old. Nurse, Papa, Mama, and How were all gone. The sky was gray, and the dinosaurs were stalking, slithering, and swimming toward the crowds.

It could not be happening, so nobody ran. An ichthyosaur grabbed a lady by her narrow waist and dragged her into the water. The two big, swollen iguanodons bit off heads without malice or passion. Needle-snouted crocodiles slithered over the grass with blinding speed, lunging for children.

None of them attacked Faith. They lurched and lunged past her on either side. She reached out one hand and felt leathery, reptilian scales slide past her fingertips. When the great megalosaurus halted before her and laid itself flat on the ground, she clambered up its foot and shoulder to sit side saddle on its rugged hump.

The megalosaurus rose to its feet again, and she was high, high enough to look out across the park and see another large dinosaur, with spikes down its back and a single rider perched on its head. As she watched, the other dinosaur broke its way out of the park, railings tumbling as easily as cricket stumps.

Seeing the other rider, she felt the strangest sense of recognition, like a glimmer of motion in an old spotted mirror.

There you are.

She could not remember who the other rider was, but she knew it was somebody like herself. She also knew that they were her enemy. They had taken someone precious from her, and she was there to pursue them.

Sensing her wishes, the megalosaurus set off in pursuit, swaying out through the break in the fence and on to the thoroughfare, followed by a rampage of other dinosaurs. Faith kept her eye on the other rider while the iguanodons overturned omnibuses and ate horses. Carts cracked and crunched under the megalosaurus's broad feet. It roared, parasol spokes caught between its teeth.

Faith was gaining on her quarry. Soon she would be able to see the other rider's face. Soon her steed would be close enough to lunge for the rear haunches of theirs.

A steely shriek split the air above her. She looked up, just in time to see a winged shape scythe down from the sky toward her, a human silhouette just visible on its back. A toothed beak gaped. Then there was blackness, and the painless, soul-sickening click of her own neck breaking.

Chapter 26

TEETH

IT WAS GOOD TO FEEL THE GRASS UNDER HER hands, under her head. Faith breathed deeply. She was not dead then. That knowledge was luxurious. She opened her eyes and looked up at the night sky. It was so clear that she could just make out the colors of the brightest stars and the faint, smoky glow of impossibly distant clusters.

I am alive, she told herself. *I did not have my neck broken by a pterodactyl. The model dinosaurs in Crystal Palace Park did not come to life and eat London.*

And then, with a little more puzzlement:

I am outdoors.

Faith sat up with a jerk, then had to support herself as the world spun and tilted. It was true. She was no longer in the cave.

She looked around, and found that she was sitting on a grassy headland. Her legs below the knee were dangling into a hole, half hidden by a thick tangle of low bushes. Peering down into the hole, she could make out the faintest glimmer of yellowish light.

"That must be my lantern," she said aloud. Now that she thought about it, it seemed that she *did* remember untying her own ropes. Her fingernails were chipped and broken. She turned over her hands, and looked at their grime and grazes. Yes, there had been climbing. Squeezing and clambering. She had delved through the cave network and found another way out.

"I have woken much sooner this time," she whispered to herself. She stood up and swayed. "And my head is clearer," she added, as the stars prickled and pulsed.

Faith looked around, trying to recognize the shapes of the headlands and fit them into her mind's map. She edged close to the precipice and peered down, feeling a tremble in the backs of her knees.

She knew where she was! She was not far from the high road that ran between Bull Cove and the town, close by the lookout hut where she had been abandoned in favor of "miscellaneous cuttings."

There is a ratting at the lookout hut on the coast road every Monday night, Paul Clay had said during their confrontation in the roof garden. *Come and find me there—we can talk about your precious murder.*

It was Monday night, and she was close to the hut. Attending the ratting had once seemed unthinkable, but now Faith could not remember why. She wanted to talk to Paul Clay.

He had dared her to come. It had been a dare he did not expect her to accept, a way of slapping her in the face with her own squeamishness and powerlessness. Now, however, she felt neither squeamish nor powerless. She could still remember the texture of dinosaur hide against her skin.

A patient, insistent wind tugged at her clothes as she walked along the road. The stars blazed with cold patience. Low trees quivered and skulked.

At last she recognized the fork in the road where she had been unloaded from the Lambents' carriage. She found the twisting path she had used before, until she saw the lumpish silhouette of the hut jutting from the rocky slope. This time its outline was complicated by a small throng of figures, and she could hear voices. An orange glow spilled from the open door.

They were men, all men. *What are you doing?* screamed a part of her mind. *Why are you here?* Panic was beating its wings somewhere in her head, but for now it was muffled. She pulled forward the hood of her cape to hide her face. She waited, just on the very edge of the halo of lantern-light.

There were three boys talking by the door. As she watched, the youngest turned his head and saw her. As he did so, the light from the doorway fell upon his face. It was Paul Clay.

He stared, and the others with him turned to peer in Faith's direction. Paul whispered something hastily to his companions, then walked quickly over to Faith.

"What are you doing here?" he asked incredulously.

"You dared me, remember?" It suddenly occurred to Faith to wonder how she looked, cowled and black clad, lurking among the shadows and furze. "I thought *I* was supposed to be frightened, not you."

"I never thought you would come!" he hissed. "Are you mad? Do you *want* people to see you here?"

"Did you tell them who I am?" demanded Faith.

"Do you think you're in disguise?" Paul rolled his eyes. "There are scarce a dozen folk our age on the whole island. Anybody who sees you *knows* who you are." He cast a glance over his shoulder. "Just now, I had to tell my friends you were touched. Struck to the brain with grief. Harmless but given to wandering. How else could I explain your turning up here?"

Faith glanced across at the hut and realized that the pair of them were drawing some surreptitious gazes.

"How else was I supposed to talk to you?" she whispered. "You never came to see me!"

"What do you expect?" Paul narrowed his eyes. "You stole our photography commissions, up at the dig! Why? Was that one of your spiteful games?"

Faith fought a mad temptation to tell him that it was, just to see if she could make him flare up.

"No," she admitted. "I needed to get on to the site, to investigate. Did your father tell you about the chain that broke on the mining basket?"

Paul nodded. "You were in the basket with your brother, he said. It wasn't dangerous though, was it? The guy ropes saved the basket from falling."

"Letting *us* ride in the basket was only decided at the last minute," whispered Faith. "It changed everything, because we were *children*. Everything was checked and tightened up again—and that was when the guy ropes were attached. If an adult had ridden down instead, or maybe two adults, like my father and the foreman . . ."

"No checks," said Paul thoughtfully. "No guy ropes."

"Smash," said Faith.

"You think it was meant to kill your father," said Paul, not bothering to make it a question.

"I think someone weakened a link," Faith agreed, "and it must be somebody allowed on the site." She did not want to mention the Lie Tree, her visions, or the fact that Paul's own father was one of her three main suspects.

Paul considered with his usual clifflike inscrutability, and gave a tilt of his head that might have been first cousin to a nod.

"It fits," he murmured quietly. "I talked to people—found out about folks in town that might have wanted your father dead, like the family of my friend Toby who got caught in the trap. They were all home that night.

"The dig then." He frowned. "Mr. Lambent. Dr. Jacklers. The foreman Crock. Stoke and Carrol. The navvies." He gave Faith a small, dark smile. "Me and my father."

"Uncle Miles," added Faith. "Mrs. Lambent. Miss Hunter."

"Not all of those would be strong enough," Paul said thoughtfully.

"It might not matter," said Faith. "I think I know why my father never fired his pistol at the murderer." She remembered her recent vision, the spined dinosaur receding into the distance, and the sudden ambush from the pterodactyl rider. That was the message of the vision, she realized. Not a solitary enemy, but a pair. "I think there were *two* killers. One to meet with him and distract him, the other to strike from behind. A pistol wasn't enough—he needed eyes in the back of his head."

Paul thought about this, then nodded slowly.

"Bodies are heavy," he said, with the confidence of experience. "Until you move a few, you don't realize how heavy. If he was put in the barrow and taken up to the cliff, that would be a lot easier with two."

"Paul!"

Looking up, Faith found that most of the milling figures had vanished into the hut. Only a ginger-haired boy of about sixteen remained peering out through the door.

"They're ready for the next dog!" he called to Paul. "Hurry up!" He gave Faith a brief, inquisitive glance. "While you're about it, be a gentleman and bring your lady friend in from the cold!"

A "no" would have been the easy and right answer, but it was not the one that Faith gave.

The hut was ill-lit and looked larger now that it was full of people. The closeness of bodies, male bodies, felt hostile and other. Their heavy boots made Faith feel fragile and pointless. Most people were looking toward the center of the room and did not notice her slipping in with Paul and the ginger-haired boy.

As she moved into the light, Paul peered at her, then frowned slightly. "What's wrong with your eyes?" he whispered.

"Nothing," said Faith, looking away from him. Paul's other friends had drawn closer as well, watching her with wary eagerness. Occasionally they darted impressed glances at Paul. It was not surprising, she supposed. They had sent him out for a mere lock of the Reverend's hair, and he had come back with the Reverend's entire crazy daughter. Fortunately, nobody else in the hut seemed to have any attention free for her.

Even from her position by the door, Faith could see that in the center of the hut wooden boards had been set up edge to edge to make a rectangular pen, about six feet by eight.

"Bessie!" announced somebody on the far side of the pen. The bellowing on all sides sounded affectionate.

Next to the pen, a man was holding up a dog. It was a bright-eyed Jack Russell terrier, and Faith was startled by how small and ordinary it looked. Somehow she had been expecting some wrinkle-faced, loose-jowled monstrosity, four feet at the shoulder.

"How much does she weigh?" shouted a man in the crowd, holding a watch in his hand.

"Fourteen pounds!" called her owner.

Men were handling bags that bulged and writhed, and emptying them into the pen. The crowd was counting to fourteen in unison, and now there were rats in the pit, skulking and scooting, finding corners and trying to climb them, boiling and tumbling over each other in their attempts to get out. Calls of Bessie's name rose to a roar of excitement.

"Now!" shouted the man with the watch, and Bessie's owner dropped her into the pit.

How fast she was, that bristle-faced little dog! It was a game. She darted, and cornered a rat, and bit down on its soft middle, and shook it, and moved on. Pounce. Grab. Shake. Another brown shape on the sawdust like a tiny sack of flour.

Faith's eyes deadened, but she kept watching. It was the same as it had been on the dreadful night when she could not take her gaze off the body on the rug.

She wanted there to be more blood and screeching. She wanted each death to detonate before her like a little black firework. She wanted it to matter. There was bellowing all around her, but the killing itself was soft and quiet and matter of fact. Life to death, life to death, with no more drama than turning over a counterpane.

"Thirty seconds left!" came the shout.

How sweet the terrier was! How businesslike! But Faith could only see its teeth now. It was only teeth.

"Only teeth," she said, and laughed. The sound was lost in the cacophony around her. Everybody was shouting, calling. Bellowing meat, laughing meat. Meat with only a tiny, brief wink of life. And what was life? Teeth. Teeth and a stomach and a blind, idiot impulse behind the eyes, telling the meat to kill and eat other meat.

And the bones fell to the ground, and other bones fell on top of them, and yet more bones, until there were whole hills and cliffs made of them. Death upon death upon death upon death. And two-legged animals dug up the old bones and wondered at them. And then they died as well and lay there, like rats in the sawdust, waiting to become old bones.

"Fourteen dead! Time!"

Bessie was scooped up, and now men were leaning over the wooden barricades, poking the dead rats with sticks to see if there was a tremor of life.

Something was tugging at Faith's sleeve. There was a voice in her ear.

"Come away." It was Paul. Paul Clay.

"No," said Faith. "I want to see this. This is funny. Let me watch." She felt light-headed. She thought of her vision, and the megalosaurus biting and biting, and the well-dressed headless corpses toppling to the ground.

Paul Clay was pulling on her arm now, and she let him lead her out of the hut, because how could it matter? She could still see it, she could still watch, it was happening in the darkness when she closed her eyes.

It was freeing to know that nothing mattered. There was a sense of space, as though the sky had lifted away and she had found out that the land and sea were made of smoke. Only smoke. She was smoke. Her body felt hot and light and airy.

"Sit down," said Paul.

"There is no need," said Faith. If she wanted, she could fly.

"Just sit down," said Paul. And she did, because otherwise he would keep saying and saying it, and what did it matter? "If you need to be sick—"

"Sick? I'm not sick!"

"You're pale as paper, and there's something wrong with your eyes."

"I have my father's eyes," said Faith. It was hard not to laugh. Paul Clay did not know how funny it was, and that made it all the funnier.

"Why did you come here?" Paul asked again, his voice edged with frustration and a hint of despair.

"I need you to do something for me," Faith admitted. "Your father changed a photograph by gluing a little boy's head on to a picture of you. Could *you* do something like that?"

"And make it look natural?" Paul frowned, regarding her warily. "Only if the parties were the right size, and looking the same way."

Faith fished out her notebook, and took out her precious only photograph of her father. She looked at it with a pang, then held it out toward Paul.

"Cut out my father's head," she said. "Glue it on to somebody in one of the excavation photos. Make it look as if my father is standing right there at the dig—haunting them all."

"Why?"

"I want to frighten a murderer."

"No," said Paul flatly.

"Why not?"

"Are you mad? The photographs might look like parlor games to you, but we need the money! My father pretends that we don't, but we do. If we get a reputation for making prank pictures with dead customers' faces, who will come to us?"

"You took a dare to cut off my father's hair!" snapped Faith. "Well, now I am daring you to cut out his face!"

"Oh, why not dare me to jump off a cliff?" Paul retorted. "There are dares *you* would not take."

"Are there?" Faith rose to her feet again. "Dare me. Dare me to do anything. And if I do it, you must make the photograph."

271

They locked gazes, and again Faith felt their conversation tipping toward a precipice of craziness and rashness, the way it always did.

"Take a rat out of that, bare-handed," Paul said, pointing to a bag on the ground with a tightly tied neck. Before Faith's eyes it stirred, three rounded shapes shifting and wriggling within. As soon as the words were out, Paul looked frightened.

"Wait!" he said as Faith crouched beside the bag and slightly loosened the stout cord around the neck. She made eye contact with him again, and plunged one hand inside.

There was rough fur against her fingers, and a spasm of movement that made her flinch. A furtive tickle of whiskers, a tiny claw-graze. She snatched toward the motion, and closed her hand about a rounded, hairy something. It was soft and frantic, twisting in her grip while she fought every instinct and kept hold of it.

There was a sharp pain near the base of her thumb, as unseen teeth fixed themselves in her flesh. Faith's arm jerked, but she kept her grip. She could not help smiling at Paul's expression of fascinated horror.

"Stop it!" Paul dropped to his knees beside her and dragged her hand out of the bag. The rat escaped her grip and fled into the darkened undergrowth. Its fellow inmates followed suit as the bag fell open.

"Why did you stop me?" Faith was furious. "I had the rat! You cannot say I failed!"

"Did it bite you?" Paul turned over her hand. There were two deep red tooth marks at the base of her thumb.

"What does it matter?" shouted Faith. "You wanted me to suffer, or you would not have given me the dare!"

"I wanted to see you back down!" exploded Paul. "Just once!"

"Get me another bag of rats!" demanded Faith.

"No!" Paul gripped his own hair, closed his eyes for a moment and let out a breath. "You win. You can have your photograph. Just . . . no more rats." He gave the empty bag on the ground a despairing look. "We should go," he said, in something closer to his usual tone, "before the rat catcher comes back and finds his wares gone."

He walked with her as far as the road, where she made him stop. She did not want him to see the opening to the Lie Tree's cave network.

"I never meant . . ." he began, then trailed off and shook his head. "Wash the wound," he said instead. "People die from rat bites."

Faith walked on, without looking back. She could not explain herself to him. The rat bite had hurt, but that had not bothered her. In a strange way the pain had been a relief, like talking to this boy who hated her.

Chapter 27

SILENCE LIKE A KNIFE

AFTER FAITH HAD BEEN WALKING FOR FIVE MIN-
utes or so, she heard the gravelly crunch of a footstep some
distance behind. Her first thought was that Paul had followed
her. When she snatched a glance over her shoulder, she saw two
figures, but neither of them was Paul. They were his friends, the
two older boys she had seen at the hut door.

"Slow down there!" called the taller, ginger-haired boy. "Don't
be frightened!"

There was something about being told not to be frightened
in that bare, moonlit scene that made Faith want to run. The
boys would be faster though, for they had no skirts to tangle
their legs.

The pair caught up, so that they were walking on either side
of her, at about two yards' distance.

"You shouldn't be walking out here alone," said the ginger-haired boy. "Why don't we come along with you, see you
home? We're friends of Paul. You'll be safe with us."

It was a natural enough offer, and perhaps even charitably
meant. The ginger-haired boy's smile was broad, but there was
a cold curiosity in his eyes. Faith knew he was not being kind

even before she caught him flicking a conspiratorial glance at his friend.

She tried walking more briskly, but they accelerated and kept up easily, and after a little while she slowed back to a normal pace.

"We can't leave you alone, miss," insisted the other boy, a tallow-haired youth with a broad nose and watchful eyes. "Chivalry don't permit it."

"We only want to talk to you," said the ginger-haired boy.

Faith slid one hand into her pocket and secretly levered open her father's folding knife. She was one rat between two dogs, but she could bite. *They outnumber me*, she thought with an odd calm, *and they are certainly bigger and stronger. But if I were to stab one of them, I think the other would be badly frightened.*

"You can tell us things," Ginger went on, "just like you would tell our friend Paul. We're all friends here, aren't we?"

Faith hesitated, then nodded, keeping her face blank and stupefied. Paul had told them she was "touched," and that was a part she could play. If she seemed dopey, any sudden moves on her part would take them by surprise.

"We were all very sad to hear about your father," Ginger remarked, without bothering to drop his smile, "and we were wondering . . ."

". . . what he did with his share of the treasure," finished Tallow.

Ginger gave a small, reproving hiss, and Faith caught him giving the other boy a pointed look.

"Ignore my friend," he said quickly. "Cartwheel went over his head yesterday, still a bit soft in the skull. We were just wondering . . . if the treasure was somewhere safe. Or . . . if you need us to move it to a better place."

"They never gave him treasure," said Faith, in a dreamy,

childlike voice. She turned to the ginger-haired boy and stared intensely at his left ear. "Is that why he was angry?"

"Your father was angry?" Ginger looked unnerved but tantalized, and Faith realized that he would snap up any scrap she threw him.

"I . . . I think so," she said. "I . . . can't remember."

"So what happened to the treasure?" asked Tallow, who appeared to have only a weak grasp on subtlety. "You been at the dig—the big hole in the ground. Did you see anybody with coins? Maybe in a bag?"

"No," murmured Faith. "Only the box." She saw both boys' faces sharpen with painful interest. She was almost starting to enjoy herself. "I don't know anything about the box!" she added for good measure, shaking her head vigorously. "I never saw it—I never saw anything! I never saw him give anyone the box."

"Who? Who was it that gave somebody the box?" asked Ginger.

"Mr. Lambent?" suggested Tallow in a none-too-quiet undertone.

Faith looked down at her own hem and did not deny it. She was watching her lie grow, nourished by nothing but hints and silences, and take a new shape before her eyes. Silence itself could be used as deftly and cruelly as a knife.

"We already know about Mr. Lambent's box," Ginger assured her swiftly and unconvincingly. "You can tell us all about that. Who did he give it to?" He watched her face carefully. "Mr. Clay? Mr. Crock?" There was a pause, and his eyes glittered with inspiration. "Or was it a lady? A lady with black hair?"

"Do you mean Miss Hunter?" asked Faith, taken by surprise. She could think of nobody else who would fit the description.

"We know she goes to the dig," said Tallow, and sniggered slightly, "and we know why."

"Why?" Faith was genuinely curious. Miss Hunter's visit to the dig had perplexed her. The postmistress was friends with Mrs. Lambent, but it would surely have been more comfortable to have visited her at the Paints.

"Well, we shouldn't be talking about that sort of thing in front of a respectable lady like you," declared Ginger. "Unless . . . you want to make a bargain. We tell you about Miss Hunter, you tell us about the box. Well?"

Faith slowly nodded.

"It's a secret everybody knows," said Ginger, with malicious relish. "Miss Hunter has a hidden sweetheart. She won't eat candied violets, but she orders them on every mailboat. She goes out riding alone in her trap at all times of the day and night, and she takes the north road, away from town. That road don't run to many places."

It was true. It led only to Bull Cove, the excavation, and the Paints.

"And sometimes," said Tallow with a grin, "they see a signal from the telegraph tower. A wink of light in the sun." He held up an imaginary something and swiveled it in the air. "Mirror," he said.

"They say Mrs. Lambent comes to the dig because she knows Miss Hunter drops by," added Ginger, with a wink. "Keeping an eye on the chicken coop, in case the fox gets in."

"Miss Hunter turned down Dr. Jacklers a dozen times," added Tallow. "Got her eye on a better bargain. Mrs. Lambent won't last forever, they say."

Faith remembered Lambent, who could not sit still for a minute, breaking off his striding and paleontology to sit and drink tea when Miss Hunter visited. It was hard to imagine anybody having a passionate affair with such a plump, snide, moorhen-like woman, but it made sense of both Miss Hunter's and Mrs. Lambent's visits to the dig.

Faith's vision had hinted at two murderers. Now that she thought of it, they might be more than allies. They might be lovers. Behind Lambent's tempestuous impulses, there might be a pair of neat, plump female hands pulling his strings.

At the same time, Faith was realizing something new. The sly, sharp Miss Hunter was a force to be reckoned with on the island, but she was not *liked*. There was no mistaking the gleeful malice in the boys' tones. Miss Hunter had poisoned the islanders' minds against the Sunderly family. Now Faith had the chance to return the favor.

"I never meant to see anything," she said in the same numb tone. "It was only an old box. And then Miss Hunter went away quickly in her trap."

The boys exchanged excited glances.

The ground was becoming more hummocky now, and dotted with small bushes. Not far away, Faith recognized the one that hid the entrance to the cavern. She slowed, slowed, stopped, then turned and stared blank-eyed back down the road.

"Who is that following us?" she asked, raising an arm to point.

Both boys started, and peered back into the darkness. At that moment a hazy clot of cloud drifted across the moon, briefly darkening the headland.

Faith ran.

She had cleared the nearest hummock and hidden herself among the low bushes before the confused shouting began. She heard feet pounding the turf this way and that. There were calls and entreaties. At last the footsteps stopped and she could hear two people panting for breath.

"I think she ran off the cliff!"

"Should we go down and look?"

"What good would that do? If she jumped, we can't nail her back together! We need to go!"

After the boys had left, Faith emerged, slipped over the quivering grass, and pulled back the bushes that concealed the aperture leading back into the cave network. The light from her lantern was still glimmering below. Guided by its radiance, she slid down inclines and squeezed through crevasses until she found herself again in the great cavern of the Tree.

The Lie Tree was waiting for her.

It had grown even in the few hours since her last visit; Faith was sure of it. She felt drained now, but as if she had come home.

A trailing loop of vines reminded her of a flowery swing she had seen in a painting. It seemed the most natural thing in the world to sit down on it. It creaked, but accepted her weight. Faith reached out to either side, stroking the backs of her hands against the cool, black foliage, then leaned back against the mesh of vines and closed her eyes.

The echoes of the sea were deafening. She could hear many sounds in them: the roaring of the megalosaurus in her dream, the bellowing in the hut, and the hostile whispering in the church. Sometimes she thought she heard her own name, lisped and mangled, as if an untried tongue was practicing it.

She had already chosen her lie.

"The smugglers' treasure is no longer at the excavation site," she told the plant. "Mr. Lambent gave it to his lover, Miss Hunter."

People were animals, and animals were nothing but teeth. You bit first, and you bit often. That was the only way to survive.

Chapter 28

WHITE EYES AND A
SHIVERED SKIN

FAITH WOKE IN, OR RATHER ON, HER OWN BED.
She was still dressed in her funeral clothes, and once again she
felt sick and exhausted. Groggily she recalled rowing back from
the cave, tottering up the stairs in the dark, and falling onto her
bed.

The memory of her night's adventures slowly unrolled itself,
like some macabre tapestry. It seemed a phantasmagoria. Riding
dinosaurs, being attacked by a pterodactyl, attending a ratting,
plunging her hand into a bag of rats . . .

Her attention was drawn by a pain in her hand. At the base
of her thumb she found two deep, ominously purple gouges,
the skin around them a startled yellow-white. Staring at it, she
remembered the pain of the rat's bite and the sting of washing
it in salt water later.

Faith really *had* gone to the ratting. She had been seen there,
a lone girl in a crowd of men. She had felt so sure and clear-
headed under the stars, but now her stomach churned at the
thought of the risks she had taken. Gossip would surely be
spreading. Her treasured invisibility would be in tatters. Again
Faith's mind was darting, ratlike, looking for corners and escapes.

She would have to deny everything outright, or say that she had gone for a walk and become lost.

She was parched. She was just draining the water from her bottle, when a terrible thought occurred to her. Suddenly she could not remember when she had last refilled the snake's water bowl.

Hastily she pulled the cloth from the cage. The snake was coiled among the rags as usual, but the gold and white flashes on its ebony scales looked dull and waxy.

"No!" Faith opened the cage door, poured water hastily into its bowl and gently stroked its coils. To her relief, it moved. When its head emerged, however, she saw that its eyes were covered by a translucent cloudy crust. "Don't die! Don't leave me! I am so sorry!" As it slid up her arm to recline across her shoulders, its scales felt papery against her skin.

There was a faint knock on the door.

"Excuse me, miss," came Mrs. Vellet's quiet voice. "If you would like to join your brother for breakfast in the nursery—"

"Mrs. Vellet!" With an impulse born of panic, Faith threw open the door. "The mouse you gave me for the snake a few days ago—how did it die? Could it have swallowed poison?"

Mrs. Vellet was a little taken aback by Faith's sudden snake-bedecked appearance at the door, but rallied well.

"The mouse was in a trap." The housekeeper looked uncertainly at the snake. "It does not seem likely that it was poisoned— but I suppose it is possible."

"Something is wrong with it—look!" Faith lifted the snake's foremost loop so that the housekeeper could see the milky eyes. "Is there anything in the medicine cabinet that might make her vomit?"

Mrs. Vellet was peering with a frown. "Miss—what happened to your hand?"

In her concern for the snake, Faith had completely forgotten to hide the bite. "There was a rat behind the barn!" she explained hastily. "It . . . It does not matter right now!"

"That wound needs more care than your pet does," Mrs. Vellet said, with surprising firmness.

"But—"

"Your snake is sloughing, miss," the housekeeper said patiently. "Nothing more."

Faith's mouth fell open. She felt like an idiot. Of course she knew that snakes shed their skin—she had seen them do so several times. However, it had not even crossed her mind as an explanation. She had only been able to think that the snake was dying and leaving her. Faith felt almost sick with relief. She had not killed the snake.

Fifteen minutes later, snakeless and dressed in her day clothes, Faith found herself sitting in the parlor while Mrs. Vellet unlocked the medicine cabinet.

The housekeeper held Faith's hand firmly but gently, and swabbed at the wound with a cloth dipped in something that stung. An acrid smell of alcohol filled the air. Faith tried not to flinch and looked away from the bite into the cabinet, which seemed to be full of bottles.

"It looks like a wine cupboard," she said aloud.

"The two invalid ladies who used to live here liked it that way." Mrs. Vellet glanced over her shoulder at the bottles. "You would be surprised at the cures they could find in it. Brandy to stimulate the heart. Cherry liqueur for fatigue. Oh, and anything mixed with tonic water is medicine against malaria, I am told."

"Is there a lot of malaria here?" asked Faith doubtfully.

"I never heard of any, miss, but I am sure the invalid ladies knew what they were about." The housekeeper's face was dead-pan, but there was a slight wry curl to her voice.

Then Mrs. Vellet frowned. She was staring past Faith and out through the window.

"Heaven save us," she murmured. "What is that?"

Turning to look, Faith could just make out a brownish-gray smear across the sky, some distance to the south.

"It looks like smoke!" said Faith. It was too close to come from the town. Only a few things lay in that direction—the church, the parsonage, the telegraph tower, the post office, and Miss Hunter's abode. A dark suspicion started to gnaw at her mind.

Mrs. Vellet stared out at the smoke, brow furrowed, appar-ently making the same calculations.

"You go to back to bed, Miss Sunderly," she said at last, with-out looking at Faith. "You need sleep, or you will make yourself ill. Prythe is taking letters to the post office this morning—he will find out if anything is amiss."

Yielding to exhaustion and the housekeeper's insistence, Faith tottered back to bed. She was sure that she could not sleep, but fell into slumber almost immediately. She dreamed that she was in a parlor drinking tea, and trying to hide the vines that crept out of her cuffs and collar. Miss Hunter sat opposite in a rocking chair, her skin papery, and her eyes frightened behind their crusted white shells.

Faith was next woken by the sound of murmurs, which sounded so close that they might have been in the room with her. It took her a few moments to realize that the muted conversation was taking place on the servants' stairs. She struggled out of bed and stole over to place her ear against the wall.

". . . preys on a man's mind." It sounded like Prythe, choosing his words carefully and solemnly as usual. "Do *you* think there is a curse?"

"I think there are as many curses in this house as unicorns," Mrs. Vellet answered drily.

"Jeanne thinks she is cursed." There was a long pause.

"How does she fare?" asked the housekeeper.

"Ill, and getting worse, even in the church. She cannot eat or sleep. She has nightmares, and is chilled to the bone. Some folk are saying that she is dying."

"Some folk say a lot of foolish things, and I hope they do not say it in Jeanne's hearing. I would not want that idea taking hold of her . . ."

The voices moved away.

Jeanne was not dying, Faith told herself. Of course she was not. There was no curse. It was nothing but Jeanne's imagination playing tricks on her. Nothing but the effects of continual fear, and sleeplessness, and lack of appetite, and sleeping in a cold church night after night . . .

There was a creeping sensation under Faith's skin. Just for a moment she wished that she could shed herself like a snake's skin, and slide away to be somebody new.

It was the middle of the afternoon. Faith had missed lunch, but a meal tray had been left outside her room, presumably by Mrs. Vellet.

Heading downstairs, she encountered Myrtle pacing the hall, fretful and intolerant of everything.

"Faith! Where in the world have you been?" She did not wait for an answer, which was just as well. "You need to look after your brother. He has been running wild this morning!"

"But I need to go to the excavation with Uncle Miles and make sketches!" exclaimed Faith.

"That dreadful place where chains snap and people throw rocks? No, Faith—I should never have allowed you to go there in the first place. Besides, your uncle left for the dig first thing this morning. Apparently they are close to breaking through into the lower chamber, and he did not wish to miss anything."

This was a blow. Now more than ever Faith wanted to be watching the members of the dig.

"Besides, I need you here to keep an eye on Howard. He has been writing—there is ink all over the nursery—and he has not been wearing his blue jacket! You know he must wear that whenever he is writing! He is going to school in a few years. . ." She paused and raised a hand to her forehead. "School," she murmured, as if the thought pained her.

"I am sorry," Faith began, "but the last time I put the jacket on him he cried so much—"

"Then let him cry!" exploded Myrtle. "It is for his own good! It will be far worse for him if we indulge this phase of his! He will be teased at school, and have his knuckles caned if he uses his left hand. And it will make a difference when he is making his way in the world—nobody will invite him anywhere if he grips his cutlery in the wrong hands! Howard's future is at stake! His future . . ." She trailed off, looking distracted.

Faith bit her lip. "What if it is not a phase?" she asked.

"Faith, your brother is *not* left-handed," Myrtle said firmly, as if Faith had made an unfair accusation. Left-handedness was seen as ill-mannered and defective, even a little twisted and unsavory. "What is wrong with you today?" She frowned, and looked at Faith properly. "You are a mess! When did you last comb your hair properly? And why do you smell of lemons?" She looked around her at the hall. "Everything is a mess! And Dr. Jacklers will be arriving at any moment." She glanced at the clock. "Where *is* he? Two hours late and not a word—something is wrong; I can feel it."

Even as she said this, a clop and crunch of horse hoofs was audible from outside.

Myrtle let out her breath. "At last!" she said.

As it turned out, it was not Dr. Jacklers. It was Dr. Jacklers's apology in paper form. He had been detained attending to Miss Hunter.

It appeared that in the dead of night Miss Hunter had noticed a gaggle of men loitering not far from her home. Although she lived with only an elderly maid for company, Miss Hunter had not felt under threat, since it was not unusual to see little ragtag groups weaving home slowly after a ratting, or sitting and drinking on the cliff-tops.

After she retired, however, she was awakened by a smash and a cry of "Fire!" She woke her maid and led her downstairs, where they discovered a haze of brownish smoke drifting from the rear of the house. Miss Hunter sent her maid to the parsonage to seek help from Clay, while she began moving valuables out of her house and out of the post office next door, starting with the precious post in her care.

Unexpectedly, she found herself helped by a group of men, who had just been passing and who ran in to move out her furniture and valuables, cloths wrapped around their faces to protect against the smoke. It was only when she saw them loading some of her trunks and furniture on to barrows, or hoisting them on to their own backs, that it became clear that these were not Good Samaritans. She had shouted at them, and finally tried to wrest her jewelry case out of the hands of one of her "rescuers." He had shoved her brutally, knocking her backward. Her head had struck the corner of the wall, hard enough to render her insensible.

"We are trying to ascertain whether there is a fracture, or bleeding within the skull," read Dr. Jacklers's letter. Faith thought of the hints she had dropped on the cliff-top. They had seemed so tiny and air-frail. But the two boys must have run straight back to the ratting hut, spreading her rumor among a gang of men already rowdy and in their cups, and not a mile from Miss Hunter's house. Faith's other lies had lit a slow fuse. This lie had thrown a spark straight on to a heap of ready powder.

The last part of the doctor's letter Myrtle did not read out loud. Instead she stood there, quivering in her beautifully tailored dress, a flush stealing its way up past her velvet choker.

Faith watched her with dread, wondering if her own name was mentioned in the letter. *It is believed that the attack took place because of scurrilous rumors spread by your daughter while she was cavorting in a den of blood sports . . .*

However, when Myrtle raised her gaze she looked through Faith, not at her, her face clouded and abstracted.

"The doctor thanks us for helping him with his investigations," she said abruptly, "and apologizes for troubling us during this painful time. He will try to avoid trespassing upon our patience any further."

"What does that mean?" asked Faith.

"It means that we shall not be seeing Dr. Jacklers again," Myrtle answered, her voice flippant, but heavy with bitterness. "He is hauling Miss Hunter from the jaws of death, and doubtless he believes that this will improve his prospects with her. If she is returned to the world an imbecile, he may even be correct."

Faith sensed that there was something in the letter that she had not been told. It sounded as if the doctor's unseemly courtship had come to a sudden end, and she wanted to feel relieved about that. However, something about her mother's expression filled her with dread. Myrtle was not belligerent or vociferous, as she might have been if her vanity had been punctured. Instead her face was stony and deeply tired, and for once she almost looked her age.

Howard was almost crazed with boredom, so Faith took him out into the garden with the family's old croquet set and pushed hoops into the stubborn earth. The grass was too long, and the balls bounced wherever they chose. Howard laughed when Faith forgot the score, and when the balls hid in tussocks or burrowed into hollows. After a couple of hours Mrs. Vellet brought out supper for them to eat on the grass, like a picnic.

As they played, Faith walked beside Howard like a sleepwalker, picturing fractures in the skull beneath Miss Hunter's neat black hair. She imagined the postmistress tossing in delirium, or reduced to a drooling simpleton.

This is what you wanted, said a voice in her mind. It was her own thought, but she could almost hear it, speaking with her own voice. *You wanted revenge on her, and now you have it.* And yet this brought Faith no happiness.

"She might be a murderess," Faith said under her breath.

She pressed her hands against the side of her head and forced herself to think. If she had understood her vision rightly, there were two murderers. Miss Hunter was rumored to be having an affair with Lambent. Miss Hunter rode out at all times of the day and night. Lambent claimed he had trouble sleeping, which gave him a good excuse to go out at strange hours.

They could be meeting in secret. They might be involved in an "intrigue."

Faith did not know why they might want to kill her father, but Lambent had written to Uncle Miles inviting the Reverend to Vane, and Miss Hunter had been the family's enemy from the start.

You must be ruthless, said the voice in her head. *You have come too far to turn back.*

"Can we play again?" asked Howard for the twentieth time, appearing at her side.

"You must be tired of it by now!" exclaimed Faith, though she could see from his face that he was not. She envied him. Had she ever been able to play and play the same game without losing joy in it, or worrying about anything else? Perhaps this knack was something she had lost, or something she had never had.

She looked around her, noticing the dulling of the sky and the fading peach halo in the west. The battered wooden hoops were becoming harder to see against the grass.

"It is starting to get dark," she said aloud. She had not even noticed. "This must be the last game, How. I mean it this time."

"Are *you* tired?" asked Howard and then he put his head to one side. "What's wrong? Are you bilious?" Miss Caudle, his nursemaid back in Kent, was often bilious, and Howard had adopted the word.

"No," Faith said, managing a smile, "but . . . I have a headache."

"Is the ghost making you ill?" There was a worried light in Howard's eyes, and Faith wondered how many conversations about Jeanne he had overheard.

"No, of course not!" Faith forced herself to smile. "You keep the ghost away, remember? By being a good boy and copying out your Scripture."

Howard dropped his gaze, and his hands curled nervously. "I couldn't make it go," he whispered. "It came back."

"No, How—"

"I *saw* it. Last night."

Faith halted, and looked down into Howard's round, earnest eyes. She was gripped by a powerful fancy that, if she looked around suddenly, she would see her father silently watching her. The thought should have comforted her. Instead she felt a creeping dread. Try as she might, in her mind's eye she could not make his expression kind or understanding.

"Where? Where did you see it, How?"

Howard turned and pointed at the greenhouse.

"It made a light," he whispered. "I saw it from my window."

Taking Howard's hand, Faith slowly approached the greenhouse. It had rained overnight, and the grass was still wet enough to dampen the hems of her skirts. The greenhouse panes were clouded with moisture. She raised the latch and entered.

Several of the plant pots had been moved slightly. Tiny clods of fresh black earth were scattered here and there. In the center of the floor, Faith found a small, gluey blob of yellow candle wax.

Faith's superstitious fear ebbed, only to be replaced by a far more pragmatic dread. Ghosts were not the only things that walked.

"What did it look like, How?" she asked gently. "What did you see?"

"It looked like a man. In a big black coat."

"Did you see its face?"

Howard shook his head, and looked a little mulish. "It was looking all everywhere. I think it was looking for me, but it didn't know I was up in the window. And then it went around the house."

Faith walked Howard out of the greenhouse and in the direction he had pointed. It led her past a flower bed to the foot of the steps that ran up to her roof garden.

There was a large, earth-laden footprint on one of the steps.

"Stay there, How." Faith walked up the steps. In the garden she found two more faint prints on the stone flags. Here too the pots had been shifted slightly, and the stone children faced in new directions as if startled into conference. Somebody had been here, in her secret haven. Perhaps their stealthy tread had been pressing the flags while she was asleep mere yards away. Somebody had been searching, and their search had brought them to her very door.

But they weren't looking for me.

The realization struck her as she slowly descended the steps. The "ghost" had searched the greenhouse, the flower beds, and her roof garden. They were looking for a plant.

Both Prythe and Uncle Miles had mentioned plants going missing, and at last she understood why. Somebody had carried away the wrong plant in haste and darkness. Uncle Miles's determination to gain possession of her father's papers and specimens also took on a deeper significance.

Somebody knew about the Tree. Somebody wanted the Tree. Her father had been right to hide it, right to fear that somebody would come for it. Somebody had tried to steal it, had asked Uncle Miles to acquire it, would stop at nothing to get it.

A Tree that could give you secrets nobody else possessed, and unpeel the mysteries of the world. A Tree that could show governments their enemies' plans, scientists the secrets of the ages, journalists the vices of the powerful. It was not just scientifically fascinating. It was valuable. Powerful. Priceless.

Someone might kill for a plant like that.

Faith's face tingled as she took up the threads of her mystery once more, looking at everything in a new way. The invitation to Vane had brought the Reverend to the island, but it had also brought the Lie Tree. He could not entrust it to anybody else, and perhaps the murderers had counted on that. All this while, Faith had been poring over her father's life, trying to work out who might have been envious, angry, jealous, or vengeful enough to kill him. But perhaps he had simply died because he owned a plant that somebody else wanted.

And now . . . it was in *her* possession.

Faith halted at the bottom of the steps. Another thought struck her, causing her to glance hastily around.

If the murderers were looking for the Tree, then they probably knew of its falsehood-based diet. They might even be looking for strange lies that spread like wildfire. Ghost stories, for example, or rumors of curiously elusive treasure. And if they tried to trace back the latest gossip about Miss Hunter, sooner or later they might find themselves talking to somebody who remembered two boys mentioning a conversation with one Faith Sunderly . . .

She remembered her vision, recalled flattening herself to the ground in terror. She was not an all-powerful puppeteer. She was nothing but a paper girl, and could be torn apart if she was discovered.

"The ghost *might* be dead," said Howard hopefully, curling one hand around hers. "I shot it with my gun."

"Oh." Faith thought of his little wooden gun and tried to sound reassured. "Did you?"

"Yes!" Howard swung her arm to and fro. "*Bang!* Except . . . it didn't say bang. It said click. But the ghost went away so I think it was shot."

Click.

Howard's wooden gun never made any noise.

"Howard," Faith said slowly, "which gun did you use to shoot the ghost?"

"The ghost-killing gun," Howard said promptly. "The one we found in the woods."

"The one we . . ." Faith lowered her face into her hands. They had searched the dell together, looking for ghost-shooting guns, but she had been too busy staring at wheel ruts to pay attention to Howard.

Faith, look! Look at this! He had found something and shouted to her, but she had not looked.

"Is the gun this big?" she asked, scarcely daring to breathe. "Made of metal, with a yellowish-white handle?" When Howard nodded, Faith crouched down until their eyes were level. "Howard, listen. That is a *real* gun. A dangerous gun. You need to give it to me!"

"No!" Howard released her hand and recoiled a few steps. "I need it! I need it for the ghost!"

Faith made a grab for his hand, but Howard turned and fled back to the house. She followed him, but could not find him in the nursery.

"Is Master Howard ready for his milk?" asked Mrs. Vellet as she passed Faith on the stair.

"Nearly ready—we are just having a game of hide-and-seek before bed," Faith said hastily. If she explained the full story, there would be a full-scale search for Howard, and the pistol would be found and confiscated. Now more than ever she needed it.

"Well, it will do him good to wear himself out a little," said Mrs. Vellet. The housekeeper looked particularly tired and care-worn herself.

Faith had already mapped out the house for hiding places, but Howard was small and could fold up into any number of corners. Furthermore, it was getting dark, and there were more shadows to hide a diminutive, stubborn form.

"Howard," she hissed as she searched, "please come out!"

At long last, as Faith was passing through the hall, she heard a muffled sound of movement from the library. She crept over and put her eye to the keyhole.

She could see nothing unusual at first, only a narrow view of the bookcase, illuminated by gentle candlelight. However, she could hear the stealthy grating of drawers being pulled out, a faint sound like rending cloth, and now and then a low, grinding creak.

Then footsteps approached and a shadow crept up the bookcase. A man came into view. He pulled books out of the case one by one, shaking them as if looking for loose papers, and dropping each as it disappointed.

He reached past the books, knocking on the back of the bookcase, perhaps testing for a hollow space. As he did so, he turned his face toward the door.

It was Uncle Miles.

Chapter 29

MYRTLE

ANGER AT THE DESECRATION OF HER FATHER'S
books overwhelmed Faith's fear. She stood up, turned the handle, and flung open the door.

"Uncle Miles! What are you doing?"

Her uncle started, the light from a single candle washing
across his face.

"A proper inventory . . . your father's possessions . . . long
overdue. All the thefts . . ."

Faith looked around the room. The cushions had been slit
and their stuffing pulled out. All the drawers were on the floor.
A few floorboards had even been pulled up.

"Does Mother know you are doing this?"

"Faith!" Uncle Miles dropped his voice to a whisper. "You
and I agreed—your mother is distressed, best left untroubled by
such things!"

Faith stared down at the leather and paper sprawl at her
uncle's feet, her father's precious, wounded books.

"Mother!" she shouted.

She glared at Uncle Miles while floorboards creaked above. Footsteps descended the stairs, and then Myrtle appeared in a rustle of crêpe.

"Mercy, what was that scream! Is Howard hurt?" She joined Faith in the doorway, and stared. "Miles!" She stared at her brother in shock.

"I had to take matters into my own hands," said Uncle Miles, reddening.

"Matters?" Myrtle advanced into the room. "These are not *your* matters to take, Miles! You have no right! These things belong to my husband! To my family! To me!"

"The time has come for that to change," said Uncle Miles. He had retreated a step, but only a step. "Myrtle, I talked to Lambent at the excavation. He told me that the inquest is scheduled for tomorrow afternoon. There is no more time."

Myrtle's shoulders drooped very slightly, and once again she looked older and more tired than usual.

"Is that true?" Faith turned to her mother. "Did Dr. Jacklers's letter say so?"

Her mother hesitated and then nodded.

"And do you think that the good doctor is so besotted that he will rally to your story?" Uncle Miles gave a small, sad chuckle as he eyed his sister. "I think given enough time you might have brought him to that, but time has run out."

"Do not be so sure." Myrtle's defiance rang hollow. "He is very fond of me."

"I daresay, but you ask too much of the man! You want him to perjure himself, or near enough. And do not forget that Lambent, as magistrate, decides whether the coroner gets paid, and will probably *not* pay if his decision reeks. No, my dear, I think that a sensible, level-headed businessman like Dr. Jacklers will choose two guineas in the hand over a pretty but unpredictable widow in the bush."

"If I have to testify myself . . ." Myrtle straightened her back.

"If you testify, you will win yourself gossip and nothing else." Uncle Miles no longer had the demeanor of a criminal caught mid-burglary. "Everybody is already talking about the way you continue to receive visitors after your husband's death. Do you think a jury will look kindly on you if you march up to give evidence, bold as a sailor? And what other witnesses do you have? I know Prythe will not lie for you—I was there when he said as much."

"Mother, let me testify!" pleaded Faith. Dr. Jacklers had not listened to her when she talked of murder, but perhaps a jury might. It was too good a chance to waste.

"No!" Myrtle snapped. She looked angry and horrified. "You have not even taken your confirmation—you have a clean, new soul, Faith, do not squander it!"

"Then let me tell the truth!" exclaimed Faith, overwhelmed with frustration. "Nobody believes our story, because it is a lie! We should have told the truth from the start!"

"Faith, go to your room!" ordered Myrtle, her face flushing.

"No," said Faith.

The two adults stared at her. For the first time Faith wondered whether there were three adults in the conversation.

"We could not tell the truth, and we cannot now!" spat Myrtle. She was breathing heavily, struggling against her corset for air. Her eyes were large, bright, and dangerous. "The truth is that your father abandoned us—left us without a thought of how it would affect us, or how we might survive afterward. He did what he always did. He took his own cold course, and left everybody else to flounder!"

Faith clenched her fists and felt her eyes sting, and wished her mother dead, dead, dead.

"And you *will* flounder," Uncle Miles cut in before Faith could reply, "unless you listen to me. Myrtle, from now on, everything is reversed. *You* need *me*. If I am to take care of you all, you must let me call the tune. All I am asking—"

"—is everything," Myrtle finished bitterly. "You want everything we have—"

"I have found a way to make us a good deal of money." Uncle Miles spoke over his sister. "There is a respectable person, right here on the island, who will pay generously for the papers and live specimens your husband brought here. If I am to provide for your family, I will need the funds!"

"Who?" demanded Faith. "Who is this 'respectable person'?"

Her uncle immediately looked annoyed, sly, and calculating. It was no good, Faith realized. The identity of the buyer was one of his trump cards. He did not want Myrtle rushing off to sell the items herself.

"You really have no choice," Uncle Miles urged gently, and Faith saw Myrtle wilt slightly.

"Mother, we do have a choice!" protested Faith. Somehow she had to persuade her mother to stop Uncle Miles from tearing up the house. "We have money put away at home, and in the bank—I remember Father saying so! There is money set aside for school and university for Howard, and a dowry for me! I am never getting married, so we can live on the dowry!"

Myrtle stared at her, blue eyes wide. A single tear slid down her cheek, and one of her hands reflexively wiped it away, drying her lower lid. She dropped her gaze and her shoulders slumped in surrender.

"Faith," she said, "go and fetch your father's papers."

"*You* had them all along?" Uncle Miles glared at Faith accusingly.

"Leave the child alone," Myrtle said wearily. "I told her to hide them and keep it secret. You win, Miles. Is that not enough?"

"No," said Faith. It was not a defiant declaration like her refusal to leave the room. It was a small, cold sound, and it lay there in the silence like a pebble.

"Faith . . ." There was a warning note in Myrtle's voice.

"No." Faith took a few steps backward, shaking her head. She had briefly considered agreeing, running upstairs, and coming down with all of her father's papers except the vision sketches and the journal. But her uncle would probably follow her. Besides, she had only looked quickly through the other papers, and could not be certain that they did not hold some crucial secret of the Tree.

"Faith, do as your mother says!" Uncle Miles advanced, his rounded face no longer kind or comfortable.

"Mother, he needs to tell us who has offered him money!" declared Faith. "Uncle Miles lied to us—he brought us here because he wanted to join the Vane dig! They told him he could only join if he persuaded Father to come. It was a bribe—"

Faith got no further because Uncle Miles had grabbed her by the arm. It hurt, and she was shocked by the realization that it was meant to hurt.

"Be quiet!" Uncle Miles was taller than he had ever been. "Where are the papers?" He shook Faith hard. She tried to pull his fingers loose, but he tightened his grip and dragged her out of the room. "Show me!"

"Miles, stop it!" called Myrtle somewhere behind them.

Faith was not strong, and nobody had ever taken advantage of that before. But now she knew the threat had always been there, lurking in every smile, every bow, every allowance made for her sex. A veil had torn, and here was the truth in all its ugliness. Her shoes slithered on the floor. At the base of the stairs she tripped on her hem and fell painfully on to the steps.

Without hesitation Uncle Miles dragged her back to her feet, and Faith turned and hit him, as hard as she could. His expression changed, anger forming soft, ugly bulges like porridge bubbles. She knew that he would hit her back. He would break her face like a meringue.

"Let go of my daughter!"

There was a *thwack*, and Uncle Miles cried out, clapping his free hand to his neck and looking over his shoulder. Beyond him, Faith could see Myrtle, a poker swung back in one hand, ready to strike again.

"Myrtle, have you gone mad?"

"Let go of her now, Miles, or as God as my witness I shall knock you silly and have the servants throw you out!" Myrtle's voice grew louder as she spoke, and the end of the sentence echoed through the hall.

Uncle Miles looked nervously about him, as if expecting Prythe to come running from a side room and bowl him over. He swallowed. There was a long pause.

"Is that your decision?" he asked.

Myrtle said nothing, but stood her ground, holding her poker in front of her like a fencer's foil.

"Then I wash my hands of your delightful mess of a family," Uncle Miles said sourly, releasing Faith. He took a step toward the stairs, but Myrtle's poker hand twitched, so instead he stormed down the hall, seizing his coat and hat from the hooks. He opened the front door and disappeared into the night, leaving the door to bang open behind him.

Myrtle's poker arm fell limply to her side. She walked to the front door, closed it, then headed slowly back into the drawing room. Faith followed, still feeling shocked and tremulous.

Myrtle dropped the poker back among the other fire irons. She stopped with her back turned to Faith, and dropped her face into her hands. Her shoulders began to shake. Faith found a handkerchief and stepped forward, putting a tentative hand on her mother's elbow.

"Mother . . ."

Myrtle twitched from her touch, turned around, and slapped Faith across the face. It was not hard, but it stung. "Why could you not give him the papers?" she cried, her voice breaking. "We needed him! Now . . . I do not know what we can possibly do."

"He betrayed Father." Faith's pain and shock gave way to anger again. "And we do not need him. We have—"

"We have nothing, Faith!" shouted Myrtle. "Nothing! Nothing! Our home was the *rectory*, for the use of the rector. With your father dead, the next rector will take his living and his house. We have no home, and no more money coming in." Myrtle drew in and released a ragged breath.

"You said we could live on your dowry," she said, with a pained grimace. "There will be no dowry, Faith, no money for Howard's education, not even money for food. If he had died in a natural way, we would have his savings . . . but suicide is a crime. The moment the inquest finds your father guilty of self-murder, everything he owns will be confiscated by the Crown."

Faith stared at her open-mouthed. At last she began to understand her mother's determination to lie about the place where the body was found, and her uncle's cryptic remarks about taking control of her father's possessions so that they would not be lost.

"But . . . why should *we* be punished? That is cruel and makes no sense!"

"The world is cruel and makes no sense," Myrtle answered bitterly. "Every suicide is treated so, aside from maniacs. I think it is too late for me to change my story and claim that your father was mad. Besides, it would blight your futures if everybody thought mad blood flowed in your veins."

"You never told me any of this." Faith felt her bruised cheek. The truth had been hidden from her, and she had been slapped for not knowing it.

"There was quite enough to bear without having to tell you what your precious father had done to us."

"How dare you speak of him like that?" Faith felt her own temper spark. "He never abandoned us! He was struck down! He was murdered!"

"What are you talking about?" Myrtle's voice was flat and weary.

"I tried to tell you, but you wouldn't listen! They killed him in the dell. They hit him from behind. They took him in a wheel-barrow to the cliff, and tipped him over the edge."

"What? Who?" Myrtle frowned, her eyes still incredulous.

"What do you care?" shouted Faith. She had gone too far and now could only go further. "Father is *dead*, and all you care about is your dresses, and your jewels, and *flirting*! You never even waited for them to bury him! I saw you! I saw you with Dr. Jacklers, when Father was lying there dead on the carpet!"

"How dare you!" Myrtle's voice was no longer girlish. It was full-lunged and hard-edged, like that of an angry cat. "Do you think that was vanity? I was fighting for my family's survival, and my looks were the only weapon I had! I *needed* Dr. Jacklers to say your father's death was an accident. I *needed* Mr. Clay to change the picture, so that we could use it to dispel rumors back in England. So I was the rich, pretty widow who counted on them, and might be grateful enough to marry them some day.

"This is a battlefield, Faith! Women find themselves on battlefields, just as men do. We are given no weapons, and cannot be seen to fight. But fight we must, or perish."

Faith's face was hot. She had heard her mother's voice properly for the first time, stripped of coy wit. It was hard, ugly, and strong.

"You disgust me," Faith said. Her voice wobbled. She wanted her own words to be true, but they were not.

For a second Myrtle's face looked hurt and a little childlike, and then the anger surged back.

"And I barely recognize you!" Faith's mother stared at her as though she were on fire. "Where did all this anger come from? I have tried so hard with you, Faith, but you were never company. It was like talking to a sleepwalker—"

"I was always awake!" interrupted Faith. "I was always angry!"

"You shut me out!" There was a tremble in Myrtle's lip that was not just anger. "You are just like your father—"

"Yes!" shouted Faith. "Yes! I am like him, and nothing like you! I am all his, and none of me is yours!"

And with that she turned and ran from the room, wishing that she could leave the memory of her mother's words behind her.

Chapter 30

A TINY DEATH

YOU DISGUST ME.

Faith put her hands over her ears as she ran upstairs, wanting to shut her own words out of her head. She had meant it, she told herself. Myrtle deserved it. But over and over she remembered Myrtle's hurt look. The pain in her mother's eyes reminded Faith of the way she had felt when her father had torn her to pieces in the library.

Myrtle had been fighting a dirty war, but fighting it for the family's survival. How could Faith claim the moral high ground? For all Faith knew, her own actions had already claimed lives.

Her ears pricked. There were faint sounds coming from the direction of Howard's nursery, scritches and scratches.

She emerged on the landing, but as she turned the handle of the day nursery she heard a scuffle and scamper from within. When she entered, the nursery was apparently empty. Howard's copybook was under the table, slowly flapping shut. An abandoned pencil rolled across the floor.

"Howard?" called Faith. There was silence. She did not want to venture into the night nursery, in case he bolted from some hiding place through the door behind her. "Come out, How!"

Silence.

"Howard, I am getting out your theatre!" she called, in a moment of inspiration. She settled herself on the floor and pulled the toy theatre out of the toy box.

There were a few creaks, and then a small figure appeared in the doorway to the night nursery. Howard was grimy and looked as though he might have been crying.

"Oh, *there* you are, How." Faith felt a flood of exhausted relief.

Howard edged into the room, looking daunted and evidently expecting a scolding. "Why was everybody shouting?" he asked.

"Never mind, Howard." Faith's voice sounded deadened, even to her. When Howard came and knelt down beside her, resting himself heavily on the side of her lap, she put her arm around him. "How," she said gently, "we need to talk about that pistol."

Howard buried his face in her arm and shook his head.

"Noooo!" was his muffled reply. "Nononono! I *need* it!" His face emerged again, glossy-eyed and desperate. "Do a show, Faith!"

Faith looked down at the little stage, and her spirits suddenly failed her. She had fully intended to reward Howard, but as she stared at the little bone-white woodland scene all she could think of was the great shadow-hand searching for her while she hid. The painted moon mesmerized her with its dead eye. She felt a surge of unexpected terror.

"How," she whispered, "I . . . I can't. Not right now."

"Please!" Howard had that shiny-cheeked, wild-eyed look. He was frightened. He wanted her to have all the answers again. Howard was very small, Faith reflected. Perhaps that was why he liked there to be a smaller world that he could study and control.

Faith took up the jester's rod and twirled it, watching the jester somersault. She thought of her lies, making people leap head over heels, and sometimes sending them crashing to earth and cracking their heads open.

Tongue dry and voice trembling, Faith danced the puppets through the colorless forest, letting them fight, taunt, spin, and die. She watched them in fascination, and her fingers felt numb. Was she really controlling them? Her hand seemed to tingle as she handled the Devil. He stared up at her, tusks bared in a snarling grin.

"I want the Wise Man," said Howard.

Faith maneuvered the tiny, smudge-faced sage onto the stage. At least the show was likely to be near its end.

"Master Howard!" shrilled Faith–Wise Man. "What can I do for you today? Do you have a question?"

Howard hugged his knees to his chest and peered over them. For a few moments he just rubbed his nose against his knees.

"Is it my fault because of the ghost?" he asked, very quietly. "Is it my fault because I couldn't do it, and I couldn't make it go away? And did that make Jeanne get ill and is that why she went away and is she dying? And is it my fault?" His voice grew louder but huskier, and now there were tears spilling out of his eyes.

"Oh no!" Faith could only just keep to her Wise-Man voice. "No, Master Howard, you are a *good* boy—"

"But I couldn't do it!" wailed Howard, hoarse with misery. "I—I tried! I tried! But I . . ." He pulled over his copybook and scrabbled it open, clawing through the pages.

The letters were almost legible at first, though some were back to front or sprawled out at the wrong angle. As the pages passed, the pencil squiggles and marks became wilder, more desperate and less like letters. Some left frantic, unsteady grooves in the paper. Pages of them. Pages and pages.

With a terrible sinking of the heart, Faith realized what she was looking at. Scripture.

Ghosts won't come after a good little boy who says his prayers and copies out his Scripture right-handed. They only hunt bad *people.*

With utter remorse, Faith imagined Howard scratching his marks in increasing panic every day, and lying awake each night listening for ghostly footsteps . . .

"Is it my fault?" he asked again, tremulously.

"No!" Faith swallowed hard but could not stop her voice from shaking. "No, none of it is your fault, Master Howard! None of it! The ghost never came here for you!"

"Then why did he come?" Howard clutched the toes of his shoes. "Why is he making Faith ill? Did he come here for her?"

Faith thought of killers hunting for the Lie Tree, and her mouth shaped an almost silent *yes.*

"Why?" demanded Howard. "Why does he want to hurt Faith?"

"Because she is a stupid, evil girl!" exploded Faith, unable to bear it anymore. "She spoils everything, and spreads poison everywhere she goes. And she is going to hell!"

She pushed the toy theatre off her lap, stood unsteadily, and ran from the room. Out on the landing she finally burst into tears. The sobs felt larger than she was, and for a while she was lost in them.

Faith was jolted out of anguish by a strange racket coming from the nursery behind her. There was a thudding, cracking, ripping, and skittering. She turned around and looked in through the door.

Howard was stamping on the toy theatre, tears streaming from his eyes, his nose running. The brightly painted proscenium arch had caved and crushed, and the whole theatre had dented and buckled. Nearby lay a snapped rod, and a tiny paper man with its head ripped off. The little head wore a Chinese hat.

"Oh, How!" Faith ran in, dropped to her knees, and scooped up the remains of the Wise Man. "What have you done?" Her little oracle was no more. She felt a terrible stinging sense of loss.

Howard came toward her, eyes gleaming with tears. "Killed him," he said in a very small voice. "I killed the Wise Man. He . . . He said you had to go to hell! But . . . But now he's dead . . . he can't make you go! I don't want you to go to hell!"

"Oh, Howard!" Faith crouched and spread her arms, and Howard tottered into them, snuffling. She squeezed him tightly.

"He can't hurt you now, can he?" whimpered Howard in her ear.

"Hush," said Faith. "No . . . I . . . no. He's dead. He can't hurt me. You . . . rescued me, How."

Howard sobbed for a long time, while Faith made hushing noises and stroked his head. When at last his tears slowed, she wiped his face with a handkerchief.

"Come on," she said, and led him into the nursery. Howard's eyes widened as she took down his blue jacket and opened her folding knife. First she hacked away the stitches that pinioned the left sleeve, then she dragged great slashes through the fabric, over and over.

"It's a stupid, ugly jacket," she said, her own breaths juddering, "and you never, *never* have to wear it again. You can write your Scripture now, How, and you can use your left hand as much as you like."

She was out of breath by the time she stopped. The two siblings stood and stared down at the ravaged jacket like conspirators. It was definitely dead. Dead as the Wise Man.

"Are you frightened of the ghost?" asked Howard.

"Yes, How," Faith said quietly.

Howard disappeared under his bed, scuffled around, then reemerged. A little reluctantly, he placed a small cold shape in Faith's hand.

"You have to give it back after you shoot the ghost," he declared.

In Faith's hand lay a little pocket pistol with a stubby barrel. It was her father's gun.

The pistol still seemed to be loaded, though the percussion cap appeared to have fallen off. To Faith's certain knowledge the gun had spent one night out of doors, but at least it had not rained that night, so there was some hope that the powder was not damp. In any case, she did not wish to try her hand at reloading it. She had seen her father doing so, but it had been a complicated process involving pins and the removal of the barrel, and she was hazy about the order of the sequence.

Instead she gingerly half cocked the pistol and put a fresh cap in place, then concealed the weapon in a reticule and tucked it in her pocket. She could only be grateful that the pistol had not been cocked when Howard had tried to make it "bang."

"You can stay in the nursery with me," Howard said hopefully. "I can be lookout. You can shoot the ghost from my window."

Faith hesitated. It was tempting to stay in the safety of the house, but the inquest was the very next day. Unless she could find some proof of the murder by then, her father would find a suicide's grave in unconsecrated ground, and her family would be turned out onto the streets.

"You keep watch," she said. "If you see anybody in the garden, run and find Mother, or Mrs. Vellet, or Prythe, and let them know. I . . . have to go on a secret mission. You won't tell anyone, will you, How?"

It had not been long since she fed the Tree the lie about Miss Hunter, but that lie had been believed enough for arson, theft, and violence. It was just possible that the Tree had borne a fruit. If it had, then at least the terrible consequences of the rumor would not have been for nothing.

The Lie Tree tugged at her thoughts. She felt as though its vines had grown into her mind, and that even now it was hauling her back to it.

Faith considered walking the safer route to the cave's secret entrance, but calculated that she would still be faster by boat, and less likely to be noticed. As she rowed to the sea cave once again, she could feel the cold wind seep in through every split and tear in her long-suffering funeral clothes. The moon was full and brilliant, painting a milk river down the gray-black swell.

Faith's excitement at the thought of the Lie Tree had soured. Now foreboding curdled in her stomach. She had to remind herself that the Tree itself had harmed nobody—her lics alone had done that. Nonetheless, it seemed to bring out the worst in her. If she gave up on it now, however, then all the damage she had done would be wasted. It was too late to admit defeat. For a moment she wondered whether her father had felt the same way, and plunged on with his frauds to the brink of destruction, rather than admit that everything he had done had been a terrible mistake. They were like gamblers who had lost too much to stop betting.

She let the wave wash her boat into the cave, felt it ground, and leapt out to tie it up. It was time to test the fruits of her experiments. She carefully removed the thick cloth covering the lantern, and swiftly replaced it with another, a mesh of layers of gauze that choked its light like cobweb but still let a faint glow through. If she was correct, this would not be bright enough to harm the Tree.

Shrouded lantern in hand, she clambered up to the main cavern, then stopped dead.

The way ahead was crisscrossed with black vines, as if somebody had scribbled over the aperture with a thick stick of charcoal. She advanced a few steps, and the cold smell seared her throat and the skin inside her nose. In her absence, the Tree had filled its cavern.

This was the stuff of fairy tales. Faith remembered an old story of children who had fled a witch's house, and had cast down a magic comb behind them, which had sprouted into a thick and enormous forest.

Tentatively Faith reached out and touched the vines, most of which seemed to be dangling from the ceiling. They were slender and supple, and yielded as she pushed them aside. Slowly she made her way into the strange, new jungle, the leaves clammy against her face.

The vines closed behind her. With no light but that of the spectral lantern, it was hard to tell which way was which. She quickly checked her father's compass clinometer and made a note of the direction and ground slope, in case she became lost.

The most recent fruit had been near the heart of the plant. She had to hope that the same would be true again, or she would never find it.

It was easier to advance than she expected, despite the vine-matted floor. She had to duck under a few thick, spiralling stems, but most of the stray vines seemed content to drape and slither across her shoulders as calmly as her snake. Irrationally, she felt that the Tree was comfortable with her.

The tough, forking vines that veined the floor were her guides. They all weaved from the heart of the Tree, and so she slowly followed them back. As she did so, the molten voices in the cavern's roar seemed to grow louder, but no easier to understand. Sometimes her ear tingled, as though somebody had placed their mouth close to it, about to whisper.

The stone shelf reared before her, now cocooned in black tendrils. The dark, spidery mound on top of it glimmered faintly in the dull, gauzy light of the lantern. She ran her fingers through the leaves here, there, and everywhere, until at last she felt something small, round, and hard dangling below a stem like a Christmas bauble. It came away in her hand, a tiny perfect fruit.

Just as Faith was putting it away in her pocket, she saw something move out of the corner of her eye.

She spun around, lantern raised, looking this way and that. On all sides her eyes were baffled by the weaving and criss-crossing of the vines. The lantern did little more than gild the murk. She could discern no rustle amid the roar and hiss of the sea, the moan and murmur of the echo-voices.

Faith reached into the pocket reticule and pulled out her father's pistol, then drew back the hammer so that it was ready to fire. She let out a long breath and managed to hold the lantern steady in her other hand.

Some ten feet away, amid the vine-tangle, the foliage shivered again. This time she knew it was no mistake, and amid the cat's cradle of stems could make out a dark blot. It was taller than her, and in the shape of a human figure.

There was nowhere to run. Standing there with her lantern,

she was obvious. Whoever they were, they had seen her, and if they moved again she would lose track of them.

Faith pointed the pistol directly at the blot, her heart hammering like a hummingbird's wing.

"I can see you! And I know you can see me! Come forward—slowly—or I fire!" She had no idea whether she had it in her to pull the trigger, even if the other leapt at her, but somehow she kept the terror out of her voice.

The dark shape stirred, swayed slightly. For a moment she thought it would duck back into the shadows and be lost to her. Then it began to approach, one arm raised to push stray vines out of the way. At last it was close enough for the dim golden light to fall upon its face.

The intruder was Paul Clay.

Chapter 31

WINTERBOURNE

PAUL CLAY, FAITH'S ALLY AND ENEMY. SHE WAS overwhelmed by fear, confusion, and distrust. He had discovered her lair, and seen more than she could allow anybody to see.

"What are you doing here?" she demanded, still aiming the pistol.

"Don't point that at me!" he protested, blinking in the dim lantern-light. "What are *you* doing here? Why is everything . . ." He looked around at the night-black jungle.

"How did you find us?"

"Us?" Paul looked nonplussed.

"Me—and the plant."

"Is it yours?" He stared up at the vines. "What *is* it? Where did it come from? And will you put down that pistol or not?"

Faith said nothing, nor did her pistol hand waver.

"Then you can stay here with your death-ivy," growled Paul, backing away a step. "I hope you have a good evening together."

"I can't let you leave." Faith knew her arm was shaking, despite the lightness of the pistol.

"What?" Paul's angry look gave way to one of alarm.

"Somebody is looking for this plant," said Faith. "And they

are willing to kill whoever has it. And that killer might be you."

"Is that a joke?" Paul gaped at her. "You asked for my help!"

"I had to trust somebody!" Faith could see that he was standing with his spare arm crooked, as if cradling something bulky. "Perhaps I chose the wrong person. There are two killers. They might be lovers or accomplices . . . or they might be a father and son."

"Hey!" shouted Paul. "My father never hurt anybody in his life!"

"How do I know that? What do I know about any of you? Your father was allowed on the excavation site—he could have sabotaged the chain of the mining basket." As she spoke, Faith recalled something else. "And the day we arrived, he came to meet us. The carriage was too heavy, so he suggested leaving the box with this plant behind—and offered to stay with it and keep watch. He would have been left alone with the box containing the plant, if my father had not refused.

"Somebody has been searching our greenhouse and the garden for the plant. They were seen, but mistaken for a ghost. And I *know* you have been searching around our house—I caught you doing so! You said you were looking for a lock of hair, but how do I know that was true?

"And now . . . here you are. Exactly where the murderer would wish to be."

There was a pause.

"I was up on the headland," Paul said at last, "and I saw you rowing by in your boat—"

"What were you doing there at this time of night?" interrupted Faith.

"Taking pictures." Paul gingerly turned about to show that the object in the crook of his elbow was a box camera.

"At night?" interrupted Faith. "Nobody can do that!"

"I was taking a picture of the moon!" Paul blurted out. "I

heard it could be done—pictures clear enough that you can see the shadows and the peaks. Whenever there is a full moon and a clear night . . . I go out and try my luck." He looked angry, and Faith realized that he was embarrassed.

"When I saw the boat, I guessed it was you. After my friends told me you 'vanished' on the headland last night, I thought maybe you had dropped down into one of the caves. When I saw you disappear into the cliff, I knew which one."

Faith chewed hard at her lip. Curiously enough, Paul's self-consciousness convinced her more than his camera.

"So that is how you found me," she said more quietly. "But why? Why did you follow me down into the cave?"

Why did you have to come down and see all of this? How can I possibly let you leave now?

"I was curious," Paul answered promptly. There was a long pause, during which he lowered his gaze and frowned slightly to himself. "No," he said. "I . . . I don't know why I climbed down a hole after a crazy woman. It makes no sense. Every time I talk to you, you make *me* crazy too.

"Everything has gone mad since you and your family came here. Vane never had riots, or people setting fire to houses! And right in the heart of it all, there is you, coming to me for no good reason with your wild tales of murder and wheelbarrows and mining baskets . . . and I can't help listening. You're ripe for Bedlam, but somehow I keep believing what you say."

"I don't want your trust!" The darkness settled on Faith again. "You do not know me! I am . . . I am poison. Every lie on Vane is my doing."

"Have you lied to me?"

Faith realized that she had not. She swallowed and said nothing.

"So your father was murdered," Paul said bluntly. "And no

photograph will make you feel better. And if you never find the killer, there will be a ghost in your head forever. I know how that feels. My mother drowned—no body, no burial, no stone in the churchyard. The only picture of her we have is a hidden-mother photograph. You saw it. It's the one on our shelf. The little boy in that picture is me. My father—he is good to me, but he smiles at me as if I'm a photograph of her. Sometimes I have the feeling he is waiting for me to leave the room so he can go on talking to her in his mind."

Faith flinched. She felt as though tentacles of sympathy were reaching out for her. She wanted to throw them off, shoot them, burn them away.

"Do you want me to weep for you?" she asked, as coldly as she could.

"I want you to make up your mind!" erupted Paul. "You want my help, you want me to die in a ditch; you tell me secrets, you hide things; you seek me out, you run away; you ask favors, you point a pistol at my head . . ." He shook his head incredulously. "Choose! Trust me or not, but choose! Once and for all!"

Shoot him. It was a consensus murmur among the floating voices. Paul knew too much. Paul wanted too much. Paul bored his way inside her head and stopped her from thinking straight.

Lowering the pistol pained Faith. As she returned its hammer to the safety notch, she thought she heard the Tree hiss and she felt as though she was betraying her father and his secrets. Paul released his breath and let his shoulders slump a little.

"Well . . . it is too late to stop you seeing the Tree," Faith said, trying not to sound too shaky. "Right now I suppose I must trust you or shoot you—and it would be annoying to have to reload the pistol." She had an uncomfortable feeling that this still sounded like an apology.

Paul advanced a few wary steps.

"I thought you were leaving," said Faith tersely.

"I will if you will." Paul looked around, and batted vines out of his face with a suspicious air. "This is not a good place. Nothing grows this fast. Nothing that was in a box two weeks ago should be this big. And I keep hearing . . ." He trailed off and shook his head. "There is something very wrong with this plant."

"I don't fully understand it myself yet," admitted Faith, feeling defensive in turn. "I can see where it gets its moisture, and maybe it takes minerals and nutrients from the cave rock, but its energy . . ." She shrugged. "It may be carnivorous."

"Does it eat people?" Paul did not look reassured.

"Not exactly." Faith reached out, stroking the nearest vine. She felt jealously possessive of *her* Tree, *her* father's secrets. But somehow she had done something irrevocable in lowering her pistol. She had agreed to trust, and torn a big, ugly gash in her own armor.

"It feeds on human lies," she said. "Human lies that are believed. It's a symbiote—a species that survives by cooperating with another species. Humans feed it lies, and in return it bears fruit that give visions of secret truths. At least that was what my father believed."

"Was he right?" Paul asked bluntly.

Of course he was right! Faith wanted to shout. *My father was a genius, of course he knew what he was doing, of course he would not have destroyed his career and his family's fortunes for no good reason!* Instead she found herself picking over the evidence with a cold, analytical brain. Could the swelling of the fruit be coincidence? What had she really learned from the visions?

"I still cannot be certain," she confessed, reluctantly. "The fruit *seem* to open up an extra sight, and show me things I did not know . . . but I cannot tell yet how true they are." She narrowed her eyes. "I will know better if we find the murderer."

"You have eaten fruit from this thing?" This seemed to horrify Paul more than the pistol.

"Yes, and I am here to do so again." Faith glared at him. "I must! If you do not like it, you can leave. Otherwise, you can make yourself useful. The fruit will put me in a trance. I tried tying myself up so I could not wander, but . . . that . . . was not entirely successful. It would help to have somebody watching over. You can make observations at the same time."

Paul approached, glancing at the rope looped over her shoulder. He looked less than happy at the suggestion.

"Five minutes ago you would not trust me to move a step. Now you trust me to stand guard over you while you are unconscious?"

"You told me to choose," Faith told him tartly.

The fruit was bitter as ever, and sent her on a dark and twisting downward road echoing with the hoofbeats of her heart.

Then it was too dark to see, but she knew that she was pushing through jungle. There was no rock floor beneath her feet. She scrambled and climbed, over the tangle of vines strung out like suspension bridges, past mighty trunks of plaited creepers, mounting vast wooden spirals as if they were stairways. All the while the air softly hummed with murmured lies.

There were kind lies. *You still look beautiful. I love you. I forgive you.*

There were frightened lies. *Someone else must have taken it. Of course I am Anglican. I never saw that baby before.*

There were predatory lies. *Buy this tonic if you want your child to recover. I will look after you. Your secret is safe with me.*

Half-lies, and the tense little silences where a truth should have been. Lies like knives, lies like poultices. The tiger's stripe, and the fawn's dusky dapple. And everywhere, everywhere, the lies that people told themselves. Dreams like cut flowers, with no nourishing root. Will-o'-the-wisp lights to make them feel less alone in the dark. Hollow resolutions and empty excuses.

Faith heeded none of them, but climbed and climbed, because she could smell her father's pipe smoke.

She found a great knot of vines, ten feet wide, hanging suspended like a spider's cocoon. Dull blue smoke eddied out through the cracks and crevices, and Faith's heart ached at the familiarity of its smell. She tore at the vines with her fingers, wrenching open a gap, then struggled through the hole.

She found herself standing in a hot, darkened cellar. The tiny specks of swatted mosquitoes could be seen against the whitewashed walls. There was one tiny, high window, showing a turbulent purple-gray sky and letting in a roar of rain and a scent of warm mud.

A man lay on the earth-strewn floor, the iron shackle on his leg out of keeping with his gentlemanly clothes. His brown mustache and beard had once been neatly clipped, but neglect had seen them break their banks, flooding his chin and cheeks with stubble. His hair was limp and dark with sweat and grime, and there were bruise-dark shadows under his eyes.

"You must help me," he said. "You must talk to them, Sunderly. Tell them who I am, why I am here. You have papers from the consul—they will listen to you. You can vouch for me."

At first Faith thought he was talking to her. Then another faint gust of blue smoke issued from beside her. She turned her head, and there was her father, the Reverend Erasmus Sunderly, shiny with the heat but otherwise immaculate.

Faith wanted to throw her arms around him, but the sight of

him held her back. She had forgotten how inaccessible he could be. With his cold, unrevealing gaze, his presence was almost as distant as his absence.

"Winterbourne, sir," he said, in his usual detached tone, "you are asking me to testify to your character—to give my word as a gentleman. I barely know you. We first met less than two weeks ago. I know only what you and your party have told me, and that was fantastical and incredible."

"Please!" Winterbourne looked desperate. "Consider that I am not alone here—I am not the only person who will suffer! Have some compassion!"

"If you can give me proof of your story," said the Reverend, "then you will convince me, and will give me the means to convince the authorities. Tell me where I may find this Mendacity Tree. If it matches your description, I shall place my faith in you."

The chained man looked astonished, then briefly angry and mulish. Winterbourne met the Reverend's gaze for a few seconds, then wilted before it, his face desolate. "I have no choice but to trust you," he said bitterly. "Before I was seized, I found some of Kikkert's notes. If I have understood his map, there is a building three miles due north of his house, on the edge of a river that runs through a bamboo forest. I believe that is where the plant is hidden. But hurry, Sunderly!"

The Reverend gave him a curt, formal inclination of the head, then turned and walked away, giving a sharp rap at the door in the wall. It opened, and he stepped through, casting a glance back into the room. For a moment he seemed to look straight into Faith's gaze. His eyes were cool as slate. Then he closed the door between them.

Faith ran to it, felt the rough grain under her hands and heard the *clunk* of a heavy bar dropping to fasten the door on the other side. She placed her ear against the wood and could just make out her father's voice.

"No." His voice was precise and cold as a scalpel. "If the gentleman believes that he knows me, he is mistaken or delirious. I have never seen his face before."

The rain became deafening applause. Darkness closed like a fist.

Faith woke, feeling cold inside and out. She had never felt so cold.

She remembered her father's account of his conversation with Winterbourne.

I promised to do all I could to secure his freedom, and he confided in me his latest suspicions about the location of the Mendacity Tree, begging me to find it if he could not.

I was unable to save him. His fever killed him in his cell before I could arrange his release.

Now she wondered whether she had always sensed something false in those words, a shimmer of deeper water. Winterbourne had not fallen over himself to divulge the location of Kikkert's precious plant; Faith's father had forced it from him. And the Reverend had not striven to save Winterbourne. He had lied to keep him in his malaria-infested cell, and seized his chance to find the Tree.

And Winterbourne had died.

She stirred a little. This time the rope around her middle was still secure. Opening her eyes she saw Paul sitting at some distance, with his back to her. His obvious indifference made her feel even more alone, until she looked down and found an unfamiliar handkerchief draped over her arm.

Faith put up one hand, and found that her cheeks were wet. She had been weeping, and she did not know how long. She dried her face quickly, took a minute or two to calm herself, then cleared her throat so that Paul knew it was safe to look. He turned immediately and came back to her, placing her water bottle in her hand. As usual, his face was carefully unemotional.

"How long has it been?" she asked, her voice creaking like old bellows.

"An hour perhaps," said Paul. "Can you see me now?"

Faith nodded. "The vision is over. How do my eyes appear?"

Paul raised the lantern and peered, then flinched back as if stung.

"Like molten butter in a pan," he said. "I never saw anything like that. What does it mean?"

"It means I am still affected by the fruit." Faith picked numbly at her bonds. "I . . . do not feel as if I am, but I did not last time either. Do not let me grab any rats."

Paul nodded, evidently putting the pieces together. "Did you find out what you wanted this time?"

"I think so." With difficulty, Faith succeeded in tugging loose the rope, and stood shakily. "But I need to look at the parish register to be certain. Where is it kept?"

"In the vestry. But should you not be resting?"

"No." Faith shook her head and steadied herself against the pillar. "The inquest is tomorrow. I need a plan by the morning. I *must* see those records tonight."

"You never ask much, do you?" said Paul grimly. Slightly to Faith's surprise, however, he did not refuse.

Chapter 32

AN EXORCISM

AS THEY WALKED, FAITH NOTICED THAT PAUL kept himself between her and the cliffs, perhaps afraid that she would dance over the edge in a fit of fruit-induced madness. They barely spoke until they approached the lean, black finger of the church spire.

"We will need to be quiet," whispered Paul as they drew near to the church's brass-bound doors. "Jeanne Bissette will be asleep on one of the pews. Wait here—I need to fetch the parish-chest keys." He disappeared in the direction of the parsonage.

Faith stood alone in the churchyard, still aching from the inside out with the cold. The bright moonlight gave the tiny panes of the windows a lizard-scale glitter.

Over to one side she could see the grave that had been dug for her father. The earth was still piled to one side, but with admirable pragmatism, sacks of something had been heaped in the hole, presumably to stop people from falling in.

If it had not been for Jeanne's spiteful gossip, Faith's father would be lying deep and safe in that grave beneath a blanket of turf, instead of in the church crypt awaiting an unknown fate.

Faith reached out and took hold of the great metal ring on the front of the church door. It turned, and slightly to her surprise the door pulled open. After a moment's reflection she realized that Clay probably did not want to leave a young woman helplessly locked in the building.

She walked in. The church seemed much larger without people and light. The moon shone through the stained glass window, spilling watery colors over the nearest pew. It was cold within, and Faith's breath steamed.

She found Jeanne Bissette near the front of the nave, huddled in one of the gentry's box pews with a blanket over her. Jeanne was asleep, and she breathed with a worrying wheeze. Her skin looked pale and waxen, reminding Faith of her snake's dull, crusted scales.

I can do nothing to help her now, Faith told herself. *One more day, that is all I need. Then it will not matter how my stories unravel.*

But the shadows under Jeanne's eyes were dark as plum-skin, and they reminded her of Winterbourne in her vision. Perhaps her father had told himself the same thing. *All I need is one day, to look for the Tree. Winterbourne can survive in that prison a little while longer. Once I have the plant, I can arrange his release.*

Faith wondered what people would do if they found Jeanne Bissette cold and blue on the pew one morning. They might pull the sacks out of the hole outside and lower her into it. There was a ghastly poetry to that idea. Once again, Faith was trembling on the brink of the impossible, just as when she had stood outside her father's library door, willing herself to knock.

"Oh, why must I do this for *you?*" she hissed under her breath. "I do not even like you!"

Her hissed words were startlingly loud in the stillness.

Jeanne's eyelids fluttered, and she woke. She started violently at seeing a black-cloaked figure leaning over her, but then she blinked and her eyes seemed to focus.

"Miss Sunderly?" she asked, her tone incredulous.

"Do you have anywhere else to go?" Faith demanded in a whisper.

"Anywhere else?" Jeanne hauled herself into a sitting position, her hair falling unchecked over half her face. "I cannot! I cannot leave here!"

"But . . . if you could? Do you have family or friends on the island?"

"An uncle . . ." The other girl was clearly still groggy, and trying to work out whether Faith was a dream or apparition. "But—"

"There is no ghost!" Faith spat it out quickly, like an insult or accusation.

Jeanne shook her head wordlessly, her face drooping with misery and exhaustion.

"There is no ghost," repeated Faith. "There is only . . . me. *I* am the ghost. I exchanged the wires of the servants' bells. I stopped the clocks, and burned my father's tobacco in the library, and moved things around the house. I left the skull in your bed."

As Faith spoke, Jeanne's grogginess melted away. By the end she was fully alert, her eyes widening, growing darker and more dangerous.

"*You?* Why?"

"I hated you," Faith answered simply. "You told everybody my father was a suicide. You left him graveless."

Jeanne struggled to her feet, staring at Faith as if snakes were tumbling out of her mouth. Her jaw set, and her breath became quick and angry. Tears of mortification and rage shone in her eyes.

"You . . . you *witch*!" Jeanne's voice broke. "I hope they do drive a stake through your precious father's heart! I hope they do it in front of you! I hope your whole family ends up in the workhouse!"

She was taller and stronger than Faith and could easily have taken her in a fair fight. But of course the fight would never be fair. Jeanne Bissette would always reap the whirlwind for striking Faith Sunderly, beyond anything that Faith Sunderly would ever suffer for striking Jeanne Bissette. Dropping retribution from a height was easier than hurling it upward, and Faith felt a sting of shame at the thought.

"I will tell everyone! Everyone! By the time I am done, you won't be able to show your nose outdoors!" Jeanne turned and broke into a staggering run, disappearing out through the church doors and into the moonlight.

A few moments later, Paul appeared in the doorway, a ring of keys in one hand. He looked pointedly out into the churchyard, then back at Faith with a questioning expression.

"She left," said Faith.

"What were you doing in here?" he asked.

"Ruining all my plans for no good reason." Something important had been missing inside Faith for a while, she realized, and now she had a tiny ribbon of it back. It made her feel worse, not better, but she clung to it anyway. "You will probably hear about it soon. Everybody will."

"What do you mean, your plans are ruined?" Paul asked sharply. "Do not tell me you no longer need that photograph!"

"I do need it!" Faith answered quickly. "Did you make it for me? Is it ready?"

Paul reached into his pocket and drew out a small card, which he frowned at, as though performing last-minute alterations through force of will.

"It was not easy," he muttered, and passed it to her, still frowning. "This was the best that I could do."

Gazing down at it, Faith felt a frisson of shock. He had used the excavation picture that had been taken on Faith's first day as draftsman. There were Dr. Jacklers and Lambent in the foreground, staring intensely at the aurochs horn. Behind them and slightly to one side were the figures of Mrs. Lambent and Faith, the latter obscured by shadow and only partially in the shot. And clawing his way around the side of the "Bedouin tent" was a half-hidden figure with very familiar aquiline features, a domed brow, and coldly distant eyes . . .

For a moment Faith could not understand how her father had been transported into the scene in his entirety. It took her a moment to remember Uncle Miles. Of course, Faith's uncle had been told to stand behind the tent and control the billowing of the cloth. Being Uncle Miles, however, he had found a way to lean across and appear in the photograph. Paul had cut out the Reverend's face very precisely and glued it over that of his brother-in-law. The effect was deeply uncanny.

"That is . . ." Faith bit her tongue. Compliments were contrary to the rules of engagement in her conversations with Paul, but in this case unavoidable. "That is very good work," she admitted gruffly. She tucked it carefully between the pages of her notebook and put it away.

She had not quite dared to hope that Paul would respond to her crazed challenge and make her the photograph. Impulsive brinkmanship was one thing, but this had involved time, effort, and cool-headed precision.

"Thank you," she added in an undertone. She was not sure whether he heard.

Lantern in hand, Paul led her through the church and into the little vestry, where he stooped and turned keys in the three locks of a battered, old-fashioned parish-chest. He opened the lid and drew out a large leather-bound book.

He passed it to Faith, and she began leafing through, focusing on marriage records. When she reached a page listing the marriages for "the Year One Thousand Eight Hundred and Sixty," she stopped.

"There," she breathed. She reached out and tapped one of the carefully written names.

"Does that name mean something to you?" asked Paul, looking over her shoulder.

Faith nodded. "It means that I know who the killers are, and how they knew about the Tree, and why they might have hated my father," she whispered.

Her father's journal had always held the key, but Faith had not seen it. Her eye had skimmed over the one little sentence that might have told her everything she needed to know.

I discovered that the Winterbournes had taken rooms in a shabby inn . . .

Not "Winterbourne," but "the Winterbournes." Hector Winterbourne had been traveling through China with his wife. The Reverend had seen no reason to mention her. Her existence would not have seemed relevant or important to him.

By the light of the lantern Faith could make out the marble plaques on the walls. Tonight her eye snagged on all the female names.

Anne, beloved mother of . . .

In memory of his dear sister Elizabeth . . .

And here also lies Amelia, his loving wife . . .

Who had they been, all these mothers and sisters and wives? What were they now? Moons, blank and faceless, gleaming with borrowed light, each spinning loyally around a bigger sphere.

"Invisible," said Faith under her breath. Women and girls were so often unseen, forgotten, afterthoughts. Faith herself had used it to good effect, hiding in plain sight and living a double life. But she had been blinded by exactly the same invisibility-of-the-mind, and was only just realizing it.

The parish register entry recorded the marriage of Anthony Lambent Esq. to Mrs. Agatha Winterbourne (Widow).

Chapter 33

THE POWDER AND THE SPARK

THE NEXT DAY DAWNED CALLOUSLY CLEAR AND heartlessly sunny. Birdsong was cruelly loud, shattering Faith's sleep. Once again she woke in her own bed with an ache behind her eyes and the feeling that her insides had been battered with a rolling pin. As she hastily gulped water, she remembered the adventures of the night before. The visit to the Lie Tree, the encounter with Paul, the journey to the church, the conversation with Jeanne, the revelations of the parish register . . . and after that hatching strategies with Paul, slipping back through the sea cave, and rowing back to shore.

She would need to act quickly, before Jeanne exposed Faith's true, dark colors to everyone on the island. Exposure no longer terrified Faith. She felt a numb resignation when she thought about it. Instead, she only hoped that she would get her chance to play her last cards before those at the excavation learned about her.

There was no carriage to pick her up that day, of course, so she put on her outdoor clothes, picked up her sketchbook, and set off on foot down the road.

"Miss Sunderly!" Ben Crock looked astonished when Faith appeared at the dig some time later, her skirts dusty and her face shiny from the heat of the sun. He cast a look down the road behind her. "Did you walk the whole way, miss?"

"My father's inquest takes place this afternoon," answered Faith, a little out of breath from all the climbs and descents of the road. "Afterward I do not think my family will stay on Vane. This may be my last chance to visit the dig." She thought of Myrtle, and made her own eyes round, vulnerable, and uncertain. "Do you think the gentlemen will turn me away?"

Crock looked indecisive for a moment, as if considering whether he himself should be sending her home. There was no handy carriage to do so, however. Faith was counting on his reluctance to force her back along the road on foot.

"I do not think that will be a problem, miss," he said, casting a glance down into the little gorge. "The gentlemen are distracted today. Yesterday the tunnel broke through into the shaft. We have been clearing the rubble to take a closer look."

"Have they found anything?" asked Faith, her manner politely curious. In truth she knew as much as he did. Paul had told her all the latest news from the dig.

"Some of the gravel is running down through cracks—there is another cavern down below the base of the shaft, just as we thought. There is a thick layer of breccia though, so we shall be using a barrel of powder to blast our way down."

"I suppose all the gentlemen will be here for the explosion?"

"I am sure they shall, miss." Crock's mouth twitched in what was almost a smile. "I do not think any of them would want to miss it."

Faith thought the same. If there was a chance of breaking into an exciting new cavern, all the gentlemen scientists would want to be "in at the kill." They would certainly not trust each other not to start stealing bones for their own collections, or naming fossils after themselves with extreme prejudice. Everybody important to the excavation would be here this day. She was counting upon it.

As she walked into the little gorge, she won a couple of curious glances as she had on her first day, but everyone was too busy to question her presence.

Uncle Miles, who was hovering like a schoolboy by the tunnel, caught sight of her and blanched. Faith gave him a small, flat smile like a dead fish. She could still feel the bruises of his fingers on her arms. He found a hundred places to look that were not her.

She passed Dr. Jacklers, who looked uncomfortable but had the good grace to bow.

"Good morning, Dr. Jacklers," Faith said mildly. "How is Miss Hunter?"

"Well enough to be making light of her doctor's advice." The doctor's brow creased. Evidently this was a sore point.

Faith was relieved to hear it. If Miss Hunter was vexing Dr. Jacklers again, there was probably hope for her recovery.

Down in the gorge, Lambent was striding about with his flywhisk. Both Clay and Paul were present, the latter laden down with a camera stand and a carry-case. There were more navvies than before, and they were busy heaping sacks of sand and gravel around the mouth of the tunnel, creating a low, horseshoe-shaped wall.

The "Bedouin tent" had been removed from its place by the tunnel, but looking up at the top of the ridge Faith could just make out its billowing roof. Evidently it had been relocated next to the mining-basket winch.

Faith settled herself on a rock in a corner, opening her sketchbook. In a short while, Paul Clay wandered over and settled his tripod on the uneven ground. Neither looked at the other. Nobody watching could have guessed at the conspiracy between the curate's stony-faced son and the rector's shy, dowdy daughter.

"Is she here?" murmured Faith, trying not to move her lips too much.

"Yes," muttered Paul, staring intensely at the foot of his tripod. "They moved her tent up to the high ground to keep her safe from the explosion, and to give her a front-row seat when people go down in the basket. Are you sure the ghost trick will work on her?"

If Faith was right, she was dealing with two murderers of different temperaments. One had distracted her father, one had struck a killing blow. One was terrified of the rumored ghost, one was content to wander the "haunted" area and be mistaken for a ghost himself. A follower, therefore, and a leader. A weak link and a strong.

"No, but I would bet on it." Faith thought of all the memento mori in Mrs. Lambent's reception room. "She thinks she is at death's door, so she spends most of her life peering through it into the gloom. She is up to her nose in prayer books and well-wishing wreaths."

"We will find out soon enough. When we tighten the screw." Paul suited action to words and gave the screw of the tripod a few quick twists. "And how sure are you of him?"

Faith managed not to glance toward the towering figure of Anthony Lambent.

"Agatha is a loyal wife," Faith said under her breath.

A wife cannot always rein in her husband's impulses, Agatha

Lambent had said, *but she must always strive to protect him from the consequences.*

"She had a motive for hating my father, but no reason to want the Tree," she went on. "*He* does. He is a collector, a natural scientist . . . and he is standing for Parliament. Nobody can spread lies like a politician."

"Then we need to get him out of the way."

Faith's plan was to put strain on the "weak link" until it broke. There was no hope of doing that with the "strong link" present.

"When they have opened up a hole into the new cavern, all the gentlemen will want to be the first lowered down." Faith narrowed her eyes. "We need to make sure Mr. Lambent gets his way."

At last the barricade of sandbags was judged sturdy enough. A barrel of gunpowder was rolled carefully into the tunnel, and then everybody emerged from the darkness but Crock. The gentlemen and laborers took up crouched positions in a ditch behind the barricade, all attention focused upon the mouth of the tunnel.

As a lady, Faith was moved to safety behind a crag, and as custodian of the precious camera, Paul withdrew behind another. Neither of them stayed there.

They met behind the huddle of tents. Faith swiftly pulled a bulky bag out from its hiding place between two rocks and handed it to her coconspirator. Paul took it without a word and scrambled up in the direction of the road.

Peering cautiously around the nearest tent, Faith was just in time to see Crock come hurtling out of the tunnel. As she watched, he vaulted the barricade of sandbags and threw himself flat on the other side.

"It is lit!" he called out. "Everybody stay down!"

Faith ducked back. There was a shattering bang that shook her in spite of her readiness. A dull dry patter twitched and jerked the tent canvas. She tasted sand.

When she risked another look, the cave mouth was invisible behind a gauzy spreading cloud of smoke and dust. Those lying behind the barricade had handkerchiefs over their mouths and were coughing vigorously. The distraction and drifting haze allowed Faith to sneak back to her "safe seat," and then reemerge more decorously and obviously.

The navvies entered the tunnel to clear the loose rock. A few barrows of rubble later, Crock reported that the newly blasted hole had indeed revealed another chamber below.

"I think the hole is wide enough to take the mining basket, sir," he told Lambent. "We can lower it from the winch at the top, right down the shaft, and into the new cavern."

"Excellent news!" Lambent rubbed his hands. "Crock, prepare the basket. You and I shall delve the depths and see what treasures your explosive has loosened for us!"

"Ah . . ." Clay cleared his throat, and tentatively raised one hand to gain a finger-hold on the conversation. "I wonder if Crock would not do better aloft, supervising the mechanism? I would be glad to join you in your descent, Mr. Lambent."

"Or perhaps myself?" Uncle Miles suggested quickly.

"Sir." Crock was shading his eyes and staring up toward the road.

With an irregular clap and clop of hoofs, a solitary horse was wandering down the incline. Its reins trailed.

"Is that my bay?" Lambent stared. "How did it become untethered?"

The horse shook its pale mane and continued its aimless yet

relentless amble along the ridge toward the "Bedouin tent." Faith could not see Mrs. Lambent, could not guess how she was reacting. Crock clambered up to intercept the horse, and after a few snorts and nervous shifts it let him draw close and take its reins.

"There are boots in the stirrups!" called down the foreman. "Stuck through backward!" He took one out and examined it closely, then stiffened. He glanced toward Faith, but it was a look of concern, not suspicion. Then Crock clambered back down and showed the boot to Lambent, whispering in his ear. Faith knew that they must be poring over the monogram.

E.J.S.

"A riderless horse with boots backward in the stirrups?" said Clay in a hushed tone. "I have heard of such a thing at military funerals."

Lambent stared unmoving at the boot for a few seconds. Then he marched over to Uncle Miles and proffered the boot, inches from his face.

"What are you about, Cattistock?" he demanded sharply.

"I beg your pardon?" Confusion made Uncle Miles's face look rounder.

"What manner of game is this?" Lambent shifted his weight and seemed to grow taller and broader, swelling with suppressed feelings. He shook the boot. "This, sir, is a boot. A thing, sir, of leather and nails. It is not fading like smoke in my hand. It is not a phantasm of ether. It is an object as solid as you or I, and I daresay if I were to clout you in the face with it, it would leave a print."

Uncle Miles took a hasty step backward. "I do not understand you, Lambent!" he protested.

"It is a boot," Mr. Lambent continued, his voice dangerously quiet and taut, "that has made its spectral journey, I believe, from *your* family abode."

Faith had never previously seen Lambent angry. After the basket incident he had been outraged and severely out of countenance, but that had not been anger of the same dye. Now that his fists were stealthily clenched, Faith realized how large they were. For a moment she sensed strength, barely controlled strength, like a river foaming against a lock and threatening its own banks.

Like most creatures at bay, Uncle Miles looked around for support or allies and found none. At the last his eyes fell upon Faith, and something moved sluggishly behind his gaze, perhaps a realization that she could, in fact, have brought the Reverend's boots to the site . . .

"Get out!" snarled Lambent.

"But I was promised—"

"No, I do not wish to hear it! Begone!"

With one last suspicious glance at Faith, Uncle Miles fled with as much dignity as he could muster.

"We have wasted enough time." Lambent gave a gruff, lion-like noise of frustration in his throat. "Crock, make the basket ready. I shall descend with Clay."

"Hold, please!" The doctor, seemingly undaunted by the magistrate's ill-temper, was still nursing some squat and bitter grievance of his own. "We have not discussed who should descend first. You are too high-handed, Lambent!"

"High-handed? Doctor, this excavation is on *my* land, and paid for from *my* purse."

"And you have already seen fit to recompense yourself for that!" the doctor answered through his teeth.

"I beg your pardon?" Lambent's voice was low and cold.

"I am simply saying, sir, that various little birds have told me that not *all* our finds make it to the sorting table, and not *all* our finds return from your house after they are varnished." The doctor had the cold, tight voice of somebody who thinks he is being tactful. Faith could not guess which of her rumors he had heard, or in which form.

"How dare you!" thundered the magistrate.

Faith could see that in another moment Dr. Jacklers was likely to find himself thrown out of the site in Uncle Miles's wake. That did not suit her purposes.

She let her knees buckle, and dropped to the earth as a deadweight.

"Miss Sunderly has fainted!" Feet pounded the dust toward her.

She was raised to a sitting position and offered water. The doctor forgot his anger and tutted over her pulse.

Faith waved a vague hand in the direction of the "Bedouin tent."

"Shade," she whispered plaintively.

She was helped up the slope and guided to a chair beside Mrs. Lambent. The magistrate's wife did not look at her. As usual she was wrapped to the gills, but today the eyes that peered out above her shawls seemed uncommonly bright and apprehensive. Her hands toyed absently with cards in front of her, like a blind seer telling out her Tarot.

They were not Tarot cards, however. They were miniature scenes, prints of the photographs taken throughout the excavation, delivered to her that morning by Paul Clay. They rippled and leapt slightly in the breeze.

"Mrs. Lambent." Paul had appeared before the magistrate's wife. He delivered a small bow, with the solemnity of a funeral mute. "My father is sending me back to the parsonage for more chemicals and wondered if you would like me to bring anything back from town for you."

"No, thank you, Master Clay."

Paul bowed again, turned to leave, then stooped, straightened with a photograph in his hand, and added it to the pile face down without so much as glancing at it. It was done deftly and naturally, so that anybody might think he had noticed it lying on the ground.

He briefly made eye contact with Faith. Neither smiled, but she closed her eyes in a slow blink, a cat smile. *Thank you.*

The winch was made ready and the curate and magistrate slowly lowered into darkness. The doctor glared at them resentfully now and then, but did not abandon his patient. Nearby, the magistrate's horse cropped the grass with remarkable calm, tethered to the winch frame by a slipknot.

After a while, Crock came over and raised a knuckle to his own forehead.

"They have touched down safely, ma'am," he said. "They say there is a large cavern down there—they will be happy for half an hour at least."

"He should never have gone down," Mrs. Lambent said under her breath. "This is an ill day, an unhappy day . . ." For an absent-minded moment, her gaze flicked down to the photographs in her hand. Her face froze and her jaw drooped. She gave a long, hoarse, lung-wrenching gasp, like a death rattle in reverse.

"Mrs. Lambent!" Dr. Jacklers sprang to his feet, and Crock hurried over as well.

The magistrate's wife was staring at the uppermost photograph, hauling in breath after ragged breath.

"That shape—clawing through the tent!"

"No, no," the doctor reassured her, "I have seen a print of that photograph; it is only Miles Cattistock battling the canvas."

"No!" Mrs. Lambent straightened in her chair and held the photograph up for the doctor to see. "Look at him! Look at his face! Can you not see who it is? It is Erasmus Sunderly! I would know his face anywhere!"

"How?" asked Faith, not loudly but clearly. "How would you know his face?" Her voice cut through the conversation like a blade, leaving a little hole of silence in its wake.

The doctor, who had been staring at the photograph, looked up in perplexity. "That . . . is a good question. How *did* you recognize him? I thought that you had never met him."

"He visited my house," Mrs. Lambent said huskily.

"But you never saw him while he was there," said Faith. "You never came to dinner, because if you had, *he would have recognized you*. He met you in China when you were traveling with your husband—Mr. Hector Winterbourne, who died of malaria.

"Some people think you have a weakness for gin, Mrs. Lambent, but I am sure Dr. Jacklers knows better. He is your doctor, so I am sure he knows why you have fevers, year in, year out. Maybe it was even Dr. Jacklers who told you that gin and tonic could be used to treat malaria."

Mrs. Lambent's breathing was developing a dangerous wheeze, and her eyes bulged slightly each time she inhaled.

"Doctor—Mrs. Lambent is unwell!" Crock's brow was furrowed as he regarded his employer's wife.

"Please, Doctor, let me tell you the rest!" Faith said urgently. "This involves my father's death—and I have proof, written proof!" She could almost see the medical man and the coroner battling inside Dr. Jacklers's head.

"Go on," he said, with a nod to Faith. For the first time the look he gave her was not indulgent or impatient.

"Mrs. Lambent's name used to be Winterbourne," continued Faith. "You can find it in the parish register. My father left a journal—he writes about meeting the Winterbournes when they were traveling upriver in search of a specimen. When Mr. Winterbourne was arrested, my father failed to arrange his release—"

"Failed!" Mrs. Lambent's deep voice throbbed with feeling. "He connived to *keep* Hector in that foul hole! He might as well have run him through!"

Faith felt a knot loosen inside her. Mrs. Lambent's outburst had confirmed Faith's story. The weak link was breaking, just as Faith had hoped against hope that it would. Now she needed to keep up the pressure, force further confessions.

"The morning before he died, my father received an unsigned letter, threatening to reveal his past and telling him to meet someone in the Bull Cove dell at midnight." Faith hesitated, then took her gamble and risked her lie. "It took a long time to find that letter. But now that we have it, it is easy enough to identify the handwriting."

For some reason the thought of handwriting made Faith briefly uneasy. Some memory fly-tapped at the window of her mind, but it was a dull buzz, nothing more.

"No . . ." whispered Mrs. Lambent. "He said that he burned the letter . . ." The whites of her eyes showed as she gasped.

"I know that the trap was your husband's idea," Faith continued. She stood, and drew closer to the older woman. "I know that you would never have risked your own soul otherwise. You were being a good wife."

"Mrs. Lambent, please tell us all you can." Dr. Jacklers was every inch the coroner now. He stooped to look the magistrate's wife in the eye, his face unusually earnest and solemn. "The law respects honesty—if you are willing to speak now, it will make a world of difference in the long run."

Mrs. Lambent opened her mouth, but all that came out were rough wheezes. At last, with visible effort, she heaved air into her lungs and forced out one loud, creaking syllable.

"Ben!"

A shadow passed between Faith and the sun. It was Ben Crock, leaping forward to fling his arm around Dr. Jacklers's neck, wrestling him backward. At the same time Mrs. Lambent lunged forward, seizing both of Faith's wrists with manacle firmness.

"Crock, what are y—erk—"

"Dispose of him, Ben!" snapped Mrs. Lambent.

Without a crease in his brow, Crock dragged the doctor backward, swung him around, and hurled him down the shaft. The doctor flailed as he fell. After he had disappeared from view, the guy ropes quivered like harp strings. Faith could only hope that they had slowed his fall.

"Did you just crush my husband, Ben?" asked Agatha Lambent in an aghast tone, still gripping Faith's arms.

Crock leaned over and listened.

"I think not, ma'am. He is shouting. Sounds healthy enough."

The navvies were watching, calmly. Not protesting, or running to wrestle Crock to the ground. They were looking at Crock . . . no, they were looking *to* Crock, for orders. They were his navvies, if indeed they were navvies at all. Crock had recruited all of them.

"Now, you little viper," said Agatha, turning her attention to Faith, "you have your father's journals. You know your father's secrets. *Where is my Tree?*"

Faith was developing an inkling that her deductions had been only partly correct.

Chapter 34

THE WIDOW

"*YOUR* TREE?"

Faith had it at last. Too late, she understood her own nagging sense of unease.

Handwriting. Lambent's handwriting on the coroner's warrant, large, flamboyant, and undisciplined. Mrs. Lambent's curt letter to Myrtle on the day of the funeral, cruelly precise in its tiny lettering. The small, neat writing on the labels in the Cabinet of Curiosities . . .

"The cabinet! That was *your* writing on the labels. All those natural-history specimens—they never did belong to your husband. They were *yours*."

The clues had been there, Faith realized. She remembered the stuffed snake strangling a mongoose. No wonder it had looked so much like her own pet. It was another Mandarin trinket snake. Agatha must have collected the specimen while she was in China.

"I have excellent taste in husbands," said Agatha, "but they do tend to be dabblers."

Her breathing was steadying now, and her eyes were steel. Faith wondered how she had ever thought that Agatha was a weak link.

344

"I made the same mistake as everybody else," said Faith wonderingly. "You were the real natural scientist all the time. Winterbourne never dragged you along in his search for the Tree—it was the other way around. And Mr. Lambent . . ."

". . . is a dear, noble soul," Agatha finished, with a devout air, "and willing to listen to good counsel."

Faith's image of a domineering husband with a loyal but frail wife faded away. Instead she saw an impulsive, enthusiastic man, led hither and thither by a clever and vengeful woman.

"You persuaded your husband to invite my father to Vane." Faith imagined Lambent seizing upon the idea like a puppy, and making it his own. "You told him to hire Ben Crock."

At last Faith realized why Agatha spent so much time at the excavation, and why Crock had kept his dancing attendance upon her. While Lambent had been strutting and posing in pantaloons, his wife had been quietly running the dig.

As she understood, Faith felt the strangest mixture of jubilation, frustration, and sadness. Here was that mythical beast that everybody had told her could not exist: a female natural scientist.

"We could have been friends," Faith said.

"As you can see, I am not without friends," Agatha answered coolly, gesturing toward the silent navvies. "Our friendship was forged in China, where your father's machinations nearly saw us all rot to death in prison."

"But this is insane!" Faith was still struggling to grasp the situation. "What are you planning to do? The people down that shaft will be missed! I will be missed! People will come to investigate." Her gaze crept to the shaft. "If you bring Dr. Jacklers up now, maybe he won't die. Otherwise it will be murder, and everyone will know you were responsible!"

"We were attacked," said Agatha, without batting an eyelid,

"by those louts from town who threw rocks at us before. They surprised us, knocked the poor doctor down the shaft, and had us at a disadvantage for a while before we chased them off and were able to haul up our friends once again. Depending on how annoying you choose to be, you may have fled in the confusion and fallen, breaking your neck."

Faith looked at Crock. *You liked me*, she thought. *You felt sorry for me.*

With whiplash force, however, the truth hit her. *You were only kind to me out of guilt. You killed my father.*

"Sorry, miss," Crock said. "I did hope to keep you as safe as possible."

In her imagination, Faith now saw Crock filing through the mining-basket chain, then adding the guy ropes in panic when two children climbed into the basket instead of his target.

"But I owe Mrs. Lambent my life," he continued. "I was Mr. Winterbourne's foreman, and they threw me into that prison too. I would have died there, but Mrs. Lambent would not abandon me. She stayed in that swamp town until she could persuade them to let me go . . . but by then she had malaria." He still had outdoor eyes, but today they held winter skies.

"The Tree, Miss Sunderly," said Agatha. "We have all earned that Tree. It is the key to prosperity that has long been denied us. It is our right."

Much as it hurt Faith to admit it, Agatha had a point. The Winterbournes had never owned the Tree, but they had given years of their lives to chasing down rumors, only to have the Tree snatched away before they could finally claim it. *They're murderers*, whispered Faith's grief. But the Reverend had caused the death of Agatha's husband. Faith understood calculated, cold-burning revenge.

Indeed, Faith might have felt real sympathy for her enemies, had she not just seen Dr. Jacklers being hurled down a shaft.

"Please, miss." Crock's smile was not unfriendly, but nor was it without menace.

"I . . ." Faith hung her head. "I did hide a plant. I . . . I can show you some of its leaves, and you can tell me whether it is the right one."

Agatha released Faith's wrists, Crock standing guard behind her so that Faith did not bolt. Faith reached into her pocket. Her fingers brushed the reticule containing the pistol and hesitated for a moment. However, if she drew the weapon half cocked, she could not stop Crock grabbing it from her. If she pulled back the hammer before drawing, her enemies would hear the click.

Instead she brought out her father's tobacco tin. She held it out, but did not move forward.

"The leaves are in there?" Agatha moved forward eagerly to take it. Just as Faith had hoped, this brought her into the sunlight.

"See for yourself." Faith flipped open the box, and flung the contents over Agatha.

The leaf fragments littered the older woman's dress, and as the sun touched them they ignited. Small fierce flames erupted on the cotton and taffeta, spitting and sizzling. Crock snatched up a rug and flung it over Agatha's dress to smother the flames.

Faith ran. Before the navvies could react, she had sprinted to the grazing horse, pulled loose the slipknot, and placed one foot in the nearest stirrup.

Then there was shouting, and rocks crackling under hasty steps. The horse's flank shivered and its back legs danced nervously sideways. Faith desperately pushed up, hoping this would seat her on top of it. Instead she found herself sprawling across the saddle like a sack of potatoes as the horse lurched into skittish motion.

Faith clung to the far side of the saddle in desperation as the horse broke into a frightened canter, the saddle pummeling her chest with each bound. Each jerk threatened to drag her fingers free and send her plummeting to the turf. Faith could hear the shoulder seams of her dress tearing.

I am so glad Mother never put me in full corsets, she thought.

The hoofs were ringing on a roadway now, instead of pounding grass. There were still shouts behind, but they grew fainter.

In this ungainly fashion she bounced along for a few minutes, before losing her grip and landing with painful force on the dusty road. The horse slowed and halted, trailing its reins. Faith rose unsteadily, feeling her knee grazed beneath her skirts, and hobbled after the horse. She made a few wobbly attempts to mount it properly, but it had been saddled for a man. She had too many skirts to sit astride, and when she tried to ride sidesaddle she slithered off. She had no choice but to continue on foot.

There was no time to lose. Faith's only advantage was a head start. Her pursuers, on the other hand, were not bruised, exhausted, suffering the aftereffects of visionary fruit or struggling with three layers of skirts.

Furthermore, her enemies knew where she was going. They knew where she lived.

By the time she reached the descent to the house at Bull Cove, Faith could feel the blood oozing from her knee and sticking to her petticoat.

Mrs. Vellet opened the door to her and stared aghast at Faith's disheveled, dusty appearance. Myrtle appeared beside the housekeeper a moment later.

"Faith, where have you been? Where . . . ? Oh, mercy, what has happened?" She dragged Faith inside and into the drawing room. While Mrs. Vellet ran off to the medicine cupboard, Myrtle stood staring at her daughter, touching tentative fingertips to Faith's hair, a cut on her ear, rips in her dress. "Darling—oh, darling—what happened to you? Has . . . ? Has somebody . . ."

It took a moment for Faith to understand Myrtle's drift.

"No." Faith clasped her hands and tried to calm herself. "No, I have not been despoiled. I am just bruised and bumped and . . . and I have been running. A band of murderers is coming this way, Mother! We all need to leave, right now, or they will kill us!"

"Murderers? Faith, what are you talking about?"

"Father did some terrible things in China," Faith blurted out. "He caused a man's death, and stole a valuable specimen, and now the people he wronged are after us for revenge. Mrs. Lambent, Ben Crock, the navvies . . . Mother, there is no time to explain it properly—we all need to go! Please, please, believe me, just for once!"

The housekeeper arrived at that moment with a bottle of medicinal brandy. Myrtle stood irresolute for a moment, tongue tip between her lips, frowning into Faith's face.

"Mrs. Vellet," she said, "please fetch Howard. We must leave now, on foot. Some murderous brutes are coming to attack us."

"Does Prythe have a shotgun?" asked Faith hopefully.

"Prythe left yesterday afternoon," Myrtle answered distractedly.

"But . . ." Faith recalled Myrtle threatening to have the servants throw Uncle Miles out of the house the night before. Her mother caught her eye and smiled.

"Yes, darling," Myrtle said crisply, "I was bluffing."

Mrs. Vellet left and returned with Howard.

"The high road or the low road?" Myrtle whispered urgently to herself. "If we take the low road, there is nowhere to hide or escape. On the high road, at least we can cut across the grass-lands, or hide behind bushes . . ."

"Madam . . ." Mrs. Vellet cleared her throat. "We . . . should take the low road."

"Why is that?" Myrtle looked surprised by the unsolicited advice.

Mrs. Vellet tightened her mouth, drew back her chin, and looked uncomfortable. If she had been able to pull her head down into her collar like a turtle, Faith fancied she would have done so.

"If we take the low road, we shall encounter a carriage," Mrs. Vellet said at last. "Somebody is coming . . . to meet with me."

The low road and the sea always flirted with each other, and today they were particularly passionate. It was high tide, and great waves could be heard crashing against the shore. The freshening wind filled the air with spray and a dusting of rainbows.

Mrs. Vellet patiently dragged Howard by the hand, while Myr-tle struggled along in her immaculate black dress, her heavy veil puffing in and out with her breaths. None of them carried lug-gage, or even a fan. Faith's limbs ached after her fall, her knee was starting to swell, and her lack of sleep was catching up with her. Now and then a woolly grogginess muffled her mind for a second, like a cloth over a lamp.

She could not help looking over her shoulder. She kept expecting to see men coming after them at a run.

The first rumble took Faith by surprise. She was too tired and sun-dazzled to work out where it was coming from. Then something cracked loudly against the road a few feet away, and she turned to see reddish-brown rock fragments fountain and scatter.

"They are above us on the cliff, dropping rocks!" Faith pulled closer to the inland side of the road. "Quick, this side! Under the overhang!"

The others followed her example and were soon in a hasty single file in the little strip of shelter.

"They must have thought"—huff—"that we would take"—huff—"the high road," Myrtle gasped as she struggled to keep up.

"They know where we are now," murmured Faith. "Some of them will double back and come down the road behind us."

Another, larger rock struck the roadway very close to the fugitives. Some of its fragments flew out and hit Howard, who gave a wail of pain and confusion. The sound cut Faith to the heart and filled her with a hot torrent of protective rage.

A little farther on, the road descended sharply, then leveled much lower down. Now the breakwater was all that defended the road from the fierce and capricious sea. The noise was deafening. Every other wave sent a gleaming arc of white foam over the top of the breakwater, falling with a slap on the roadway and spattering the cliff with dark splashes.

One seething white arc drenched them all, making them gasp. The way was sloppy with broad, salt puddles. With a chill, Faith remembered that this road had been dangerously flooded on the day of their arrival. She could not remember the tide table, or be sure that the waters would not rise higher.

Worse, as Faith peered back over her shoulder she could just make out distant figures through the haze of sunlit spray.

"They are coming!" she called.

"Where is the carriage?" cried Myrtle.

"Listen!" shouted Mrs. Vellet.

There was a clatter so faint that it was almost imperceptible. Then it became clearer and louder, until at last a pony and trap rounded the distant bend and came into view, hoofs echoing and bells ringing.

There was a single figure in the trap, wearing a maroon riding coat and bonnet and driving with an eager, cavalier speed. As the trap drew closer, Faith could make out black hair, and heavy bandaging across the forehead. It was Miss Hunter.

Upon seeing a group approaching at a run, Miss Hunter's expression changed from happy anticipation to surprise and doubt.

"Jane!" she called. "You have brought the family?"

"Desperate times, Leda," called Mrs. Vellet, hurrying forward with Howard in her arms. "They are under attack—I needed to help them escape." Her eyes were bright, and she looked younger than usual.

"Of course you did." Leda Hunter's smile had the slight sadness that often mingles with true fondness.

"Can you turn the trap around on this road?" Even as Faith spoke the words, another rock smashed down, showering the carriage wheels with gravel.

The road was just wide enough, so Miss Hunter started turning her trap about. Some of her black hair had come loose from its coiled plaits, making her look playful and reckless.

"You should not be riding with that injury!" Mrs. Vellet whispered chidingly as she passed Howard up into the trap. The two women exchanged a slight and hasty smile. And that flash of a smile was enough for Faith to understand that Mrs. Vellet was not dry, and Miss Hunter was not cold, and to sense a moment of rightness like two notes in accord, the tiniest fragment of a melody that she did not understand.

"Quickly!" shouted Myrtle.

The distant men were becoming less distant by the moment. They had reached the steep descent in the road and were running down it as fast as they dared, feet sliding on the spray-moistened surface. One was carrying a barrel the size of a large hatbox.

Miss Hunter completed the maneuver. Myrtle was helped up into the trap, next to Howard. Mrs. Vellet clambered up and squeezed in as well, the little carriage creaking and protesting at the unusual burden.

"Faith! Climb up!"

Faith cast one last glance behind her, then stopped. The men had not pursued. They had halted at the base of the hill, and they had been busy. The barrel had been set against the breakwater, and rocks heaped haphazardly over it. And now the men were running back up the hill, as fast as they could . . .

The barrel was twenty yards away. She broke into a run, in spite of her swollen knee and the weight of her wet skirts. She sprinted toward the sinister makeshift rockery, knowing that if she was correct, it could blow her apart at any second.

It was probably Crock's plan, and bore the marks of his ruthless good sense. There was no need to catch and kill five fugitives in a carriage, if you could blow a hole in the breakwater and let the sea do your dirty work.

She reached the pile of rocks, heart hammering, expecting to feel her flesh blasted from her bones. She could just see the wooden spars and hoops of the buried gunpowder barrel. A faint fizzling sound caught her ear. There was a foot of fat, varnished rope protruding from the rocks. A flower of fierce orange flame wavered at its loose end, eating the rope down to a stump.

Faith grabbed the fuse, just above the flame, and yanked

it away from the barrel. It came away easily, and she threw it across the road, to languish and hiss in a puddle. She kicked away the rocks, until she could reach down and grab the barrel. It was heavy, but she heaved it up onto her shoulder, and then hurled it over the breakwater.

"Faith!" screamed Myrtle.

There were footsteps running down the hill toward Faith. She turned to flee for the trap, but she knew it would be too late. She had known it even as she sprinted for the barrel.

Somebody grabbed her by the back of her collar, and then an arm gripped her about the middle, bruising her innards and lifting her off the ground.

Myrtle was screaming and screaming her name, as other men ran past Faith after the trap. There was shouting and the *crack-a-crack* of more rocks falling, then a screech of a terrified horse. The trap jolted into flight as the horse bolted, weaving wildly but gathering speed, and vanished around the corner in the road.

"Come back!" called a familiar voice. The sprinting navvies slowed down, turned about, and walked slowly back. "We have the one we want," said Ben Crock, setting Faith back on her feet.

Chapter 35

SURVIVAL AND THE FITTEST

UNDER A BRILLIANT BLUE SKY, FAITH WALKED down the path to the beach, the crunch of her enemies' boots behind her. The back of her neck tingled with a sense of danger.

This is the last time I shall walk this path, thought Faith, strangely calm.

She had already calculated her own odds of survival. Agatha Lambent and Ben Crock could not afford to leave her alive. They would kill her once she had served her purpose.

Once Faith was dead, it was unlikely that anybody would be able to prove anything against Agatha and her accomplices. Dr. Jacklers might testify against them if he survived, but his survival seemed unlikely. The group who had escaped in the trap knew only what Faith had gabbled to them. They had seen little—only a gang of men in the distance and some falling rocks. Uncle Miles knew a little, since Agatha Lambent had almost certainly been the "respectable person" offering to buy the Reverend's papers and specimens from him. He would not understand the significance of this, however, and was very unlikely to tell anyone about it. Paul knew some of what Faith had discovered, but Agatha and Crock did not know that, and Faith was in no hurry to tell them.

She could almost feel the presence of other Faiths from other times. Faith striding guiltily to the beach to hide her gloves among the rocks. Faith creeping through darkness with her father. Faith discovering the human horseshoe hanging from the cliff tree. Faith sneaking to the boat in her ravaged funeral gown, mad with grief and a hunger for revenge. Perhaps even a far younger Faith, on another beach, finding her first fossil and looking for her father's approval.

These other selves all seemed lifetimes away. Faith barely knew what she might say to any of them.

"Is that the boat ahead?" asked Agatha Lambent's deep, contralto voice behind her.

"Yes," said Faith. She tipped her head back, watching a ballet of tiny white gulls riding the high back of the strengthening wind.

She could no longer understand the Faith from the night of the ratting, who had believed that the world was only teeth and hunger, nothing but killing and dead bones in the dust. *Hunger cannot explain why I love the blue of this sky*, she thought.

Somebody took her by the arm and led her firmly on to the shingle. Faith could not help limping, her swollen knee hard to bend.

"Show us the cave," said Crock.

Faith raised her arm and pointed. "You cannot see it properly from here."

"And there is no other way in?" asked the foreman.

Faith turned and looked straight into Crock's clear, sky-colored eyes.

"Do you *really* think that I would be taking a boat out on these currents, over and over again, if there was another way in?"

Crock studied her for a moment, then gave a small nod,

acknowledging her point. It amused Faith. Even now, at death's brink, she could still tell a lie.

The boat was too small for many occupants.

"Sit in the stern and give directions," Agatha told Faith. "I shall take the prow, and Mr. Crock shall row."

When all three were seated, the "navvies" pushed the boat into the water. Clearly Faith's nocturnal voyages would have started far more easily with a host of deadly enemies to assist her.

The green glassy waves and crashing foam had a false brilliance like a lunatic's smile. The boat reared and bucked, leaving a playful pearly wake, but Crock managed the oars more easily than Faith ever had. The sun gleamed through the fabric of Agatha's bonnet, casting a peacock-tinted shadow across her face. They might have been a family of day-trippers.

Right now Faith was dancing to her captors' tune, doing the very thing that would make her expendable. However, this also meant that she was now faced with two enemies, not seven.

"What will you do with the Tree?" she asked aloud.

"Will I publish papers on it, stagger the scientific world, and become the toast of the Royal Society?" Agatha's deep voice was laden with cynicism and bitterness. "I think not. I had ideas of that sort once. I understand the world better now."

"You think that nobody would believe you?" suggested Faith.

"I know that they would not. It is too new, too strange; it would push too many other scientists out of their comfortable seats. Perhaps it might sound better coming from a gentleman of good breeding, but if *I* talked of it? I should probably find myself in a lunatic asylum."

"So you plan to keep it secret and feed it lies." Faith found that she was angry. If she was to be murdered for a plant, then at the very least the murderers should make the best use of the thing.

"Soon, God willing, my husband will be a member of Parliament," Agatha said calmly. "He will be well-placed to feed the Tree, and will say what I tell him to say."

The thought made Faith queasy. As a member of Parliament, Anthony Lambent could spread grand, far-reaching lies through the House of Commons to the whole Empire.

"Secrets are power," continued Agatha, "and money, if one uses them correctly. If I cannot be famous, I may as well be rich."

"But surely you intend to study it!" exclaimed Faith. "You *must* plan to do so! How can you bear to use it without trying to understand it!"

"There are things that science cannot explain," remarked Crock with a frown, as he drew on the oars.

Both Faith and Agatha instantly spluttered in disagreement.

"What nonsense!" cried Faith. "Just because something has not been rationally explained does not mean it never will be! They used to think flint arrowheads were elf-bolts! The Angles thought Roman ruins were built by giants!"

"There may be questions still unanswered, but that means that we *need* science, not that science is useless," Agatha retorted tartly. "There are fish in the sea as yet uncaught, but that does not mean that fishing nets have failed and should be thrown aside."

Faith found herself nodding.

"But we all know what the Tree is!" protested Crock. He glanced at Faith. "You're a parson's daughter—you know the good book inside and out—you *must* know what I mean."

It took a moment for Faith to grasp Crock's meaning. As she did so, she recalled cryptic fragments from her father's journal and at last understood them.

I have wondered whether the Tree may date from the Earliest Days . . . a more Fortunate Age, now lost . . .

"The Tree of Knowledge," breathed Faith, and felt a sudden, deep sadness. "Father thought so. No . . . he *hoped* that it was so. He wanted scientific proof of the Bible."

"Hope is a dangerous thing for a scientist," Agatha said coolly.

"I do not think it *is* the Tree of Knowledge," said Faith slowly. It hurt to contradict her father, and it was strange to be debating the matter with her nemeses, but she could not help herself. "Why would the Tree be out of Eden, and eating lies? Besides, the fruit do not give you godlike knowledge. Sometimes I even wonder . . ." She stopped and frowned, as a hazy suspicion took shape in her mind. "The 'secrets' might only be things that one has already guessed, deep down."

Crock continued rowing, but he was scowling now. Faith sensed a simmering, angry discomfort with the conversation. It was the first time she had noticed any hint of disagreement between her enemies. Crock seemed less than certain that the Tree was not a forbidden plant destined to damn his soul. Faith could see that he would follow Agatha Lambent into hell, but perhaps he believed that that was exactly what he was doing.

Faith noticed where they were. "That is the cave! Let the wave wash us in!"

She had never arrived at high tide before, and the water was lapping near the top of the cave's mouth. As the wave hurled them forward with dizzying force, all three had to duck down inside the boat, in order to pass through un-stunned.

Faith heard her companions gasp as the boat surged through the roaring cavern, spinning about and rattling against the walls. At last it settled, not on the shingle as usual, but on the stone plateau beyond it.

"What is that smell?" asked Agatha. The aroma of the Tree drove ice needles behind the eyes and nose. It chilled the lungs.

"The Tree," said Faith.

Crock clambered out first. When Faith climbed out, he took a firm hold of her arm.

"I don't want to lose track of you in the dark," he said.

A light quivered then glowed in the boat, showing Agatha nursing a lantern's flame into more life.

"You cannot take that in there!" Faith declared promptly. "A light that bright will destroy the Tree! You saw what happened to the leaves. You need to smother the lantern, so only a little light shines through."

After some suspicious looks and exchanged glances, Faith's enemies followed her advice. She saw the entrance cave dim around her.

As they approached the other cavern, even Faith could not suppress a small gasp. Ahead lay a mass of writhing black creeper, so dense and dark that it looked like a portal into an abyss. Huge, muscular wooden vines arched and weaved among the black tendrils, like sigils in some vegetable language.

Lantern aloft, Agatha led them toward the gently swaying curtain of black tendrils. She reached out one lace-gloved hand and gently stroked the nearest vines, rubbing finger and thumb together to test the consistency of the sap. Her eyes were bright, entranced. At the same time there was something lost and distant in her smile. Even the brightness seemed empty, like the reflection of gold in a prospector's eye.

"This is the Tree," she said, her voice awed but strangely flat. "We found it. After all these years."

Without warning, Agatha stepped into the black tentacular jungle and vanished, taking the lantern with her and leaving the entrance cave in darkness. Ahead, the glow of the lantern shifted and swayed among the vines, a will-o'-the-wisp in a sunless forest.

"Come along, Ben," Agatha called, her voice muffled. "It will not hurt you."

Crock followed, dragging Faith through the shifting, slithering tendrils.

Faith tried to keep track of their route, so that she would know how to find the hidden passage to the cliff-top. Unfortunately Crock kept too firm a grasp on her arm for her to slip his hold and escape amid the vines. In any case, even if she did, Agatha's lantern would help them track her down before she got far.

Unobserved, she slipped one hand into her pocket and sought the handle of her father's pistol. The little weapon had only one bullet, however, and she was faced with twice as many murderers.

"You can track the floor roots to the heart!" said Agatha, raising her lantern and beckoning. "They are like the slats of a fan!" As she advanced, the hanging tendrils whispered against the taffeta of her full skirts and trailed inquisitively over her shoulders. Agatha and the Tree seemed to be taking a liking to each other, and Faith felt a foolish sting of jealousy.

Crock, on the other hand, flinched whenever a vine stroked his face.

"Pay no attention to the voices," Faith whispered. "You get used to them." It pleased her to see Crock tense as he noticed the piecemeal murmurs for the first time.

As they progressed, however, the voices grew louder, and began to unnerve Faith as well.

The heart of the Tree was now a vast tortured tangle of trunk-wide wooden vines, buckling and puckering. Staring up at it,

Faith could hear her eardrums beating, with a sound like rending paper. With each beat, the twisting wood seemed to pulse and glare. In her peripheral vision she thought she saw tender wisps of blackness leaking from the knot to darken and thicken the air.

Agatha laughed, and placed one foot on a thick lower coil. Faith did not know whether the older woman was claiming conquest of the Tree, or about to climb it like a child. Crock stared at it with a suspicious frown.

"We have seen what we came to see," said Crock. "Shall we go?" He glanced across at Faith, and his face saddened. He was already thinking of her dead, she realized. He was readying himself to murder her, and already trying out the regret he would feel. He was thinking of ways to make it quick.

If she gave her captors nothing else to think about, they would think about killing her.

"Why are you in such a hurry, Mr. Crock?" Faith demanded, with a boldness she did not feel. "Are you *afraid* of it? After everything you have done, and the people you killed to be here? It is only a *plant*. It eats lies and feeds secrets, but that is easily explained. It forms a bond with one person, and then the rest is just a matter of currents in the magnetic fluid."

Agatha stiffened and turned to glare. "I beg your pardon?"

"Animal magnetism," Faith continued brightly. "It induces trances, unobstructed visions, allows living things to affect each other without touching, causes physical effects—"

"I know of the theory of animal magnetism!" snapped Agatha. "It is an absurd, exploded notion that nobody of sense now believes! Only charlatan healers still talk of it! How dare you apply such old-fashioned nonsense to my Tree?" There was a fierce light in her eye that was almost joy.

"How would you explain it then?" retorted Faith, wondering

how long it had been since Agatha had had the chance to debate anything with anybody.

"Well, obviously the Tree is some sort of spiritual carnivore." Agatha drew closer. "I would surmise that it consumes ghosts, and is able to provide answers using the knowledge of the spirits within—like a vegetable medium. My theory is that a powerful lie takes on a life of its own, almost becoming a miniature spirit. The Tree absorbs such lies, and uses their spirit energy to sustain the ghosts inside it."

She was standing close to Faith now, her eyes shining in the dim lantern-light. She was the same age as Myrtle, Faith realized, but disappointment had scored its grooves deep. There were creases at the corners of her mouth, the marks of too many words bitten back.

"Thank you," said Faith humbly. "That was . . . very enlightening." Then she struck the lantern from Agatha's hand, so that it smashed on the cave floor.

There was darkness, and smells of oil and green wood singeing. Faith tried to snatch her arm from Crock's grip, but his fingers bit into her and held. His other arm grappled her, and tightened about her throat as she struggled.

Faith pulled the pistol out of her pocket, fumbled blindly until the hammer clicked back, then raised the gun so that it was pointing backward past her head. She fired.

The bang was like a blow to the side of her head. The pistol jerked and jumped out of her grip, its hot metal bumping against her shoulder as it fell. Somebody behind her was screaming, and nobody was holding her anymore.

Faith plunged into the pitch black ahead of her, hearing glass crunch under her feet. There were shapes behind her thrashing, rustling, and panting like great beasts in the undergrowth. Faith's own blundering caused just as much noise. Vines slapped her face, tangled about her neck, tripped her feet, hooked her sleeves, trailed into her pockets, reached invisible fingers into her eyes.

She needed to find the cave wall. Once she had it she could follow it and find her way out. But her fingers met dangling vines and more vines and the clammy stickiness of leaves. There came into her head a deep soul-fear that she and her pursuers were no longer in the cave but in a wall-less, endless jungle of the Tree, a private hell where they would hunt each other for eternity.

No, she told herself, *no. There is a wall. There is a wall.*

Amid the fluttering of leaves and the matted strands of foliage, her fingers touched stone.

She followed the wall, tearing her fingers on the vine-knots in her haste. She stumbled on steps and slopes, found footholds, climbed. She clambered and squeezed, feeling her way by touch. The apertures were narrower than they had been, padded out with sprawling, crawling vines. She lost precious time sawing through her hoop ties and disentangling herself from them, so that she could squeeze through narrower gaps.

But she thanked each desperate cranny, each painful fissure, knowing that if they were hard for her they would be doubly so for the crashers and thrashers behind her. She was the rat in the crack, escaping the terrier's jaws.

There was something above her, a glimmer that could scarcely be called light. She fought and struggled and wriggled like a fish, striving toward that pale promise. Her fingers found holds and her arms found strength and she hauled herself upward. The tunnel grew lighter and at last there was a triangle of blue sky above. Faith smelled fresh air with a scent of hot grass, and felt soil between her fingers.

But as she tried to haul herself into that light, the vines tightened and held her. They were tangled about her shoulders and waist, her arms and neck, biting and knotting. She had reached the full extent of the Lie Tree's leash, and felt her fingers rake through earth as she started to slide back down the tunnel.

"No!" whispered Faith, but her whisper was not the only noise. The voices thronged about her, and now she knew why they disturbed her. They spoke in her own voice, mangled and maddened into the gargling of a cat.

He was a genius, the voices wailed and growled. *He was wronged and misunderstood. He was a good man. We had a special bond . . .*

Words that she had never spoken to the Tree. Thoughts that she had whispered to nobody but herself. And lies. Beloved, choking lies.

Faith managed to struggle one hand down into her pocket and pull out her tiny hand mirror. Reaching upward at full stretch, she could just move its glass face into the shaft of sunlight and reflect its light toward herself.

There was a fizzle and flare as the vines binding her burst into flame. She ignored the sudden burning pain and the smell of her hair scorching. Her sap-smeared clothes fizzed, but they were still damp with seawater. As the vines loosed their grip she scrambled upward and heaved herself out of the hole, belly down, like a landed fish. She rolled over and over to put out the flames, then lay gasping.

For a few moments she had no breath, no sense of anything but the sky over her head. Then she became aware that a smoke was coming from the hole. She had thought only to singe the tendrils that bound her, but now she imagined fire chasing its way down vine after vine, like the orange flame along the blast-powder fuse.

Plumes of gray smoke yielded to great, black billows. Beneath her, the Tree was burning.

Faith pulled her feet and ankles away from the hole, covering her mouth to shield it from the smoke. She could do nothing for Ben Crock and Agatha Lambent but fetch help. Unsteadily Faith stood up, then nearly collapsed again as the world turned carousel, her ears roaring.

She saw the distant spire of the church, and staggered in that direction. Her feet did not seem to be her own, and she could not keep her route straight. Somehow the cliff-edge kept sidling in on her right and surprising her. Once she caught herself irritably answering a question that nobody had asked her.

Fumes. It must be the fumes.

She glanced over her shoulder, and saw that there was still a glowering column of smoke rising from the hidden entrance. It was spreading as it rose, an unhealthy sallow smudge against the blue.

Far closer, however, was a figure. A blackened phantasm, soot-stained and relentless, hair drifting on the breeze like a warning flag. Red burns blistered her face and showed through the charred holes in her mermaid-green dress. Agatha was gaining fast, eyes fixed upon Faith, and only Faith.

Faith's legs failed her, and she fell to the ground again. Beneath her, one hand scrabbled for something to throw, and closed upon a pebble. A small, perfectly round pebble.

"Stay back!" she called, as the figure drew ever nearer. She held up the stone, hoping that Agatha saw nothing but a round, dark shape. "This is a fruit—all that is left of the Tree! Leave me alone . . . or I will throw it into the sea!"

Agatha did not slow.

"You can still run!" called Faith, scrabbling backward over the turf, her hand still raised to throw. "Go to the port! Find a boat!"

Agatha looked directly into Faith's eyes as she strode on. Her look of despair was as flat and empty as her gaze of joy had been.

"Stop!" shouted Faith. "I mean it!"

Agatha lunged forward, fingers curled to grab at the "fruit," and Faith threw it past her, toward the cliff-drop. It was all she could think of—a distraction to give her time to get away.

The older woman twisted round and stared after the small, round shape as it bounced and ricocheted toward the edge. She turned and chased it.

It bounced, and the sunlight gleamed on its slate-gray surface. It was a pebble, plainly no more than a pebble. It was bounding away faster than anybody could catch, and still Agatha ran.

"Stop!" Faith found herself shouting. "Stop! I lied!"

But as the pebble plummeted over the edge, Faith realized that Agatha was no longer even looking at it. Near the brink Agatha accelerated, and then spread her arms as she took her longest stride into eternity.

Then there was nothing but the heartless blue of the sky, the smoke-scented wind, and the crickets gossiping amid the dry grass.

Chapter 36

EVOLUTION

THINGS MIGHT HAVE BEEN DIFFERENT IF DR. Jacklers had not survived. Survive he did, however, with a very ill grace but some prospect of regaining the use of his broken leg.

He even presided over the postponed inquest of the late Reverend Erasmus Sunderly, loath to leave the task to a lesser man, and badgered the jury so severely that some of them clearly thought that they were the ones on trial. He was kinder in speaking of Faith Sunderly, but did upbraid her for failing to share her suspicions with him earlier.

The Reverend was found to have died at the hands of persons known. Ben Crock was found in the cavern, alive but badly singed, powder damage from a pistol marring the vision in his left eye. The "navvies," all men who had worked with Crock under Winterbourne, were rounded up and arrested.

The body of Agatha Lambent was found at the base of a cliff. However, her part in the skulduggery was played down. Faith knew that this delicacy was a kindness to her memory and the feelings of her husband, who had been devastated to hear of his late wife's crimes. At the same time, it made Faith feel uncomfortable. Agatha was disappearing. Her cunning, her villainy, her scientific zeal, her brilliance, and her obsessions were melting into air like steam. Soon she would be just another "beloved wife" on a marble headstone.

Faith's part in the events would become invisible as well. If the newspapers mentioned her at all, she would be an artless young girl who had stumbled upon the truth, just as she had once stumbled upon a valuable fossil. Perhaps they would even use the photograph of her at the age of seven, proudly gripping her find.

No trace was found of the Tree. The fire had consumed it, leaving only blackened cave walls and a singular smell. Faith mourned the loss to science, but could not be entirely sorry that it was gone.

Evidence inconclusive, she wrote in her notebook under her own theories and those of her father. And then: *Observations unreliable. Objectivity compromised.*

On a quiet morning the Reverend's grave was cleared and his coffin lowered into its final resting place. Watching the clods thud softly on the wood, and the turf fold over like a blanket, Faith felt a wound close at last.

My father will never understand or forgive me. But I can understand him, and forgive him in time. And that is probably enough.

"There was some good in him," Myrtle told Faith later, during a long evening where they talked about everything over cake, which was now an extravagance. "You and Howard meant something to him at least."

"What about you?" asked Faith.

Myrtle shook her head. "I told myself that I was lucky," she said. "Your father never struck me, never drank and if he had mistresses he had the good grace to be discreet. He provided for me and my children, and yet I tried, year after year, to make myself his companion. The doors never opened, Faith. In the end I lost hope.

"Ah, but I cannot complain!" Myrtle swatted away the past with one delicate little hand. "It has made me what I am. When every door is closed, one learns to climb through windows. Human nature, I suppose."

Anthony Lambent received Myrtle and Faith in his wife's Cabinet of Curiosities. He was a wreckage of his erstwhile boisterous self, his gaze roaming disconsolately from case to case.

"She was my anchor," he said, "my port in the world's storm. I could *sleep* knowing she was there. How will I ever sleep again?"

He looked across at Faith, and she was taken aback at seeing such a big man look so small.

"I am the magistrate," he said miserably. "I must enforce the law, and there are laws regarding burial of suicides—you know this better than most. Miss Sunderly . . . you saw her at the end. Did she . . . ?" He could not finish the sentence.

Faith remembered Agatha's bold leap into space. Then she looked into the widower's face and decided the cosmos would forgive her one more lie.

"She lost her footing," she said.

Lambent closed his eyes and let out a long breath. "I should not care," he said, "but . . . I would have done anything for her. These . . . all of these . . ." He walked around case after case. "The excavation was for her. All I wanted was to make her happy . . ." Bright tears oozed out of his eyes, and his lost look reminded Faith of Howard.

Lambent's mood whiplashed too quickly for anybody to react. He seized the nearest display case, wrenched it from the wall and flung it to the ground. It smashed, scattering glass shards, labels, and birds' egg fragments across the floor.

He turned to the next case.

"No!" Faith threw herself in front of it. At that moment she would have fought to the death to defend the life's work of her mortal enemy.

"Please, Mr. Lambent!" Myrtle cried out at the same time. "If you wish these things out of your house . . . then let us take them. I am sure that, ah, Howard would greatly appreciate them once he is older."

On a gray morning a few days later, an innocent mailboat docked at Vane's harbor town, unaware that it was about to take away the island's most notorious intruders.

Transporting the Sunderly luggage and Agatha's sizeable natural history collection to the harbor had been a lengthy business. It might have proved impossible without unexpected assistance from the Clays and Miss Hunter.

Faith rode to the harbor in Miss Hunter's trap, hearing slithers from the crate in her lap. Her snake had at last shed the dry sheath of its old skin to reveal new colors, vibrant and unabashed.

Scowls blistered from side streets and doorways, and Faith thought she recognized Jeanne amongst the scowlers. The Reverend's family had once been a target for mockery, resentment, and suspicion. Now truths and half-truths were spreading across Vane, and hostility had given way to a fear almost superstitious.

The night-clad Sunderly women were mistresses of deception and seduction. It was dangerous to meet their eye.

Miss Hunter, on the other hand, seemed unfazed. When Faith took her courage into her hands and began a stumbled confession, the postmistress cut her short with surprising good humor.

"We both played the gossip game." Miss Hunter wielded the reins with the confidence of practice. "After your mother upset Jane Vellet, I was angry and told everyone about that *Intelligencer* article. You spread a rumor in turn, but you were not the one who set fire to my house. A woman like me makes enemies."

Faith wondered what "a woman like me" meant. Perhaps a wilfully happy spinster with a sharp tongue and a good salary. In Faith's eyes, Miss Hunter had always seemed icily smug and unassailable. Now Faith saw glitters of defiance, and a tightrope beneath her feet.

Faith had always told herself that she was not like other ladies. But neither, it seemed, were other ladies.

As they passed Dr. Jacklers's house, Miss Hunter raised her hand in a salute. A hand waved curtly back from a top window.

"Why do you tease Dr. Jacklers for being short?" It was Faith's last chance to ask the question.

"Ah." Miss Hunter gave her small, cool smirk. "Well, at one point he grew very impatient with my refusal to marry him, so he explained to me that women lacked the intelligence to look after their own affairs. He tried to prove it by showing me his patients' skull measurements. On average, male skulls *are* bigger than female skulls.

"Unfortunately for the doctor, his records included his patients' other measurements as well. After which I told him that I was quite convinced by his evidence, and would do my best to marry the very tallest man I could find. You see, the taller men usually had larger skulls. And the doctor could not say that this was *not* a sign that they were cleverer than him, since that would tear apart his claim to be cleverer than me.

"Large people tend to have large heads. Men are no cleverer than we are, Miss Sunderly. Just taller."

On the quay, Faith stood beside Paul Clay, watching the mailboat's crew load the boxes. It was strange to be standing next to him by daylight, without secrecy. She felt too self-conscious to look at him. The arguments had been easier, theatre-vivid, full of stage lighting and dramatic gestures. Now there was a chance that their little time would run out without anybody speaking at all.

"I will write to you," she said.

"Why?" Paul examined her face, apparently looking for a trap. "So that you can tell me that you hate me? Do you think I ever want to hear from you again?"

"Yes," said Faith.

A rain shower was rehearsing. A few experimental droplets filled the silence.

"I have a confession to make," said Faith.

"Bleeding saints, is there *more*?" Paul stared. "How much worse can it be?"

This was the hardest part. It was easier to be the witch, the harpy. Being human was dangerous.

"I . . . am sometimes kind," admitted Faith. "I . . . love my little brother very much."

There was a long pause.

"The first time I saw a ratting," Paul said, without looking at her, "a dog lost an eye, and I was sick. I go back to prove I can without spewing."

"When I was seven, I found a fossil on the beach," Faith said quietly, "and my father was very proud of me. At least . . . that is what I thought happened. But it was one of his fake fossils—he thought it would look more convincing if an 'innocent child' discovered it. He laid it down for me to find."

Her golden moment on the beach, her great instant of connection with her father, had been a self-serving lie and fraud. Deep down, her suspicions of the truth had been growing, but only when she found a copy of the infamous *Intelligencer* had her worst fears been confirmed. In the middle of the page there had been a picture of "her" fossil, with a detailed account of the methods used to forge it.

She bit her lip hard. "I . . . think perhaps I went a little mad after he died."

"You put your hand into a bag of rats!" said Paul. "You pointed a pistol at me!"

"Looking back, that . . . does seem a little drastic, yes."

There was another pause, during which it turned out that nobody needed to apologize.

"I want to be a photographer," said Paul, "but not like father. I want to photograph faraway places nobody has ever seen. I want to try *new* things—find ways to take pictures of birds in flight, and scenes at night."

His confession was angrily earnest. Faith thought of him standing out on a cold headland for hours, minutely adjusting his camera to track a brilliant, contrary moon.

"I want to be a natural scientist," confessed Faith. The words sounded fragile as soon as they were out in the air.

She glanced at Paul, but he showed no sign of laughing.

Instead he was nodding quietly to himself, as if the revelation surprised him not a jot.

The deck moved under Faith's feet as the mailboat drifted away from the shore. The people shrank, the houses withdrew into ranks. They were preparing to become memories.

Faith felt an unexpected burst of nerves. Her weeks on Vane had been so painfully vivid that it had seemed like the only real place. Her other memories had become a faintly daubed backdrop. Now she was going back to England, and had to face the fact that England really did exist. The scandal about her father would be coming to the boil. The family would lose friends, and their home at the rectory. Compared to the disasters that had threatened not long ago, however, these problems now seemed like a manageable apocalypse.

"Why is it that the sweet-tempered men *never* have any money?" Myrtle said with wry wistfulness as she waved her handkerchief to Clay.

"He may have even less now," said Faith. "The whole island just saw him helping the Sunderly witches. He may find himself preaching to an empty church on Sunday."

"He needs a decent living, poor fellow, and I am sure he is too meek to ask for one." Myrtle narrowed her eyes, and Faith knew she was making calculations. "Oh—I *know* what I must do! I shall put in a good word for him."

A good word for him? With a mixture of horror and admiration Faith realized where her mother's mind had sped. Her father's living had just fallen open, and nobody else knew it yet. A replacement would be needed quickly. Myrtle knew the local squire in whose gift the living lay, and could put a word in his ear . . .

Or was Myrtle perhaps thinking even further ahead, of the

day when her mourning would end and she would be looking for a husband with a large house and a decent income?

"It would be perfect!" Myrtle breathed, very softly. "We would not even need to redecorate!"

"Mother!" hissed Faith, but she found she did not feel the utter recoil and outrage she would once have experienced. Myrtle was dreadful, but without such dreadfulness where would the family be in a year's time?

My mother is not evil, Faith reminded herself. *She is just a perfectly sensible snake, protecting her eggs and making her way in the world as best she can.*

"Well," Myrtle said, defending herself against the accusation Faith had not made, "if you are to continue with these antiquarian enthusiasms of yours, it will not be cheap. You do wish to persist in them, do you not?"

Faith nodded.

"Then heaven send you a husband with patience and money." Myrtle gave Faith an anxious glance.

Faith knew now that her mother was not worried about the embarrassment of having a dull, eccentric bluestocking daughter. Myrtle was concerned for Faith, and rightly so. If Faith pursued natural science, as a female she would probably be mocked, belittled, patronized, and ignored her whole life. She might well make herself unmarriageable. How would she live, and find money to pursue her passion?

Perhaps she would go abroad to visit excavations, and be despised as a scandalous woman traveling alone. Perhaps she would marry, and have all her work attributed to her husband, like Agatha. Perhaps she would end up a penniless old maid, with only a coral collection for company.

And perhaps some other later girl, leafing through her father's library, would come across a footnote in an academic journal and read the name "Faith Sunderly." *Faith?* she would think. *That is a female name. A woman did this. If that is so . . . then so can I.* And the little fire of hope, self-belief, and determination would pass to another heart.

"I am tired of lies," said Faith. "I do not want to hide, the way Agatha did."

"So what do you want?" asked Myrtle.

"I want to help evolution."

Evolution did not fill Faith with the same horror her father had felt. Why should she weep to hear that nothing was set in stone? Everything could change. Everything could get better. Everything *was* getting better, inch by inch, so slowly that she could not see it, but knowing it gave her strength.

"My dearest girl, I have not the faintest idea what you are talking about."

Faith thought about the best way to rephrase her resolution.

"I want to be a bad example," she said.

"I see." Myrtle stirred herself, ready to walk to the prow. "Well, my dear, I think you have made an excellent start."

ACKNOWLEDGMENTS

I WOULD LIKE TO THANK MY AGENT, NANCY Miles; my editor, Rachel Petty; Rhiannon Lassiter, for her support and robustly clear-sighted critiques; my boyfriend, Martin, for remaining patient even through my welter of all-nighters; Plot on the Landscape; Dr. Ruth Charles, for all the fascinating and entertaining information about nineteenth-century archaeology and paleontology; Heather Kilgour, for introducing me to the Crystal Palace Park dinosaurs; Sandra Lawrence, for taking me to the excellent seminar "Creepy Victorians: After-Death Photography" at The Old Operating Theatre Museum; Sarah Blake, for information on geology; *The Mismeasure of Man* by Stephen Jay Gould; *Victorian Religion: Faith and Life in Britain* by Julie Melnyk; *The Victorian Celebration of Death* by James Stevens Curl; *Crinolines and Crimping Irons: Victorian Clothes: How They Were Cleaned and Cared For* by Christina Walkley and Vanda Foster; *The Victorian Undertaker* by Trevor May; *Food and Cooking in Victorian England: A History* by Andrea Broomfield; *Cave Hunting: Researches on the Evidence of Caves Respecting the Early Inhabitants of Europe* by William Boyd Dawkins; *The Idea of Prehistory* by Glyn Daniel.